Cucumber QUEST 4

The Flower Kingdom

Gigi D.G.

First Second

New York

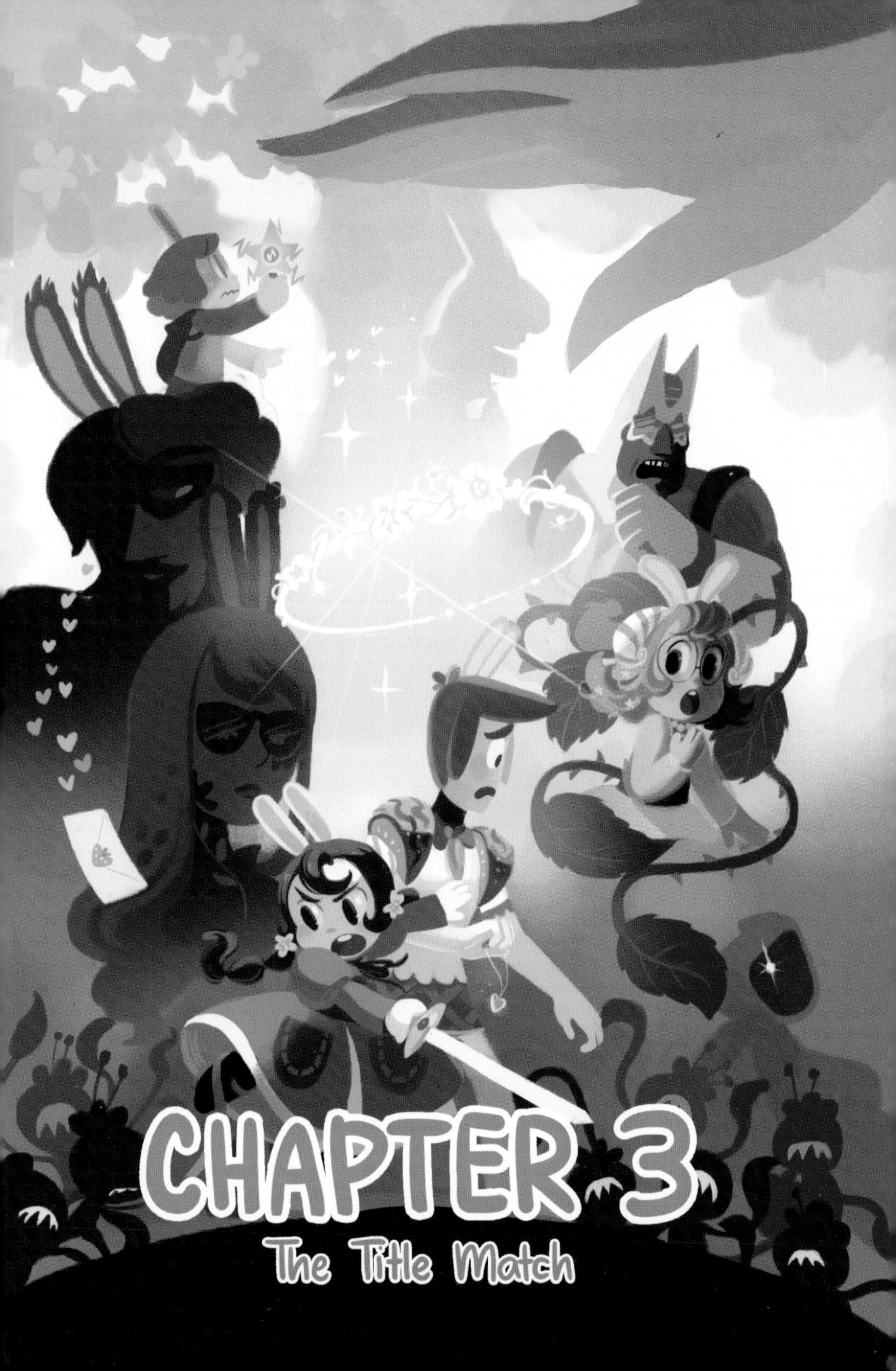

CHAPTER 3

The Title Match

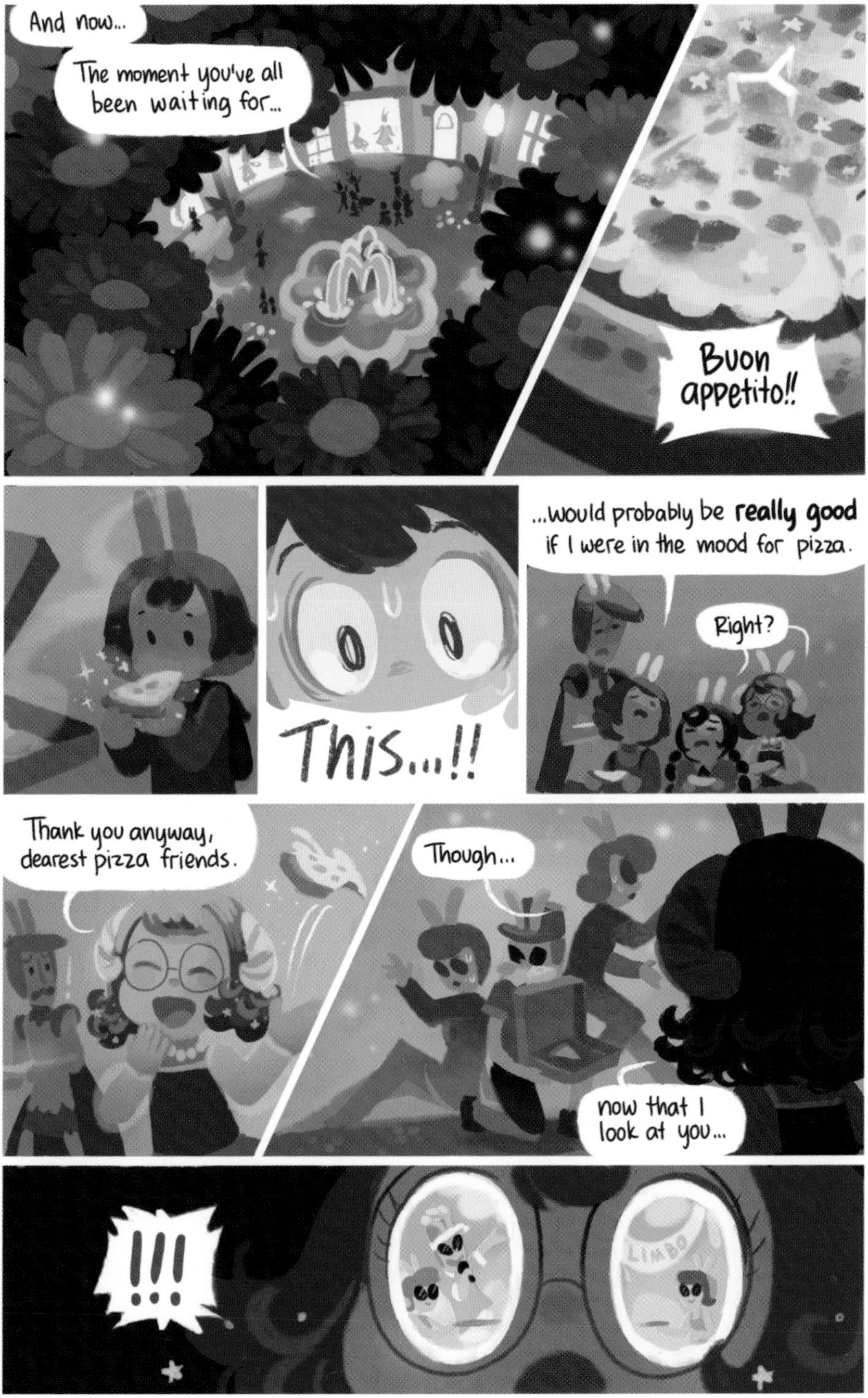
And now...
The moment you've all been waiting for...
Buon appetito!!
This...!!
...would probably be **really good** if I were in the mood for pizza.
Right?
Thank you anyway, dearest pizza friends.
Though...
now that I look at you...
!!!
LIMBO

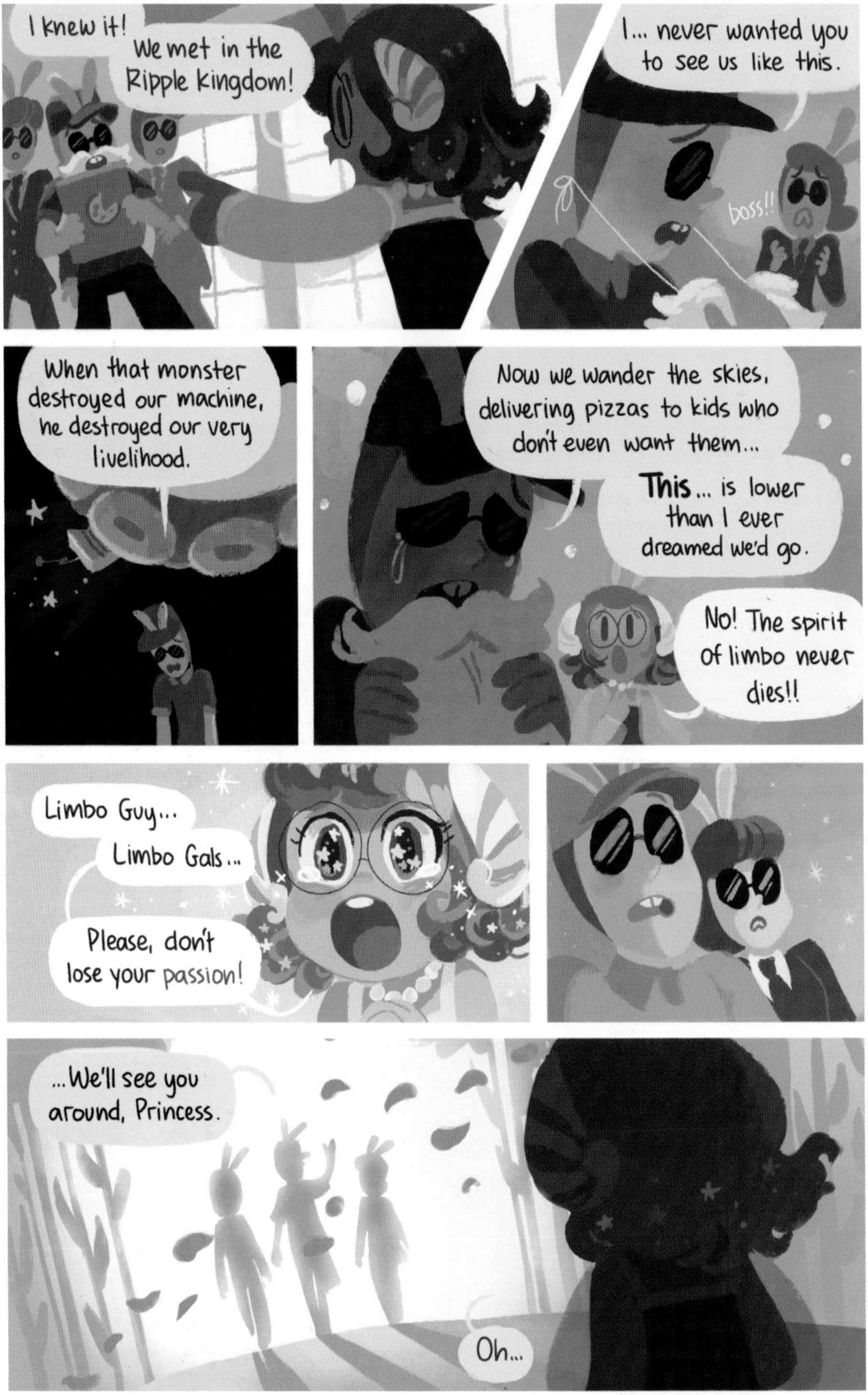
I knew it!
We met in the Ripple kingdom!
I... never wanted you to see us like this.
boss!!
When that monster destroyed our machine, he destroyed our very livelihood.
Now we wander the skies, delivering pizzas to kids who don't even want them...
This... is lower than I ever dreamed we'd go.
No! The spirit of limbo never dies!!
Limbo Guy...
Limbo Gals...
Please, don't lose your passion!
...We'll see you around, Princess.
Oh...

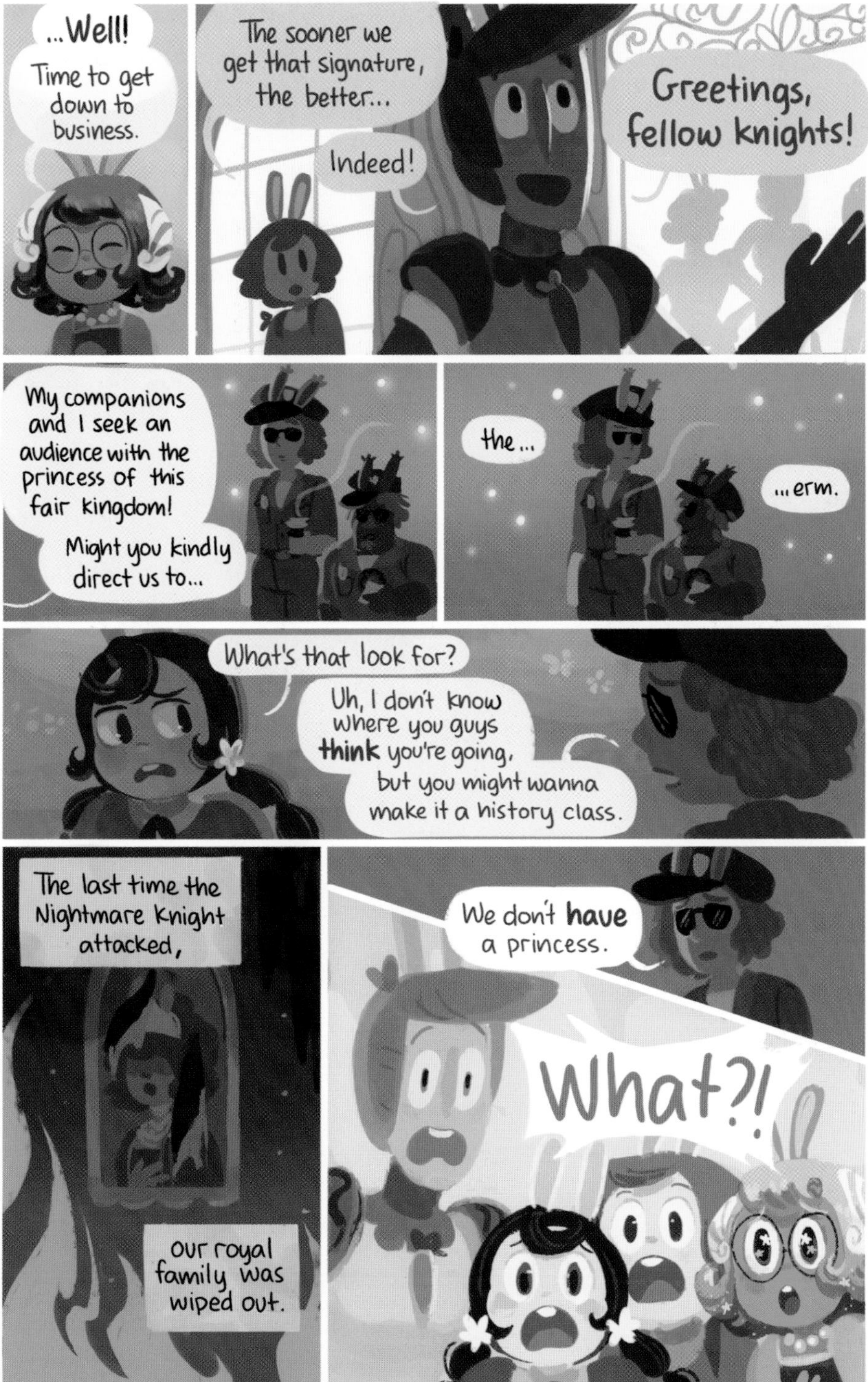
...Well!
Time to get down to business.
The sooner we get that signature, the better...
Indeed!
Greetings, fellow knights!
My companions and I seek an audience with the princess of this fair kingdom!
Might you kindly direct us to...
the...
...erm.
What's that look for?
Uh, I don't know where you guys **think** you're going,
but you might wanna make it a history class.
The last time the Nightmare Knight attacked,
our royal family was wiped out.
We don't **have** a princess.
What?!

The heroes approach.

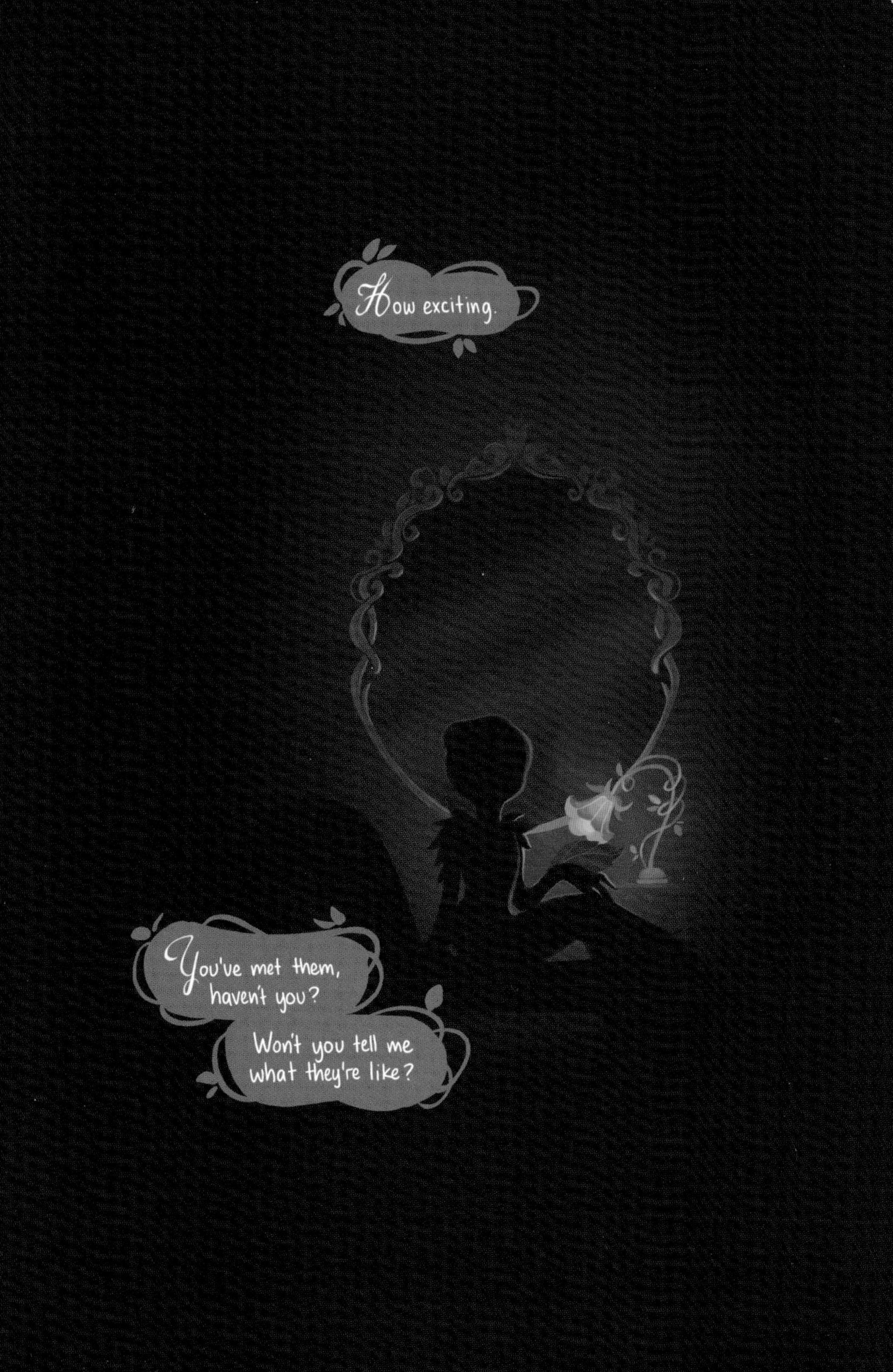
How exciting.
You've met them, haven't you?
Won't you tell me what they're like?

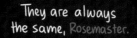

They are always the same, Rosemaster.

Expect nothing different.

You've got to let me dress for the **occasion**, at least.

I've got my eye on the most darling little accessory.

You'll adore it.

Don't I even deserve "clever"?

Yes... This convoluted plan of yours.

Come, now.

After all my hard work.

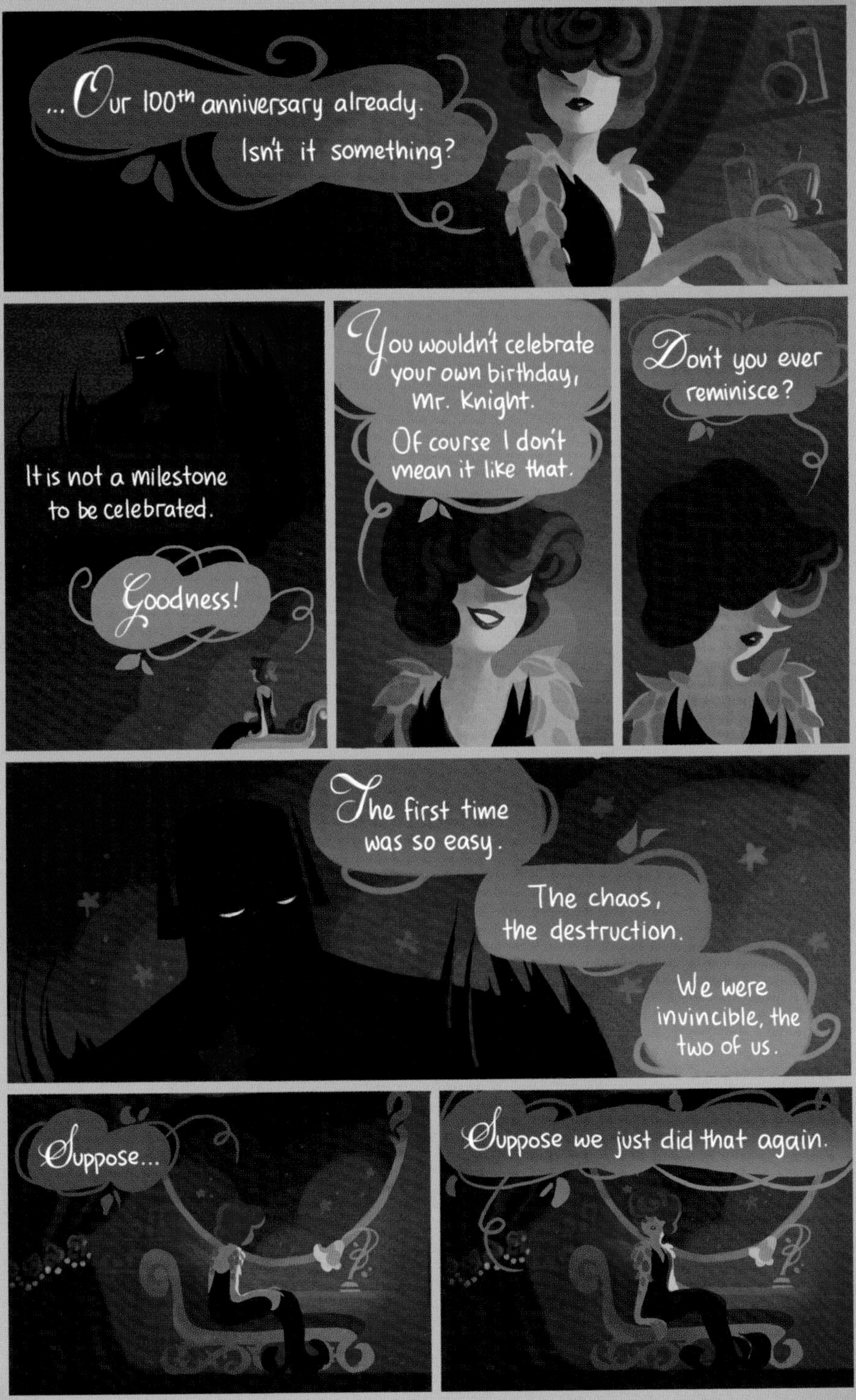

...Our 100th anniversary already.
Isn't it something?
It is not a milestone to be celebrated.
Goodness!
You wouldn't celebrate your own birthday, Mr. Knight.
Of course I don't mean it like that.
Don't you ever reminisce?
The first time was so easy.
The chaos, the destruction.
We were invincible, the two of us.
Suppose...
Suppose we just did that again.

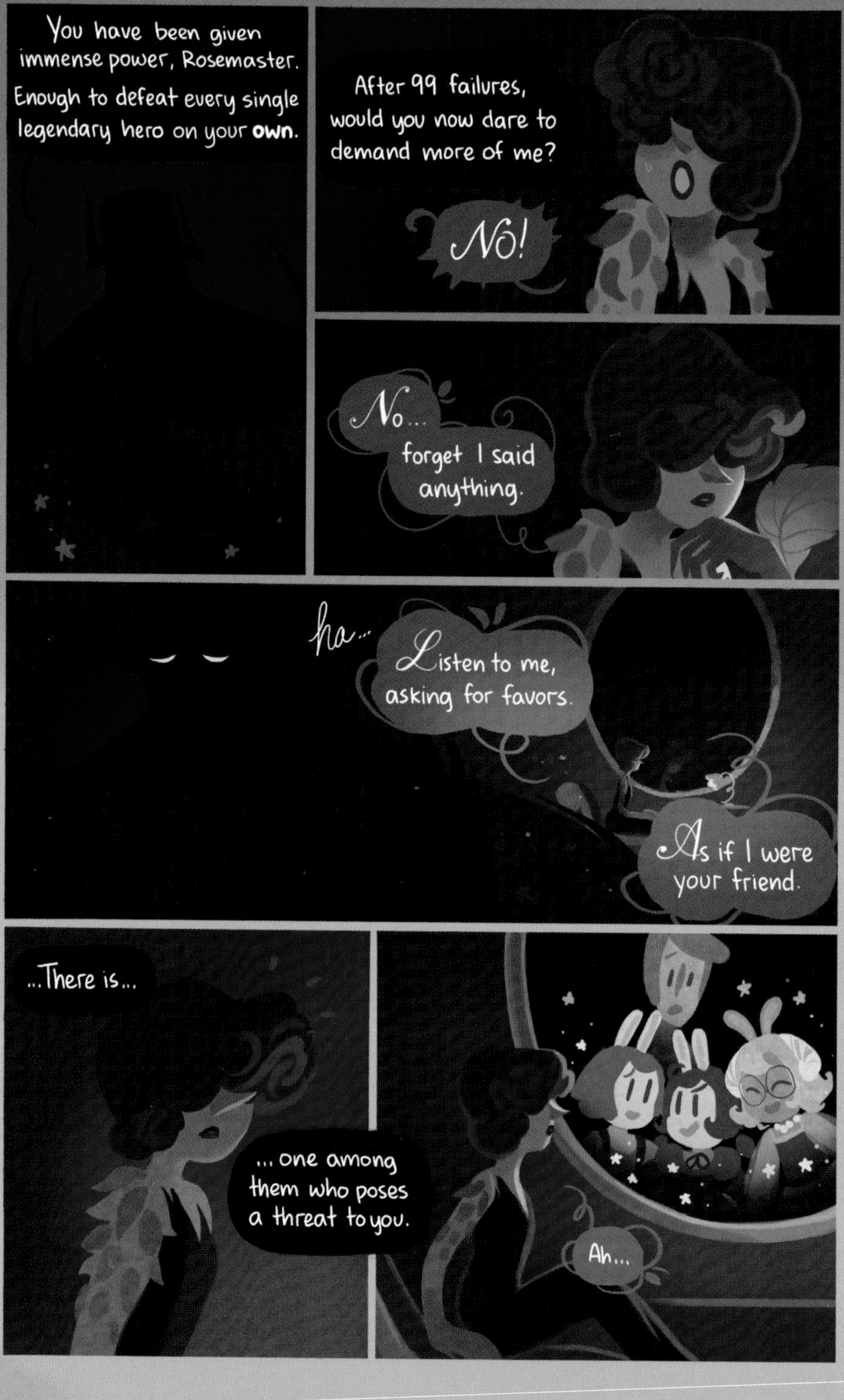
You have been given immense power, Rosemaster.
Enough to defeat every single legendary hero on your **own**.
After 99 failures, would you now dare to demand more of me?
No!
No... forget I said anything.
ha...
Listen to me, asking for favors.
As if I were your friend.
...There is...
...one among them who poses a threat to you.
Ah...

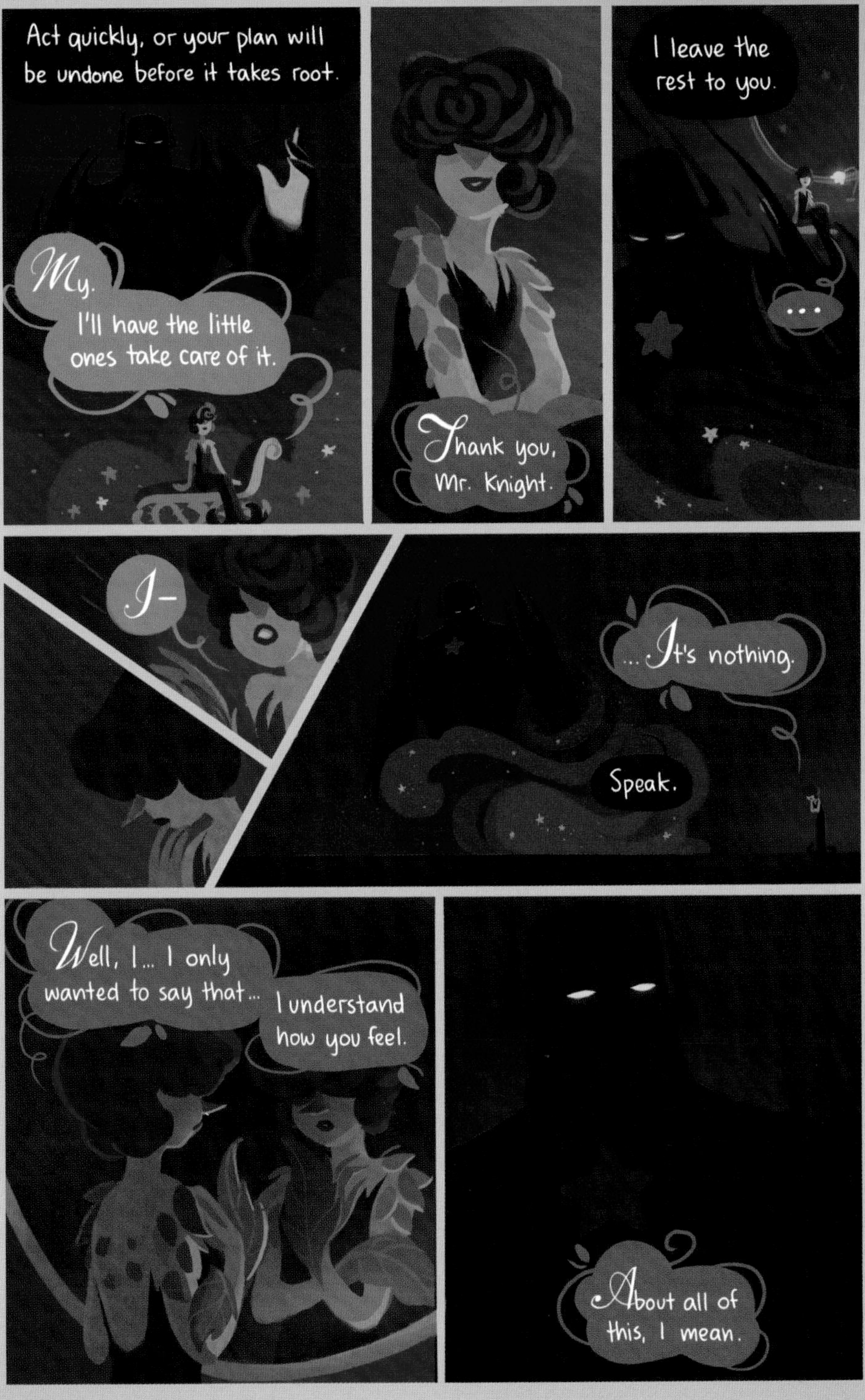
Act quickly, or your plan will be undone before it takes root.
My.
I'll have the little ones take care of it.
Thank you, Mr. Knight.
I leave the rest to you.
...
I–
...It's nothing.
Speak.
Well, I... I only wanted to say that...
I understand how you feel.
About all of this, I mean.

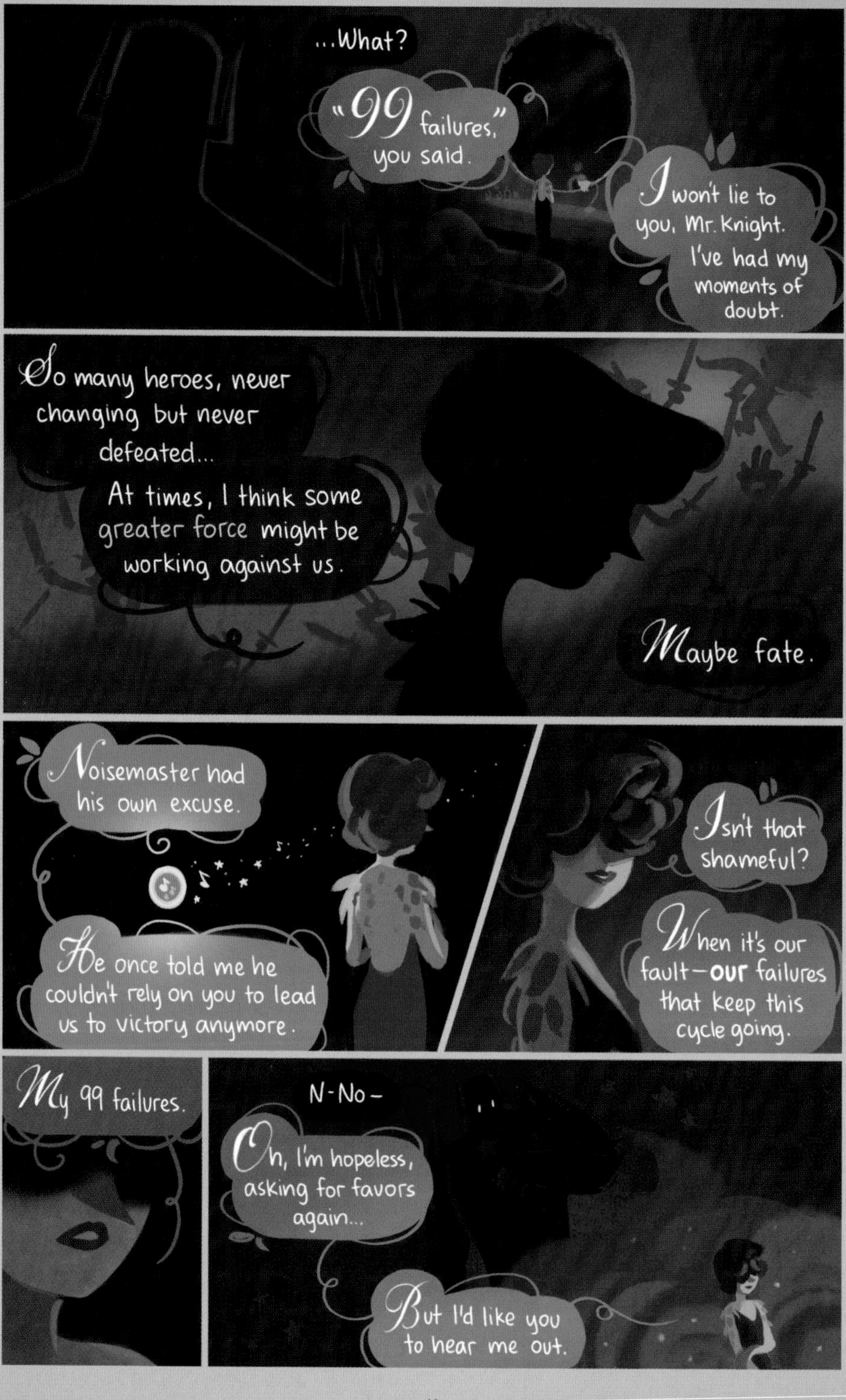
...What?
"99 failures," you said.
I won't lie to you, Mr. Knight.
I've had my moments of doubt.
So many heroes, never changing but never defeated...
At times, I think some greater force might be working against us.
Maybe fate.
Noisemaster had his own excuse.
He once told me he couldn't rely on you to lead us to victory anymore.
Isn't that shameful?
When it's our fault—**our** failures that keep this cycle going.
My 99 failures.
N-No—
Oh, I'm hopeless, asking for favors again...
But I'd like you to hear me out.

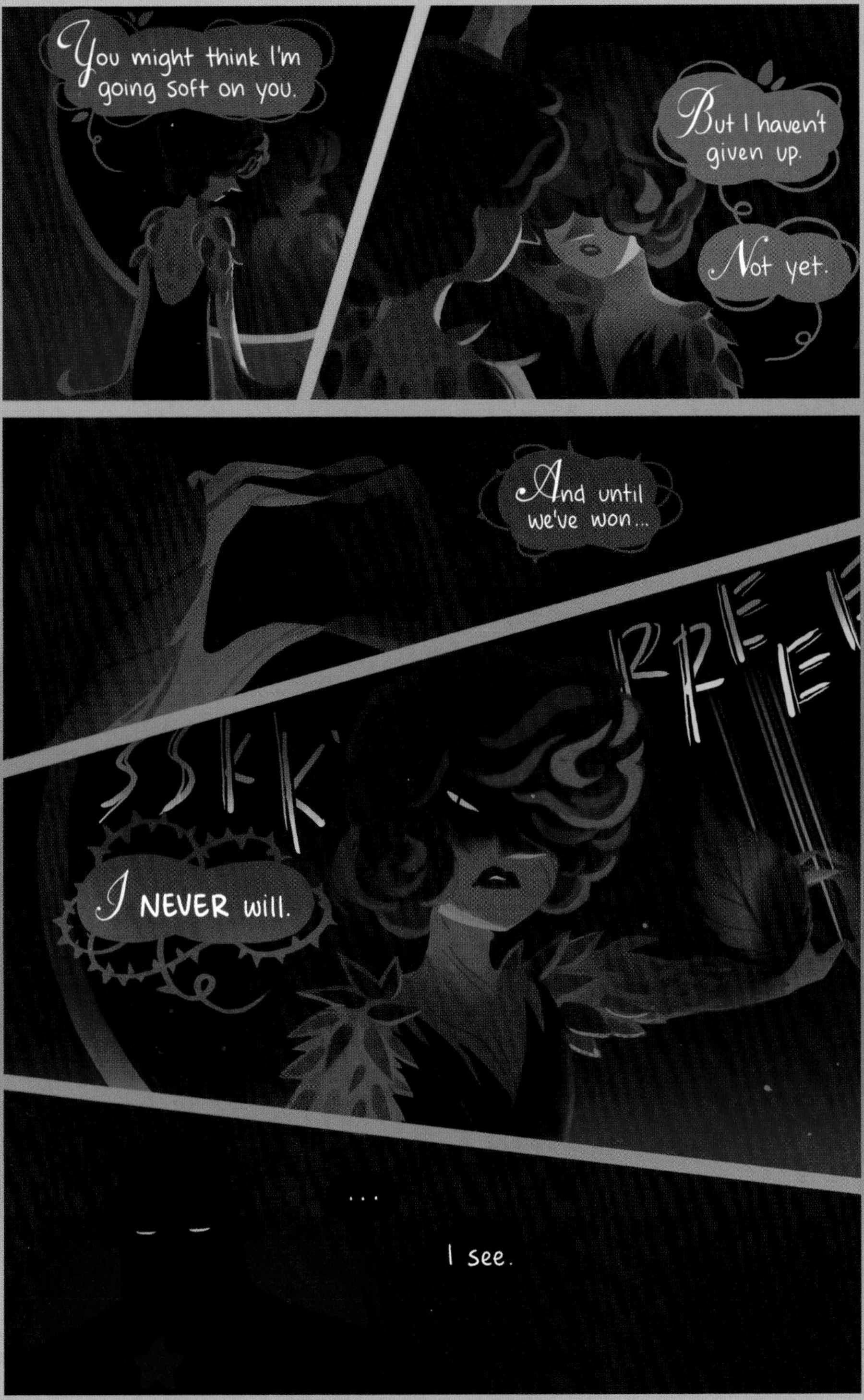
You might think I'm going soft on you.
But I haven't given up.
Not yet.
And until we've won...
SKK
RREEE
I NEVER will.
...
I see.

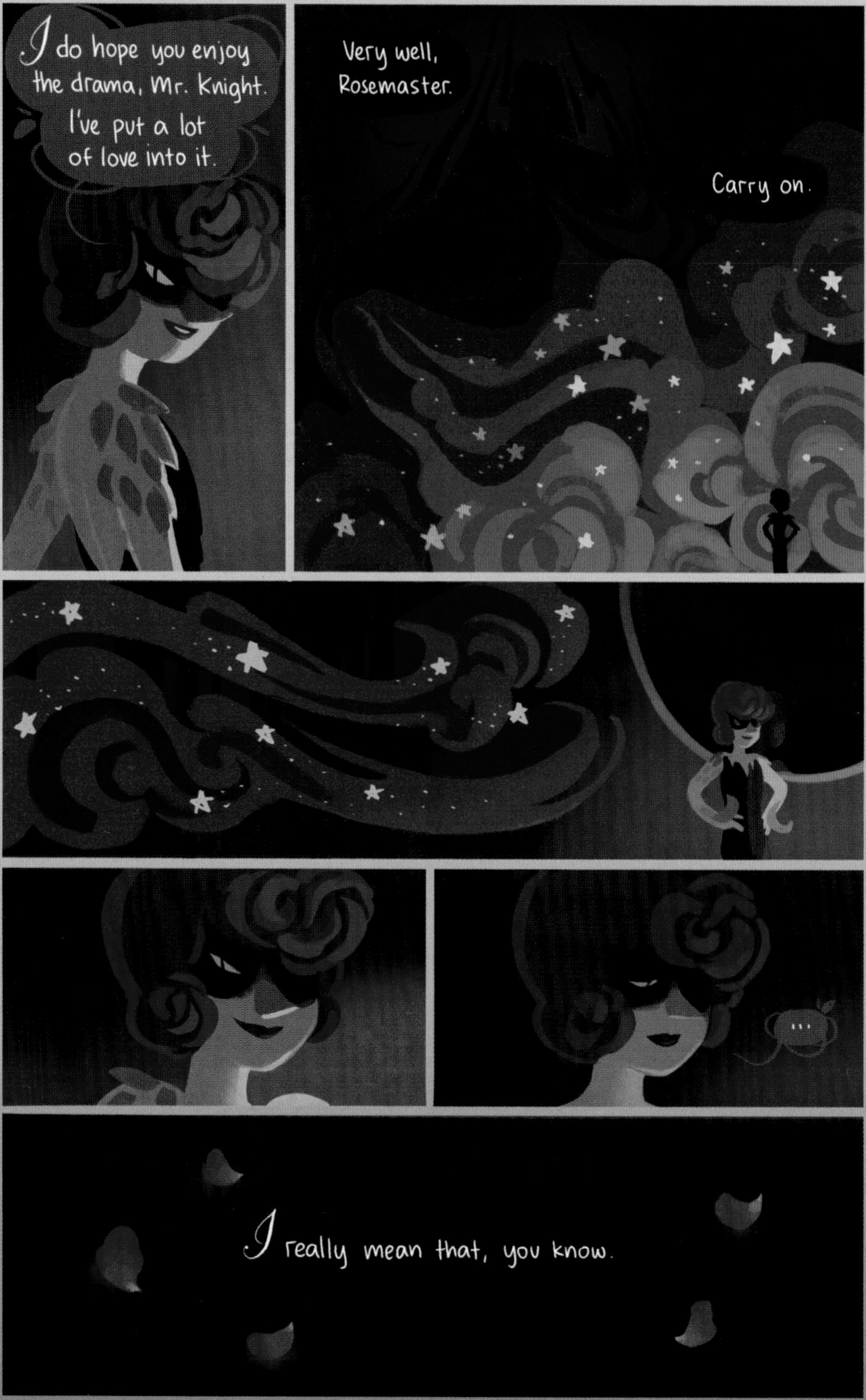
I do hope you enjoy the drama, Mr. Knight. I've put a lot of love into it.
Very well, Rosemaster.
Carry on.
...
I really mean that, you know.

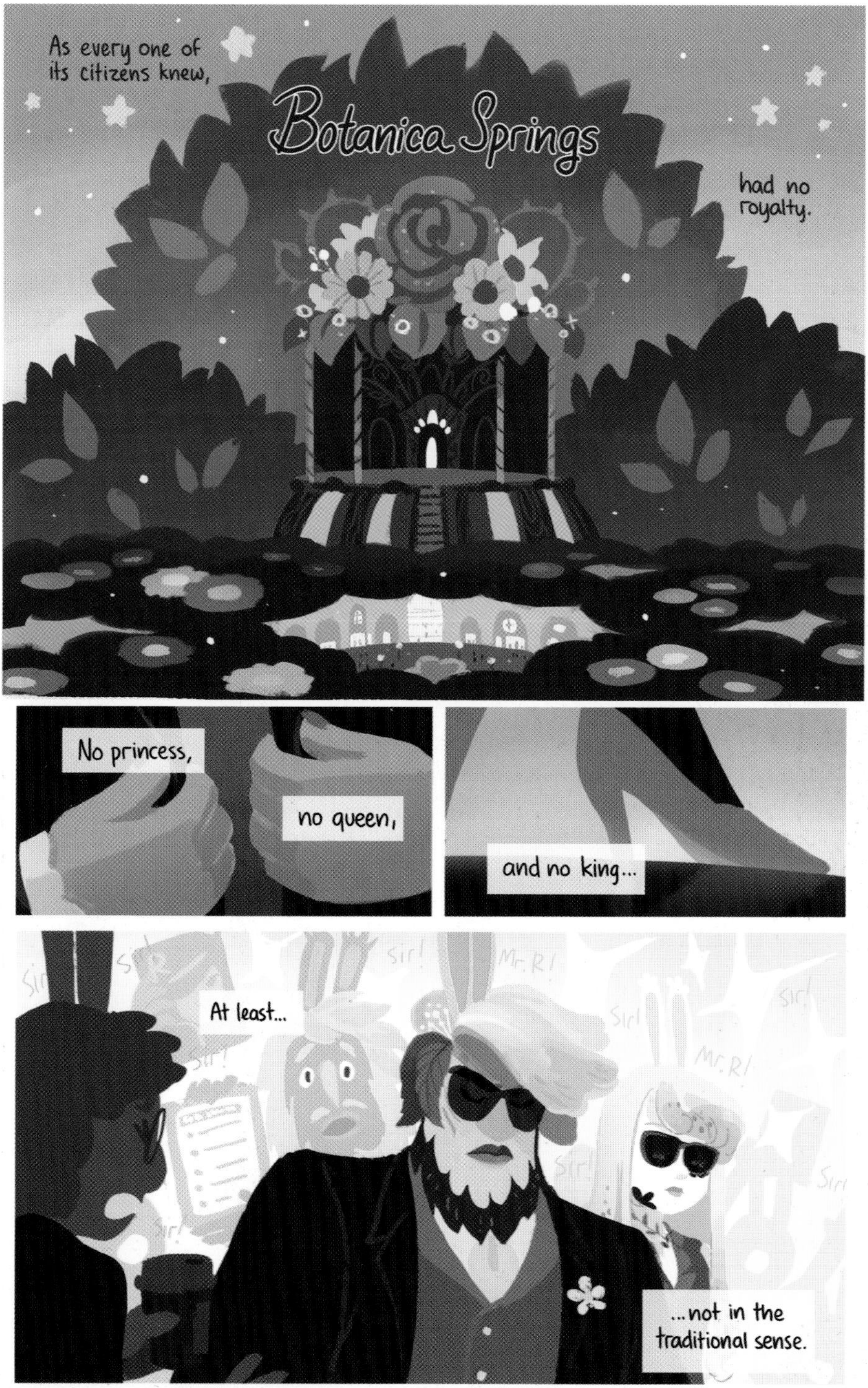
As every one of its citizens knew,
Botanica Springs
had no royalty.
No princess,
no queen,
and no king...
At least...
...not in the traditional sense.

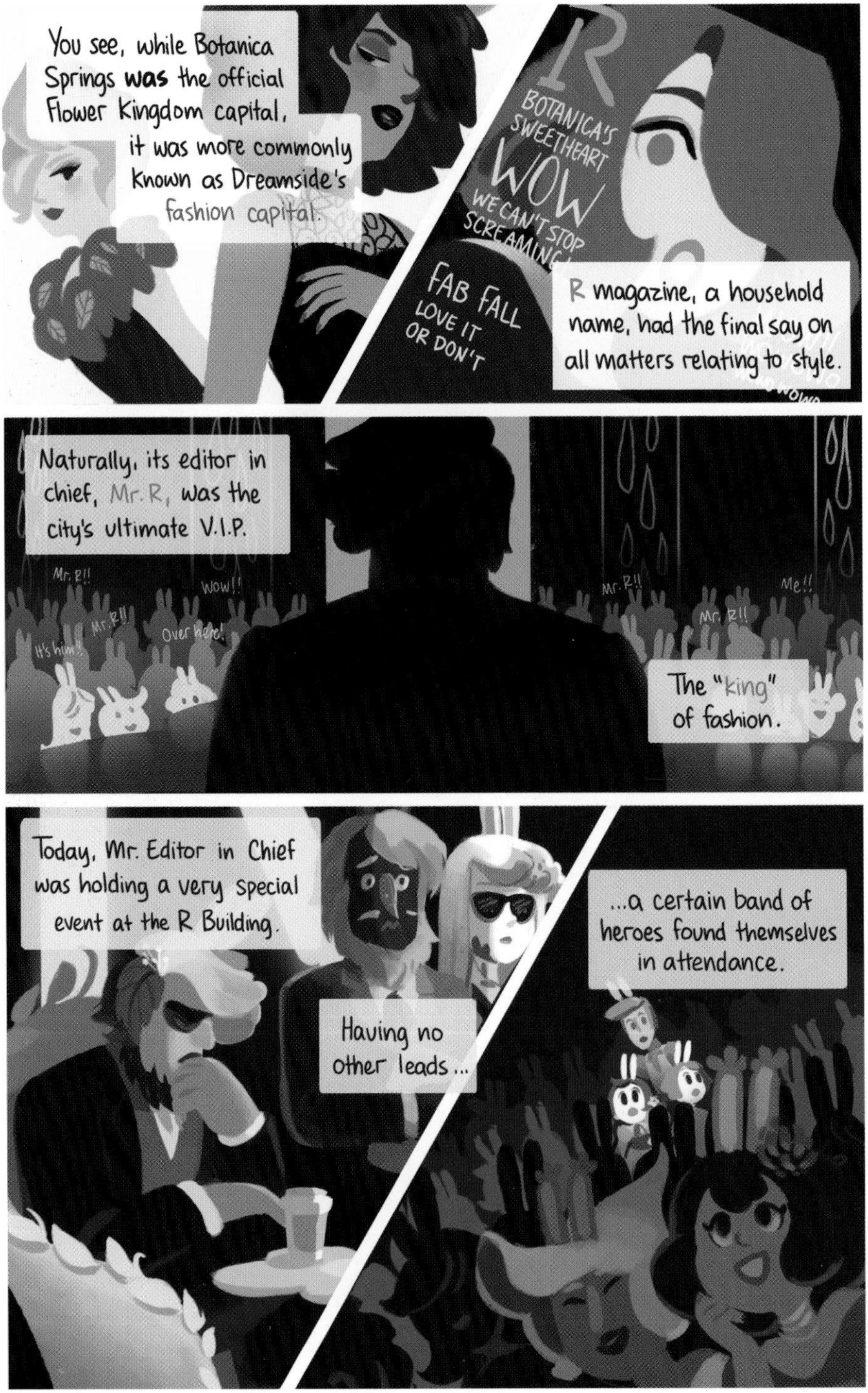
You see, while Botanica Springs **was** the official Flower Kingdom capital,
it was more commonly known as Dreamside's fashion capital.
R
BOTANICA'S SWEETHEART
WOW
WE CAN'T STOP SCREAMING!
FAB FALL
LOVE IT OR DON'T
R magazine, a household name, had the final say on all matters relating to style.
Naturally, its editor in chief, Mr. R, was the city's ultimate V.I.P.
Mr. R!!
Wow!!
Mr. R!!
Over here!
It's him!!
Mr. R!!
Me!!
Mr. R!!
The "king" of fashion.
Today, Mr. Editor in Chief was holding a very special event at the R Building.
Having no other leads...
...a certain band of heroes found themselves in attendance.

What is this **about?**

I feel a bit underdressed...

Look.

I think they're starting...

siiiii ighhh

Ahem... Mr. R is very distressed.

A-As you know, the new face of R magazine will be chosen tonight...

But he's lacking inspiration.

siiiighhhhhh

He needs a "vision," he says.

Something "fab."

Wait, that's it!

What's what?

What those officers said has been bugging me...

How the royal family was wiped out "last time."

We're the only ones who know the Nightmare Knight keeps coming back, which means they meant the first time.

And if there were no princesses after that...

Who could have signed the Dream Sword for every other legendary hero?

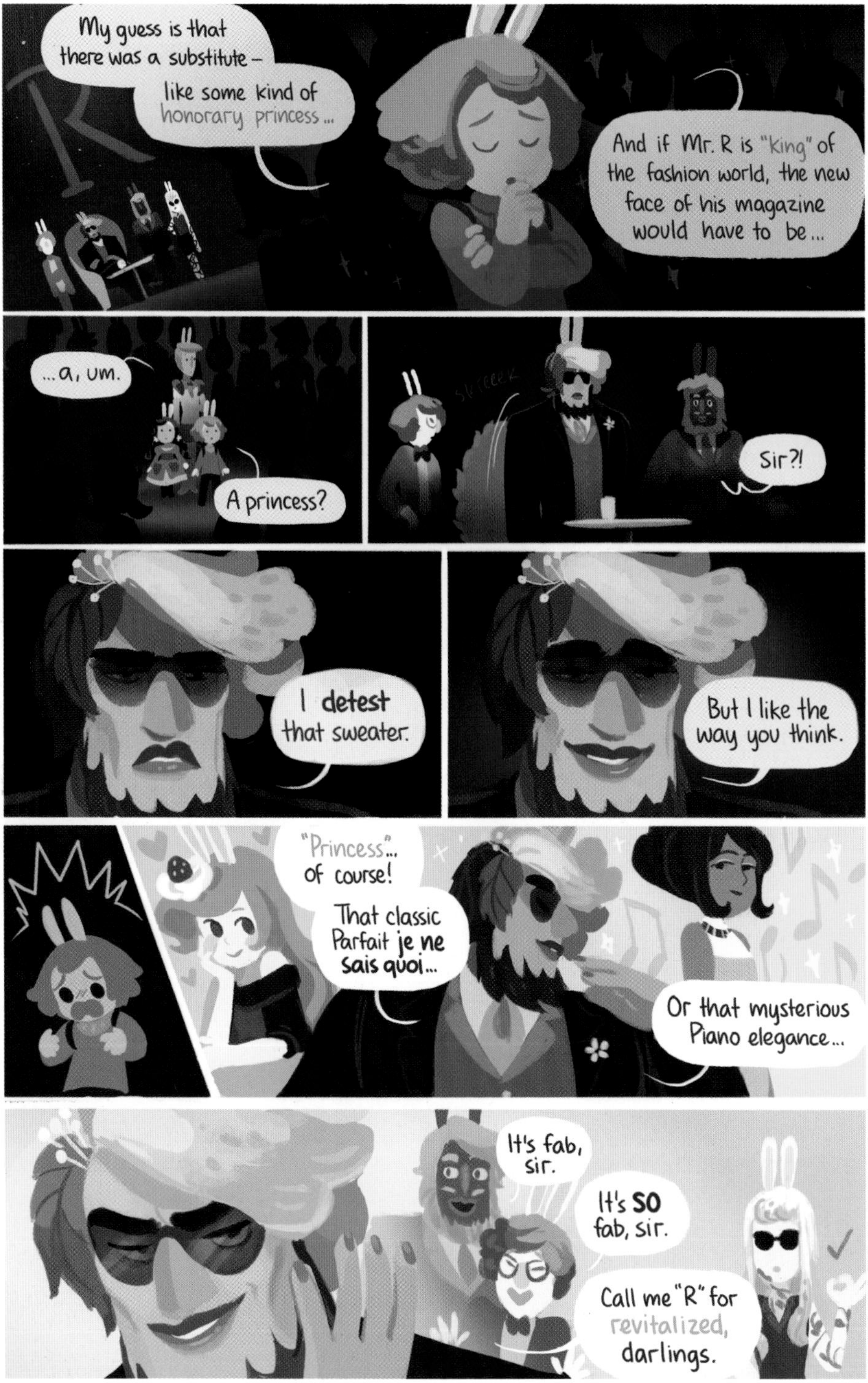
My guess is that there was a substitute –
like some kind of honorary princess...
And if Mr. R is "king" of the fashion world, the new face of his magazine would have to be...
...a, um.
A princess?
SKRREEK
Sir?!
I detest that sweater.
But I like the way you think.
"Princess"... of course!
That classic Parfait je ne sais quoi...
Or that mysterious Piano elegance...
It's fab, sir.
It's SO fab, sir.
Call me "R" for revitalized, darlings.

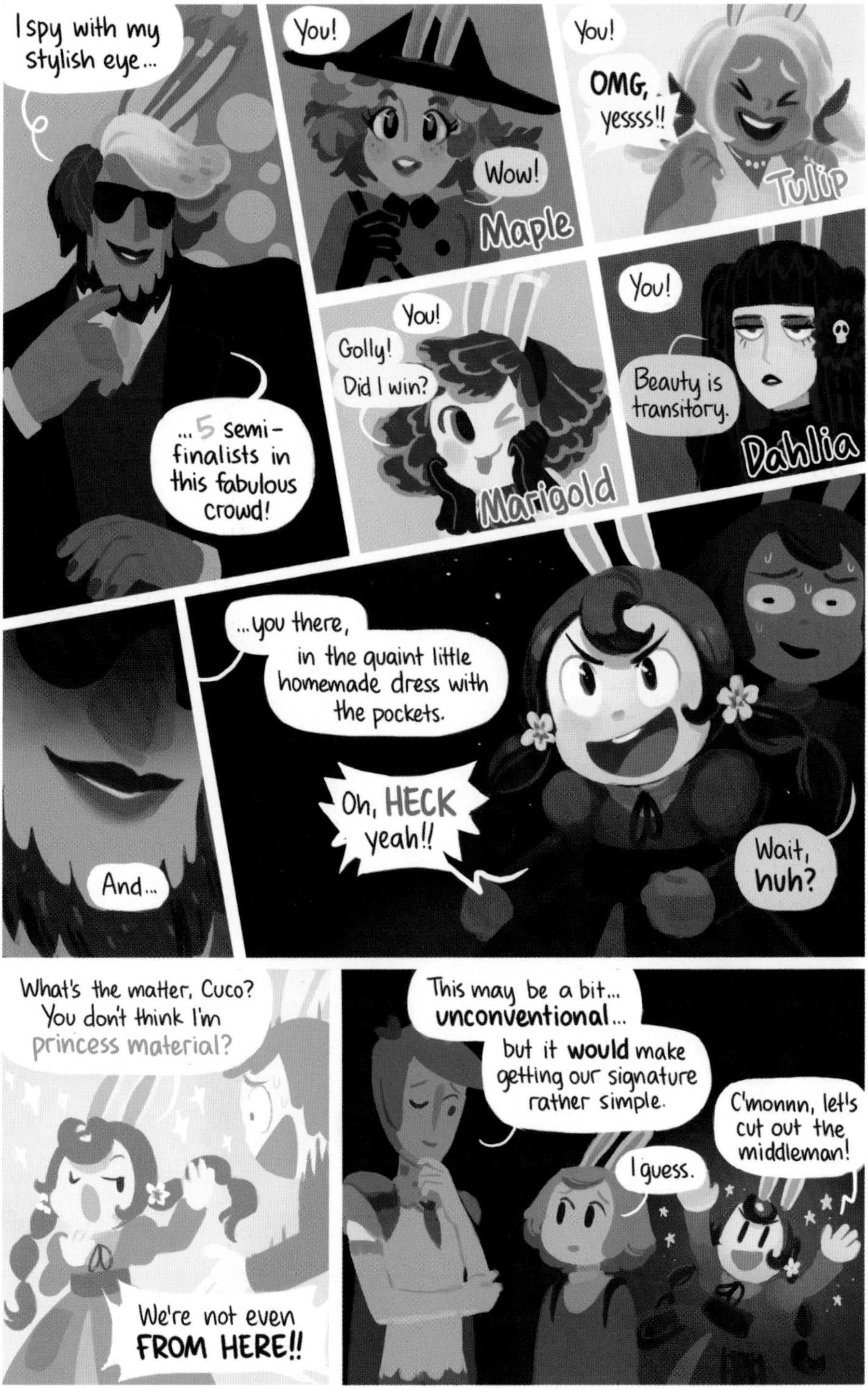
I spy with my stylish eye...
You!
Wow!
Maple
You!
OMG, yessss!!
Tulip
You!
Golly! Did I win?
Marigold
You!
Beauty is transitory.
Dahlia
...5 semi-finalists in this fabulous crowd!
And...
...you there, in the quaint little homemade dress with the pockets.
Oh, HECK yeah!!
Wait, huh?
What's the matter, Cuco? You don't think I'm princess material?
We're not even FROM HERE!!
This may be a bit... unconventional...
but it would make getting our signature rather simple.
I guess.
C'monnn, let's cut out the middleman!

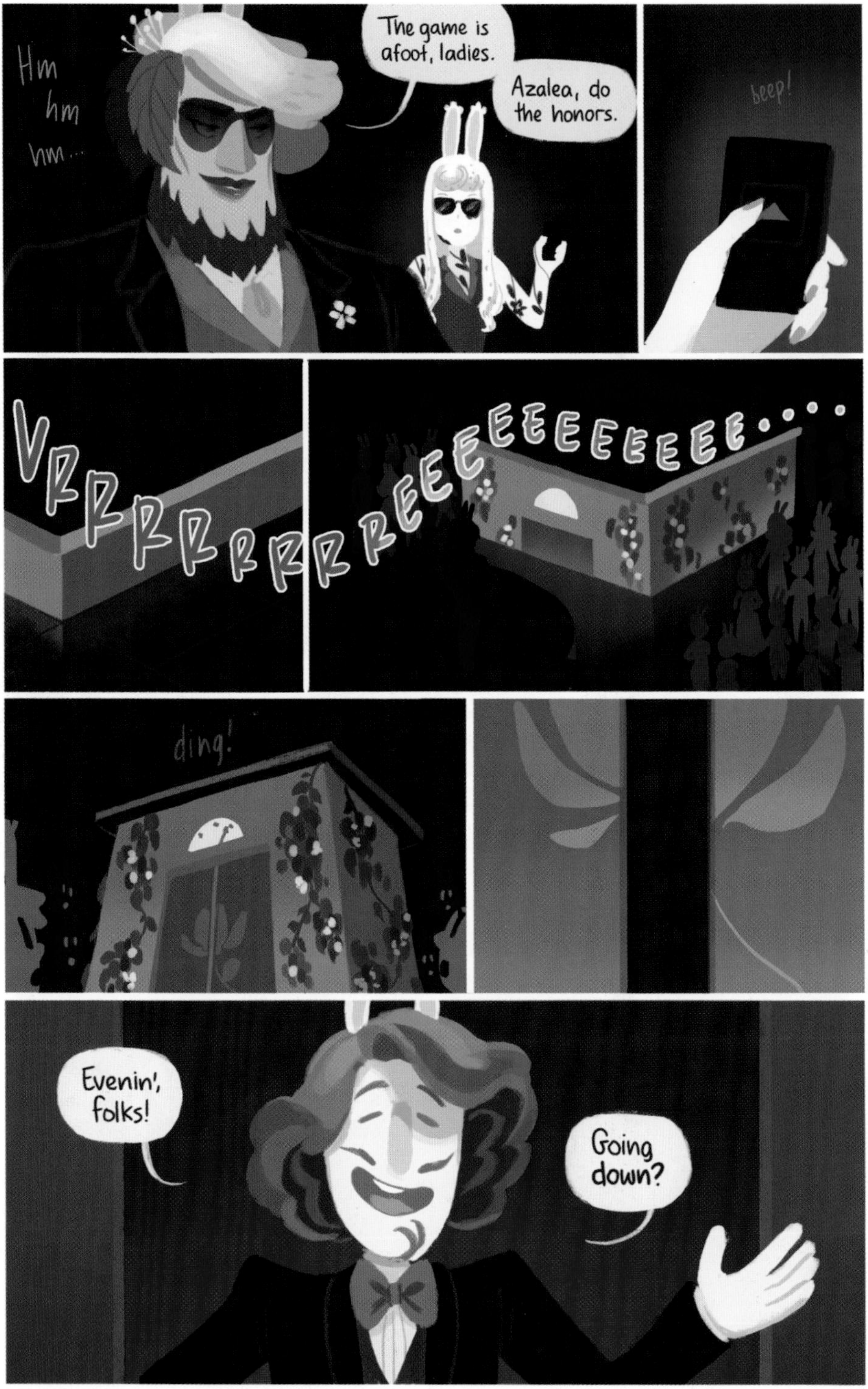
Hm hm hm...
The game is afoot, ladies.
Azalea, do the honors.
beep!
VRRRRRRRRREEEEEEEEEEEEE.....
ding!
Evenin', folks!
Going down?

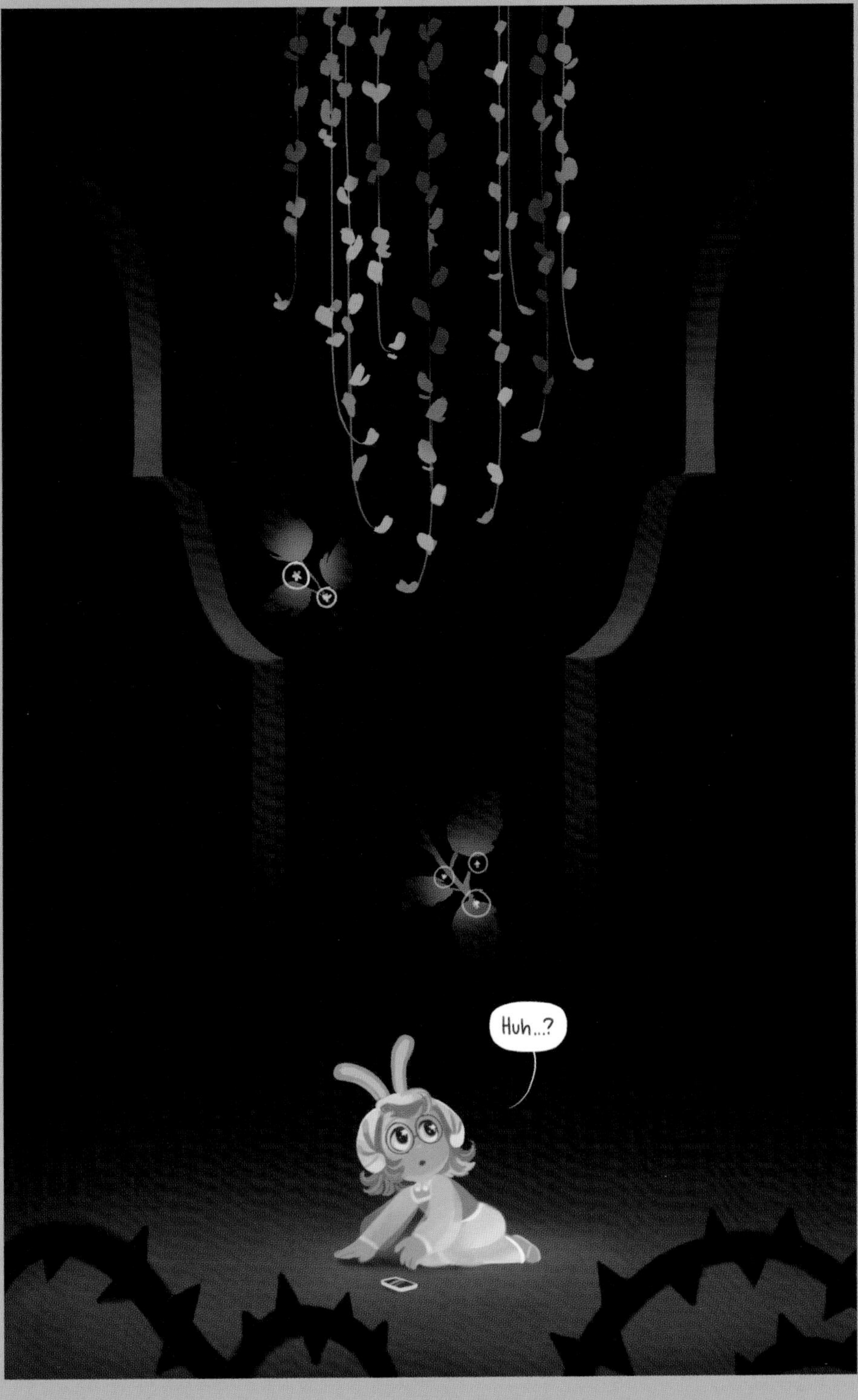
Huh...?

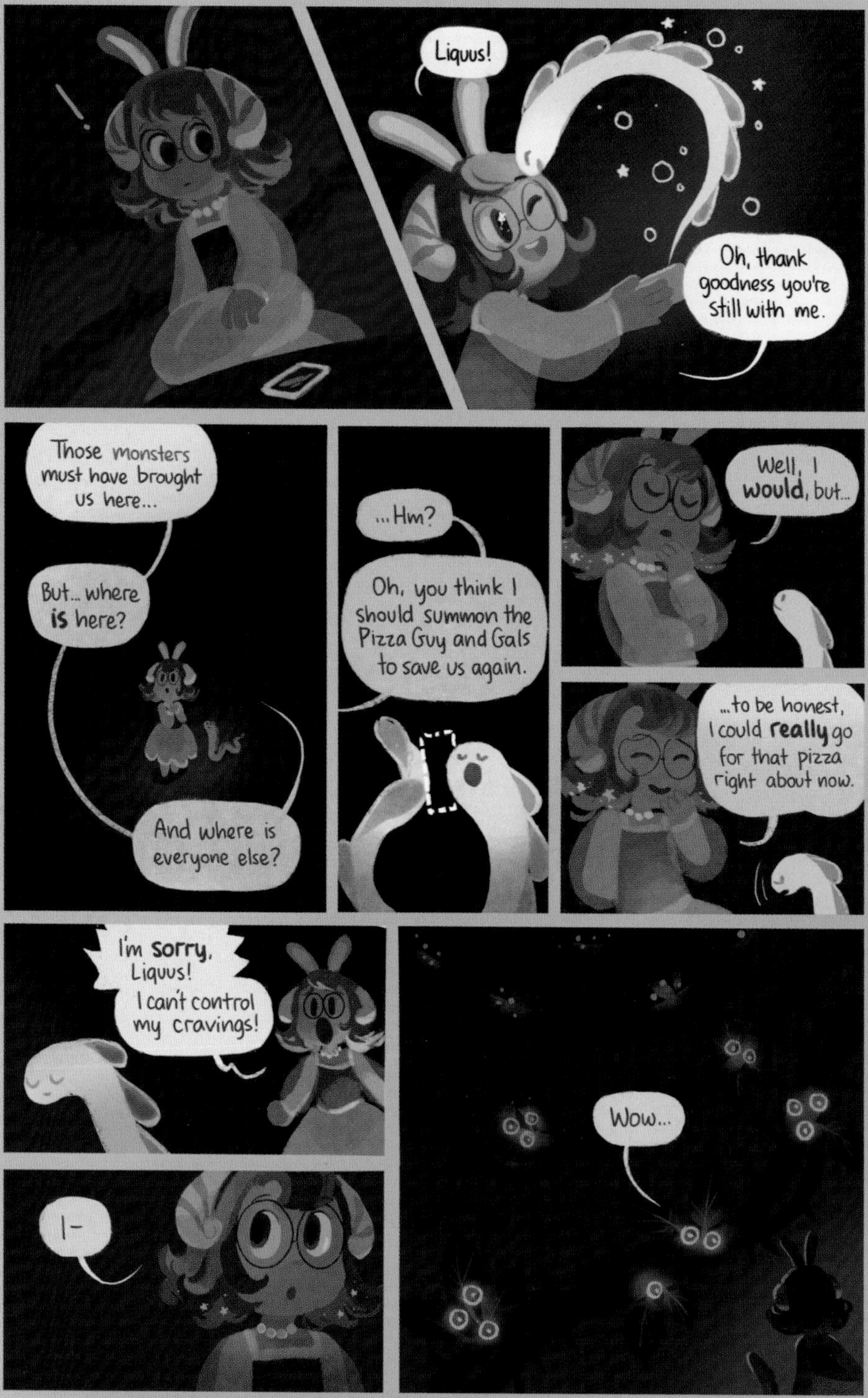
!
Liquus!
Oh, thank goodness you're still with me.
Those monsters must have brought us here...
But... where is here?
And where is everyone else?
...Hm?
Oh, you think I should summon the Pizza Guy and Gals to save us again.
Well, I would, but...
...to be honest, I could really go for that pizza right about now.
I'm sorry, Liquus! I can't control my cravings!
I-
Wow...

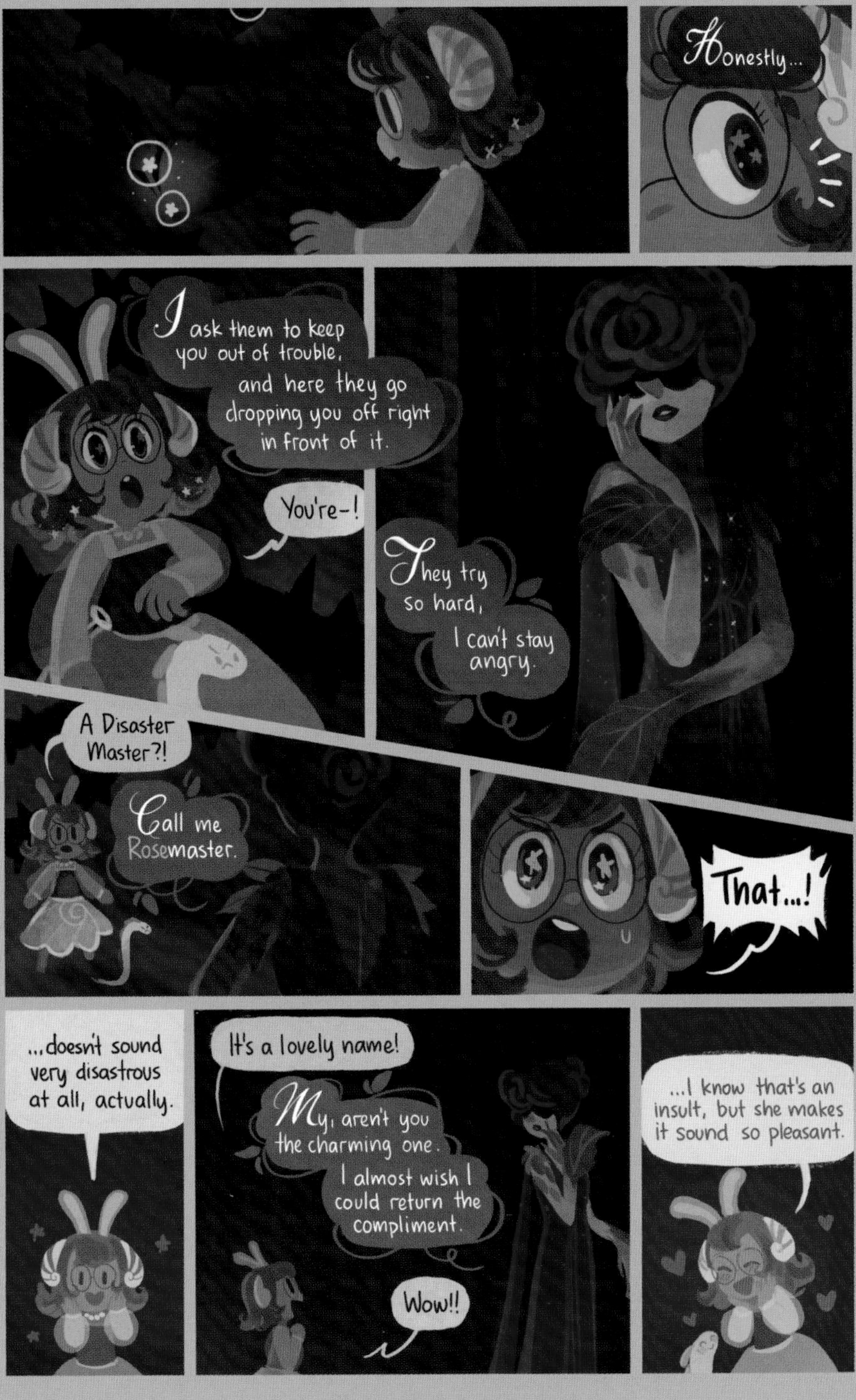
Honestly...
I ask them to keep you out of trouble, and here they go dropping you off right in front of it.
You're-!
They try so hard, I can't stay angry.
A Disaster Master?!
Call me Rosemaster.
That...!
...doesn't sound very disastrous at all, actually.
It's a lovely name!
My, aren't you the charming one. I almost wish I could return the compliment.
Wow!!
...I know that's an insult, but she makes it sound so pleasant.

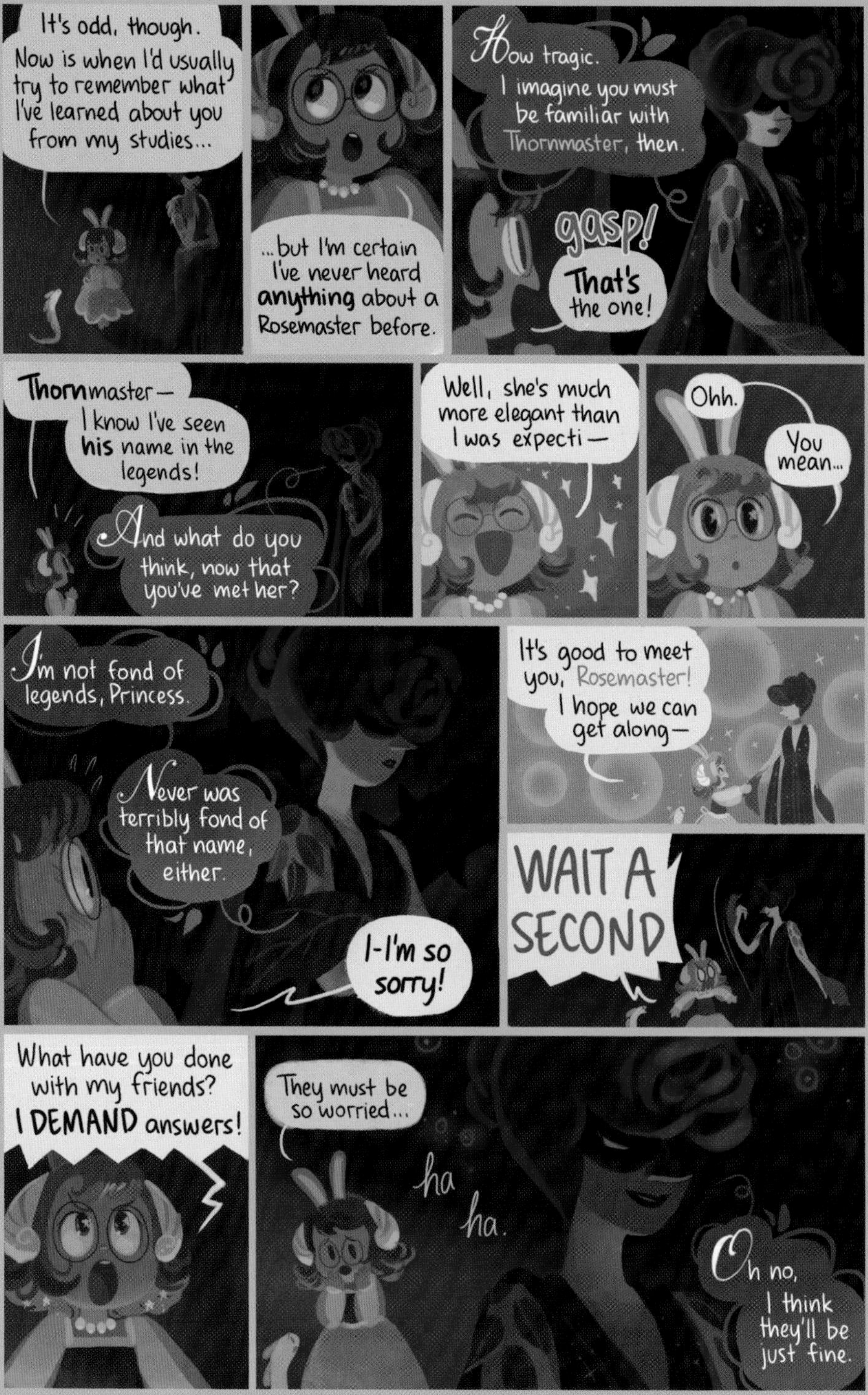
It's odd, though. Now is when I'd usually try to remember what I've learned about you from my studies...
...but I'm certain I've never heard **anything** about a Rosemaster before.
How tragic. I imagine you must be familiar with Thornmaster, then.
gasp!
That's the one!
Thornmaster— I know I've seen **his** name in the legends!
And what do you think, now that you've met her?
Well, she's much more elegant than I was expecti—
Ohh.
You mean...
I'm not fond of legends, Princess.
Never was terribly fond of that name, either.
I-I'm so sorry!
It's good to meet you, Rosemaster! I hope we can get along—
WAIT A SECOND
What have you done with my friends? I **DEMAND** answers!
They must be so worried...
ha ha.
Oh no, I think they'll be just fine.

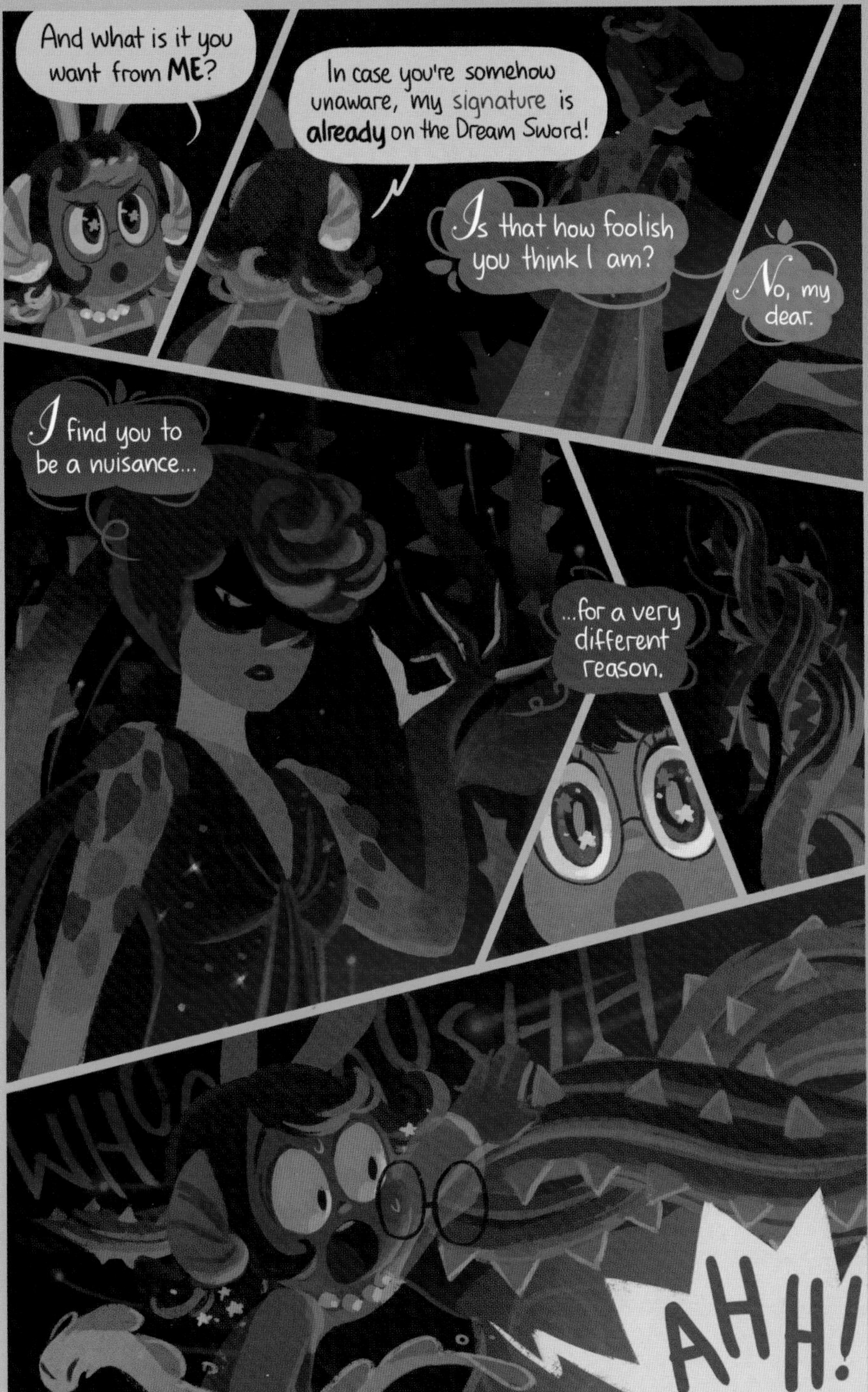
And what is it you want from ME?
In case you're somehow unaware, my signature is already on the Dream Sword!
Is that how foolish you think I am?
No, my dear.
I find you to be a nuisance...
...for a very different reason.
AHH!

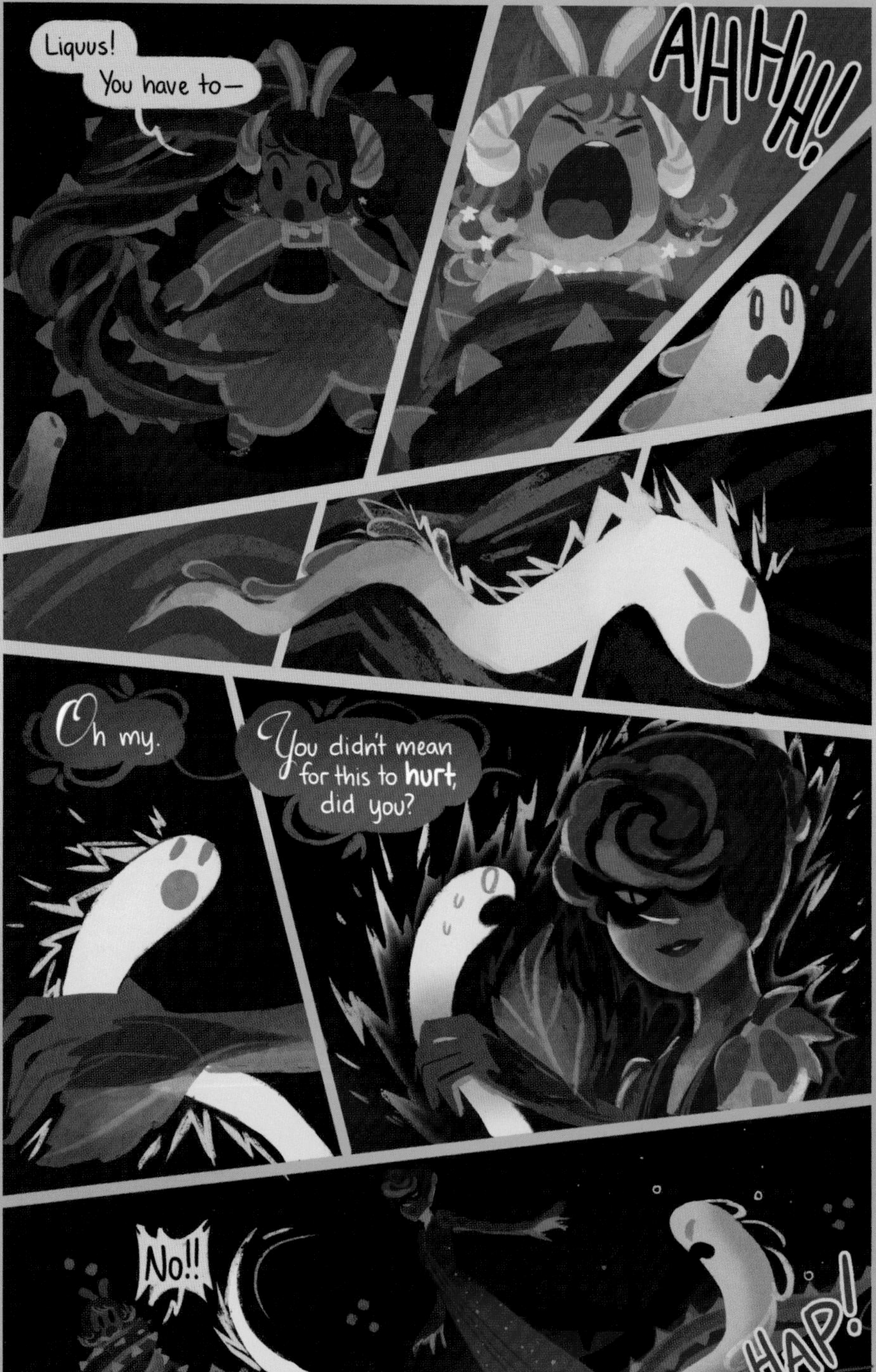
Liquus!
You have to—
AHHH!
Oh my.
You didn't mean for this to **hurt**, did you?
No!!
WHAP!

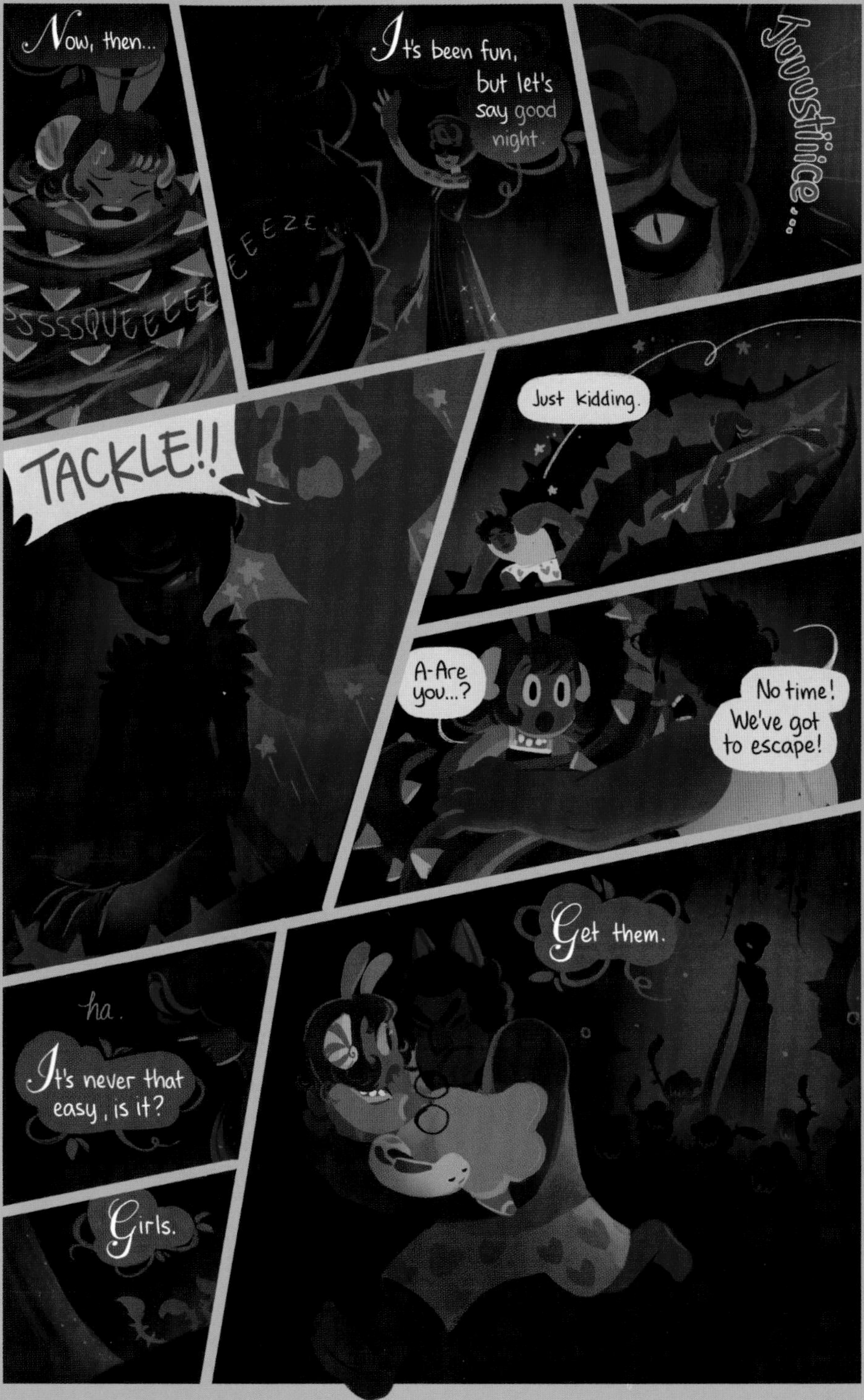
Now, then...
SSSSQUEEEEEEEEEEEZE...
It's been fun, but let's say good night.
Juuustiiice...
TACKLE!!
Just kidding.
A-Are you...?
No time! We've got to escape!
ha.
It's never that easy, is it?
Girls.
Get them.

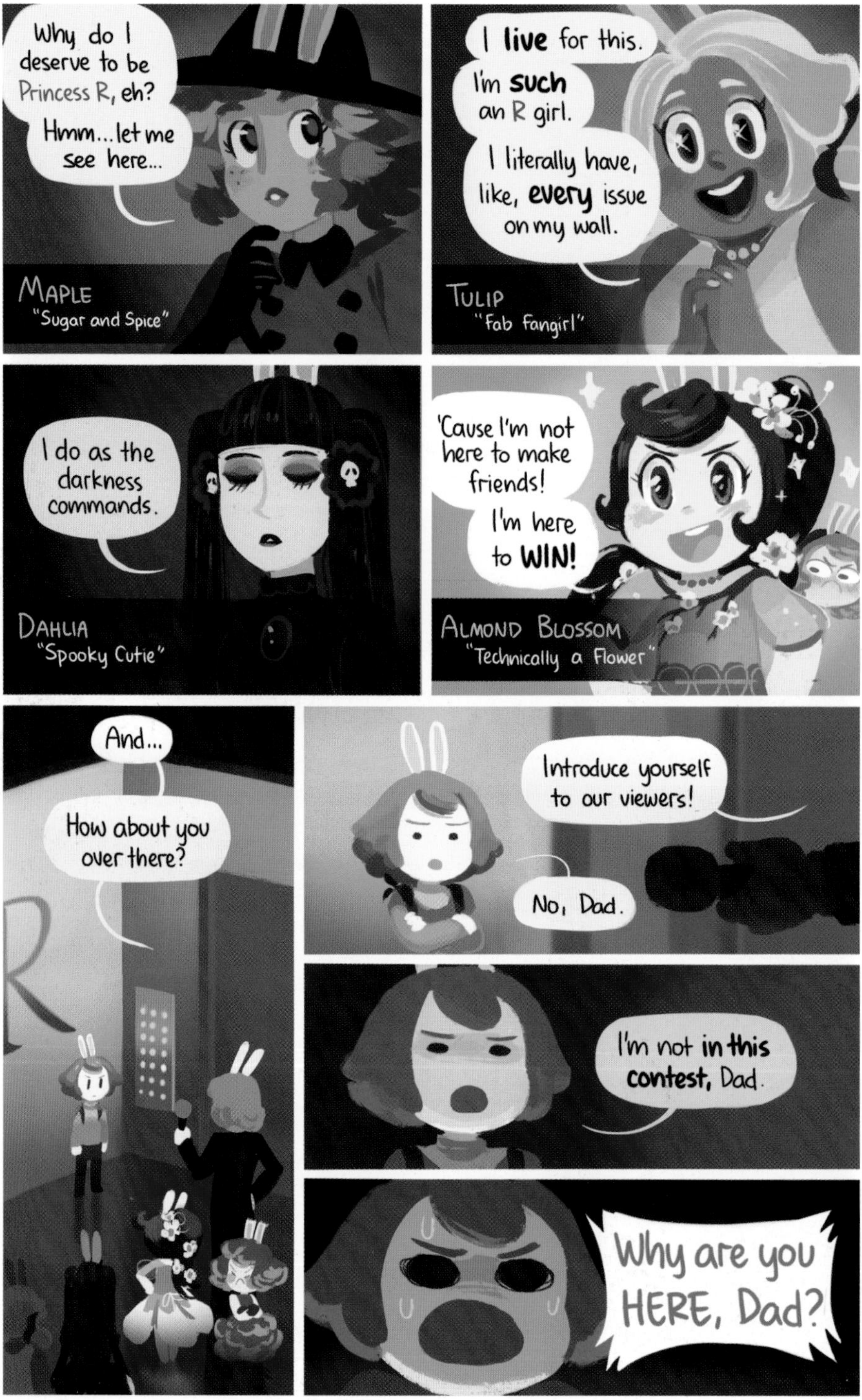
Why do I deserve to be Princess R, eh?
Hmm... let me see here...
MAPLE
"Sugar and Spice"
I live for this.
I'm such an R girl.
I literally have, like, every issue on my wall.
TULIP
"Fab Fangirl"
I do as the darkness commands.
DAHLIA
"Spooky Cutie"
'Cause I'm not here to make friends!
I'm here to WIN!
ALMOND BLOSSOM
"Technically a Flower"
And...
How about you over there?
Introduce yourself to our viewers!
No, Dad.
I'm not in this contest, Dad.
Why are you HERE, Dad?

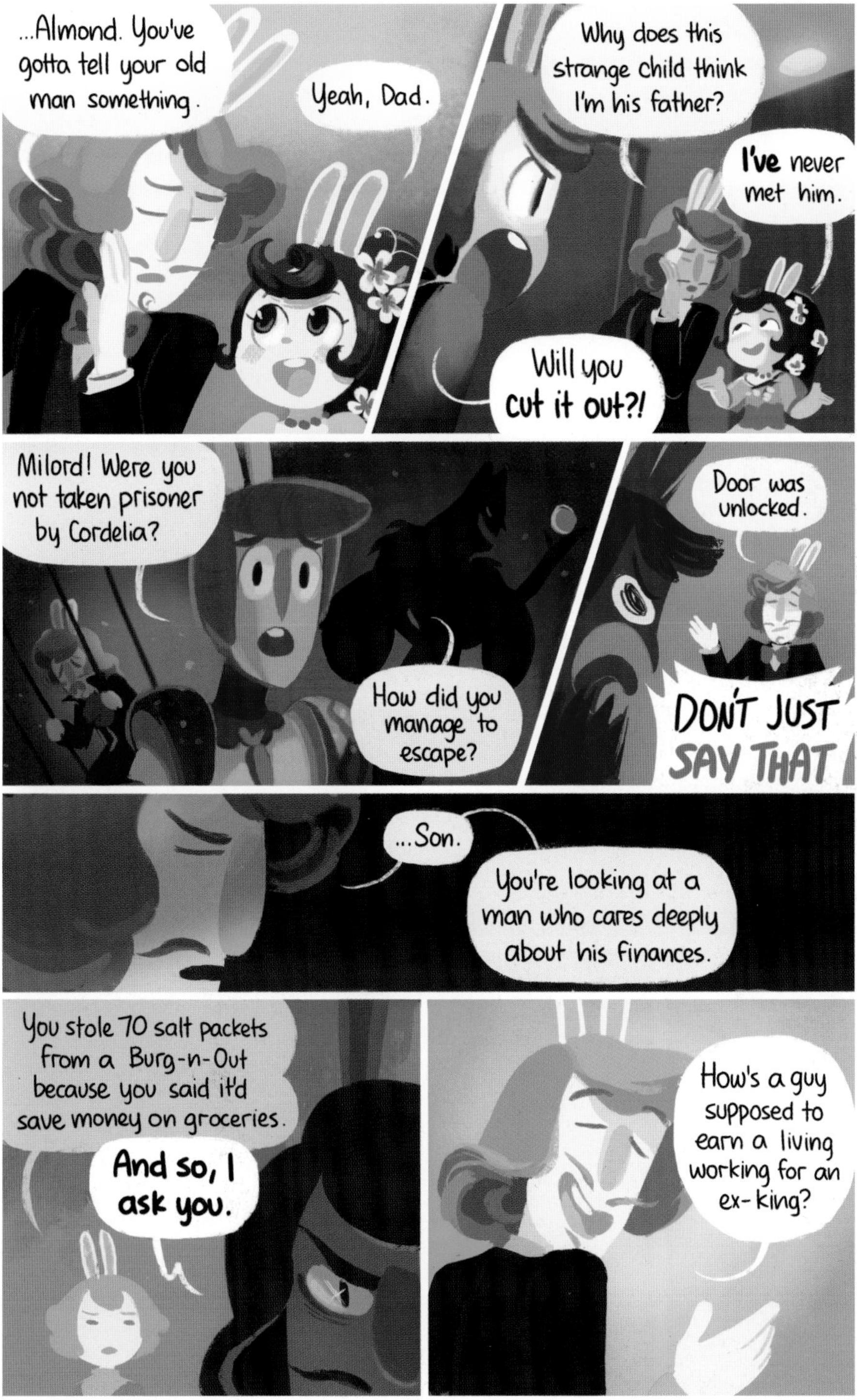

...Almond. You've gotta tell your old man something.
Yeah, Dad.
Why does this strange child think I'm his father?
I've never met him.
Will you **cut it out?!**
Milord! Were you not taken prisoner by Cordelia?
How did you manage to escape?
Door was unlocked.
DON'T JUST SAY THAT
...Son.
You're looking at a man who cares deeply about his finances.
You stole 70 salt packets from a Burg-n-Out because you said it'd save money on groceries.
And so, I ask you.
How's a guy supposed to earn a living working for an ex-king?

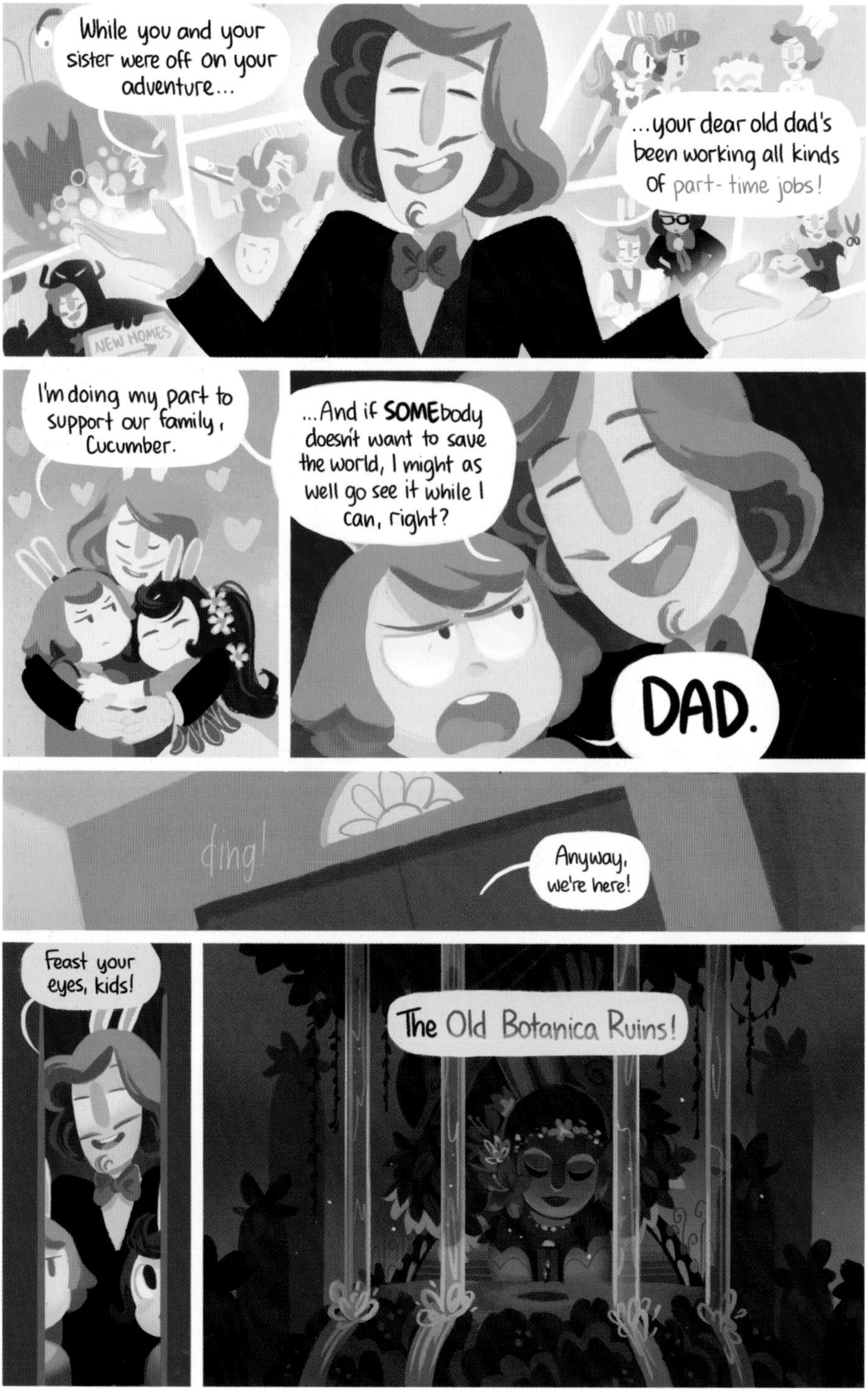
While you and your sister were off on your adventure...
...your dear old dad's been working all kinds of part-time jobs!
NEW HOMES
I'm doing my part to support our family, Cucumber.
...And if SOMEbody doesn't want to save the world, I might as well go see it while I can, right?
DAD.
ding!
Anyway, we're here!
Feast your eyes, kids!
The Old Botanica Ruins!

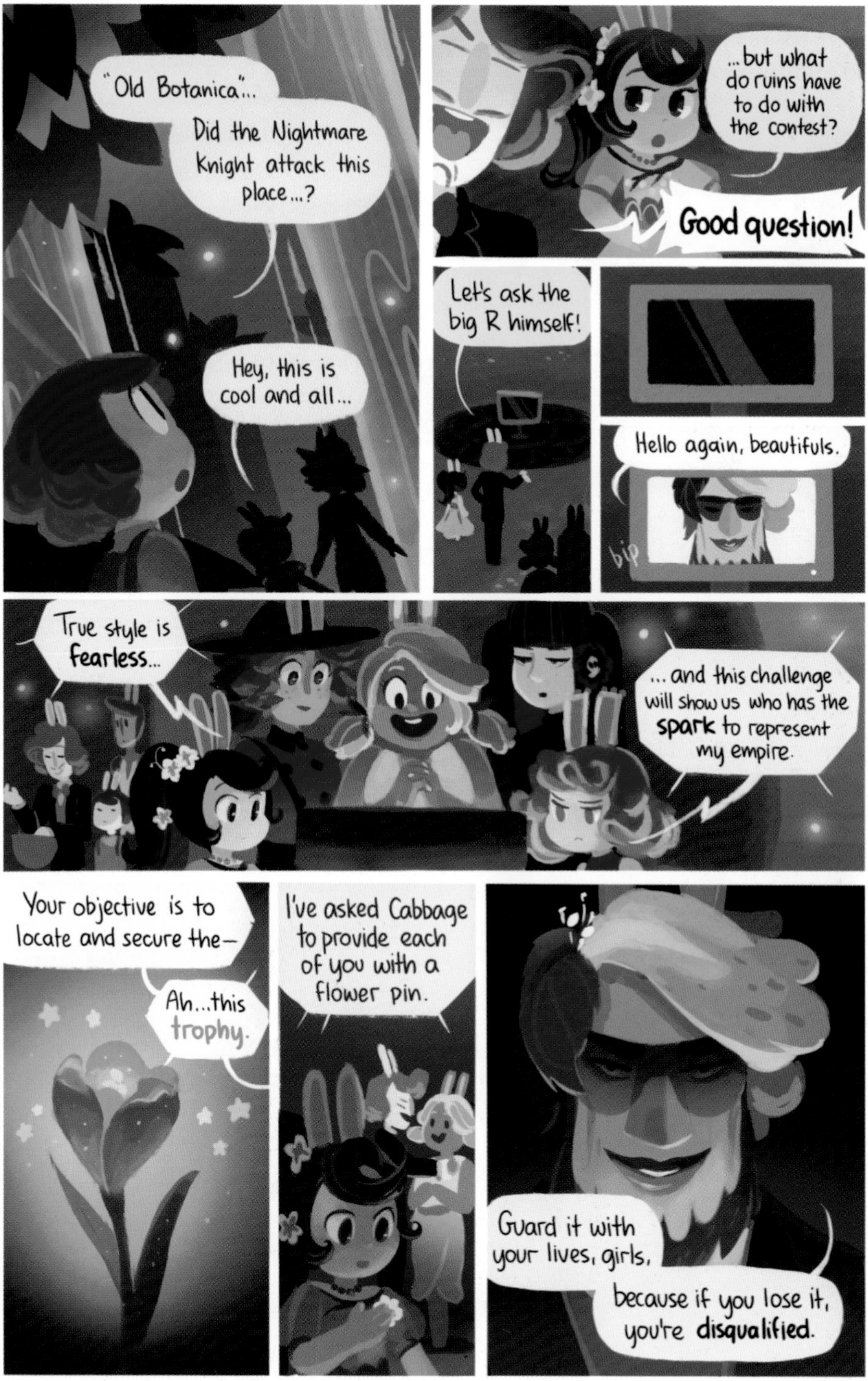
"Old Botanica"...
Did the Nightmare Knight attack this place...?
Hey, this is cool and all...
...but what do ruins have to do with the contest?
Good question!
Let's ask the big R himself!
Hello again, beautifuls.
bip
True style is fearless...
...and this challenge will show us who has the spark to represent my empire.
Your objective is to locate and secure the—
Ah...this trophy.
I've asked Cabbage to provide each of you with a flower pin.
Guard it with your lives, girls,
because if you lose it, you're disqualified.

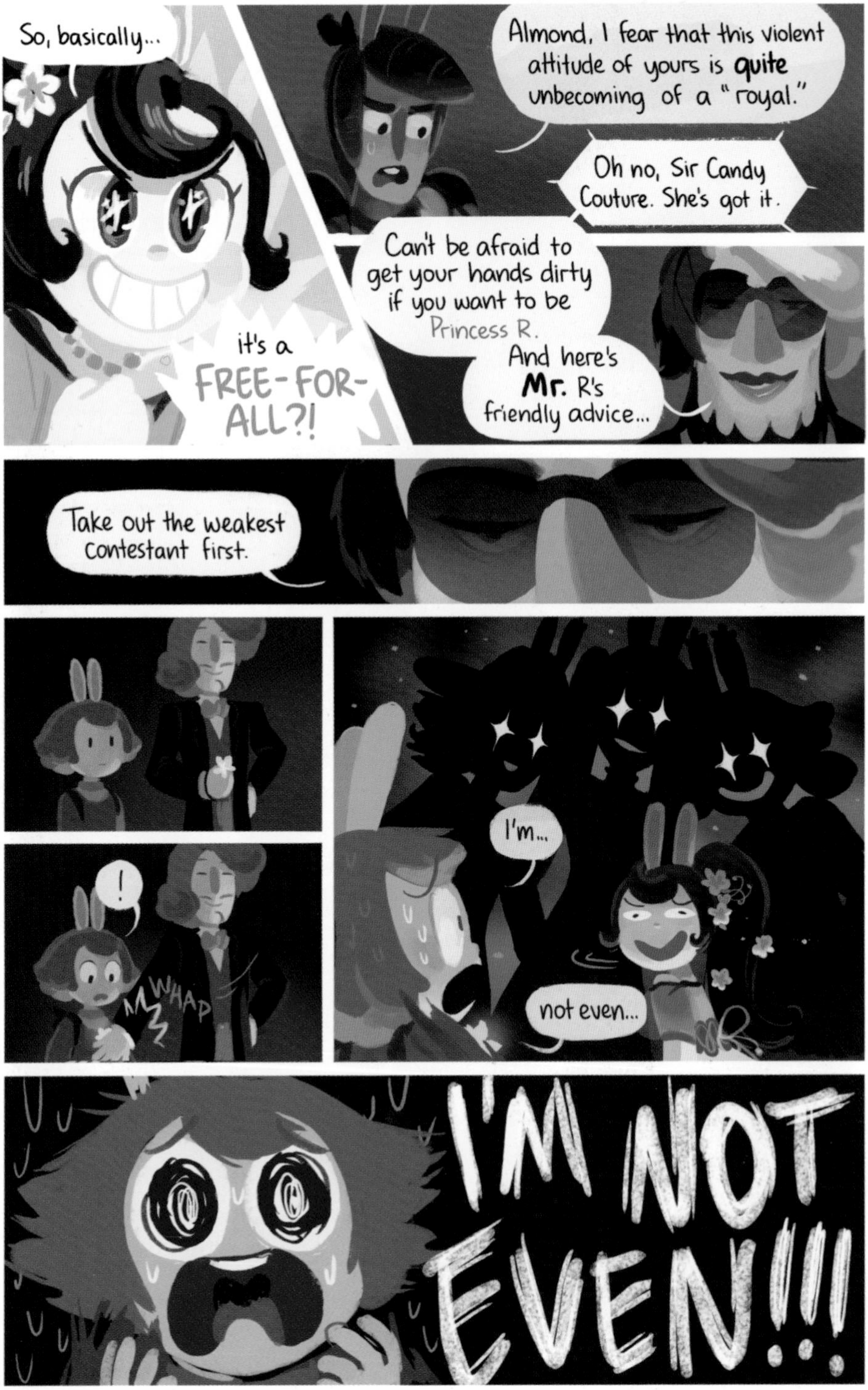
So, basically...
it's a FREE-FOR-ALL?!
Almond, I fear that this violent attitude of yours is **quite** unbecoming of a "royal."
Oh no, Sir Candy Couture. She's got it.
Can't be afraid to get your hands dirty if you want to be Princess R.
And here's **Mr.** R's friendly advice...
Take out the weakest contestant first.
!
WHAP
I'm...
not even...
I'M NOT EVEN!!!

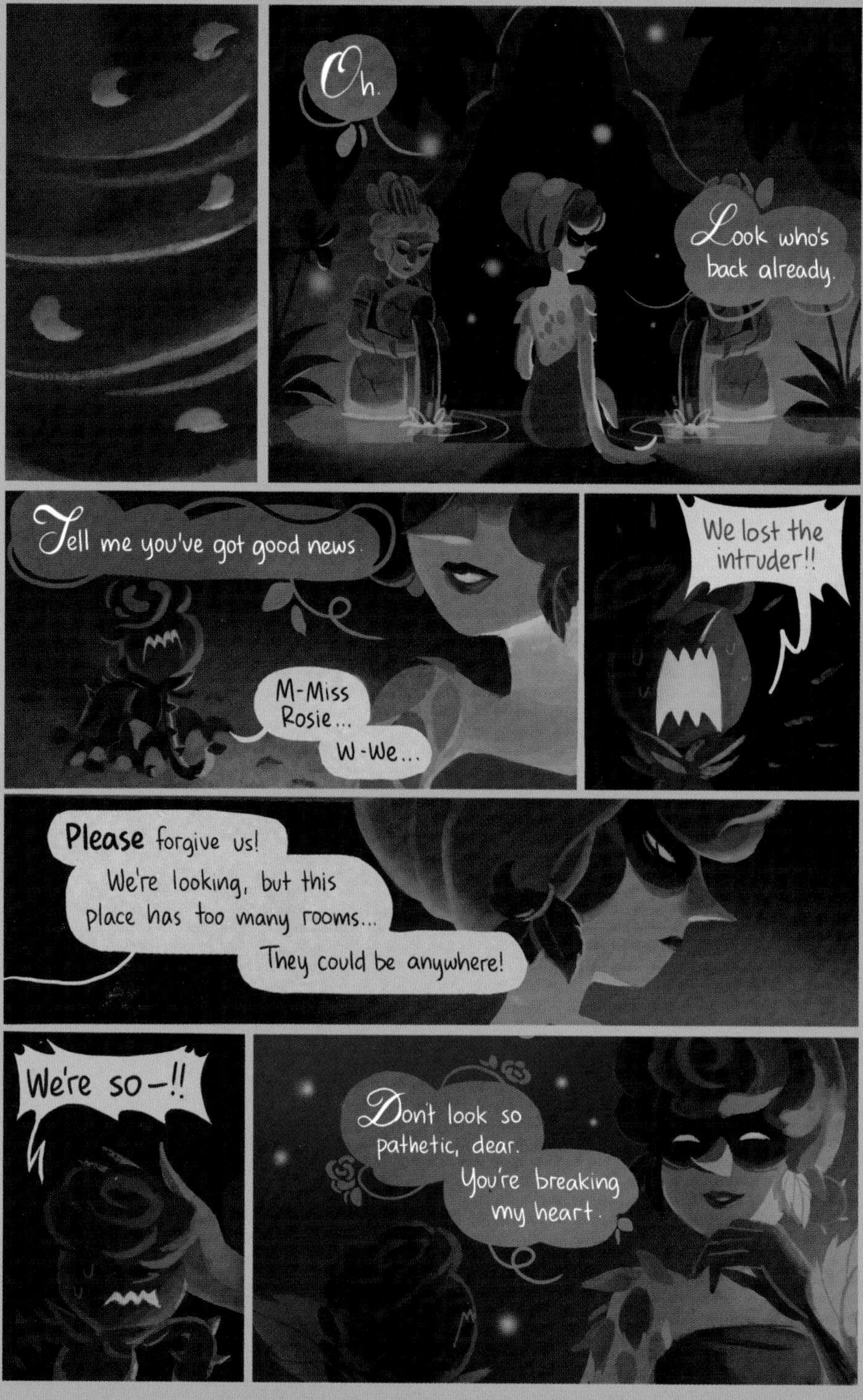
Oh.
Look who's back already.
Tell me you've got good news.
M-Miss Rosie...
W-We...
We lost the intruder!!
Please forgive us!
We're looking, but this place has too many rooms...
They could be anywhere!
We're so–!!
Don't look so pathetic, dear.
You're breaking my heart.

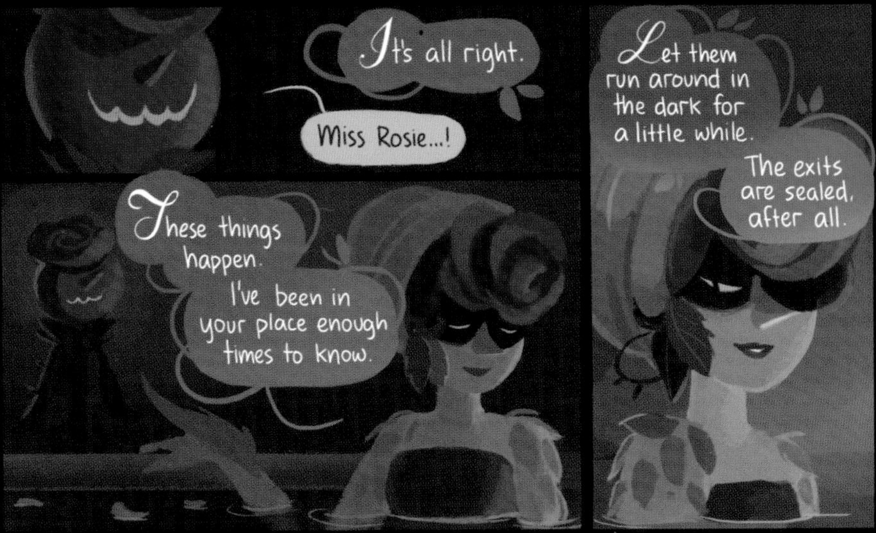
It's all right.
Miss Rosie...!
These things happen.
I've been in your place enough times to know.
Let them run around in the dark for a little while.
The exits are sealed, after all.

Our orders?

Focus on the contest.

I want you to make sure no one else like her slips in.

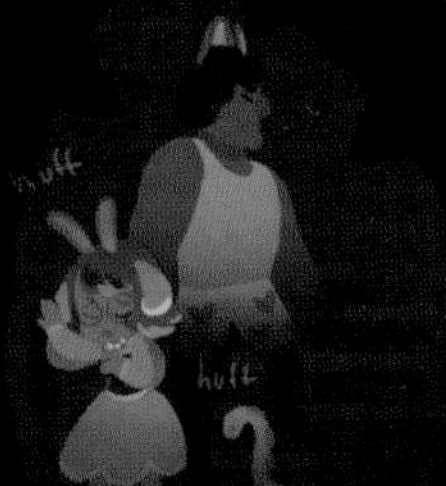
huff
huff

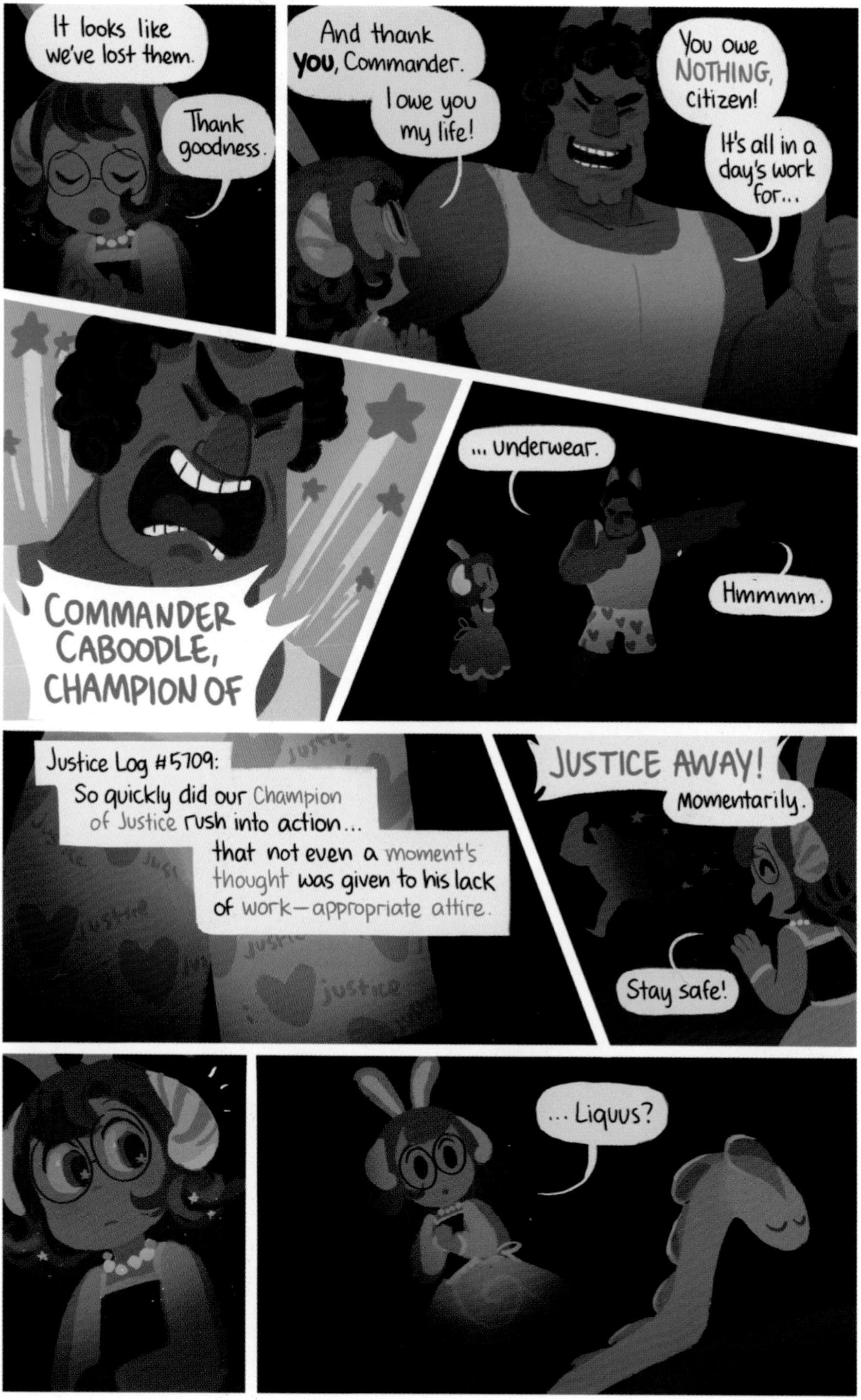
It looks like we've lost them.
Thank goodness.
And thank YOU, Commander.
I owe you my life!
You owe NOTHING, citizen!
It's all in a day's work for...
COMMANDER CABOODLE, CHAMPION OF
... underwear.
Hmmmm.
Justice Log #5709:
So quickly did our Champion of Justice rush into action...
that not even a moment's thought was given to his lack of work—appropriate attire.
JUSTICE AWAY!
Momentarily.
Stay safe!
... Liquus?

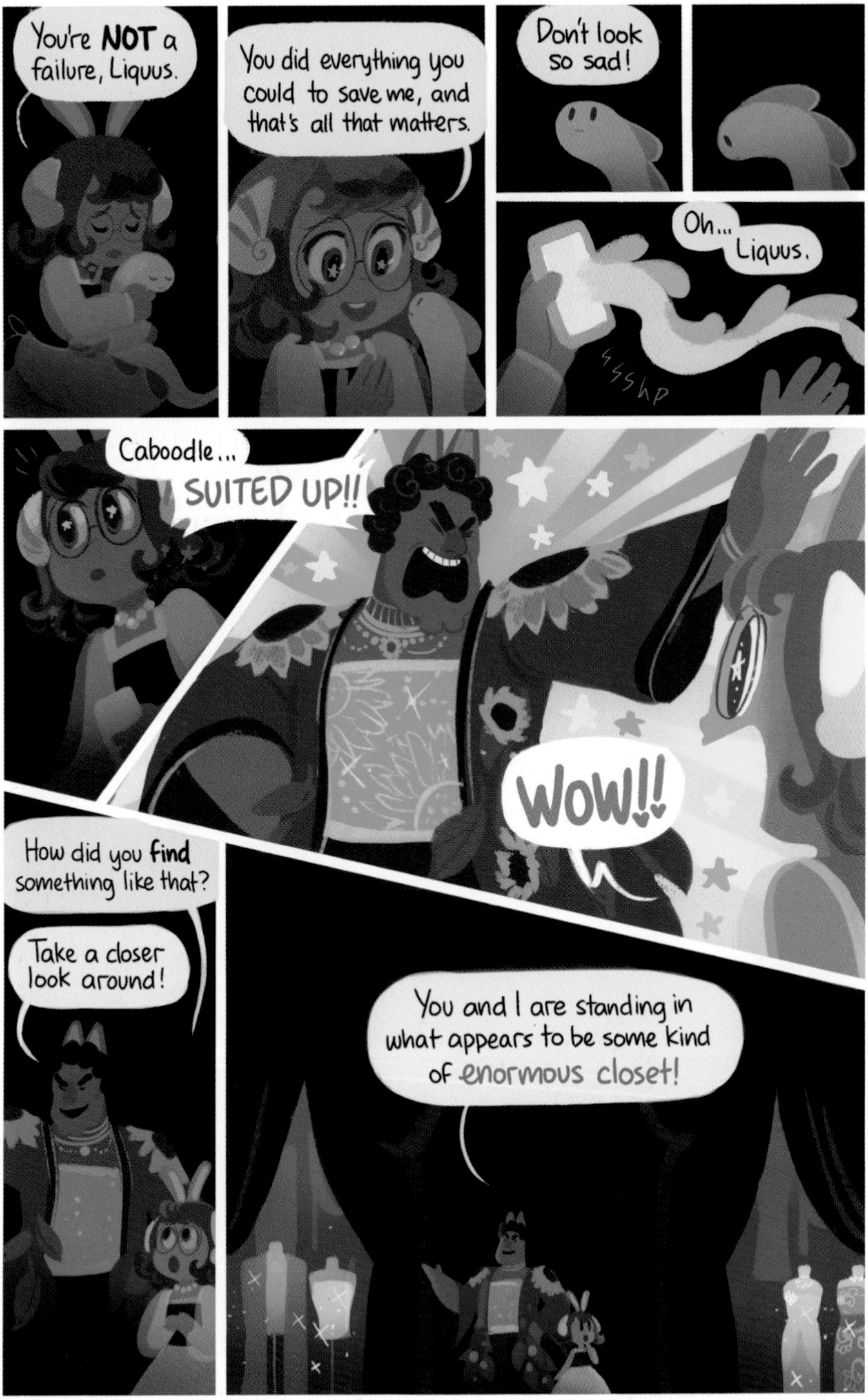
You're NOT a failure, Liquus.
You did everything you could to save me, and that's all that matters.
Don't look so sad!
Oh... Liquus.
ssshp
Caboodle...
SUITED UP!!
WOW!!
How did you find something like that?
Take a closer look around!
You and I are standing in what appears to be some kind of enormous closet!

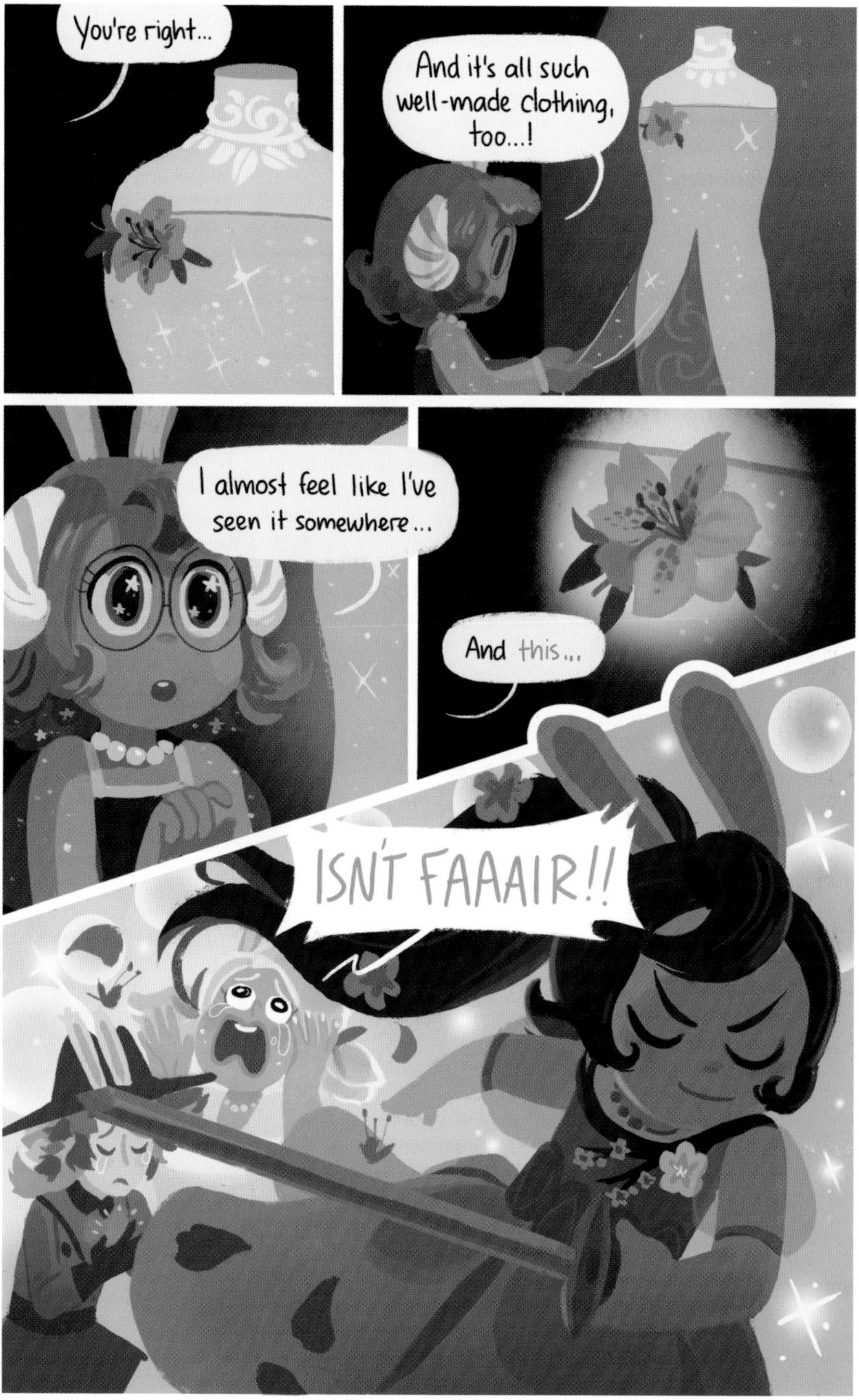
You're right...
And it's all such well-made clothing, too...!
I almost feel like I've seen it somewhere...
And this...
ISN'T FAAAIR!!

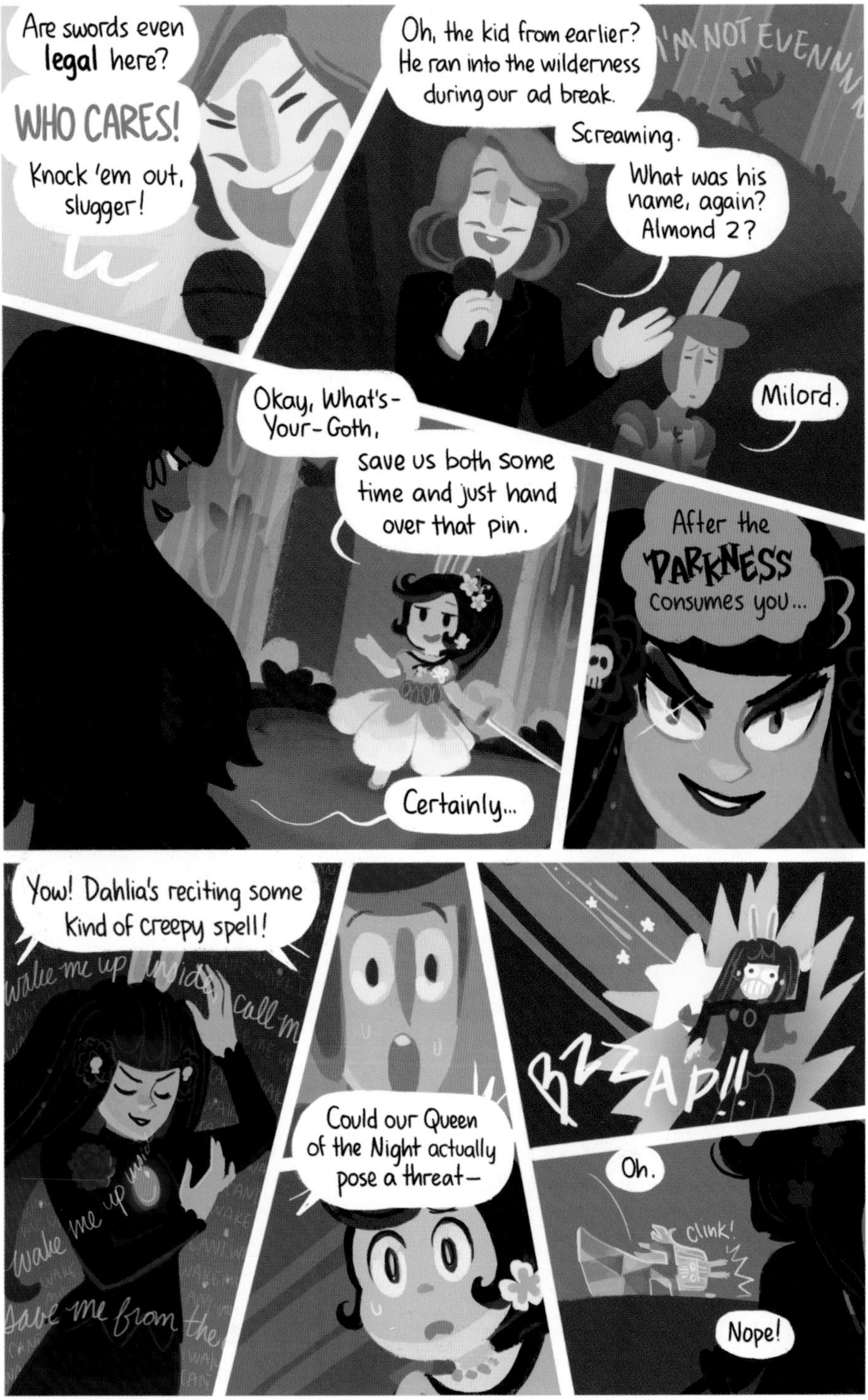

Are swords even **legal** here?
WHO CARES!
Knock 'em out, slugger!
Oh, the kid from earlier? He ran into the wilderness during our ad break.
I'M NOT EVENNNN
Screaming.
What was his name, again? Almond 2?
Milord.
Okay, What's-Your-Goth,
save us both some time and just hand over that pin.
Certainly...
After the DARKNESS consumes you...
Yow! Dahlia's reciting some kind of creepy spell!
wake me up
call me
wake me up
save me from the
Could our Queen of the Night actually pose a threat—
BZZZAP!!
Oh.
CLINK!
Nope!

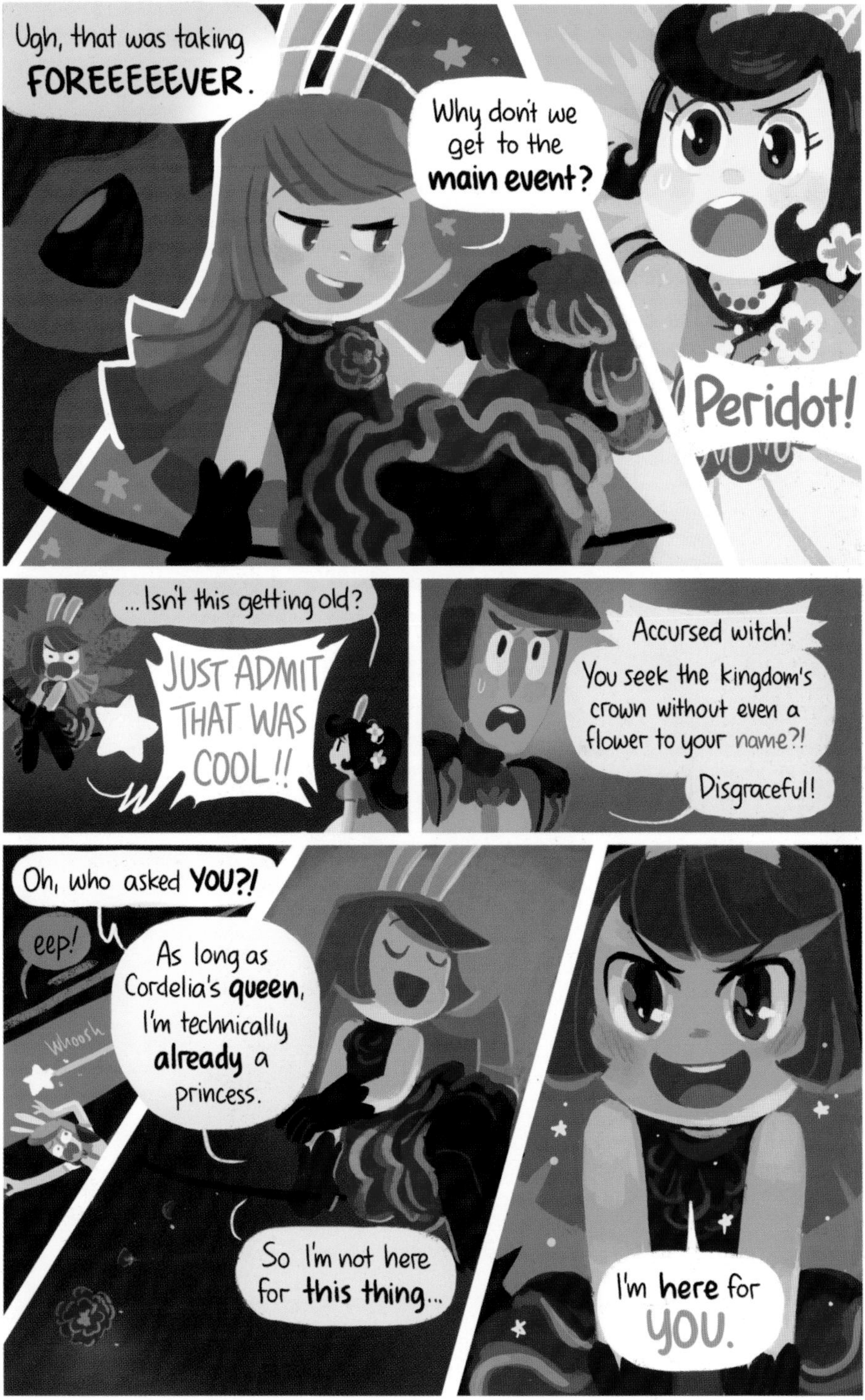
Ugh, that was taking FOREEEEEVER.
Why don't we get to the main event?
Peridot!
...Isn't this getting old?
JUST ADMIT THAT WAS COOL!!
Accursed witch!
You seek the kingdom's crown without even a flower to your name?!
Disgraceful!
Oh, who asked YOU?!
eep!
Whoosh
As long as Cordelia's queen, I'm technically already a princess.
So I'm not here for this thing...
I'm here for YOU.

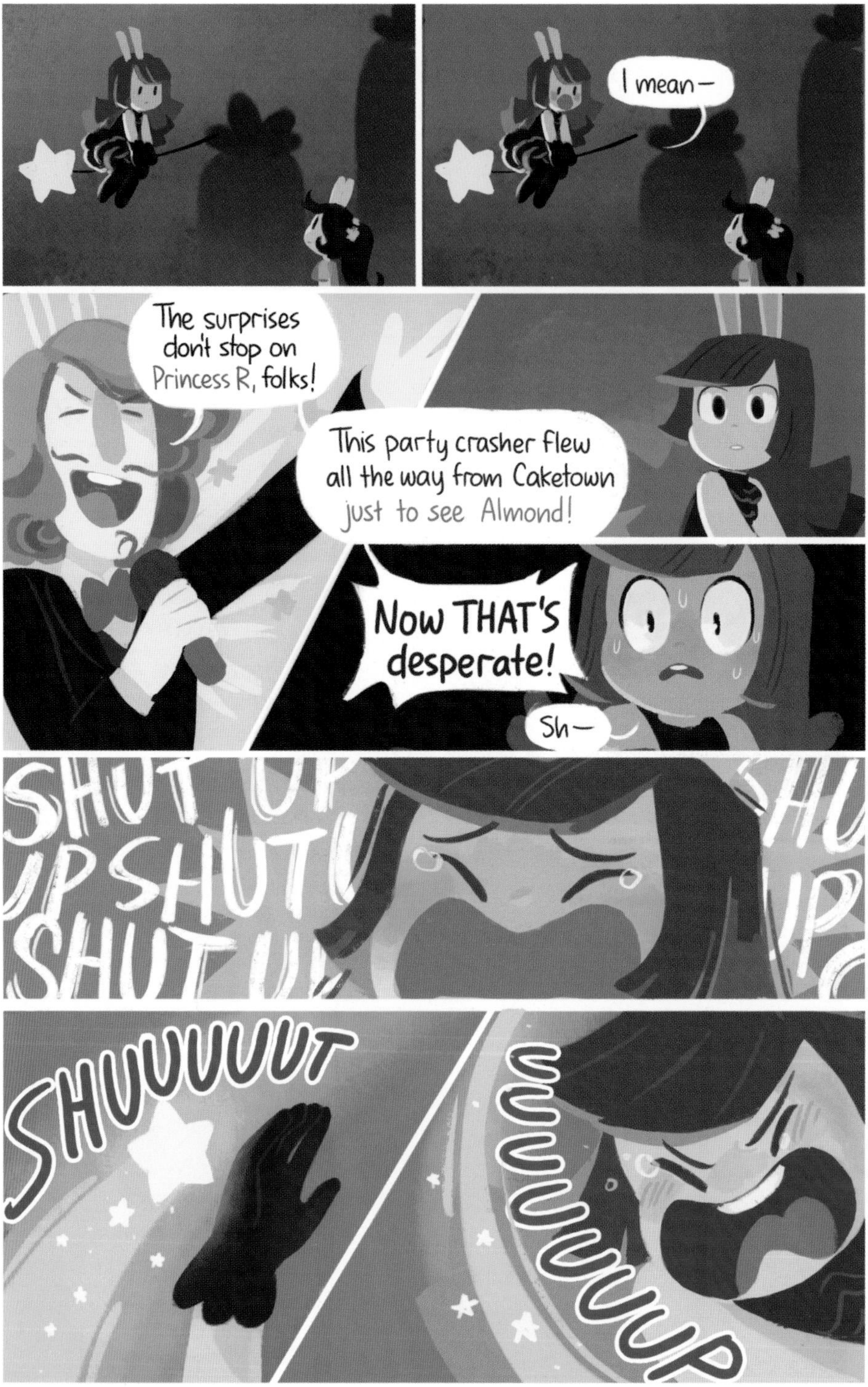
I mean—
The surprises don't stop on Princess R, folks!
This party crasher flew all the way from Caketown just to see Almond!
Now THAT'S desperate!
Sh—
SHUT UP SHUT UP SHUT
SHUUUUUT
UUUUUUUUP

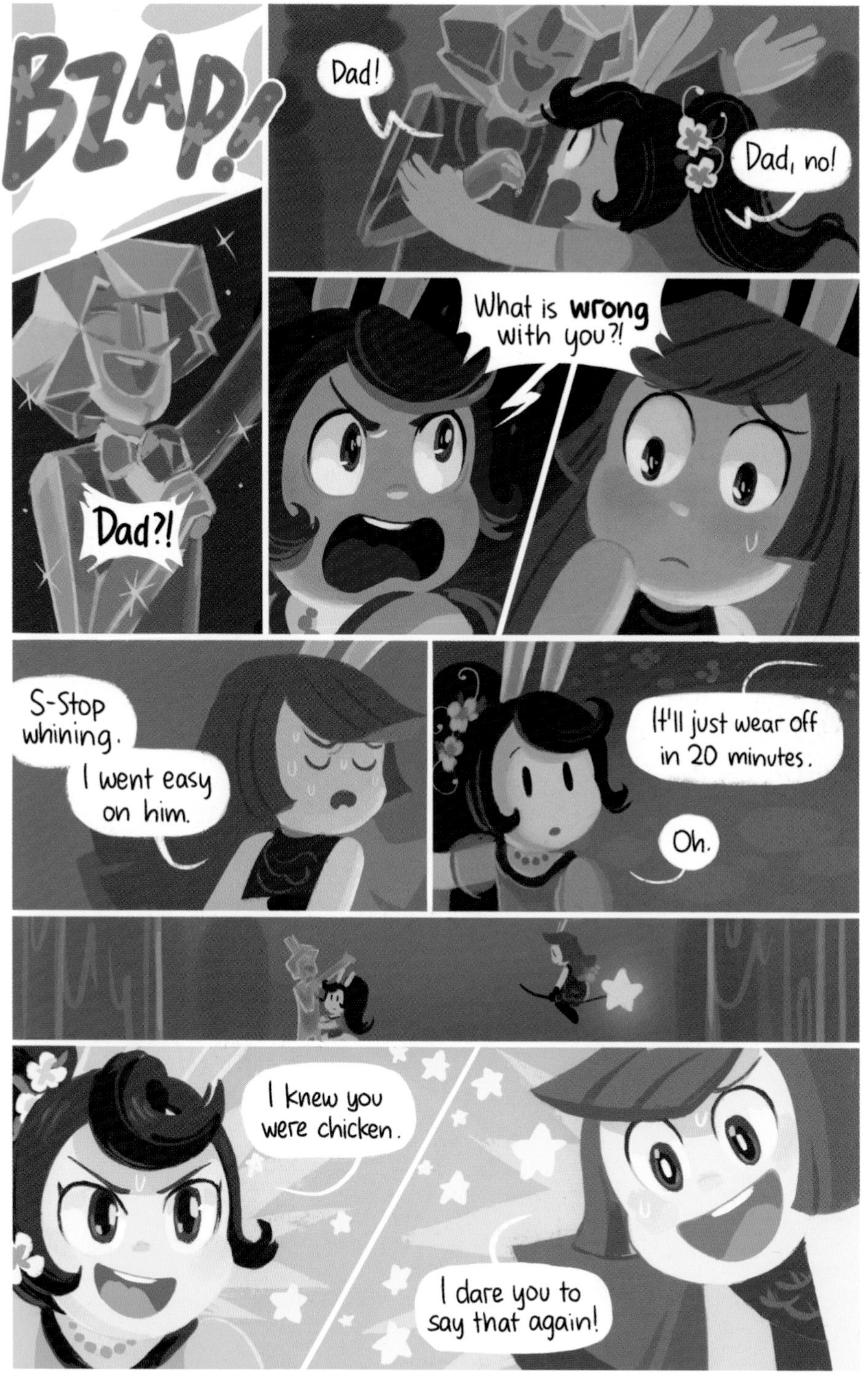
BZAP!
Dad!
Dad, no!
Dad?!
What is **wrong** with you?!
S-Stop whining.
I went easy on him.
It'll just wear off in 20 minutes.
Oh.
I knew you were chicken.
I dare you to say that again!

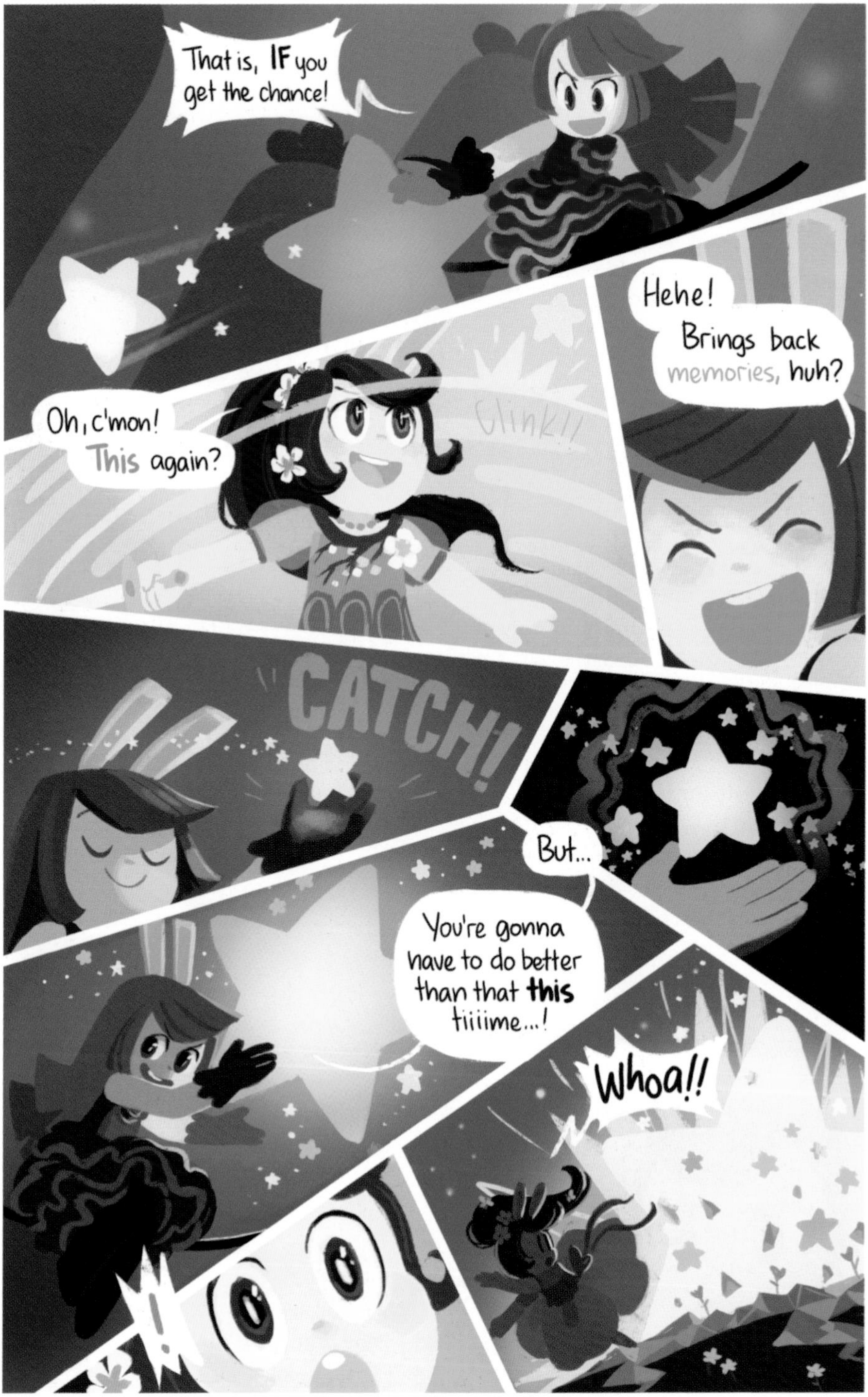

That is, IF you get the chance!
Oh, c'mon! This again?
Clink!!
Hehe! Brings back memories, huh?
CATCH!
But...
You're gonna have to do better than that this tiiiime...!
Whoa!!
!

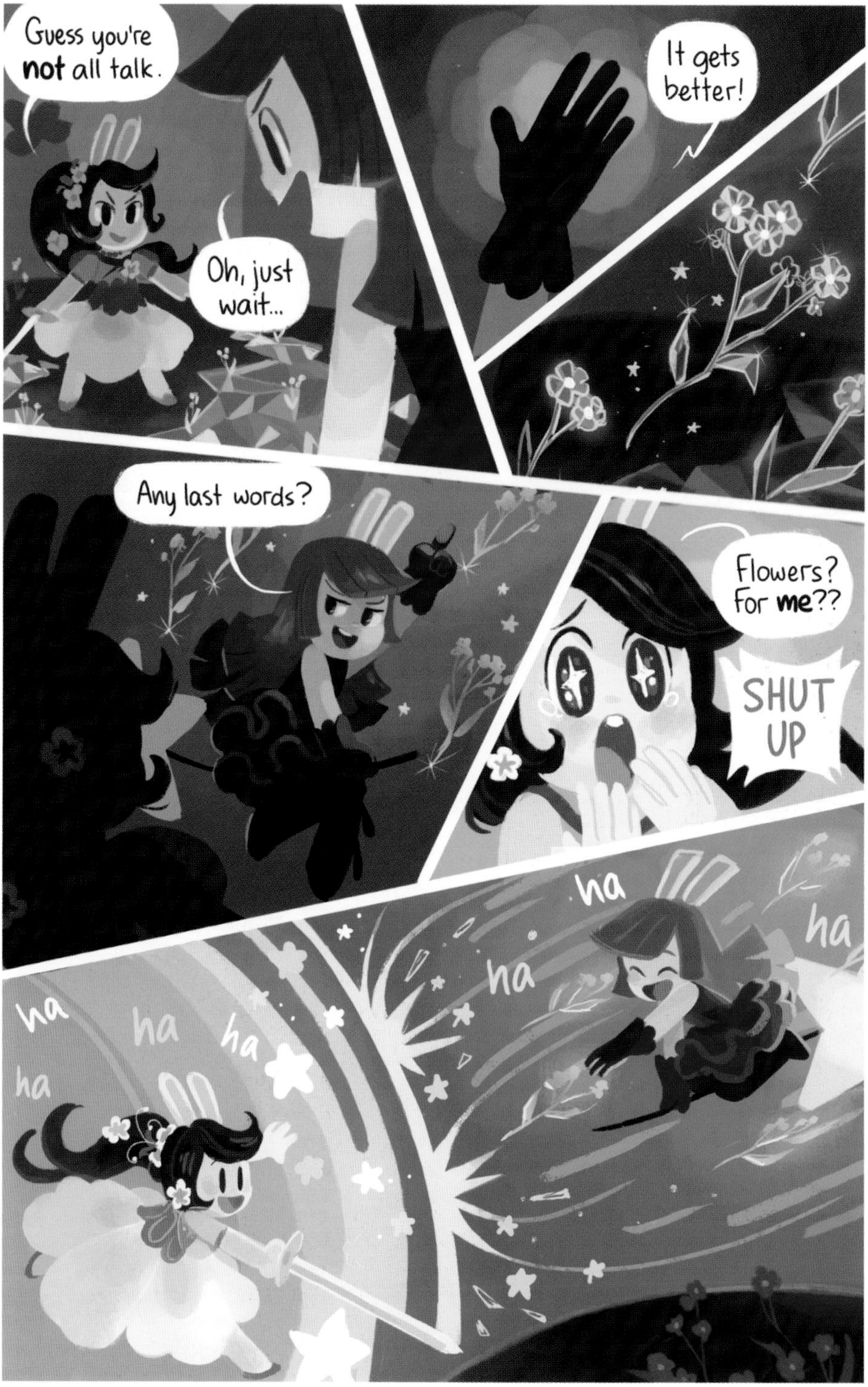
Guess you're **not** all talk.
Oh, just wait...
It gets better!
Any last words?
Flowers? For **me**??
SHUT UP
ha
ha
ha
ha
ha
ha
ha

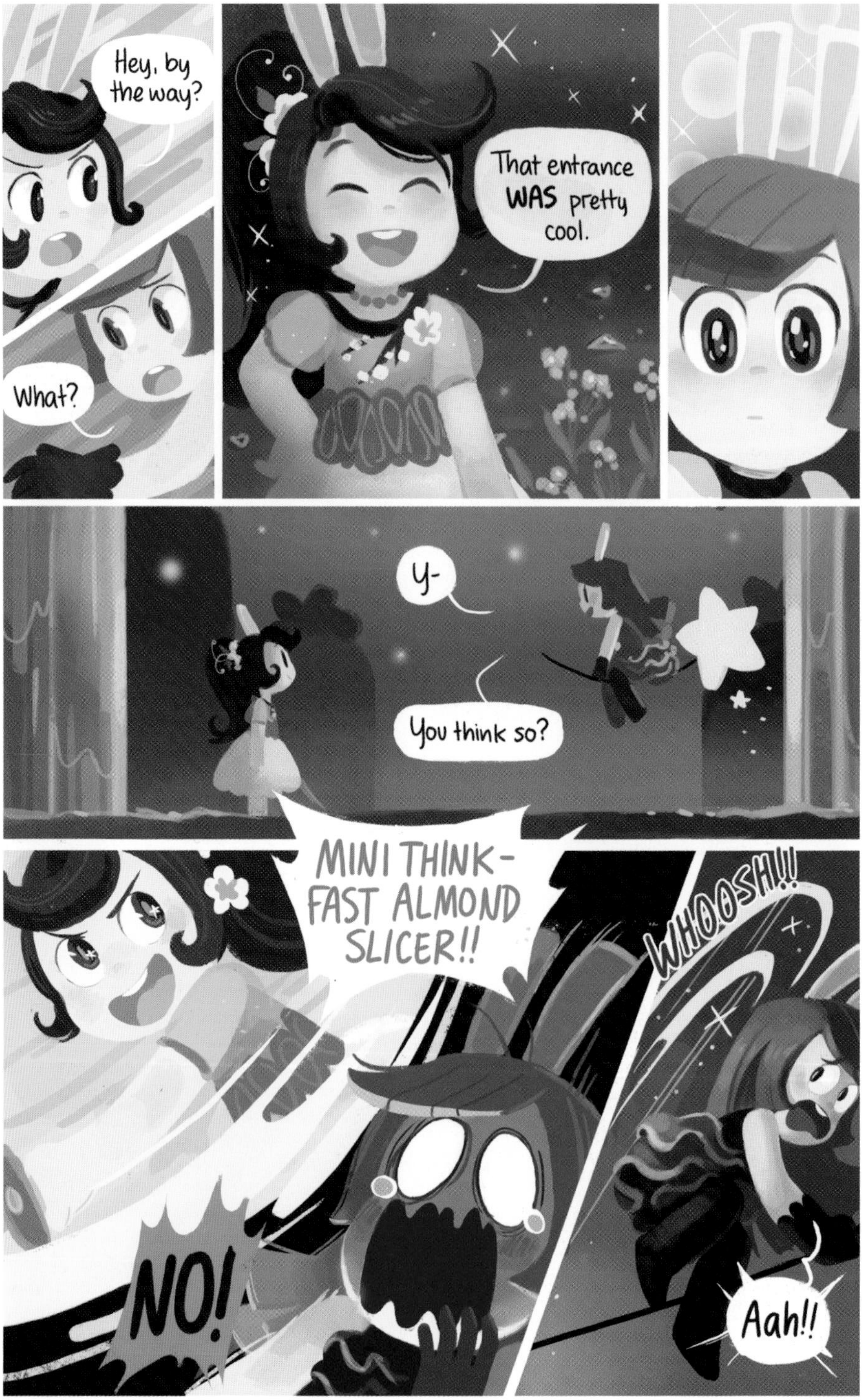
Hey, by the way?
What?
That entrance WAS pretty cool.
Y-
You think so?
MINI THINK-FAST ALMOND SLICER!!
WHOOSH!!
NO!
Aah!!

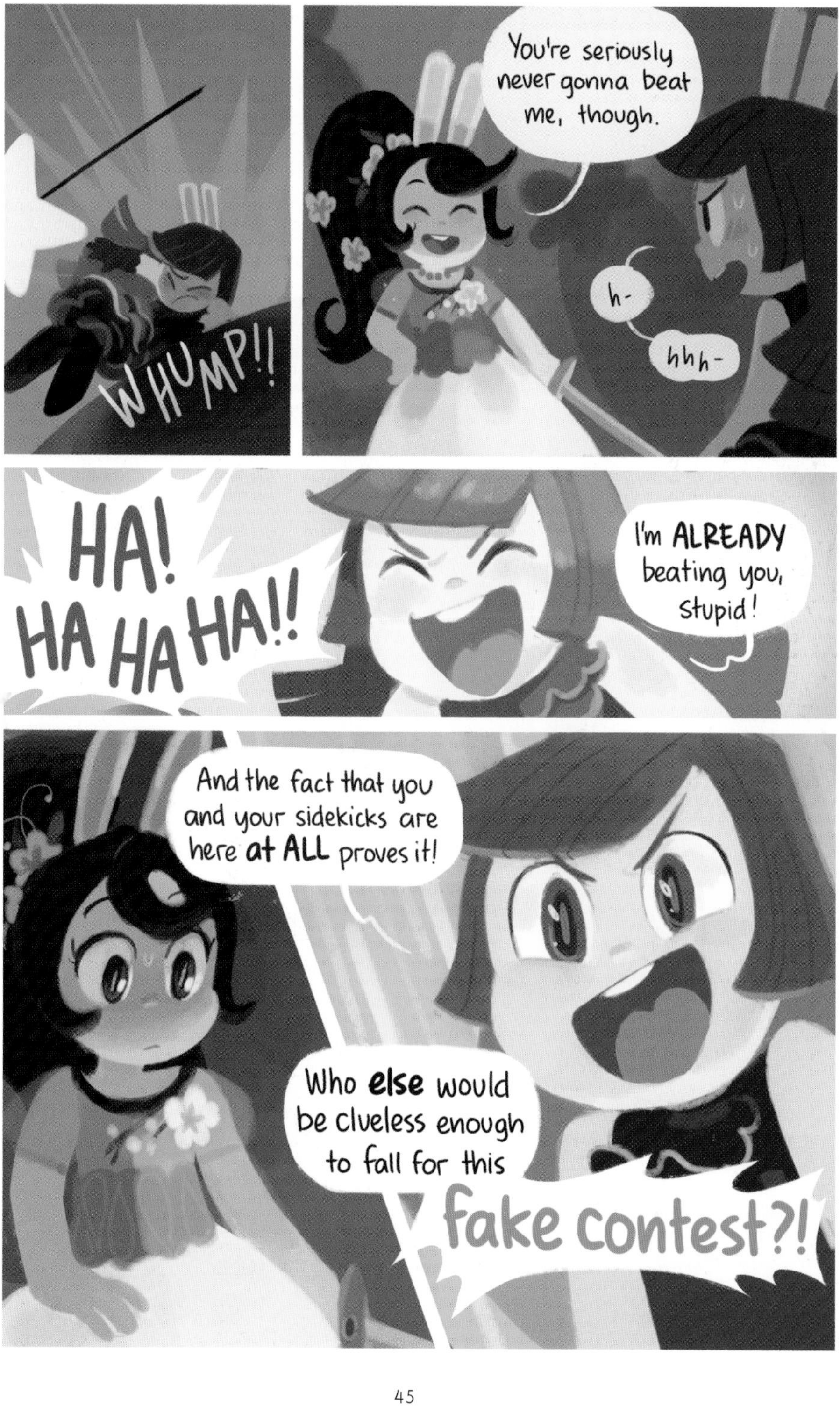
WHUMP!!
You're seriously never gonna beat me, though.
h-
hhh-
HA! HA HA HA!!
I'm **ALREADY** beating you, stupid!
And the fact that you and your sidekicks are here **at ALL** proves it!
Who **else** would be clueless enough to fall for this
fake contest?!

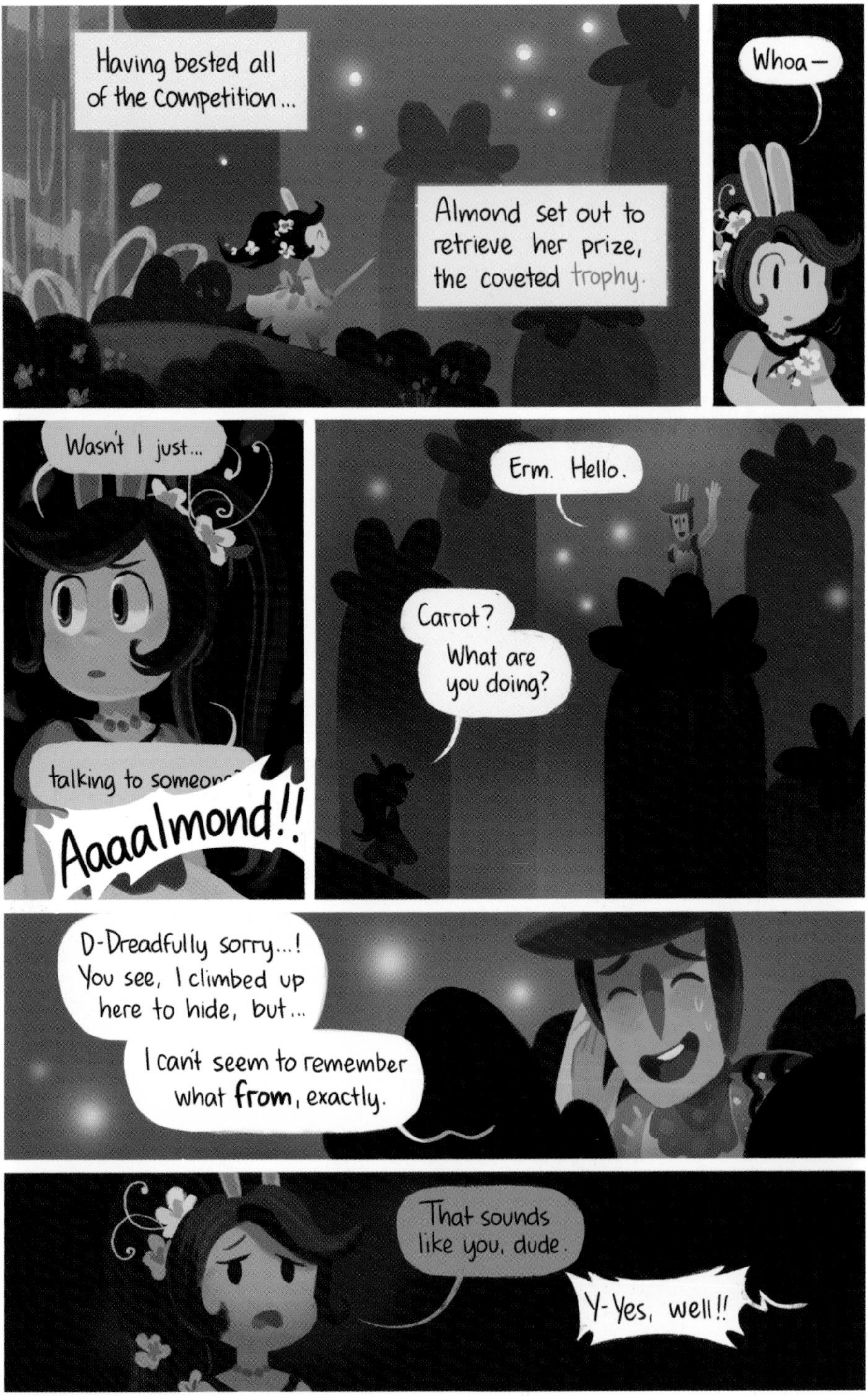

Having bested all of the competition...
Almond set out to retrieve her prize, the coveted trophy.
Whoa—
Wasn't I just...
talking to someone?
Aaaalmond!!
Erm. Hello.
Carrot?
What are you doing?
D-Dreadfully sorry...! You see, I climbed up here to hide, but...
I can't seem to remember what **from**, exactly.
That sounds like you, dude.
Y-Yes, well!!

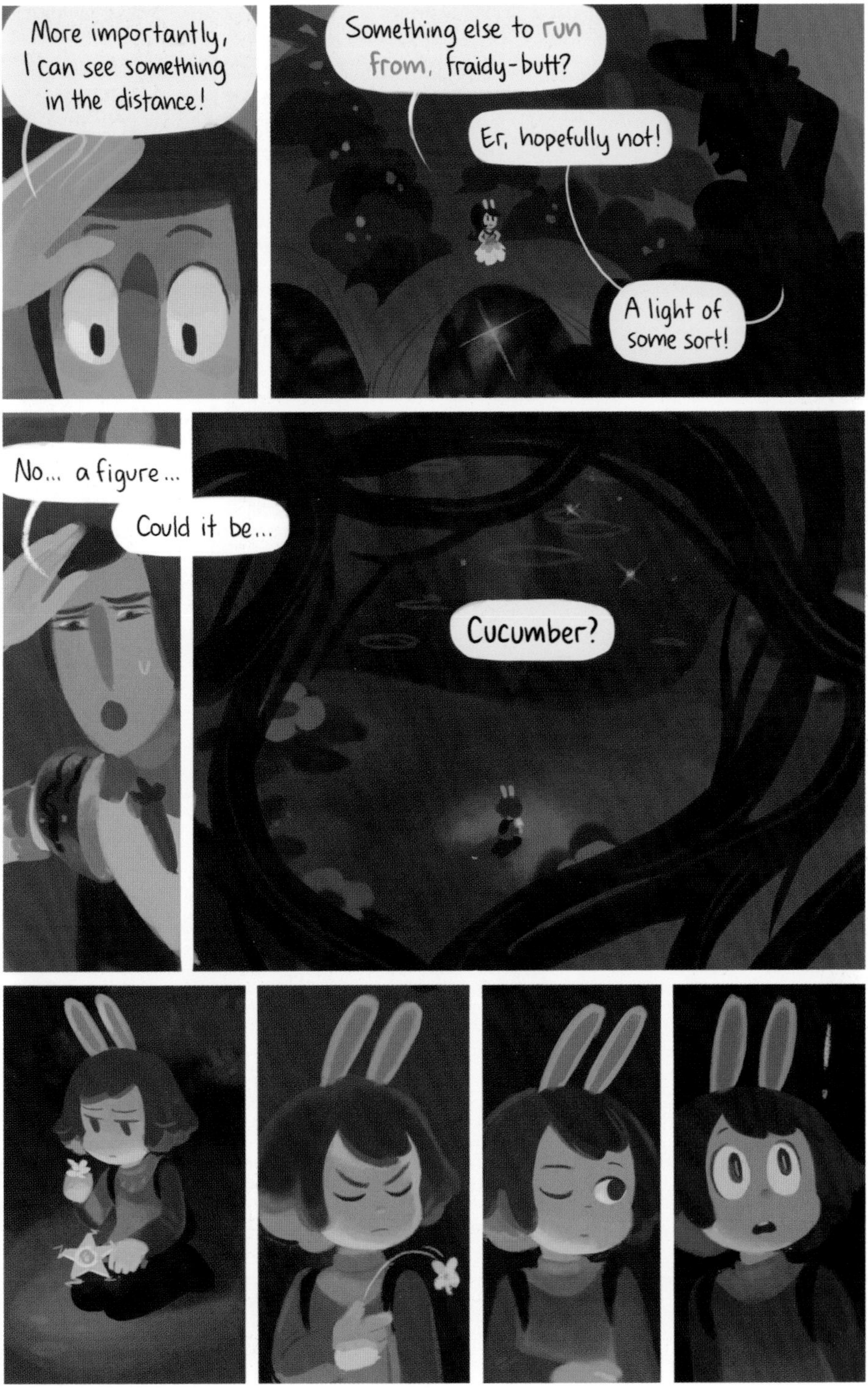
More importantly, I can see something in the distance!
Something else to run from, fraidy-butt?
Er, hopefully not!
A light of some sort!
No... a figure...
Could it be...
Cucumber?

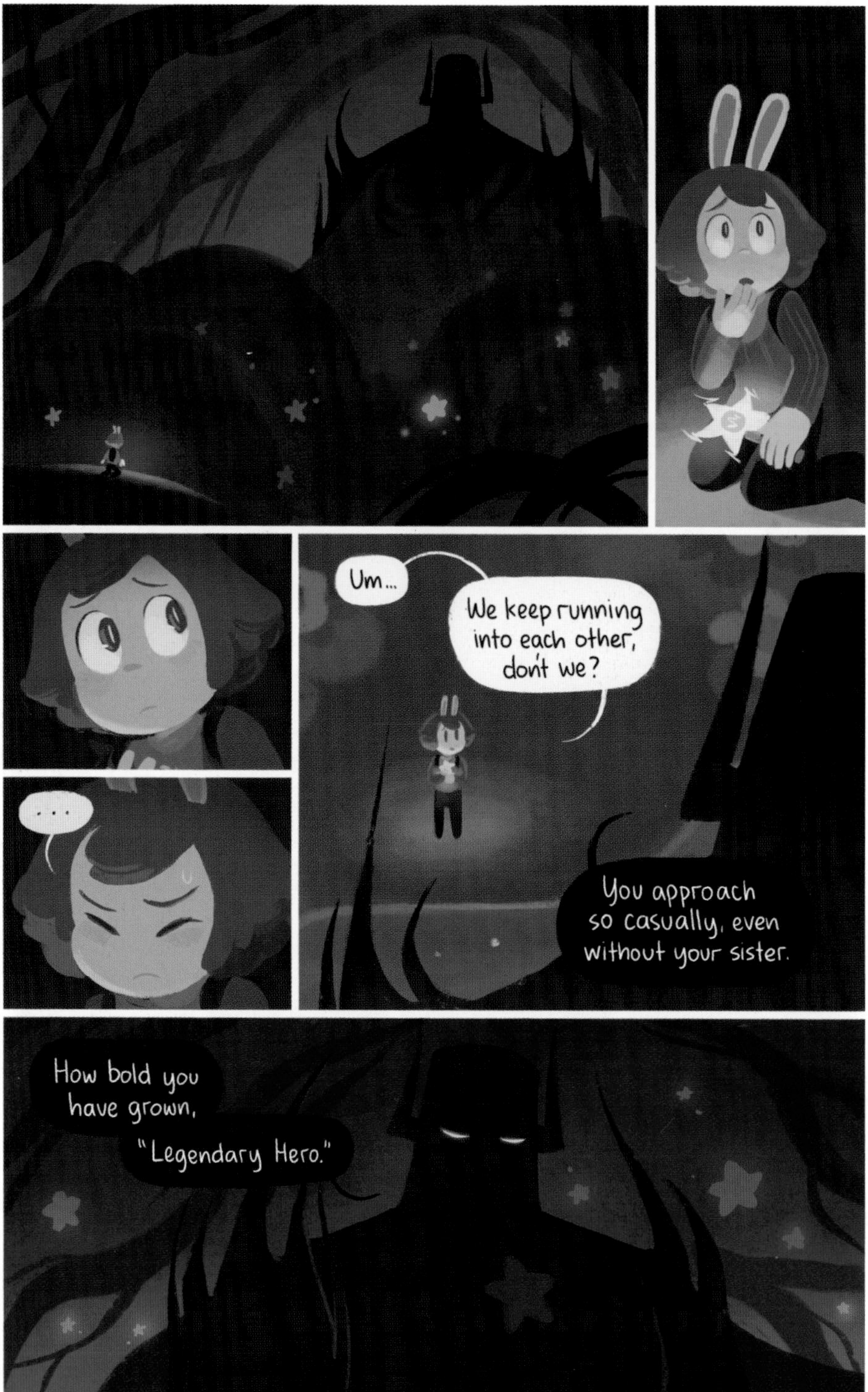
Um...
We keep running into each other, don't we?
. . .
You approach so casually, even without your sister.
How bold you have grown,
"Legendary Hero."

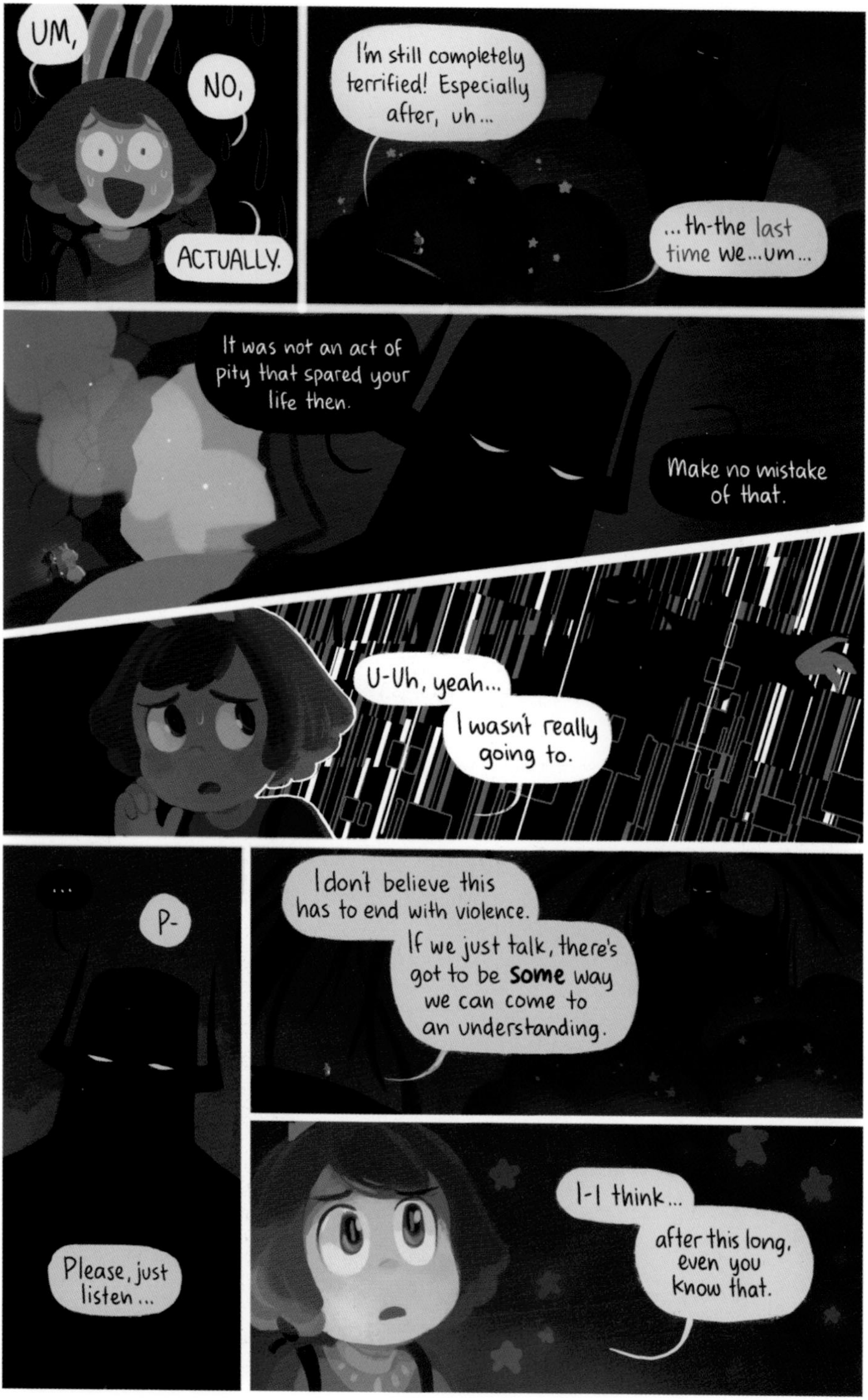
UM,
NO,
ACTUALLY.
I'm still completely terrified! Especially after, uh...
...th-the last time we...um...
It was not an act of pity that spared your life then.
Make no mistake of that.
U-Uh, yeah...
I wasn't really going to.
...
P-
Please, just listen...
I don't believe this has to end with violence.
If we just talk, there's got to be **some** way we can come to an understanding.
I-I think...
after this long, even you know that.

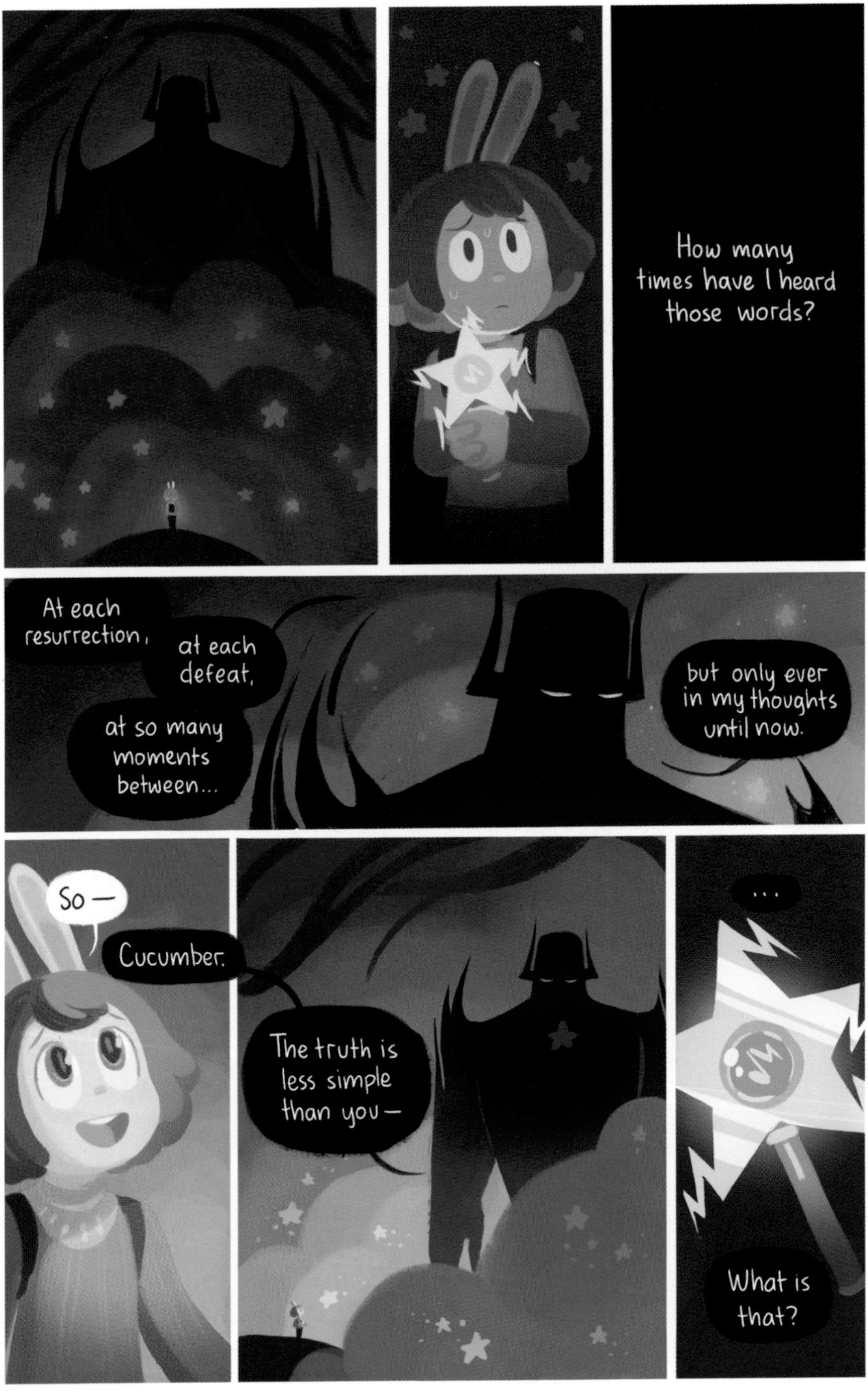
How many times have I heard those words?
At each resurrection,
at each defeat,
at so many moments between...
but only ever in my thoughts until now.
So —
Cucumber.
The truth is less simple than you —
...
What is that?

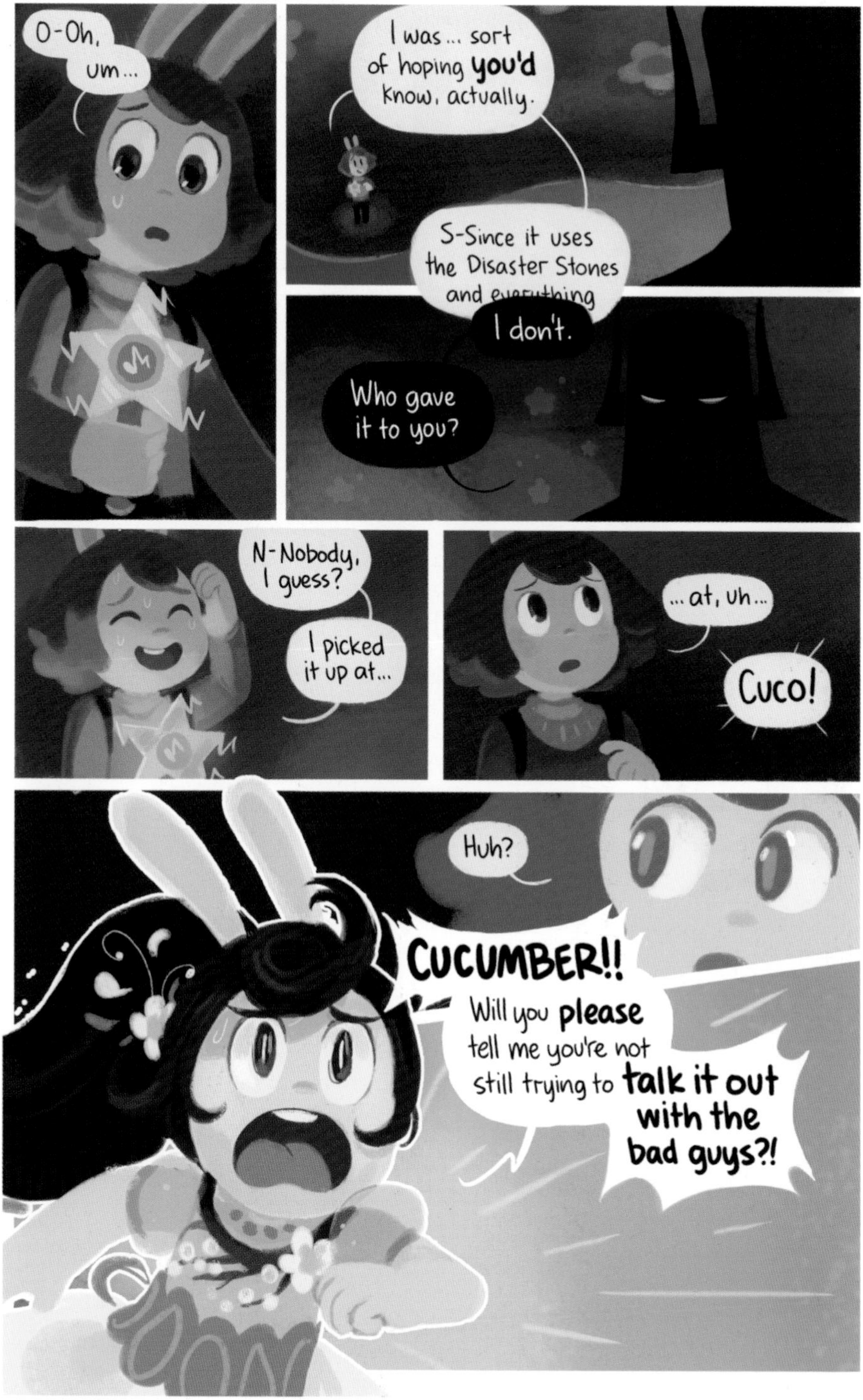
O-Oh, um...
I was... sort of hoping you'd know, actually.
S-Since it uses the Disaster Stones and everything
I don't.
Who gave it to you?
N-Nobody, I guess?
I picked it up at...
...at, uh...
Cuco!
Huh?
CUCUMBER!!
Will you please tell me you're not still trying to talk it out with the bad guys?!

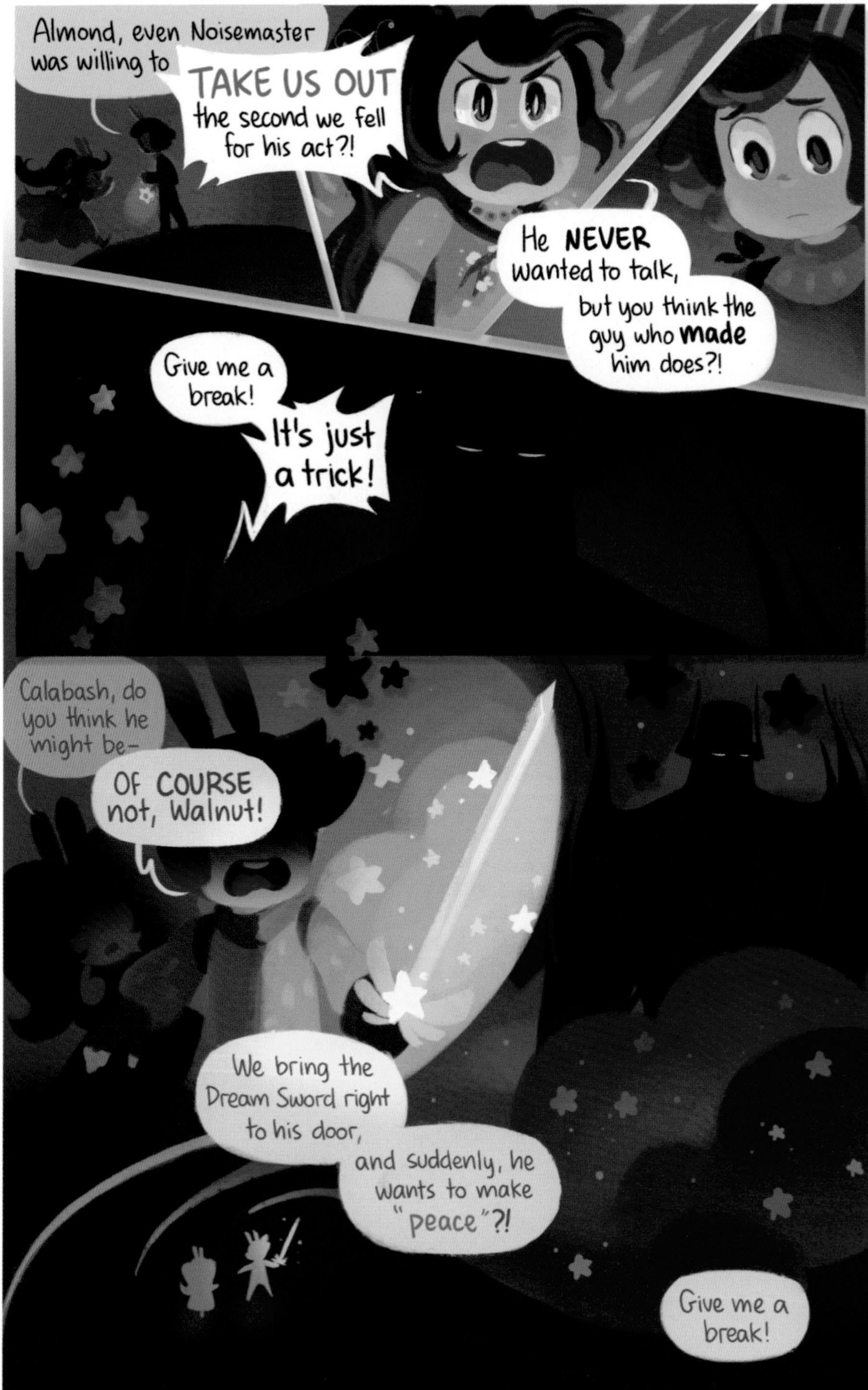
Almond, even Noisemaster was willing to
TAKE US OUT the second we fell for his act?!
He NEVER wanted to talk,
but you think the guy who made him does?!
Give me a break!
It's just a trick!
Calabash, do you think he might be—
OF COURSE not, Walnut!
We bring the Dream Sword right to his door,
and suddenly, he wants to make "peace"?!
Give me a break!

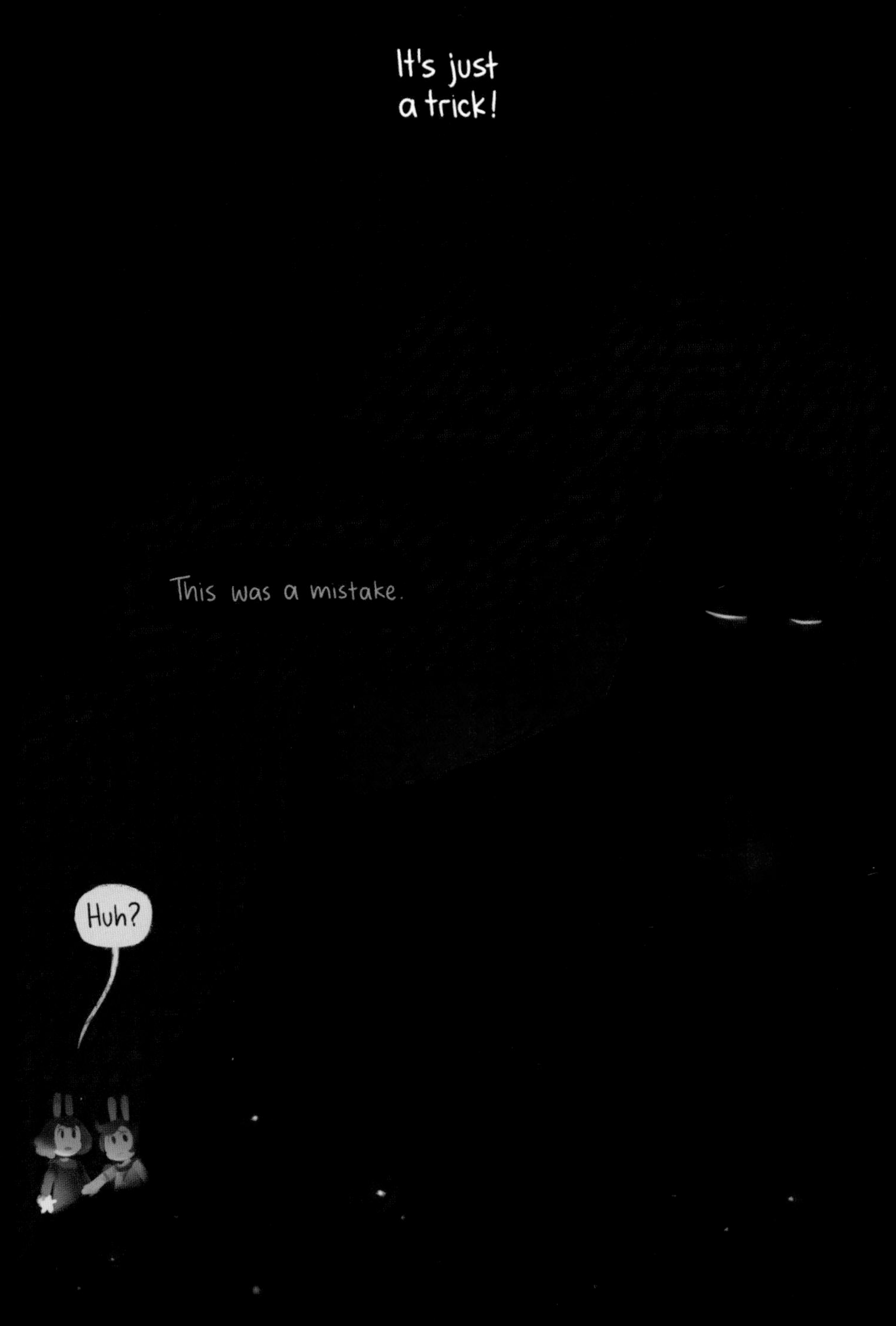
It's just
a trick!
This was a mistake.
Huh?

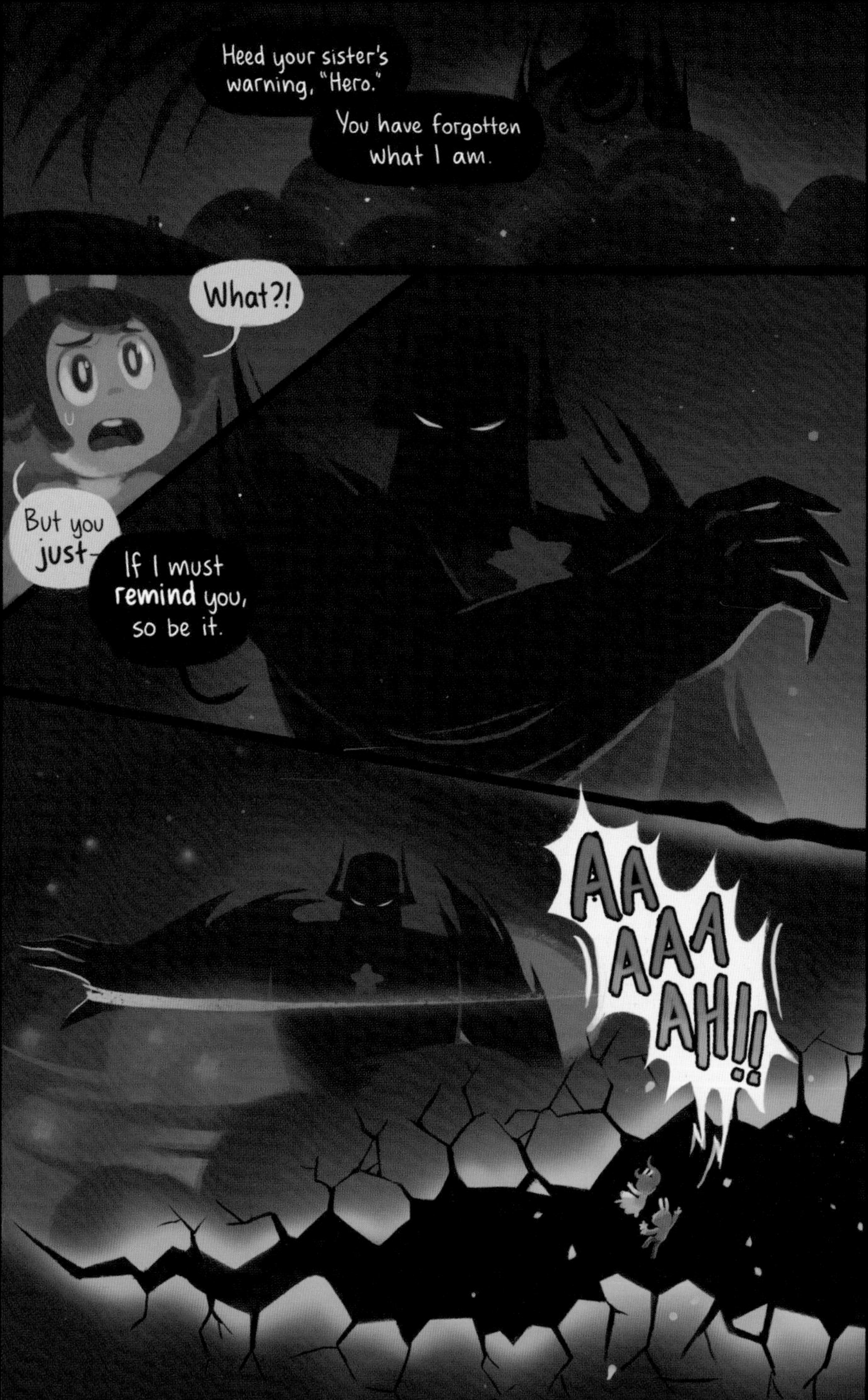
Heed your sister's warning, "Hero."
You have forgotten what I am.
What?!
But you just-
If I must **remind** you, so be it.
AAAAAAH!!

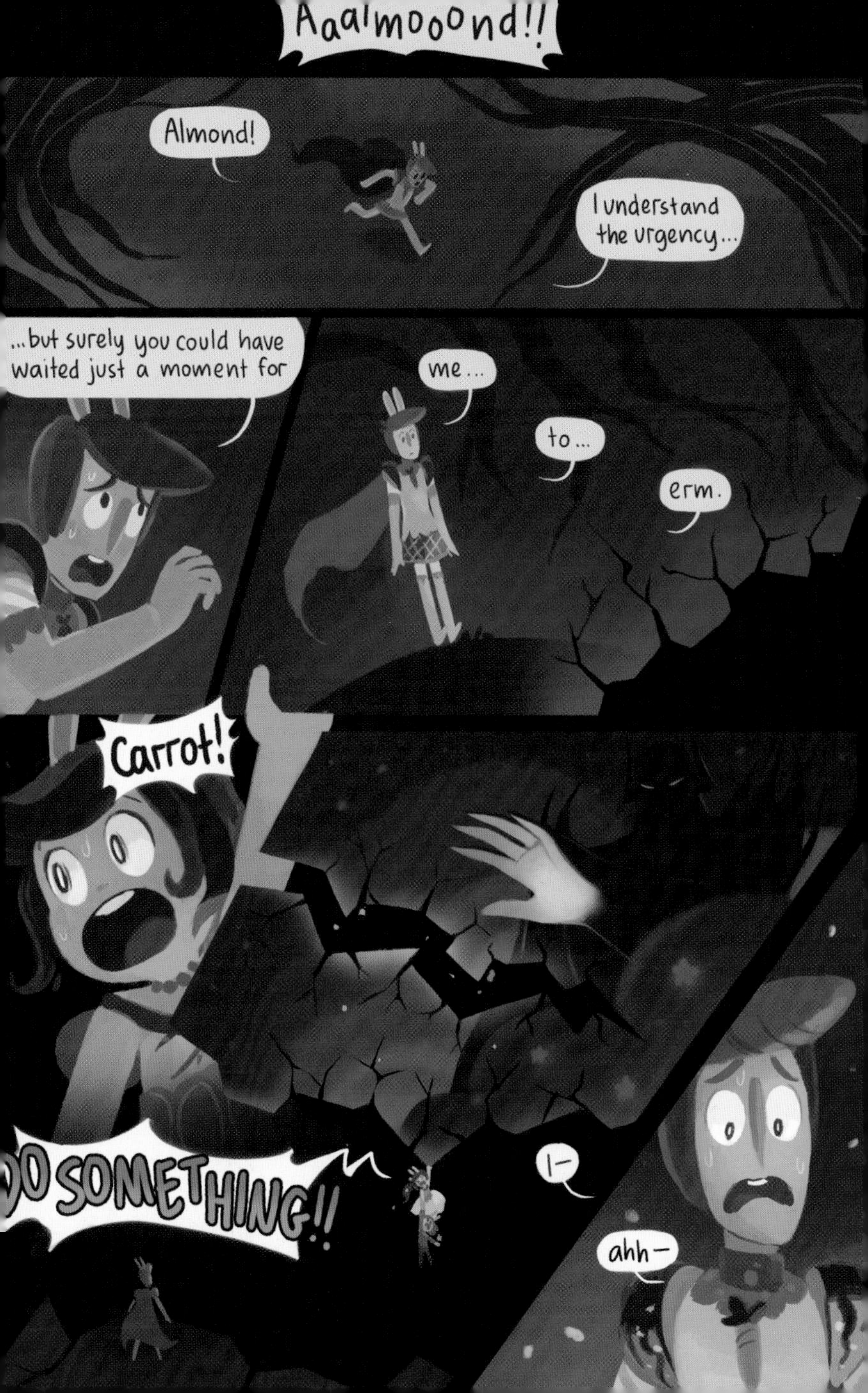
Aaalmooond!!
Almond!
I understand the urgency...
...but surely you could have waited just a moment for
me...
to...
erm.
Carrot!
DO SOMETHING!!
I–
ahh–

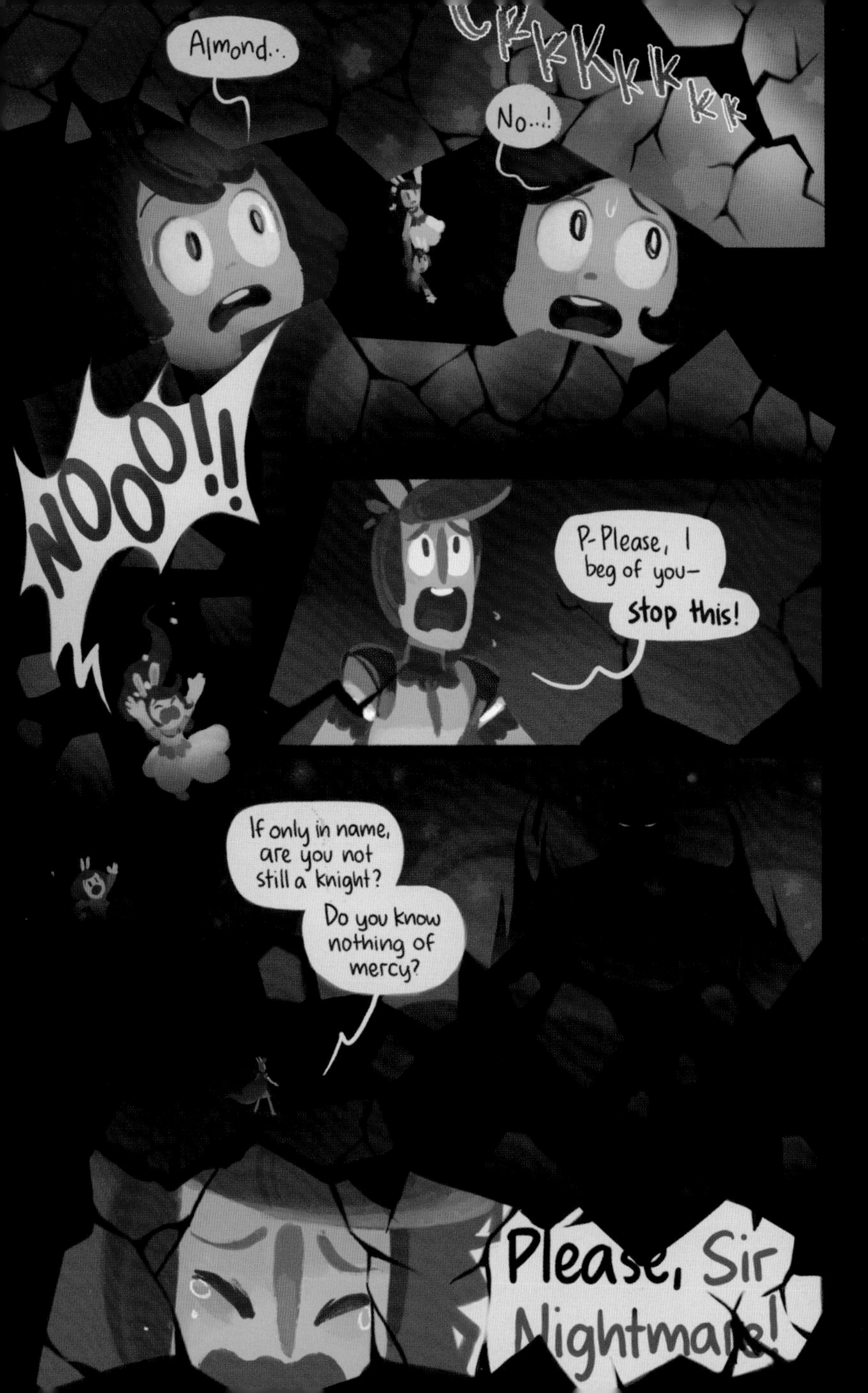
Almond...
CRKKKKKKK
No...!
NOOO!!
P-Please, I beg of you— stop this!
If only in name, are you not still a knight?
Do you know nothing of mercy?
Please, Sir Nightmare!

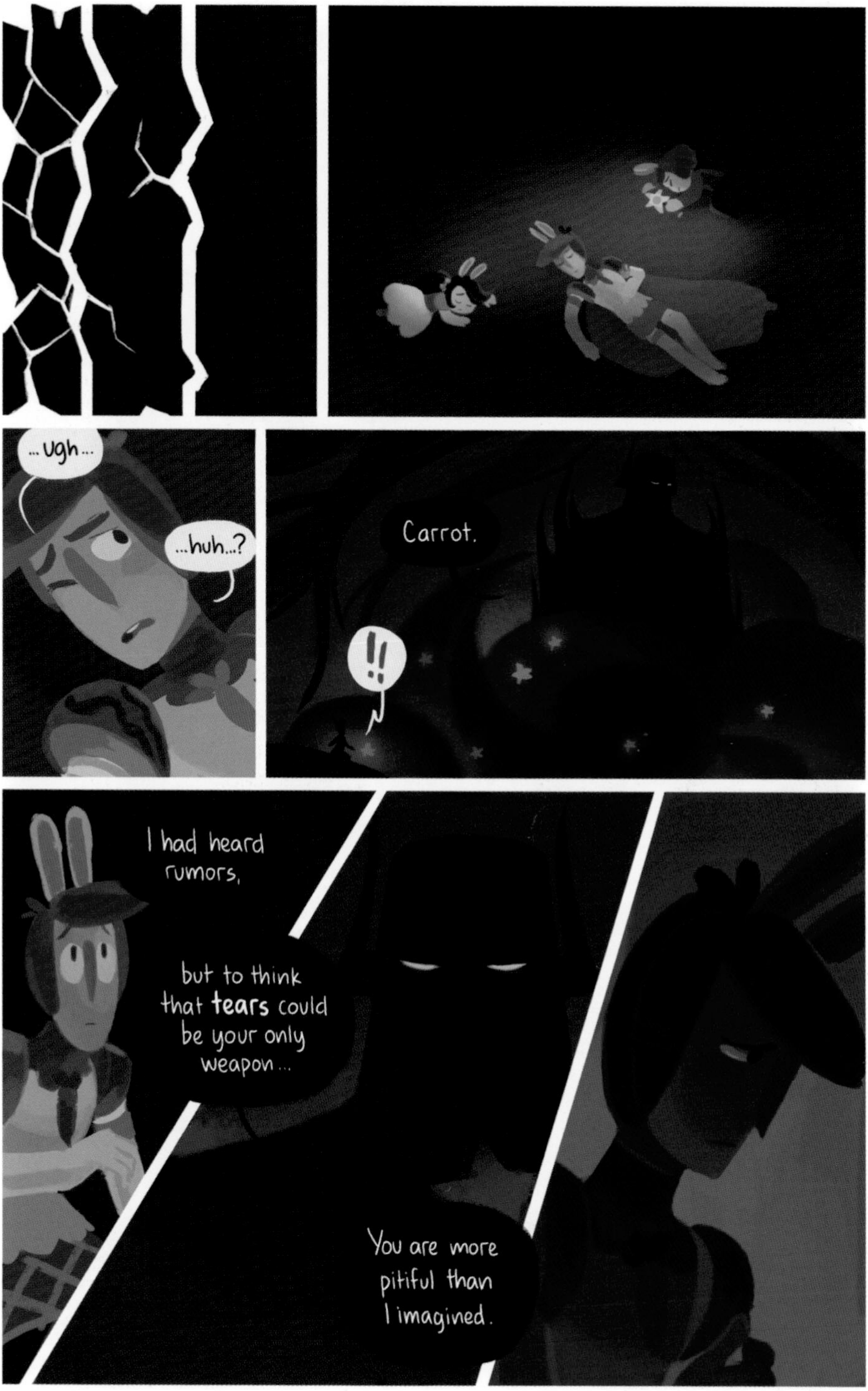
...ugh...
...huh...?
Carrot.
!!
I had heard rumors,
but to think that **tears** could be your only weapon...
You are more pitiful than I imagined.

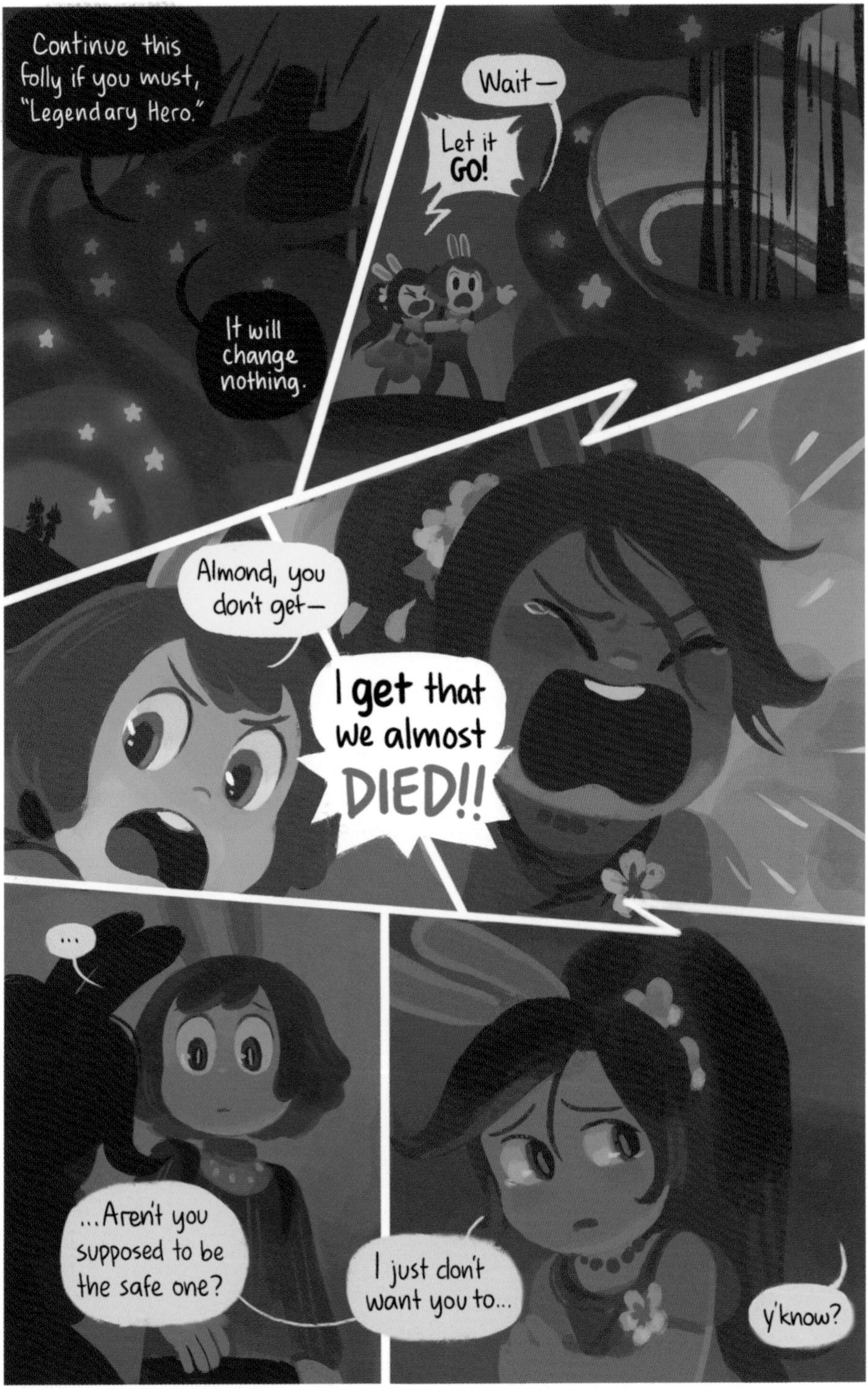
Continue this folly if you must, "Legendary Hero."
It will change nothing.
Wait—
Let it GO!
Almond, you don't get—
I get that we almost DIED!!
...
...Aren't you supposed to be the safe one?
I just don't want you to...
y'know?

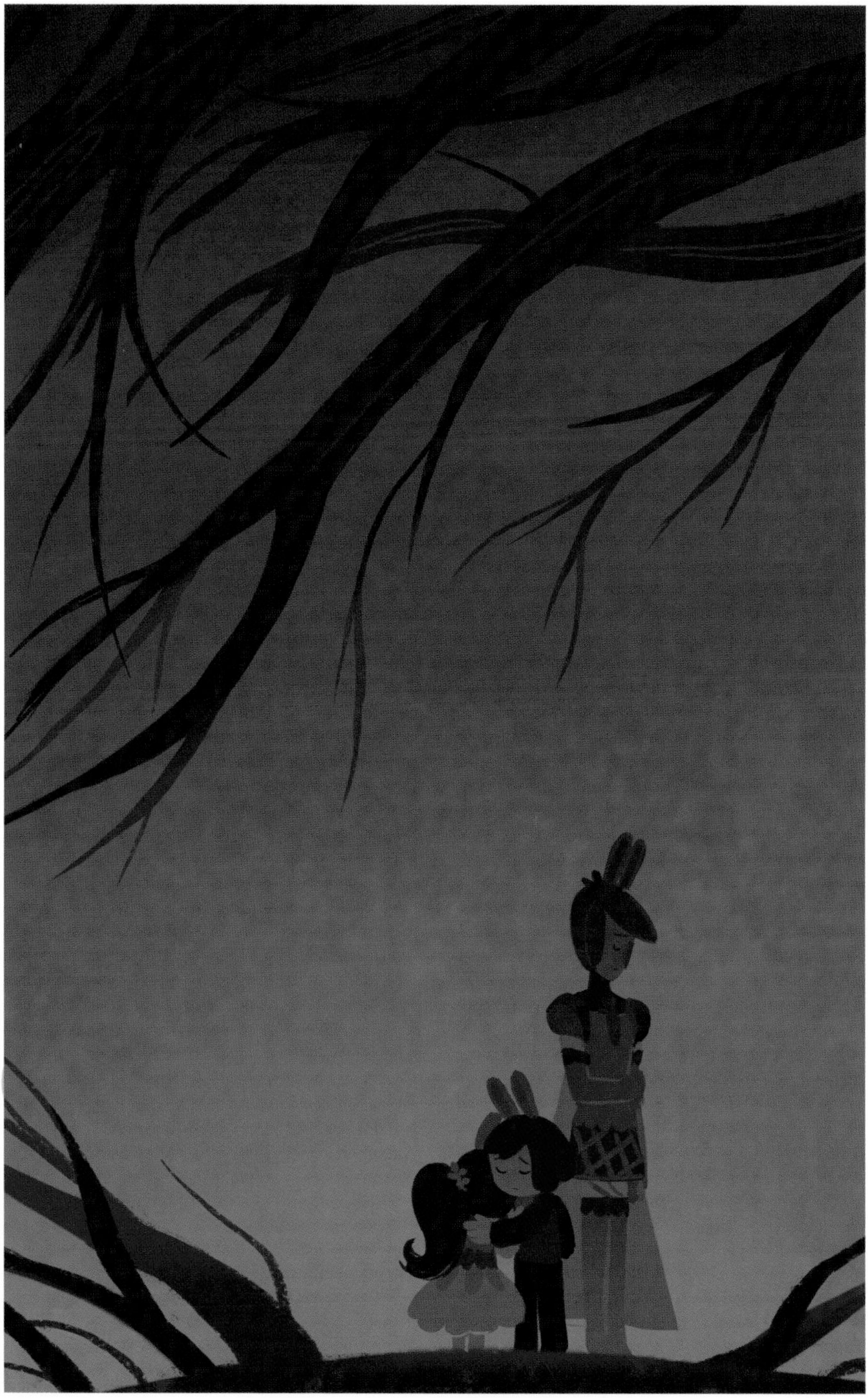

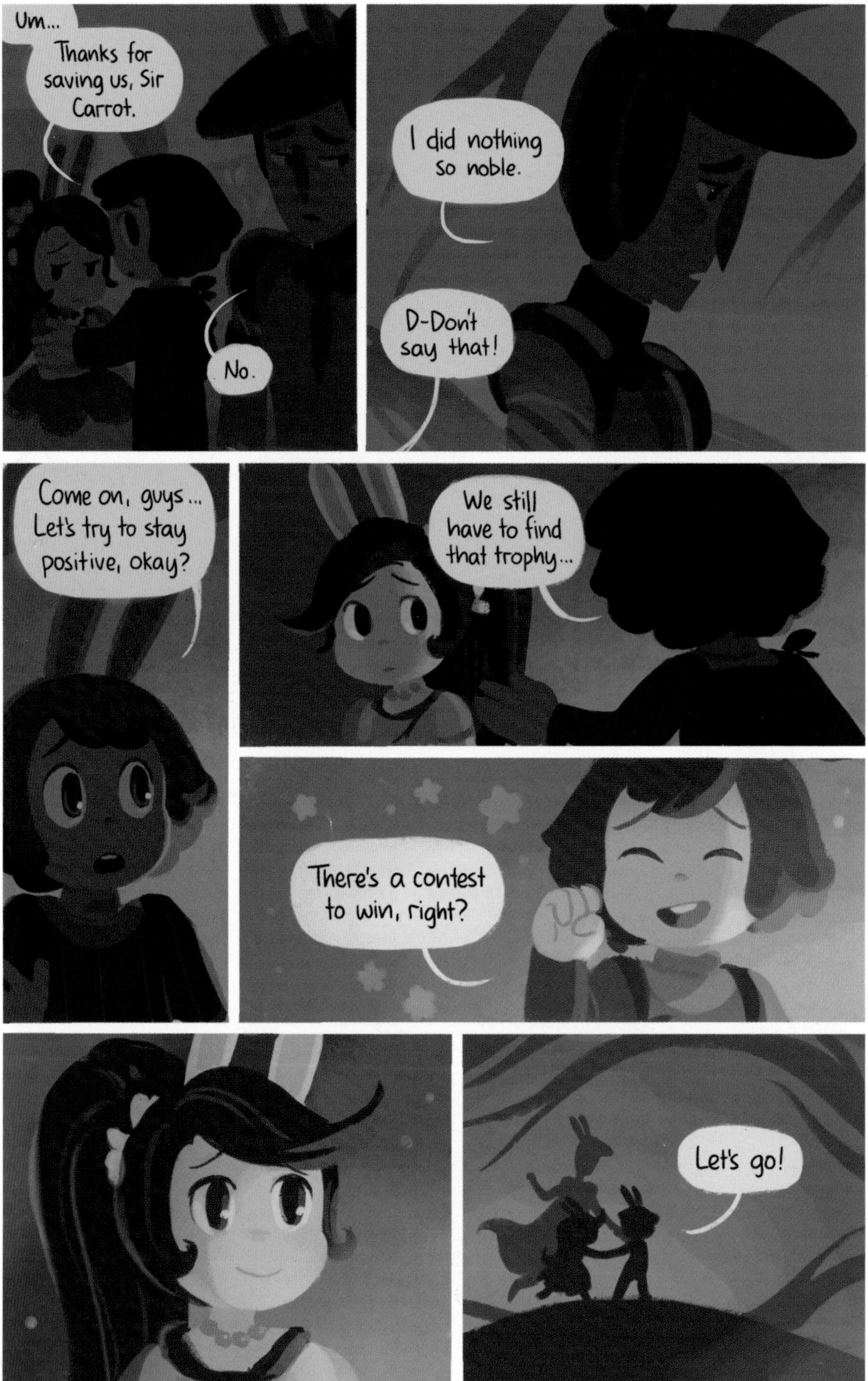
Um...
Thanks for saving us, Sir Carrot.
No.
I did nothing so noble.
D-Don't say that!
Come on, guys... Let's try to stay positive, okay?
We still have to find that trophy...
There's a contest to win, right?
Let's go!

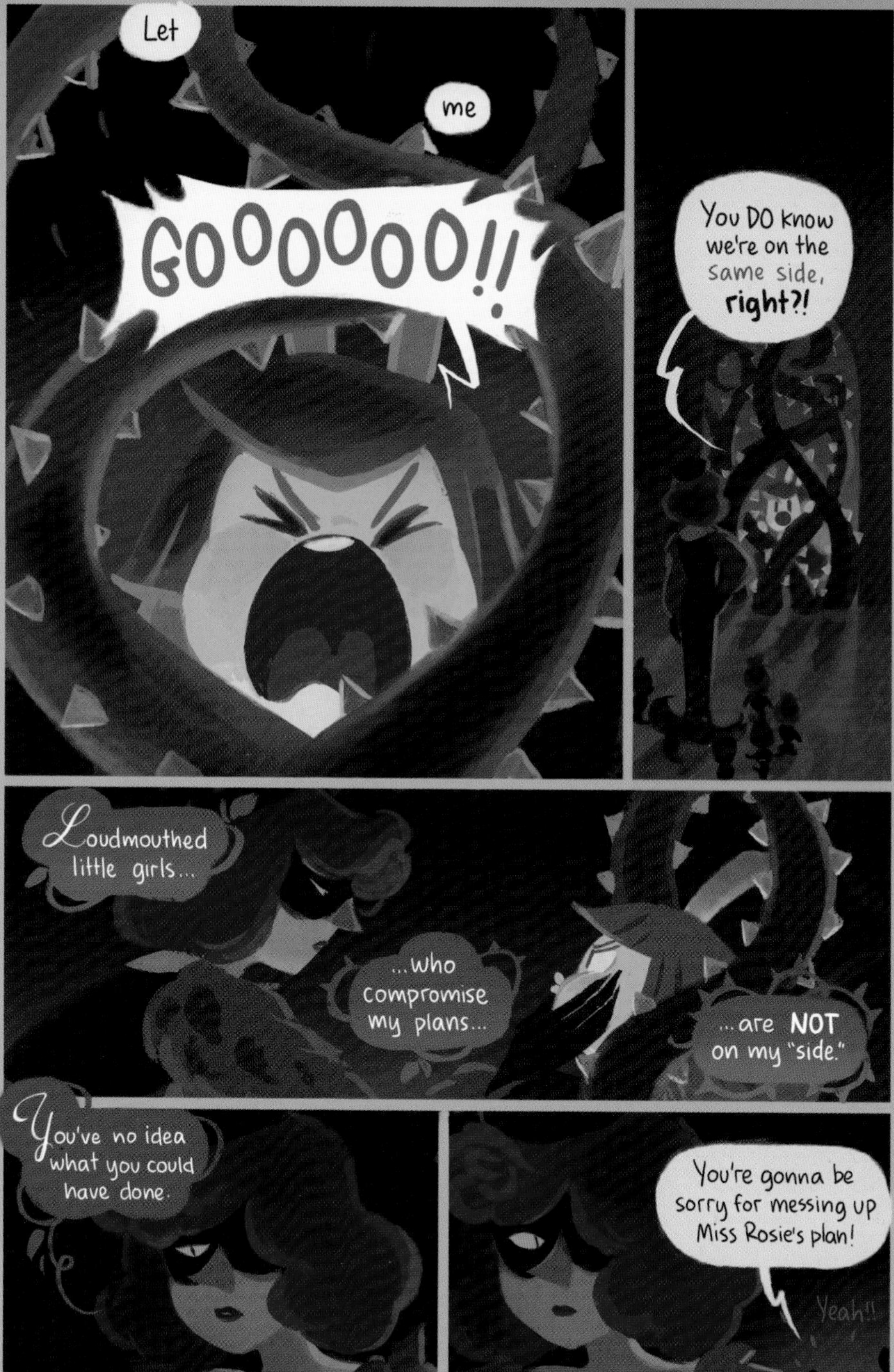
Let
me
GOOOOOO!!
You DO know we're on the same side, right?!
Loudmouthed little girls...
...who compromise my plans...
...are NOT on my "side."
You've no idea what you could have done.
You're gonna be sorry for messing up Miss Rosie's plan!
Yeah!!

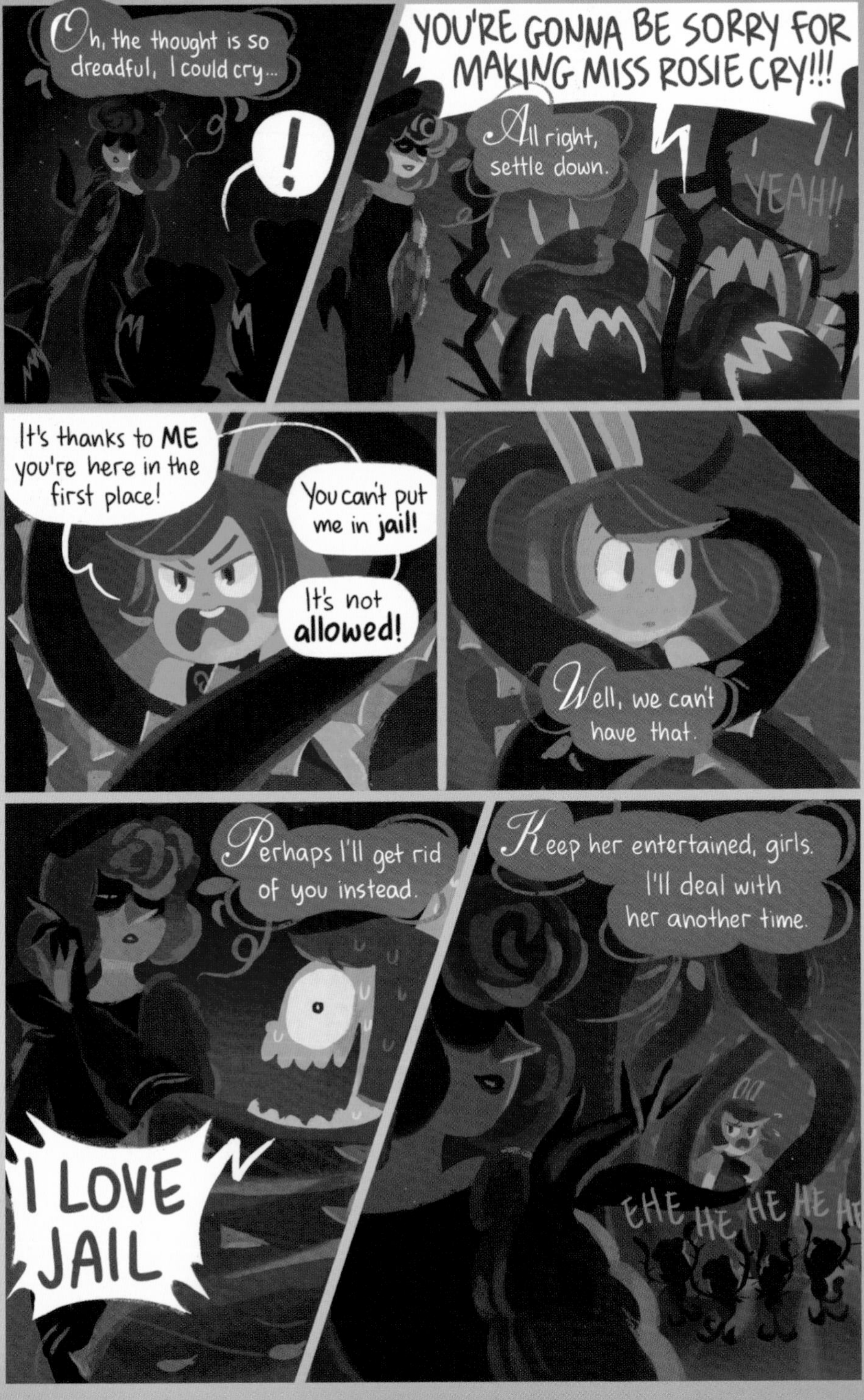
Oh, the thought is so dreadful, I could cry...
!
YOU'RE GONNA BE SORRY FOR MAKING MISS ROSIE CRY!!!
All right, settle down.
YEAH!!
It's thanks to ME you're here in the first place!
You can't put me in jail!
It's not allowed!
Well, we can't have that.
Perhaps I'll get rid of you instead.
I LOVE JAIL
Keep her entertained, girls. I'll deal with her another time.
EHE HE HE HE HE

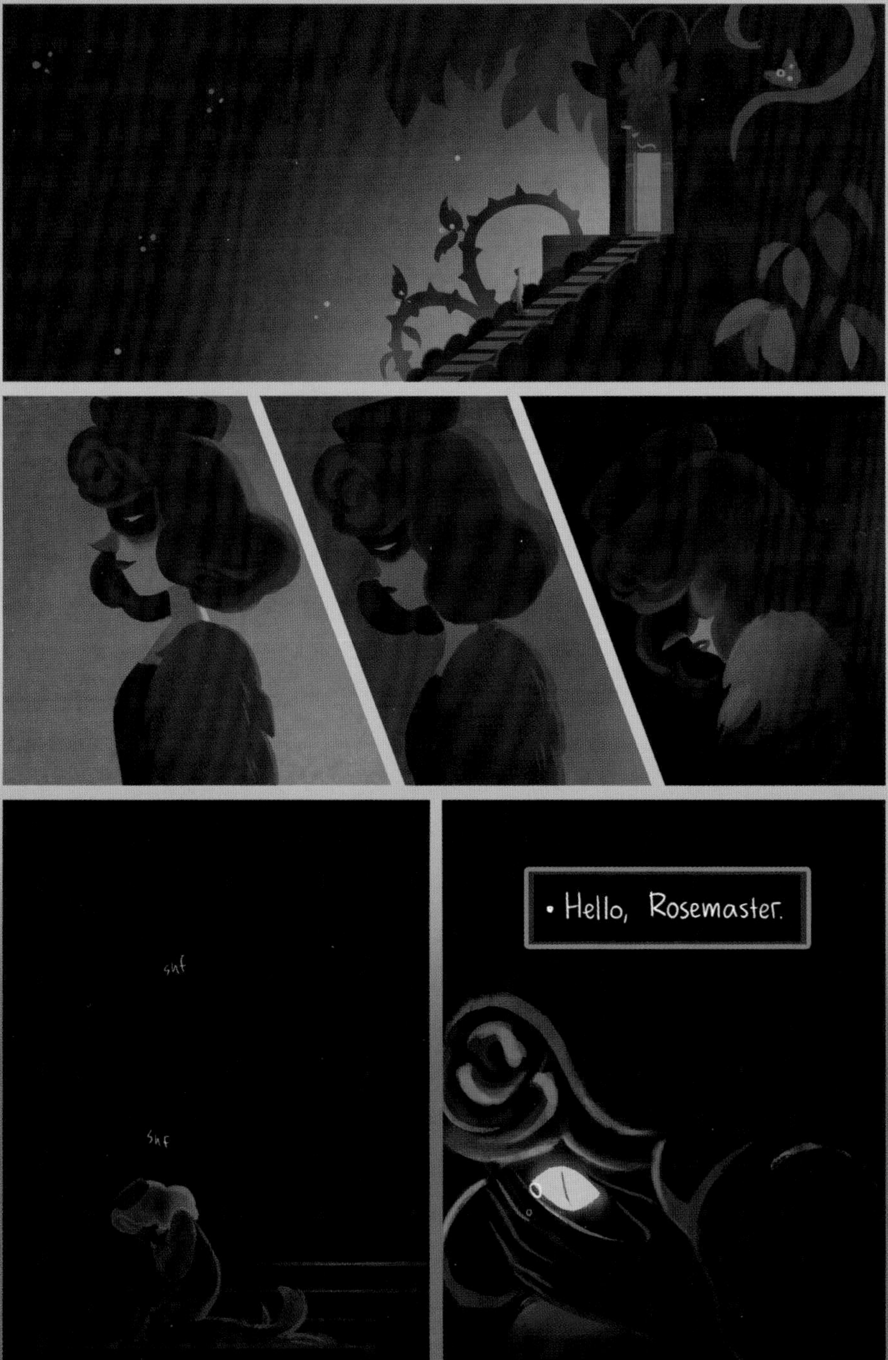
snf
snf
• Hello, Rosemaster.

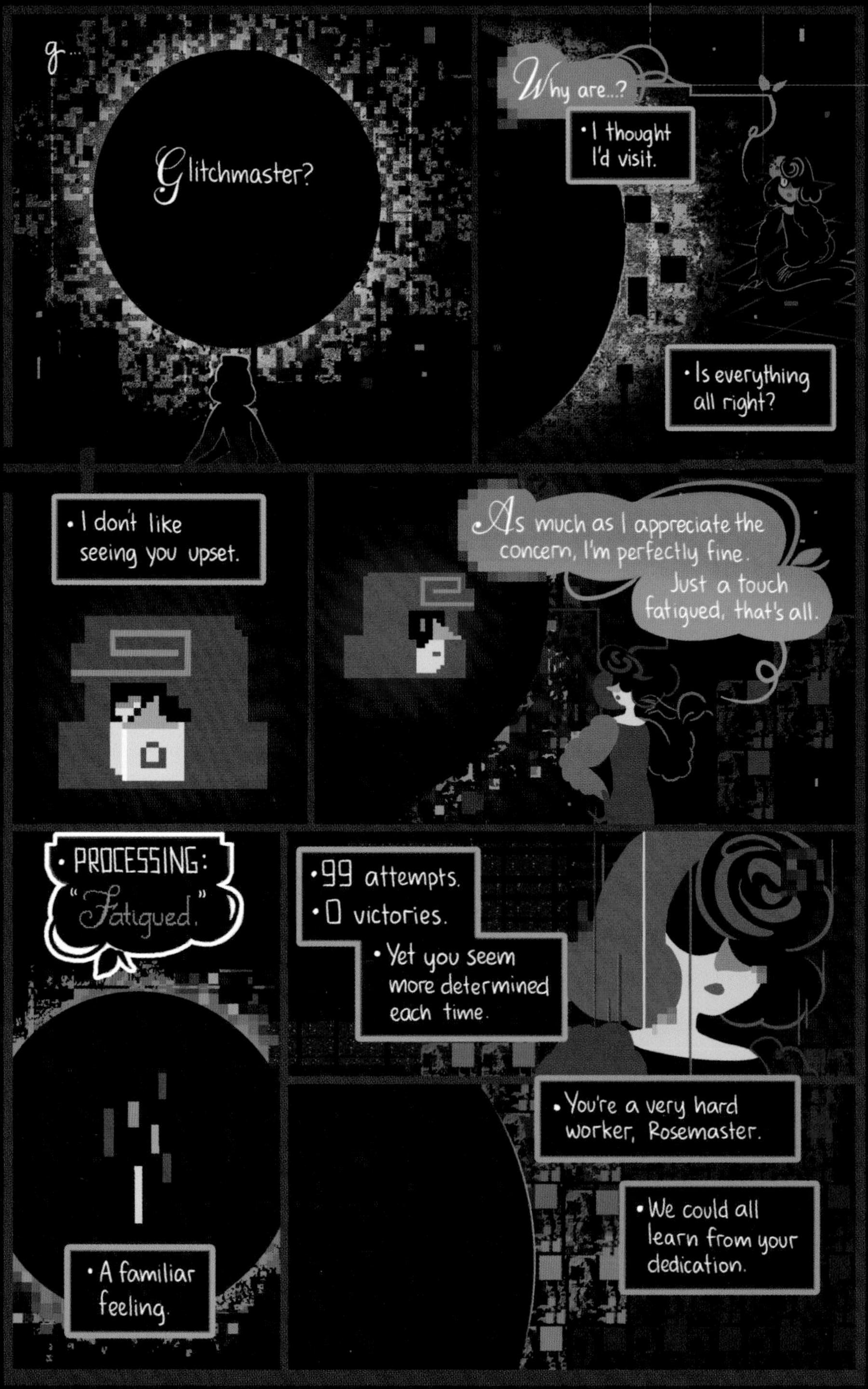
g...
Glitchmaster?
Why are..?
• I thought I'd visit.
• Is everything all right?
• I don't like seeing you upset.
As much as I appreciate the concern, I'm perfectly fine.
Just a touch fatigued, that's all.
• PROCESSING: "Fatigued."
• 99 attempts.
• 0 victories.
• Yet you seem more determined each time.
• A familiar feeling.
• You're a very hard worker, Rosemaster.
• We could all learn from your dedication.

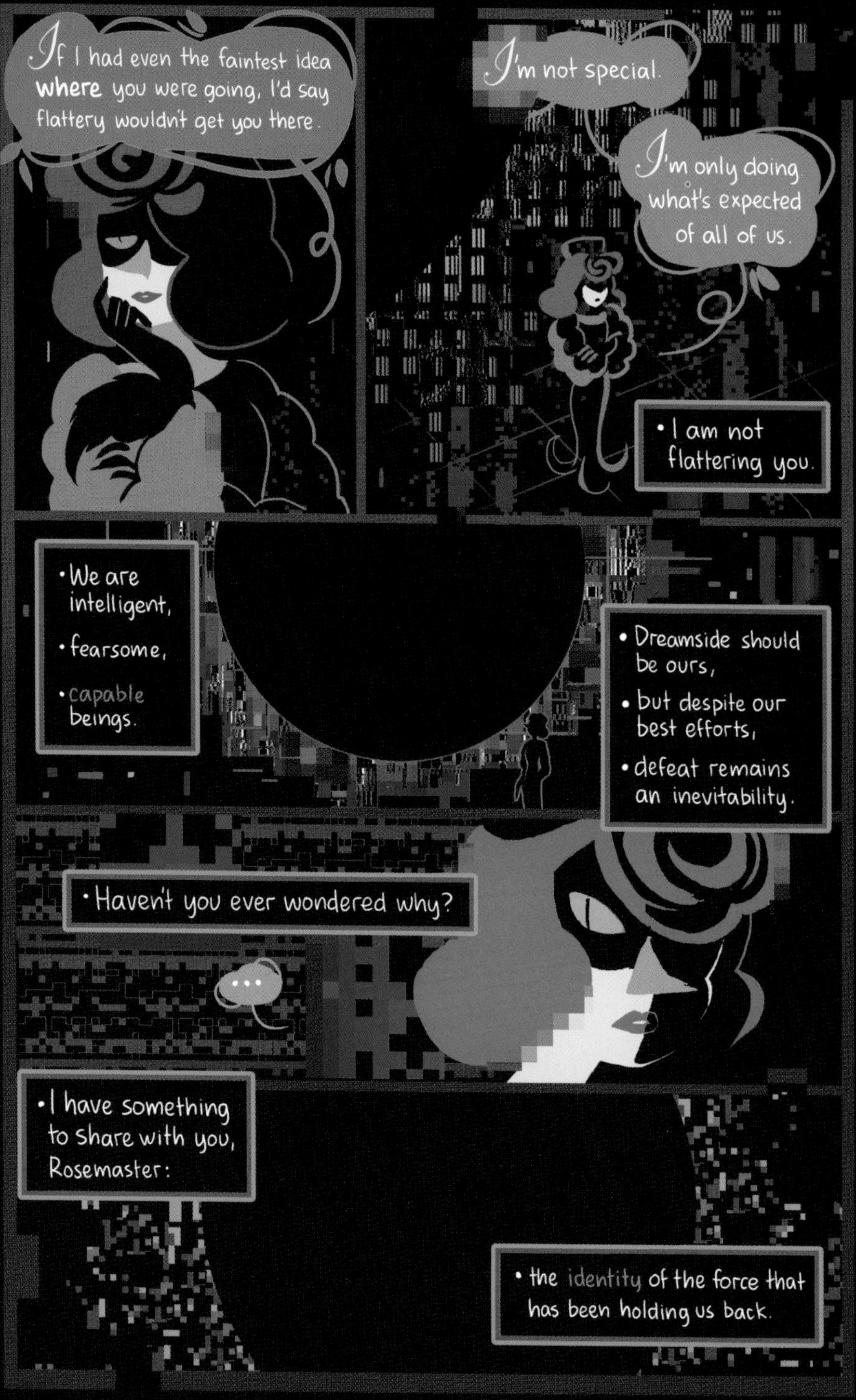
If I had even the faintest idea where you were going, I'd say flattery wouldn't get you there.
I'm not special.
I'm only doing what's expected of all of us.
• I am not flattering you.
• We are intelligent,
• fearsome,
• capable beings.
• Dreamside should be ours,
• but despite our best efforts,
• defeat remains an inevitability.
• Haven't you ever wondered why?
...
• I have something to share with you, Rosemaster:
• the identity of the force that has been holding us back.

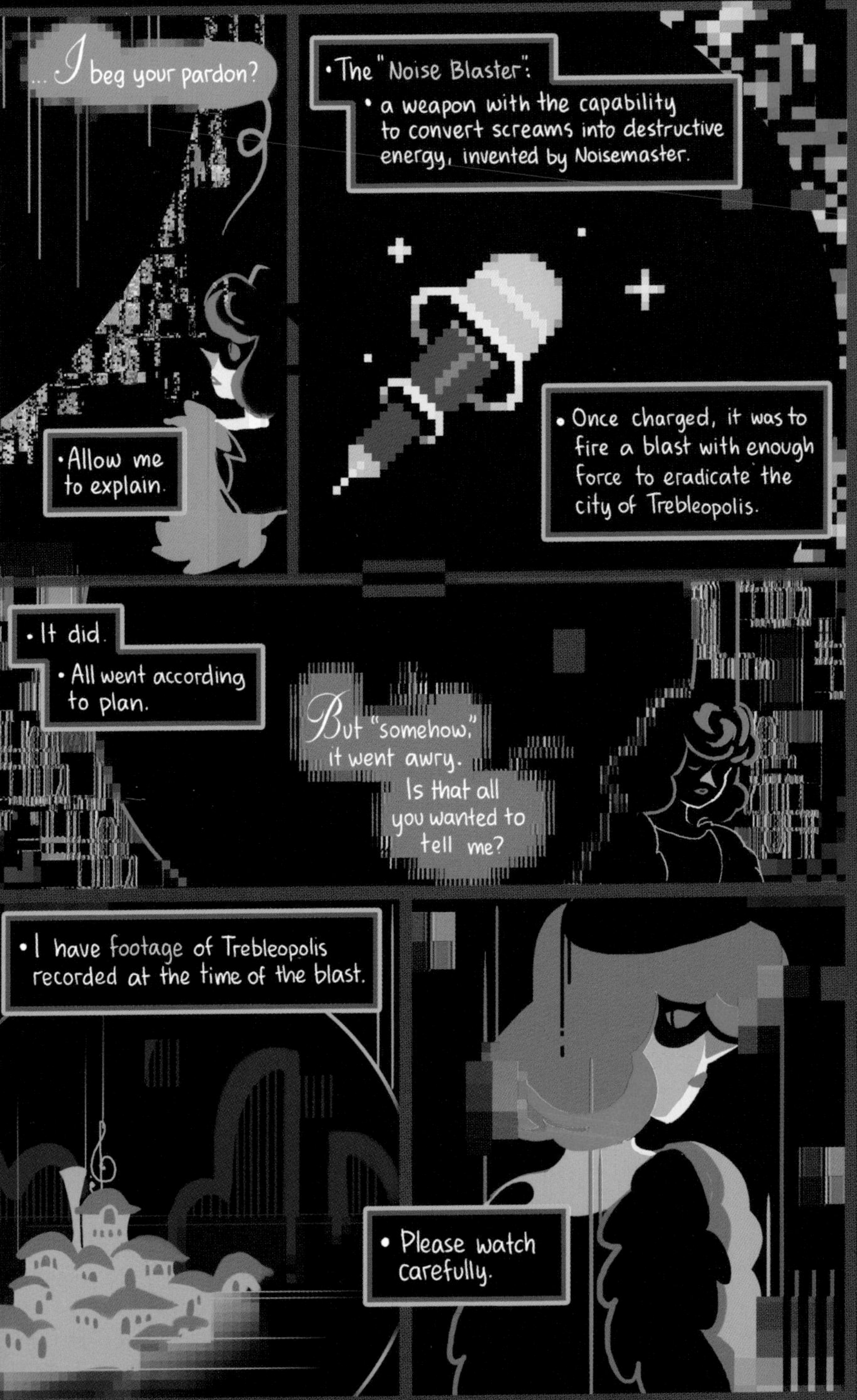

...I beg your pardon?
•The "Noise Blaster":
• a weapon with the capability to convert screams into destructive energy, invented by Noisemaster.
•Allow me to explain.
• Once charged, it was to fire a blast with enough force to eradicate the city of Trebleopolis.
• It did.
• All went according to plan.
But "somehow," it went awry.
Is that all you wanted to tell me?
• I have footage of Trebleopolis recorded at the time of the blast.
• Please watch carefully.

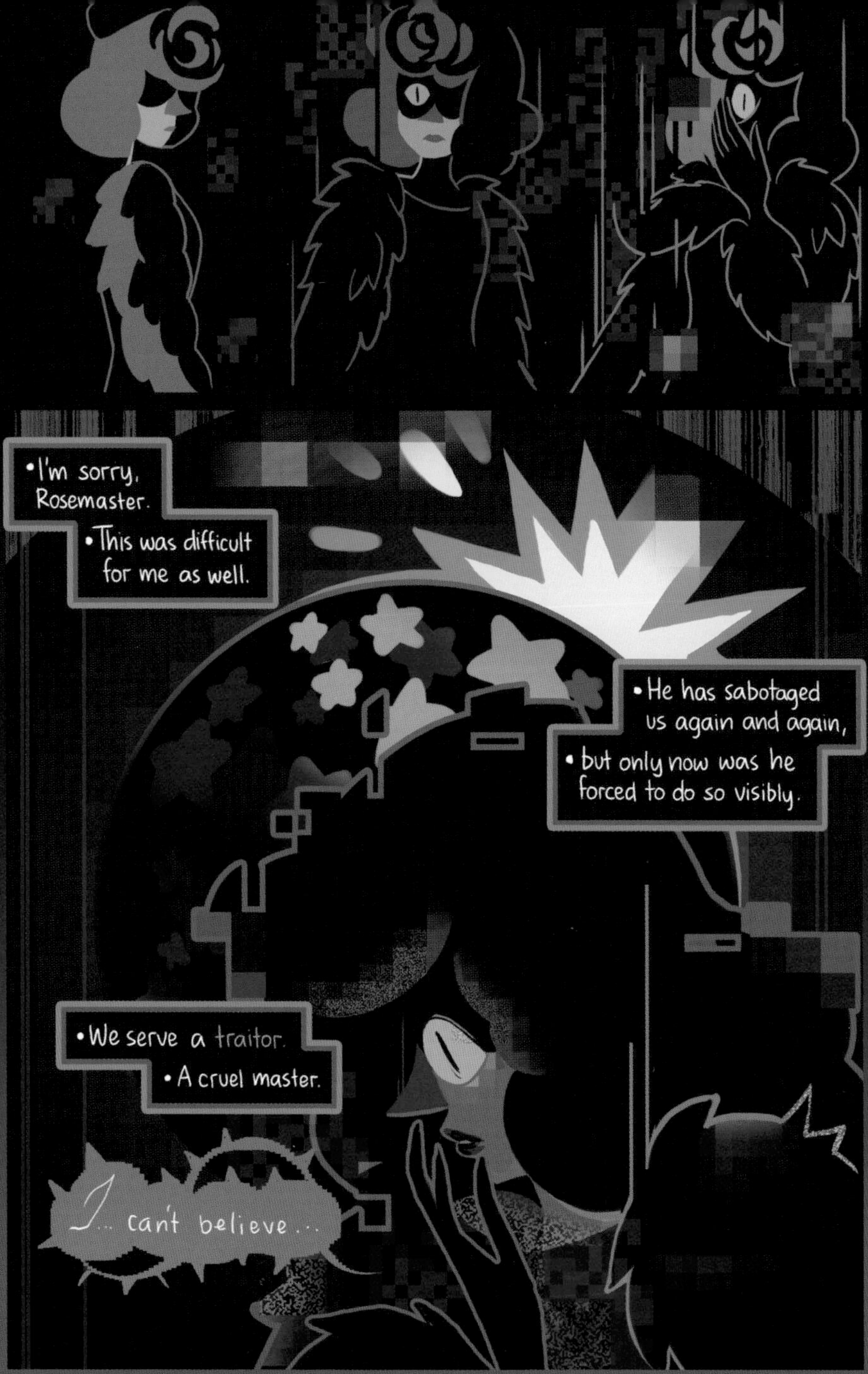

• I'm sorry, Rosemaster.
• This was difficult for me as well.
• He has sabotaged us again and again,
• but only now was he forced to do so visibly.
• We serve a traitor.
• A cruel master.
I... can't believe...

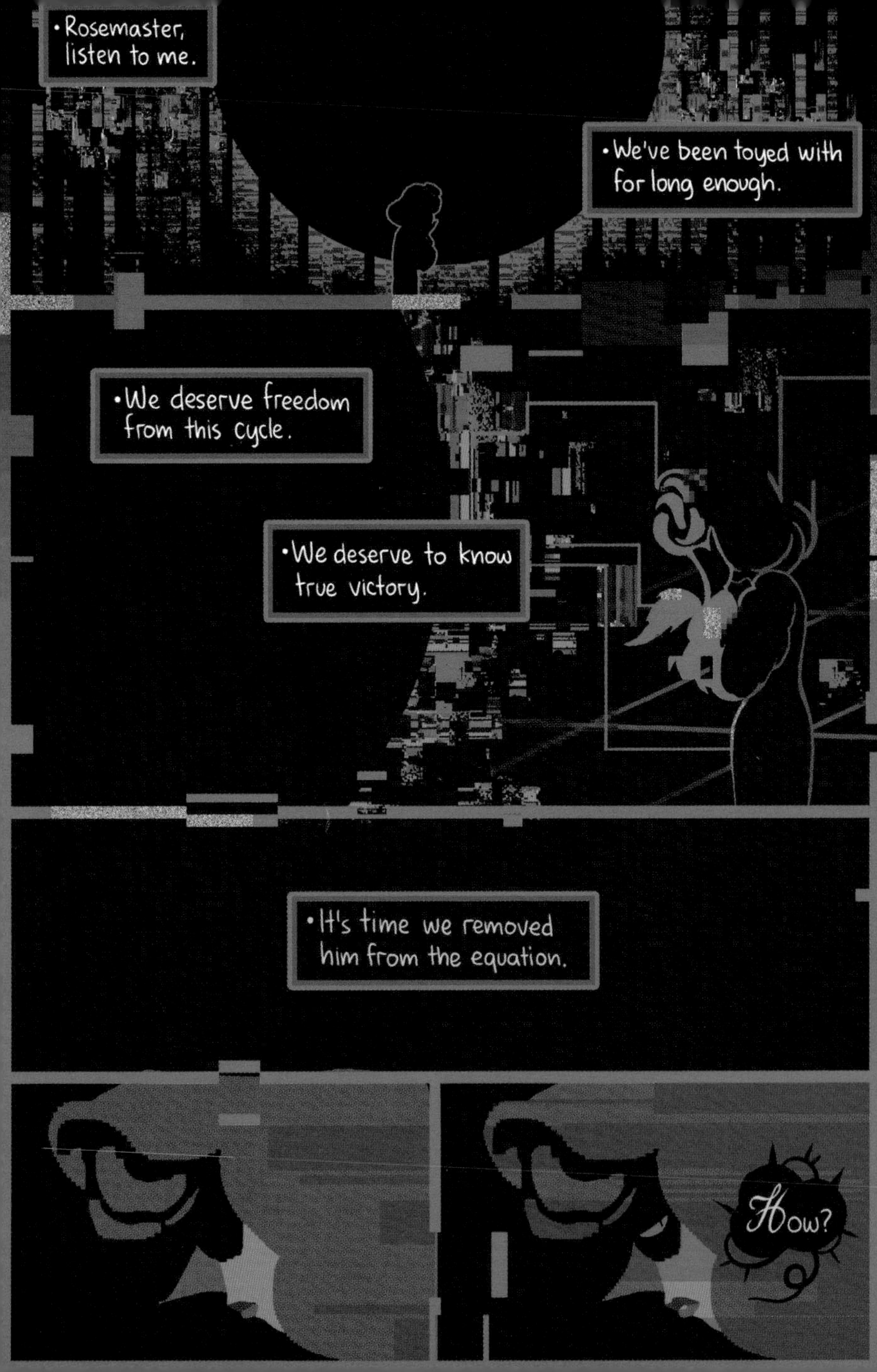
•Rosemaster, listen to me.
•We've been toyed with for long enough.
•We deserve freedom from this cycle.
•We deserve to know true victory.
•It's time we removed him from the equation.
How?

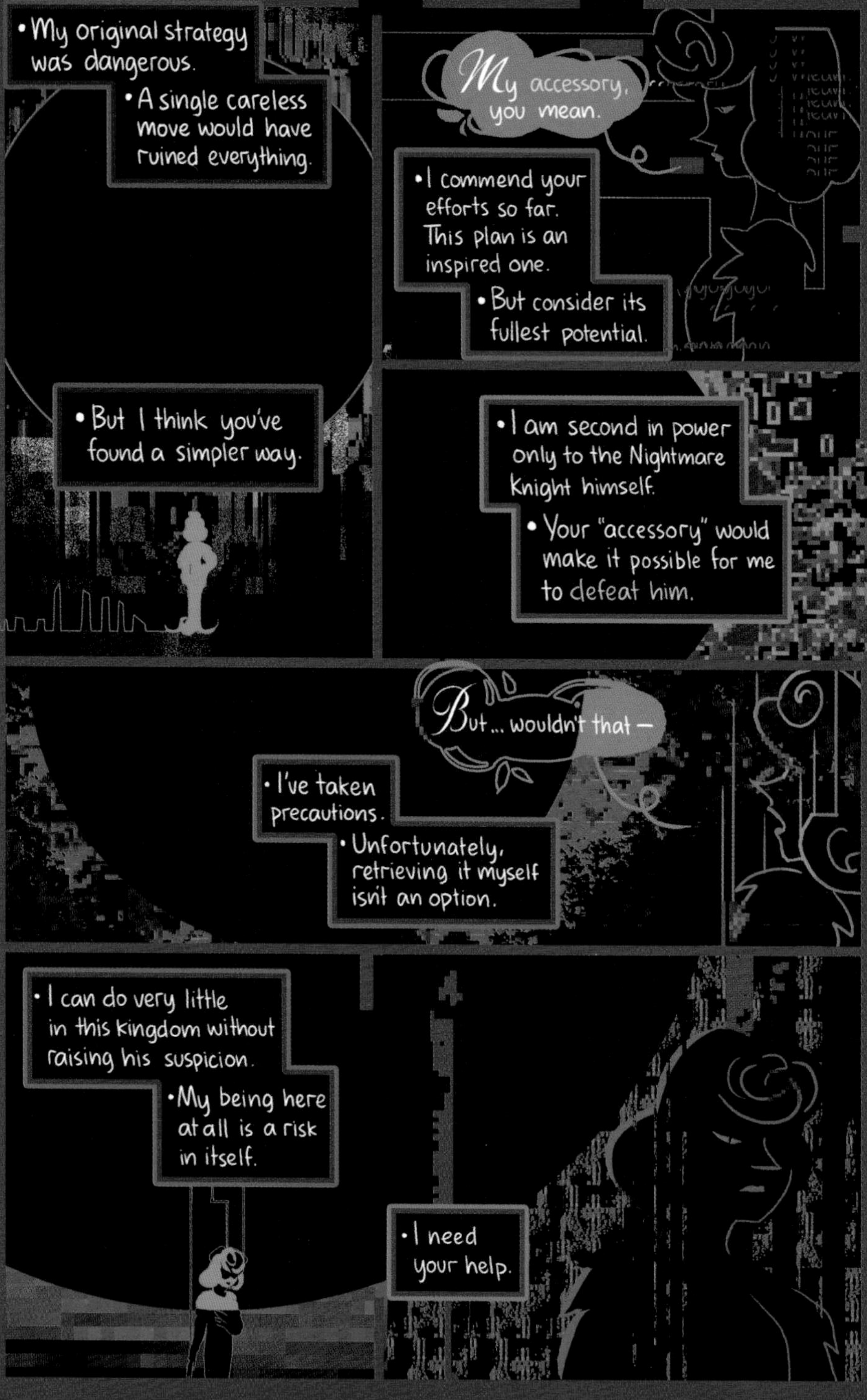
• My original strategy was dangerous.
• A single careless move would have ruined everything.
My accessory, you mean.
• I commend your efforts so far. This plan is an inspired one.
• But consider its fullest potential.
• But I think you've found a simpler way.
• I am second in power only to the Nightmare Knight himself.
• Your "accessory" would make it possible for me to defeat him.
But... wouldn't that —
• I've taken precautions.
• Unfortunately, retrieving it myself isn't an option.
• I can do very little in this kingdom without raising his suspicion.
• My being here at all is a risk in itself.
• I need your help.

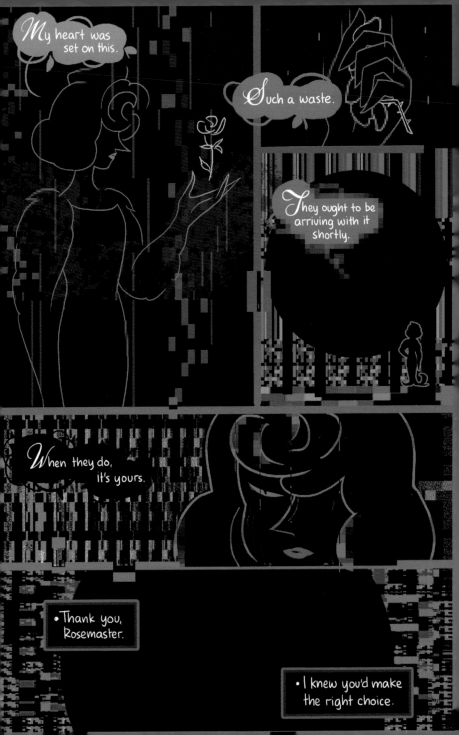

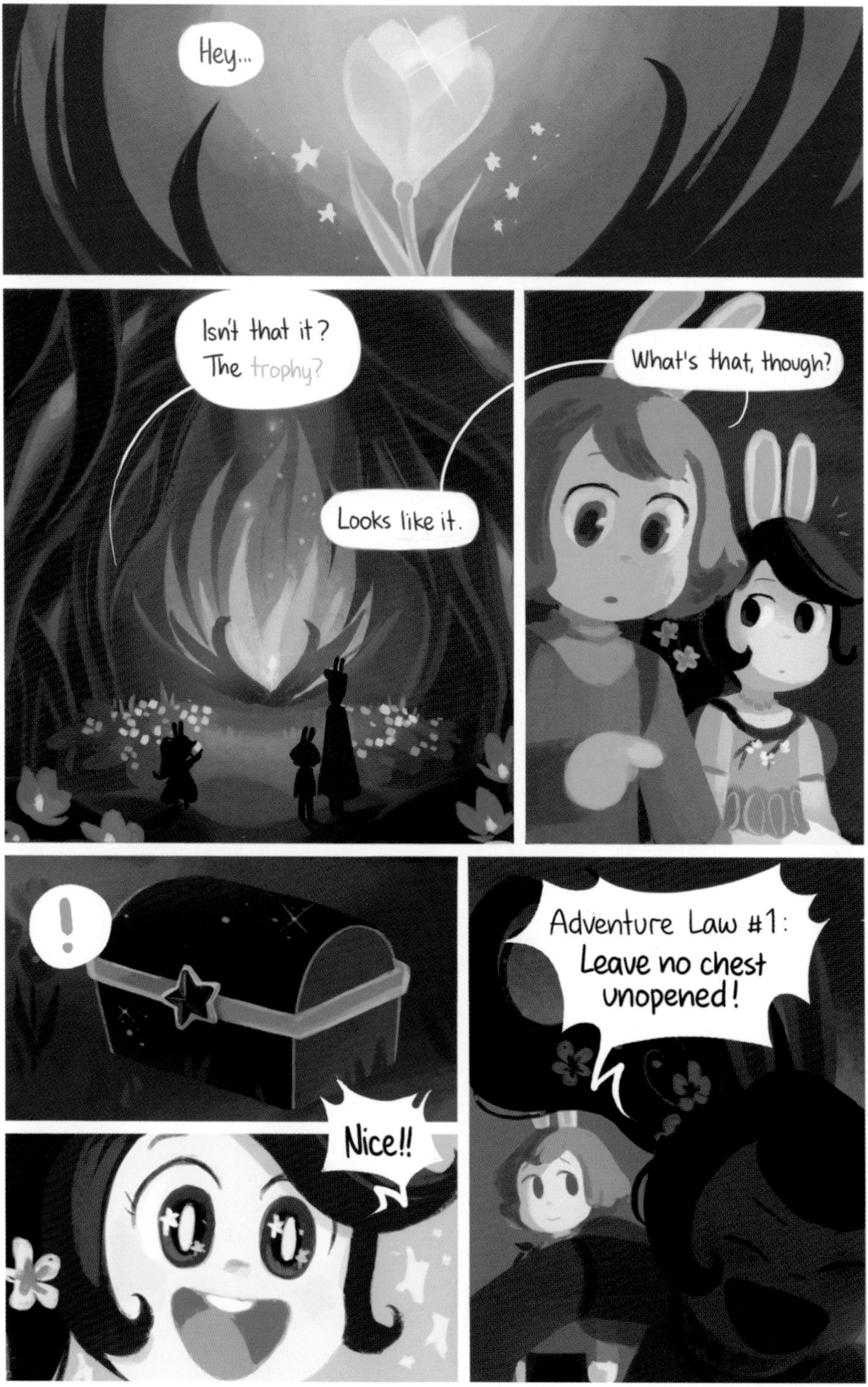

Hey...
Isn't that it? The trophy?
Looks like it.
What's that, though?
!
Nice!!
Adventure Law #1: Leave no chest unopened!

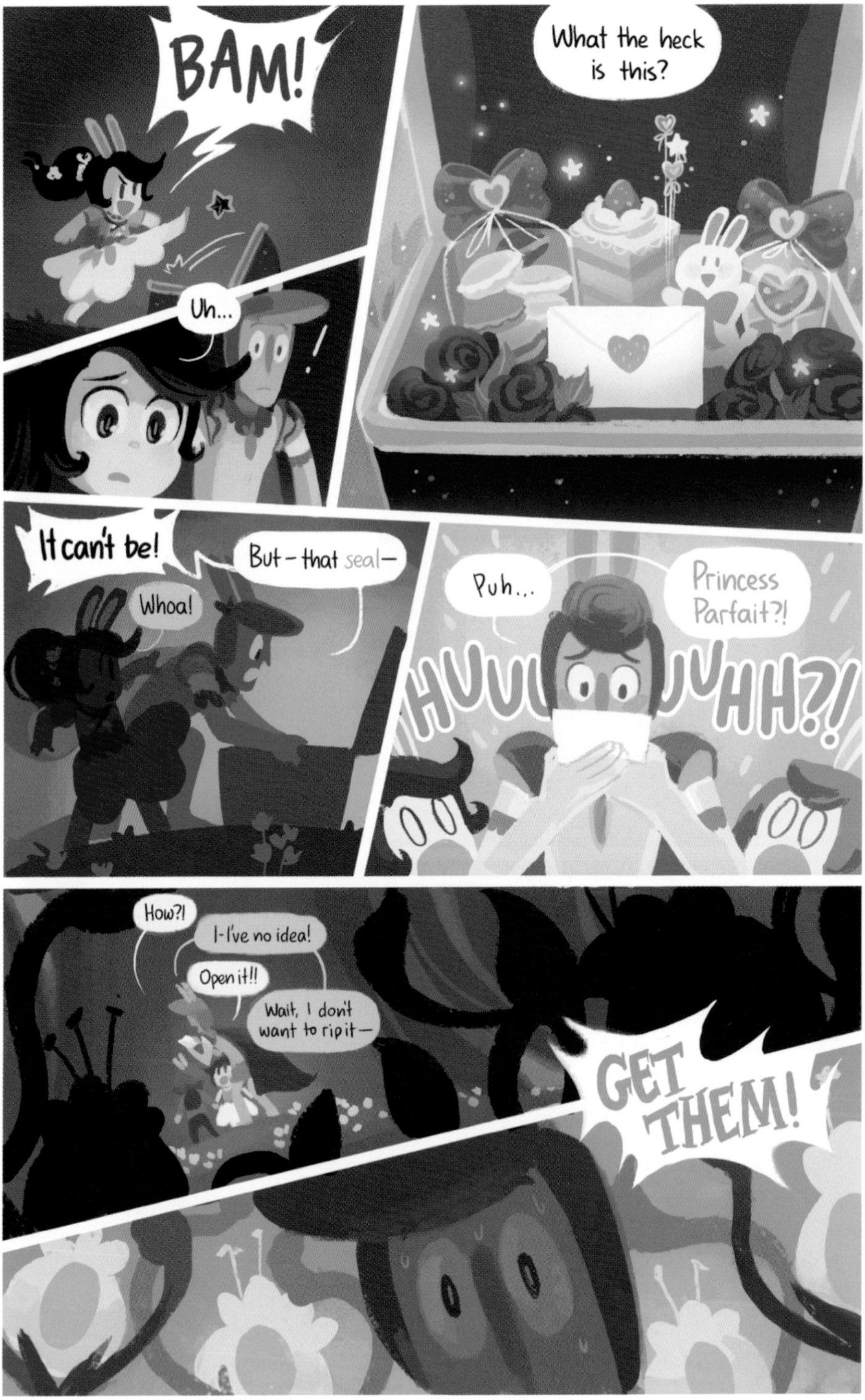
BAM!
What the heck is this?
Uh...
It can't be!
Whoa!
But—that seal—
Puh...
Princess Parfait?!
HUUUUUHH?!
How?!
I-I've no idea!
Open it!!
Wait, I don't want to rip it—
GET THEM!

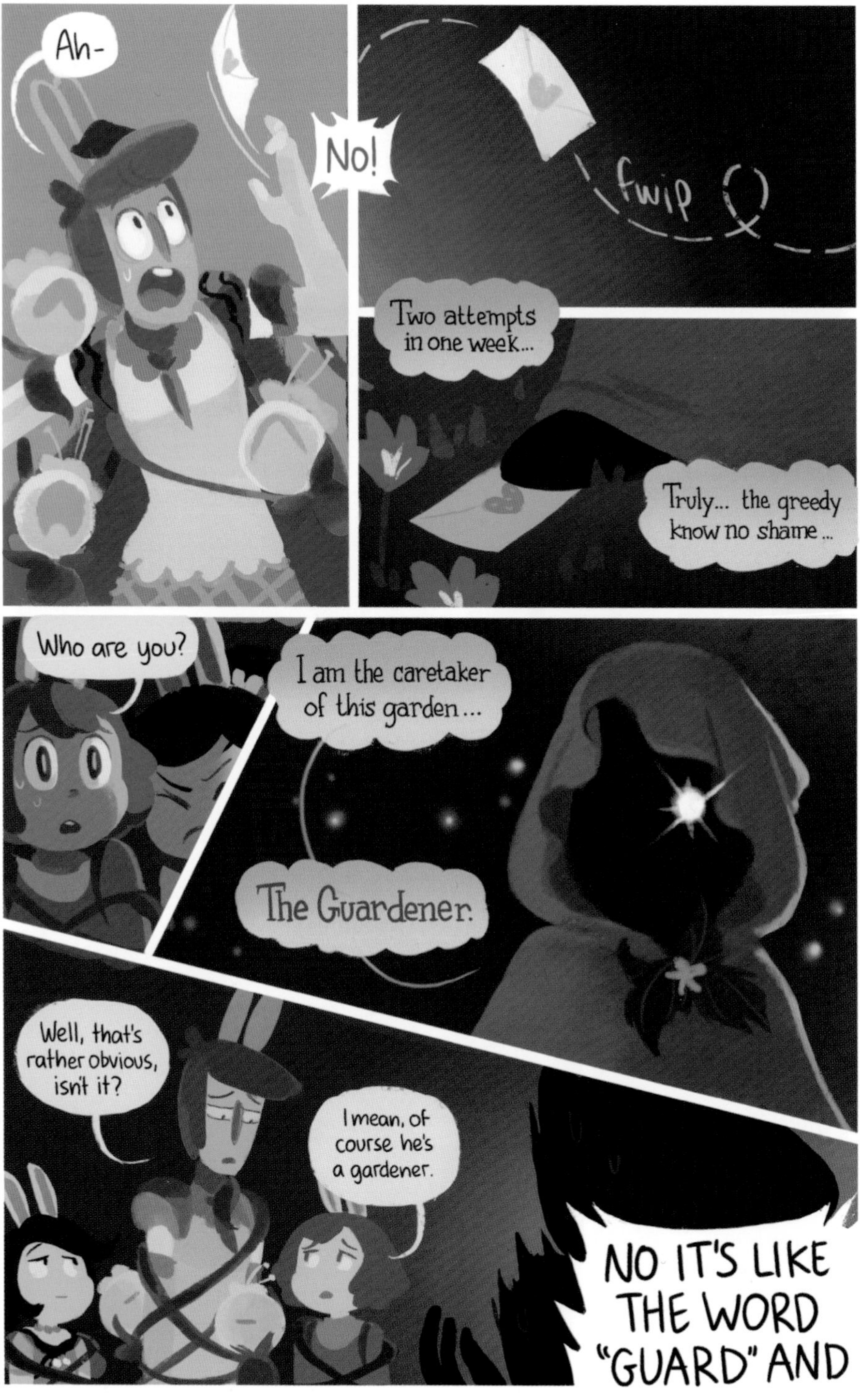
Ah-
No!
fwip
Two attempts in one week...
Truly... the greedy know no shame...
Who are you?
I am the caretaker of this garden...
The Guardener.
Well, that's rather obvious, isn't it?
I mean, of course he's a gardener.
NO IT'S LIKE THE WORD "GUARD" AND

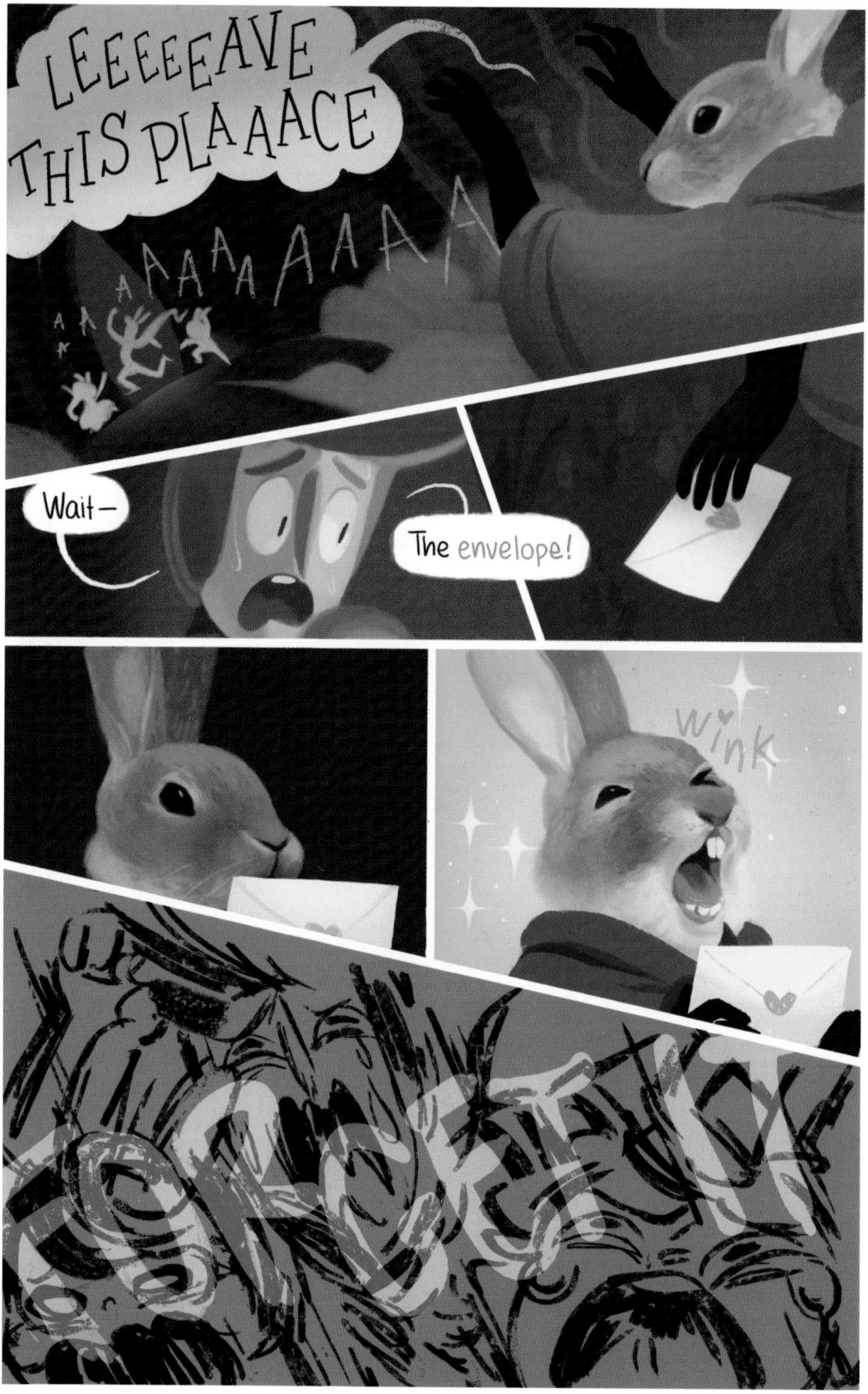
LEEEEEAVE THIS PLAAACE
Wait—
The envelope!
wink

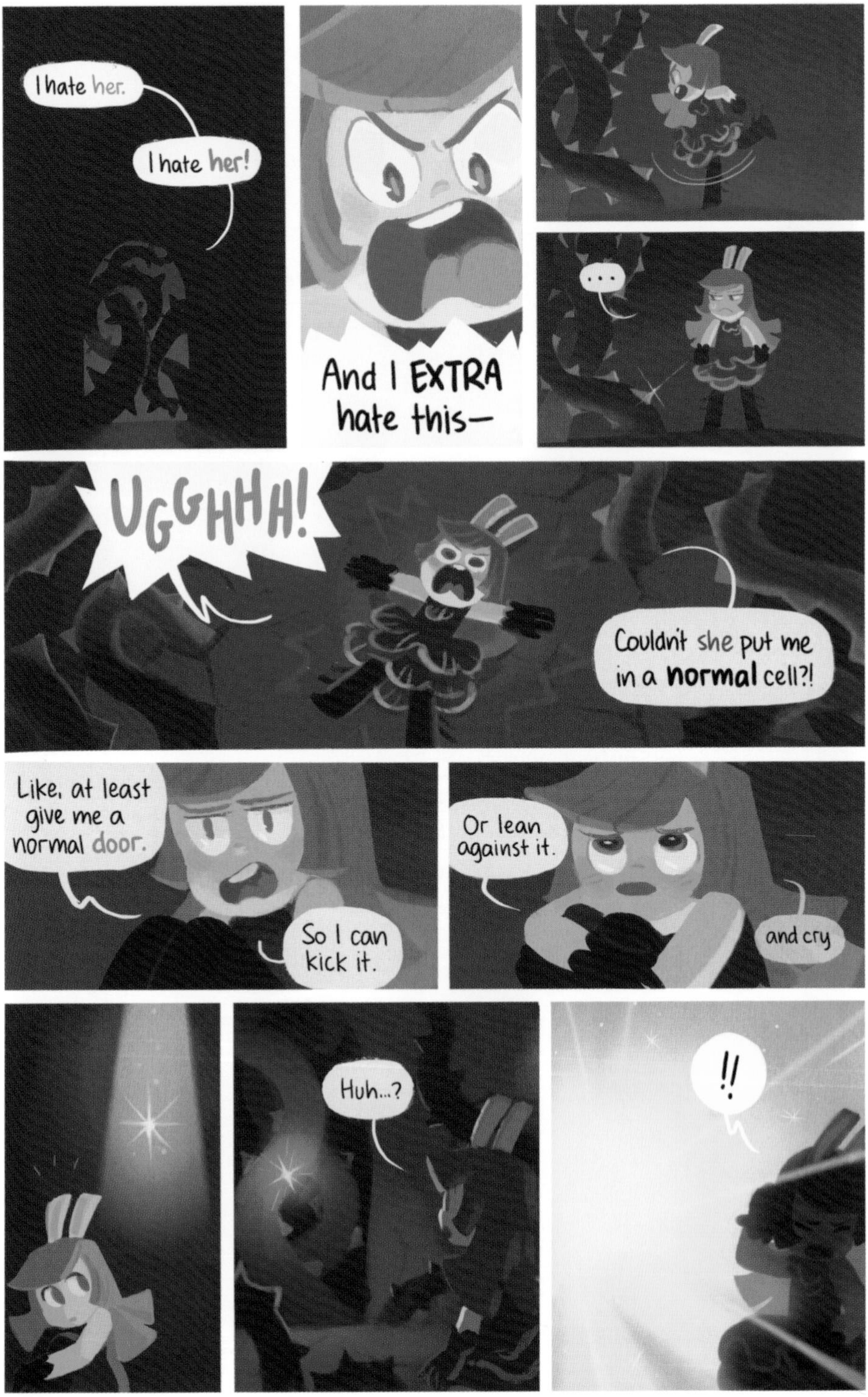
I hate her.
I hate her!
And I EXTRA hate this—
...
UGGHHH!
Couldn't she put me in a normal cell?!
Like, at least give me a normal door.
So I can kick it.
Or lean against it.
and cry
Huh...?
!!

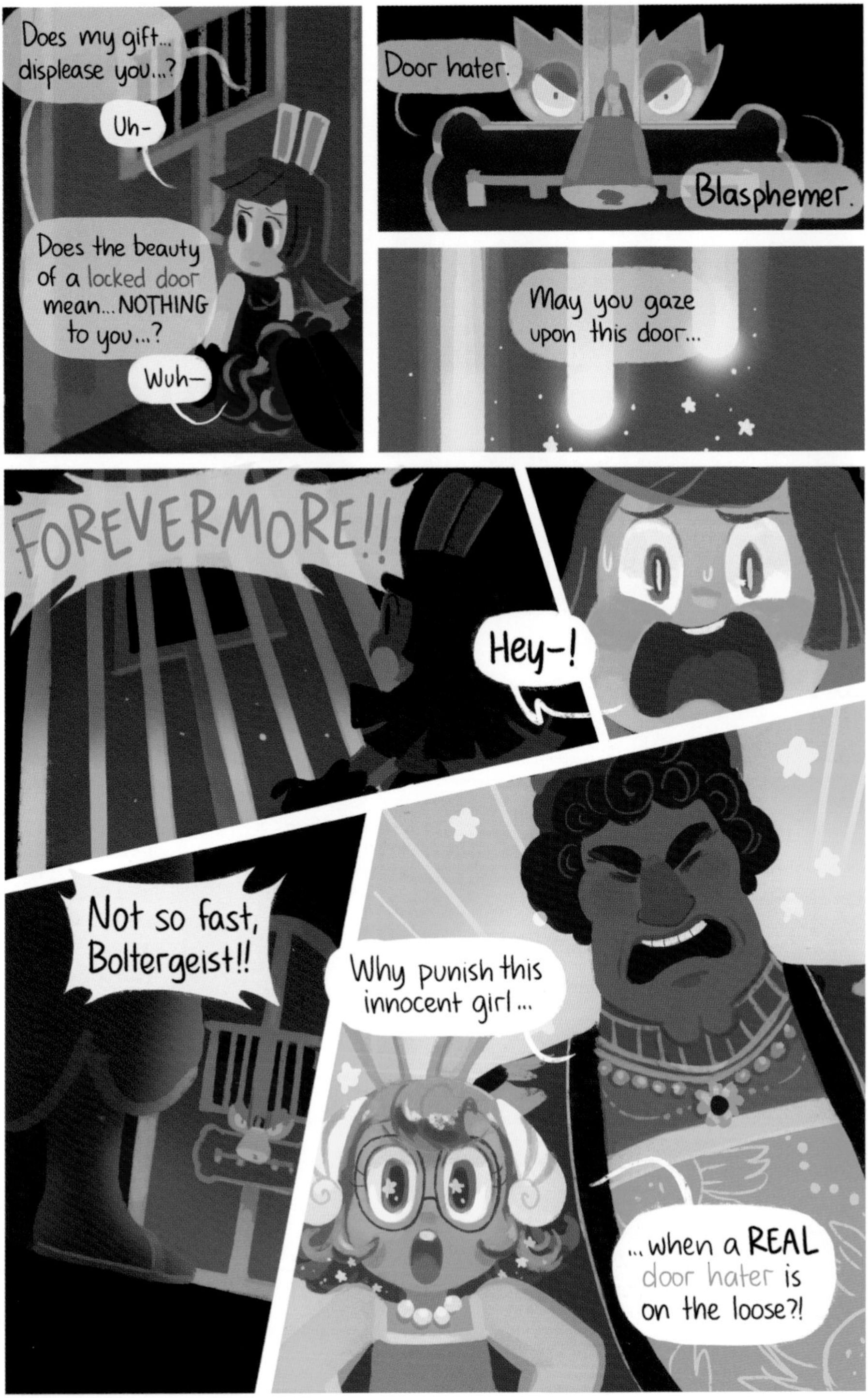
Does my gift... displease you...?
Uh-
Does the beauty of a locked door mean... NOTHING to you...?
Wuh-
Door hater.
Blasphemer.
May you gaze upon this door...
FOREVERMORE!!
Hey-!
Not so fast, Boltergeist!!
Why punish this innocent girl...
...when a REAL door hater is on the loose?!

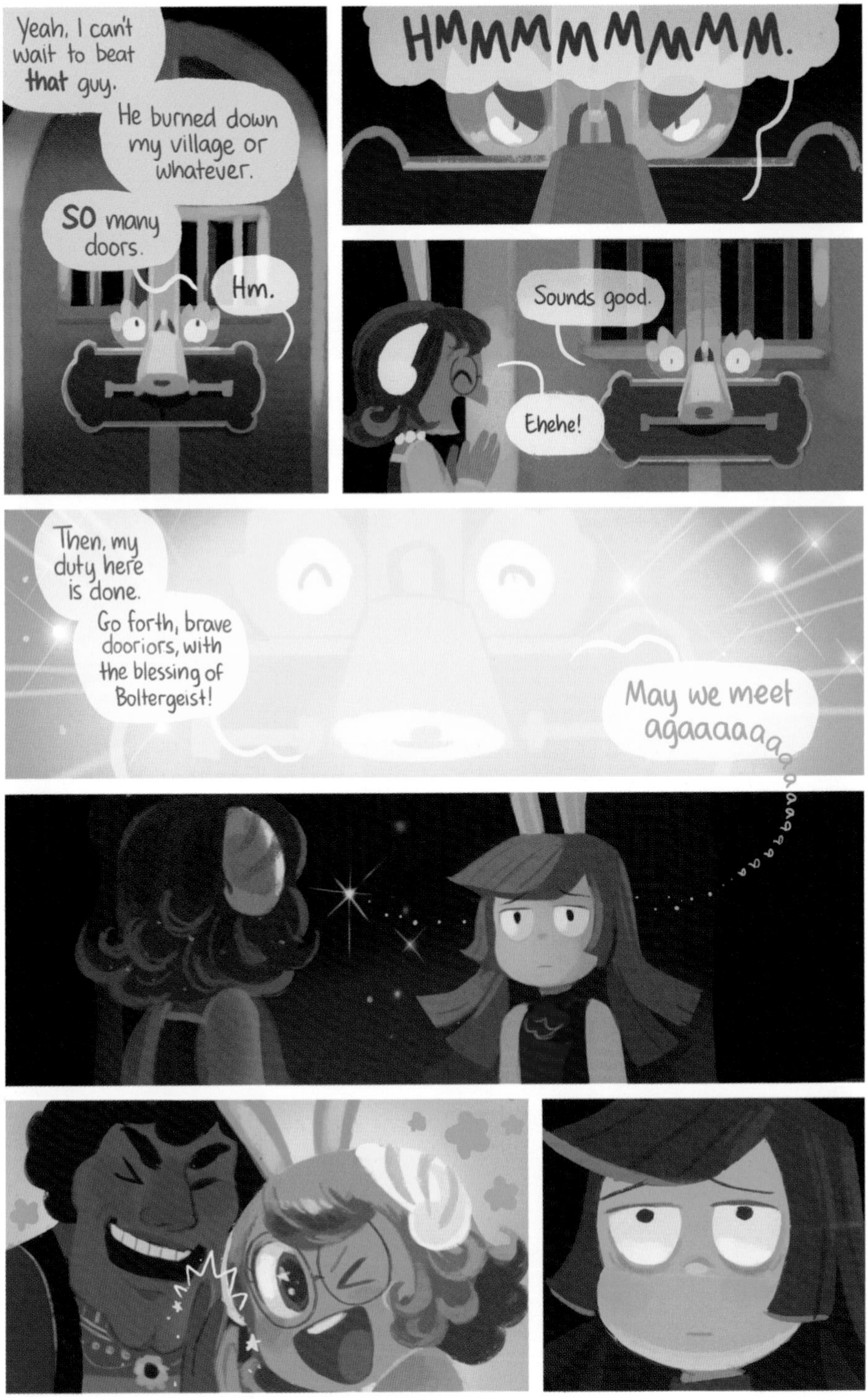
Yeah, I can't wait to beat **that** guy.
He burned down my village or whatever.
SO many doors.
Hm.
HMMMMMMMM.
Sounds good.
Ehehe!
Then, my duty here is done.
Go forth, brave dooriors, with the blessing of Boltergeist!
May we meet agaaaaaaaaaaaaaa...

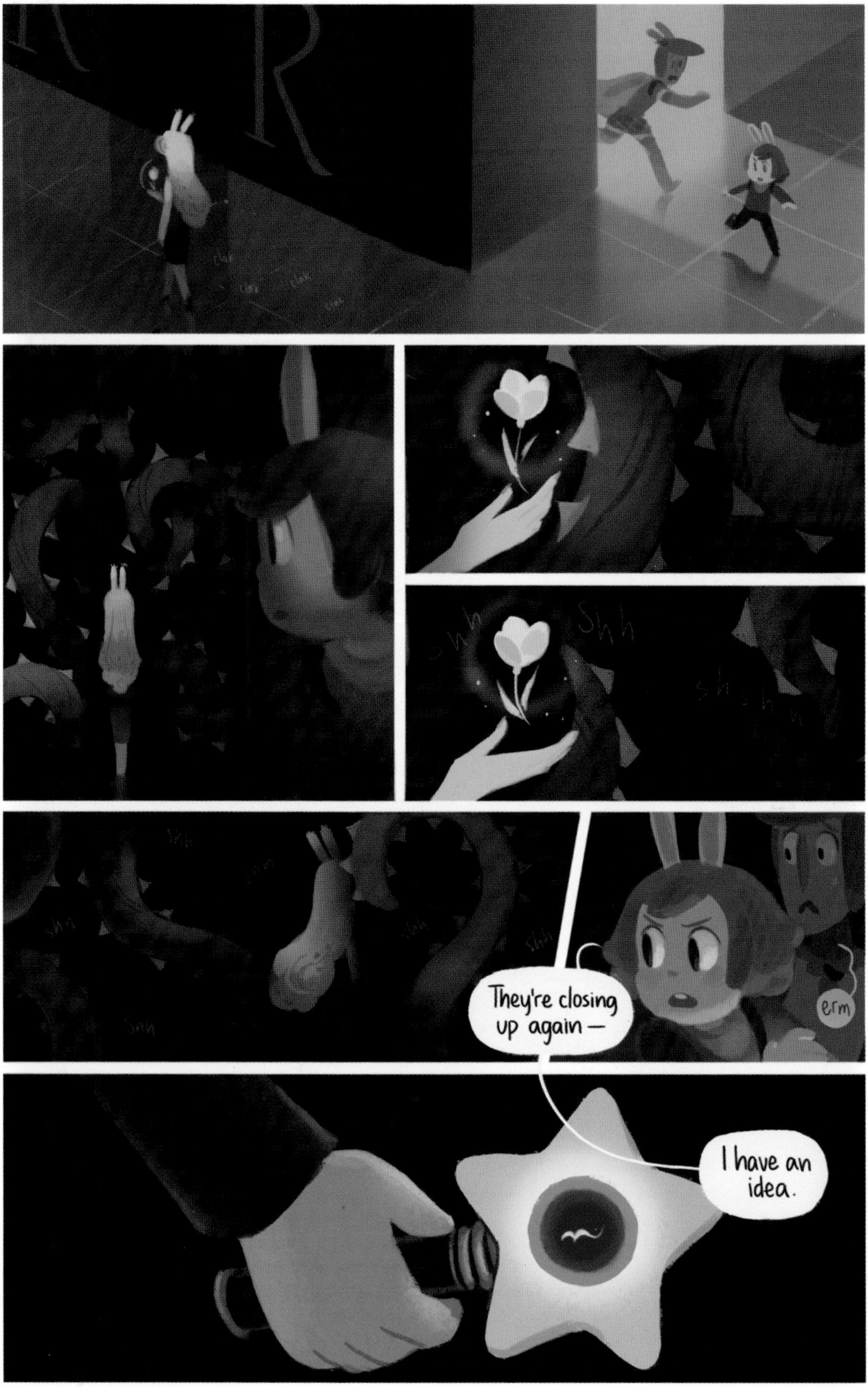
They're closing up again—
erm
I have an idea.

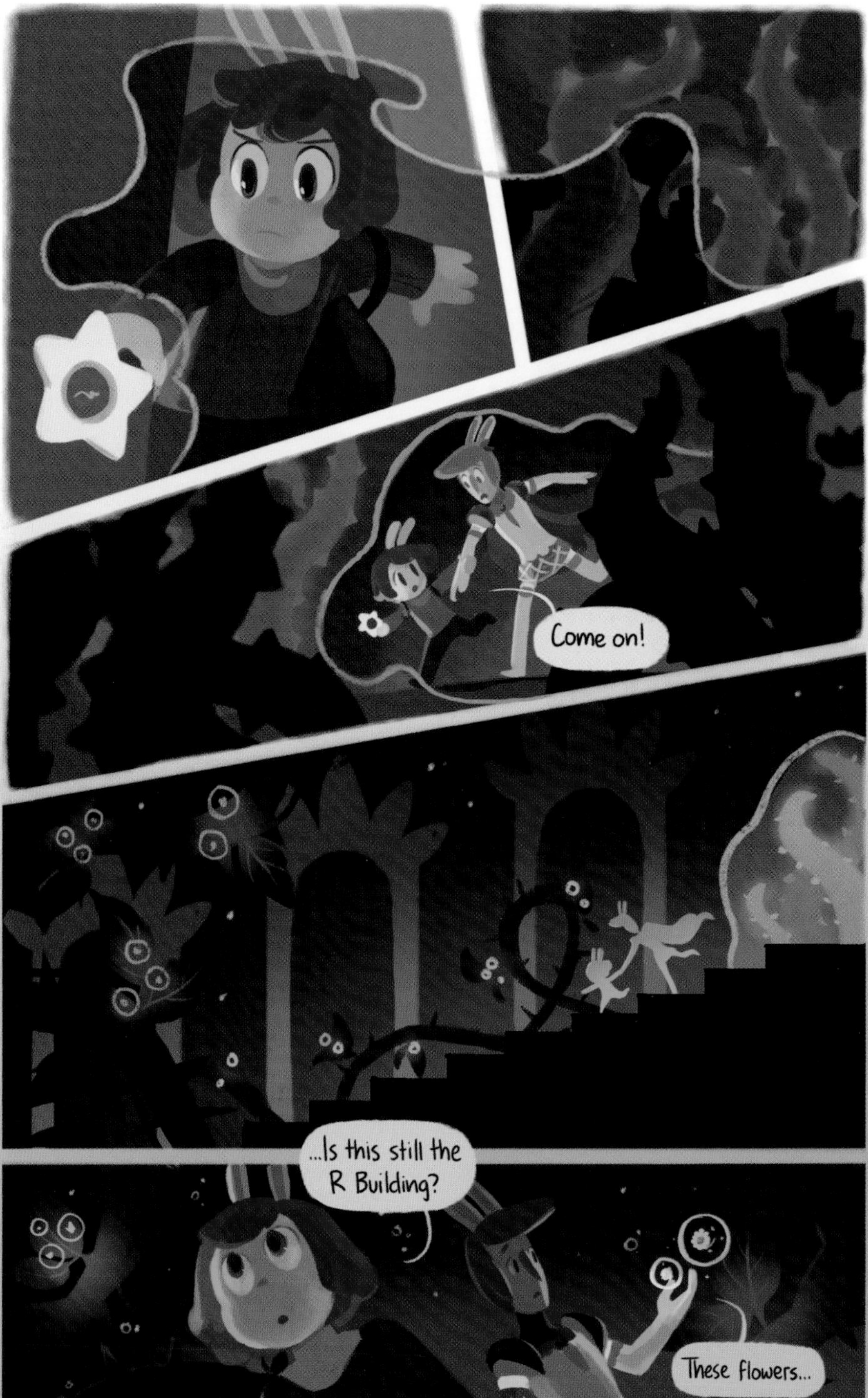
Come on!
...Is this still the R Building?
These flowers...

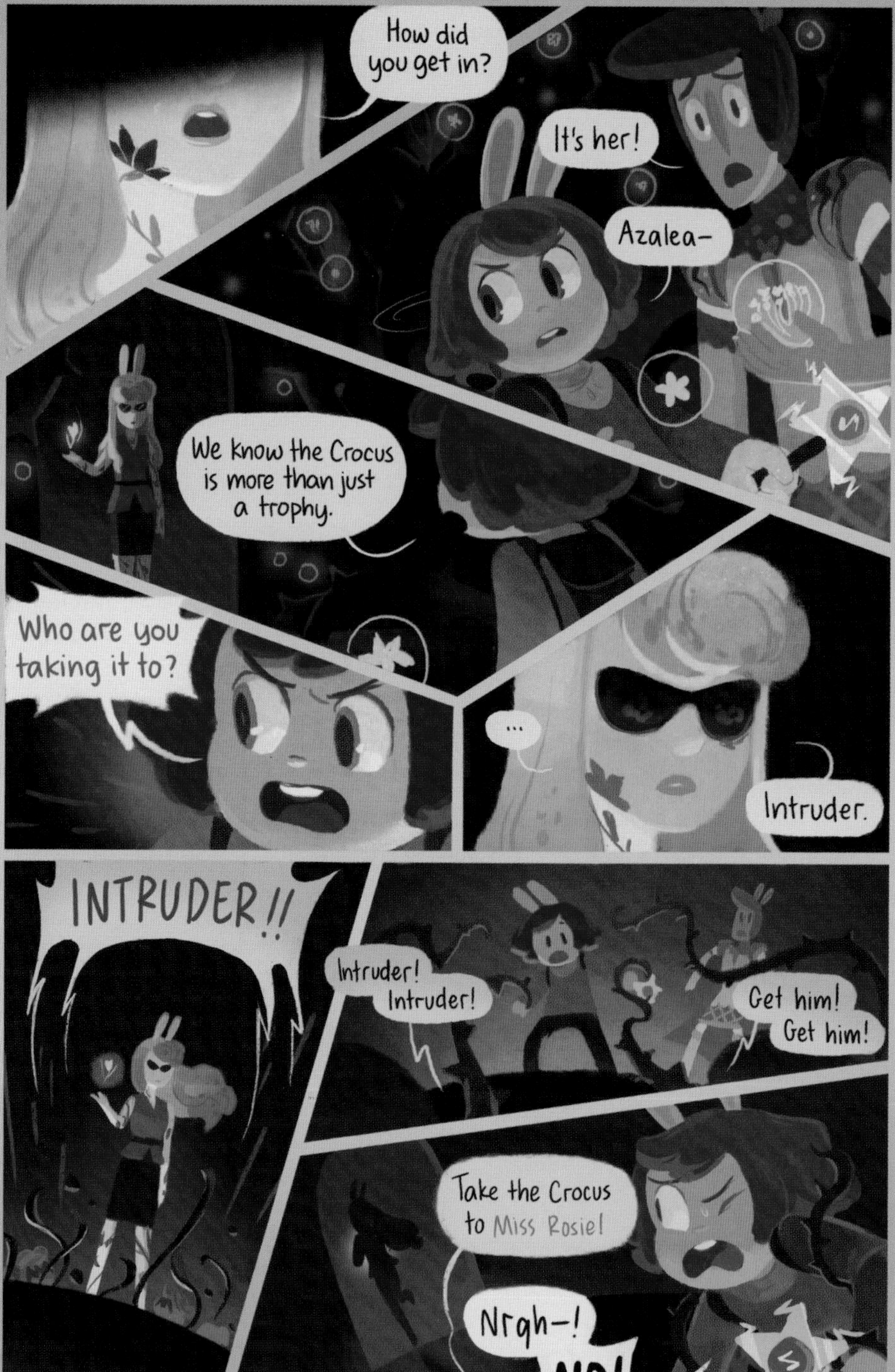
How did you get in?
It's her!
Azalea-
We know the Crocus is more than just a trophy.
Who are you taking it to?
...
Intruder.
INTRUDER!!
Intruder!
Intruder!
Get him!
Get him!
Take the Crocus to Miss Rosie!
Nrgh-!
NO!

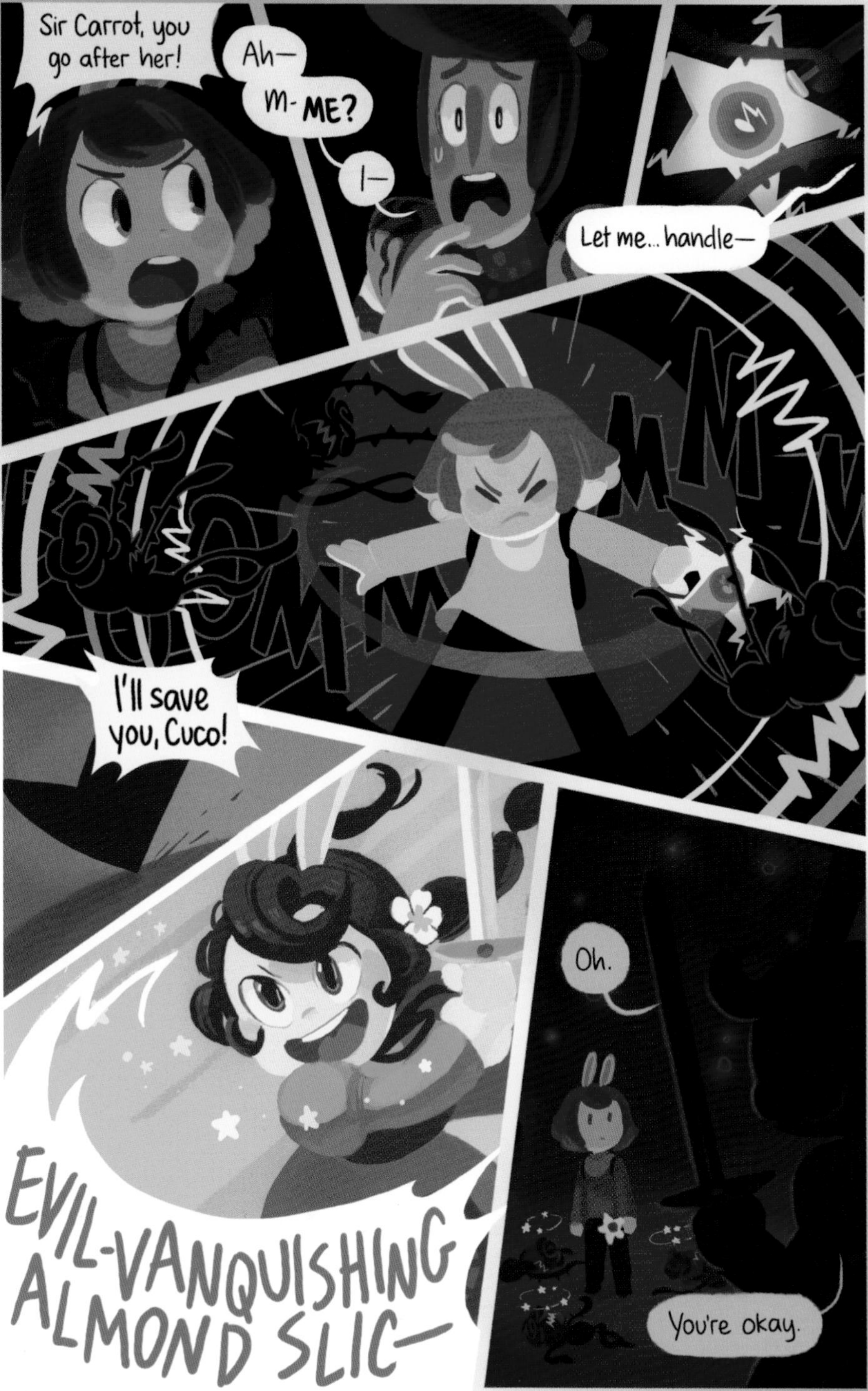

Sir Carrot, you go after her!
Ah—
m-ME?
I—
Let me... handle—
I'll save you, Cuco!
EVIL-VANQUISHING ALMOND SLIC—
Oh.
You're okay.

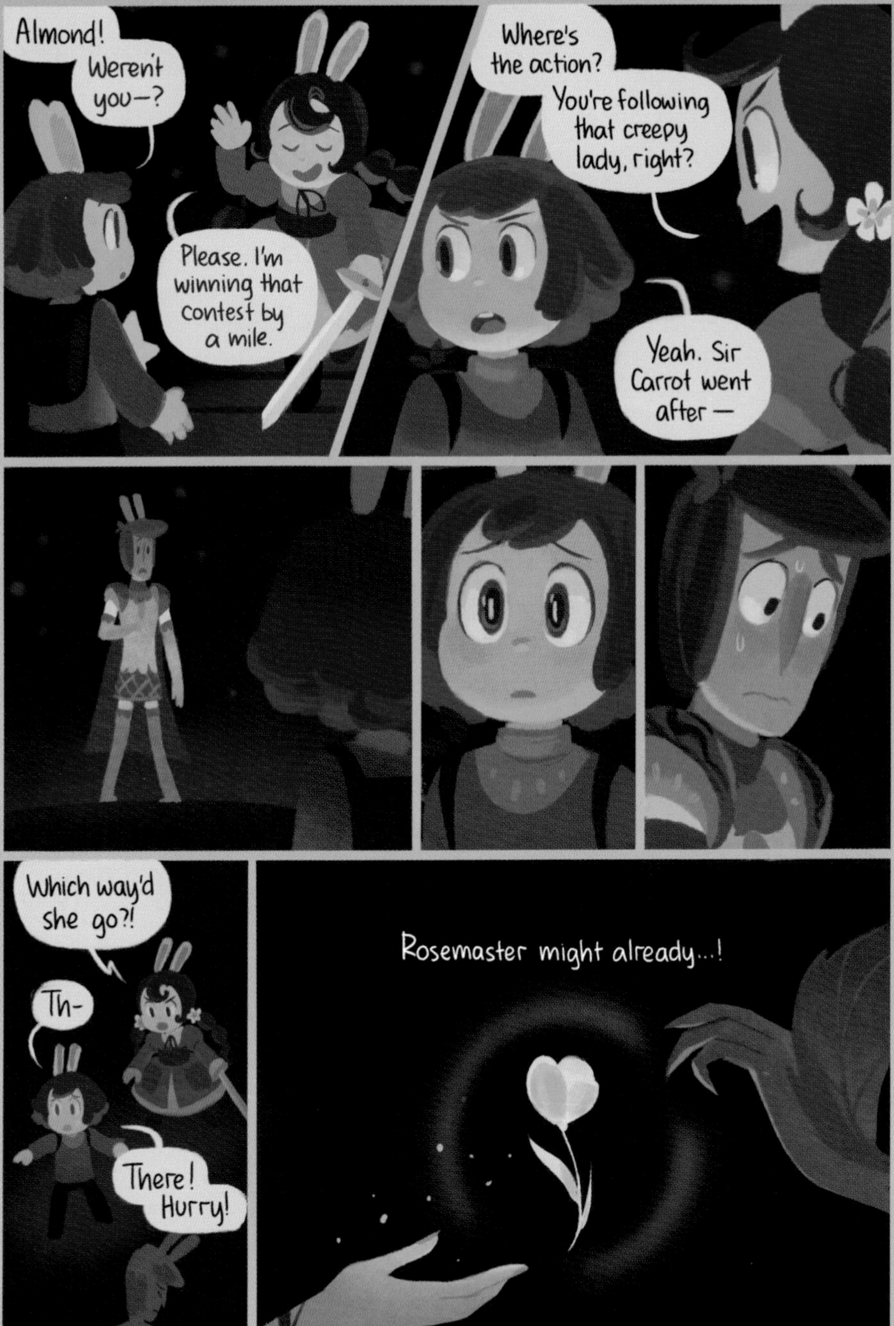

Almond!
Weren't you—?
Please. I'm winning that contest by a mile.
Where's the action?
You're following that creepy lady, right?
Yeah. Sir Carrot went after—
Which way'd she go?!
Th-
There! Hurry!
Rosemaster might already...!

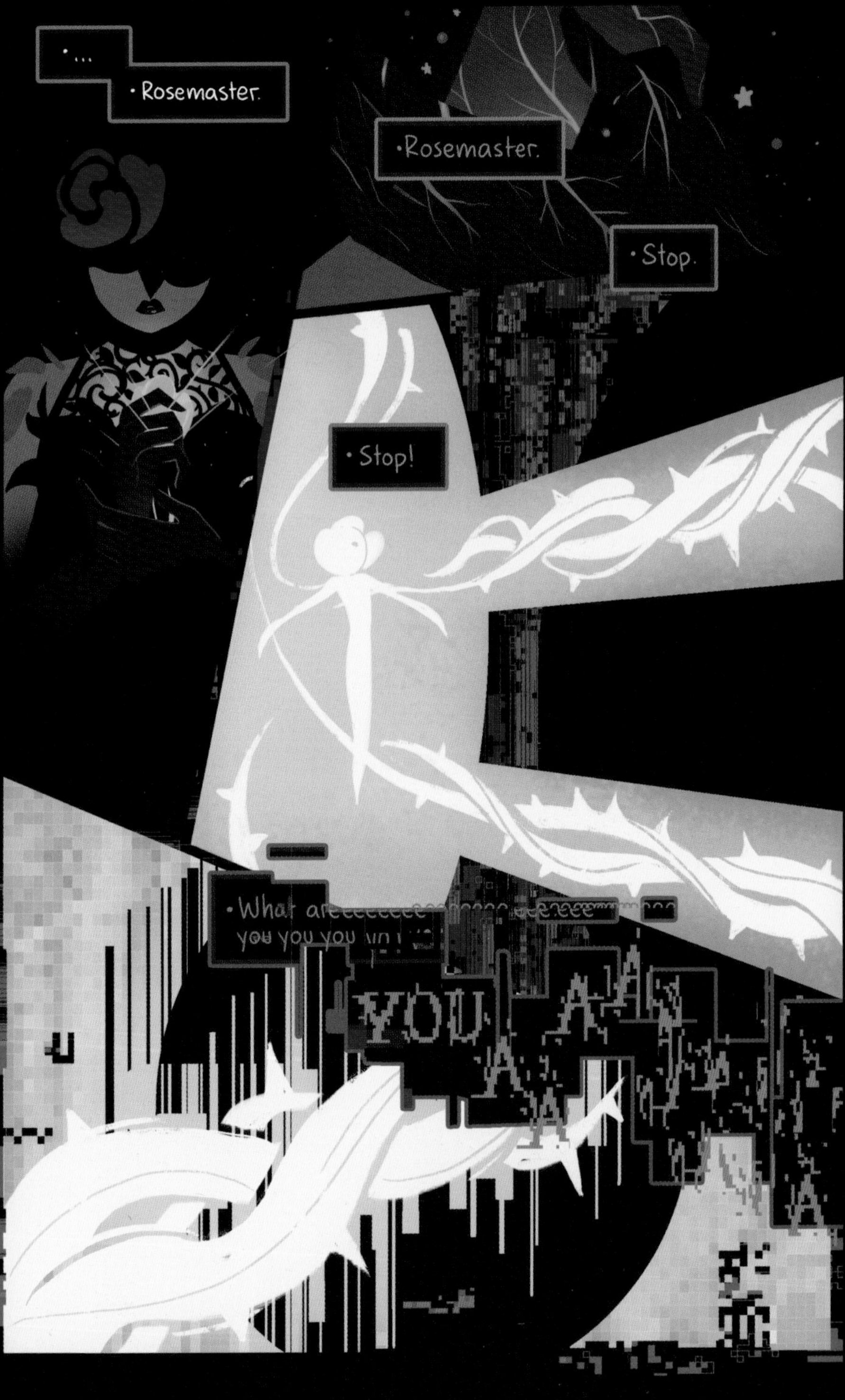
•...
•Rosemaster.
•Rosemaster.
•Stop.
•Stop!
•What areeeeeee
you you you
YOU

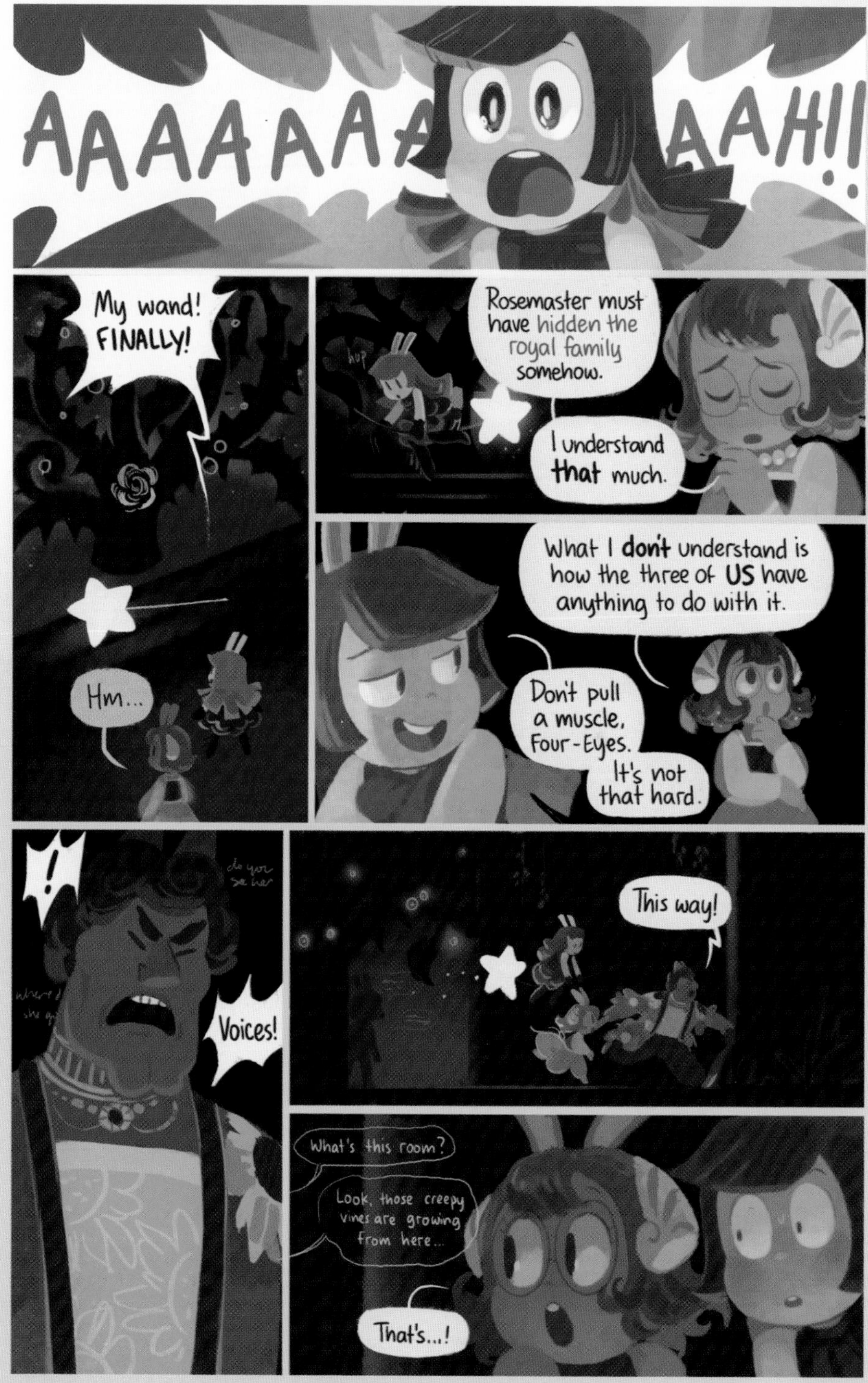
AAAAAAA AAH!!
My wand! FINALLY!
Hm...
hup
Rosemaster must have hidden the royal family somehow.
I understand that much.
What I don't understand is how the three of US have anything to do with it.
Don't pull a muscle, Four-Eyes.
It's not that hard.
!
Voices!
This way!
What's this room?
Look, those creepy vines are growing from here...
That's...!

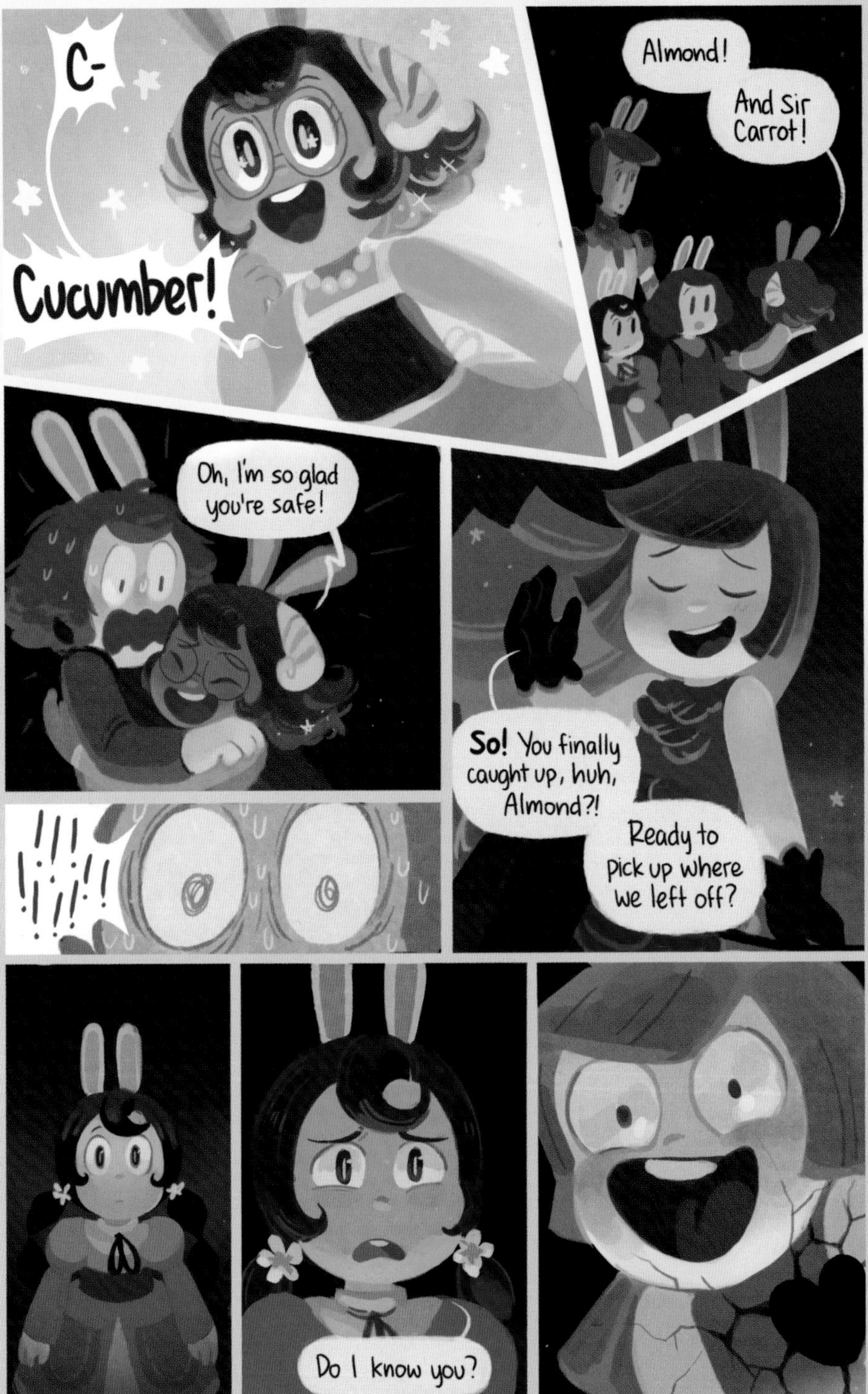
C-
Cucumber!
Almond!
And Sir Carrot!
Oh, I'm so glad you're safe!
!!!
So! You finally caught up, huh, Almond?!
Ready to pick up where we left off?
Do I know you?

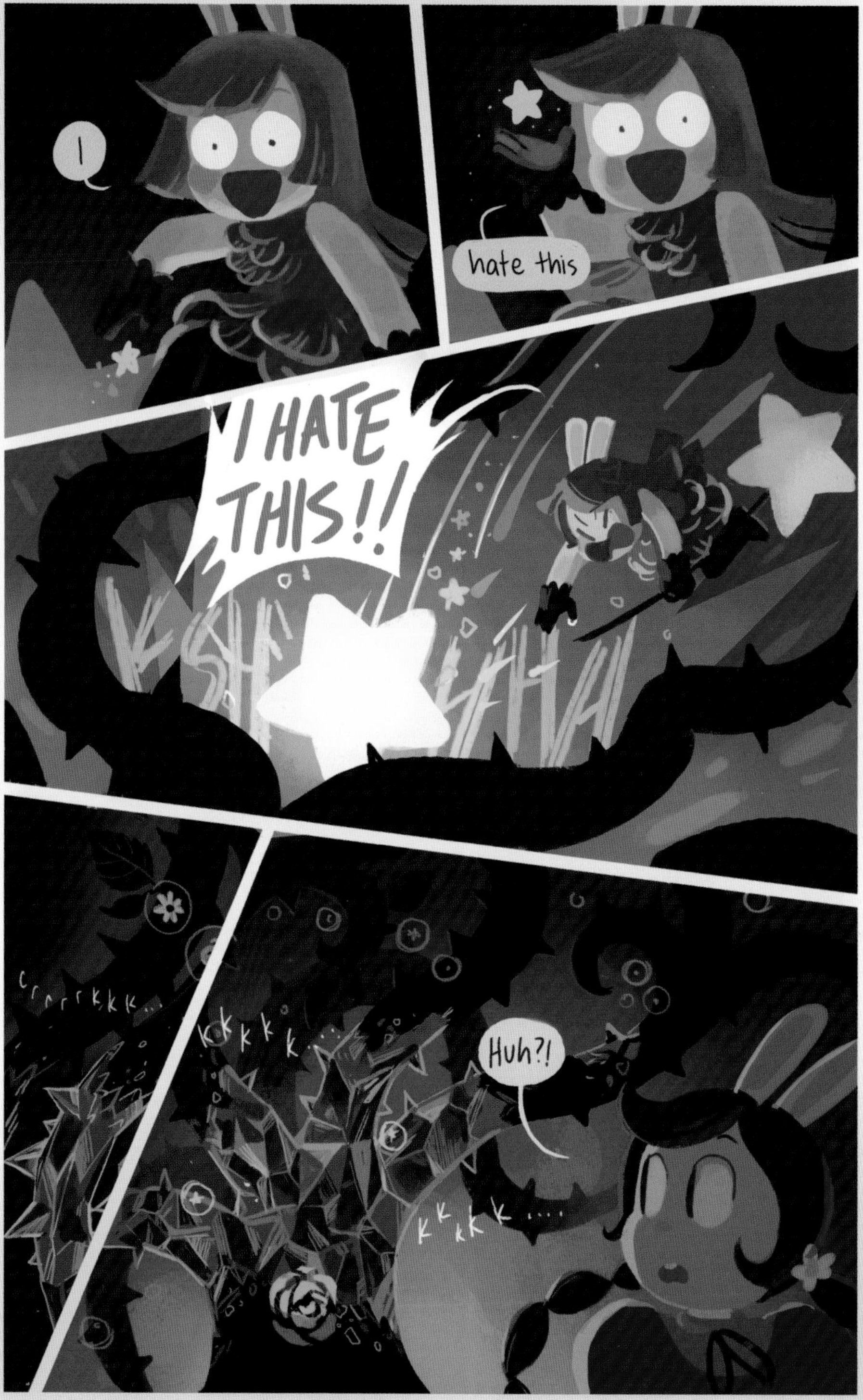
I
hate this
I HATE THIS!!
KSHHHHA
crrrrkkk...
kkkkk...
Huh?!
kkkkk....

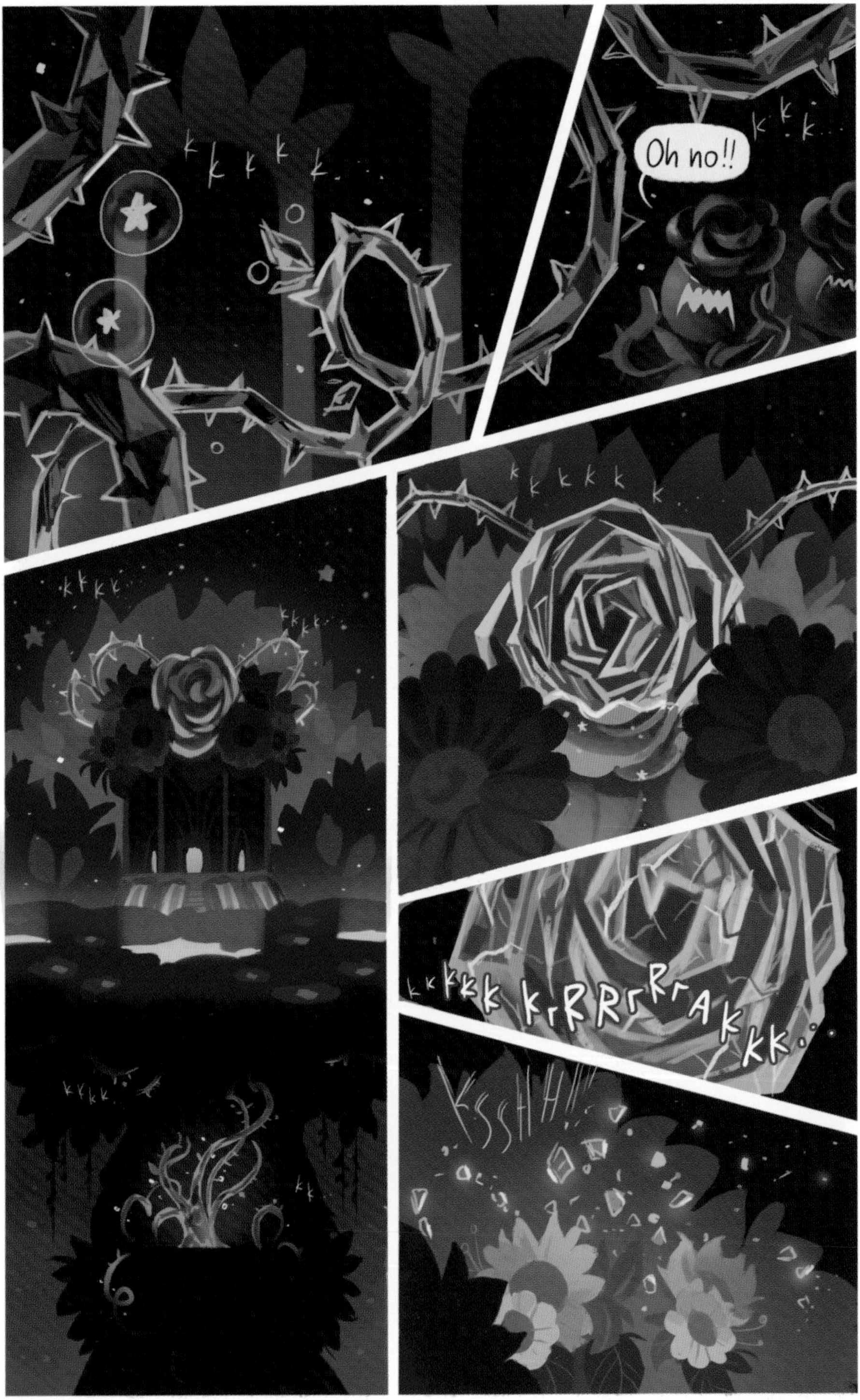
kkkkk
Oh no!!
kkk
kkkkkk
kkkk
kkkk
kkkkk KrRRrRrAKKK
KSSHH!!!
kkkk
kk

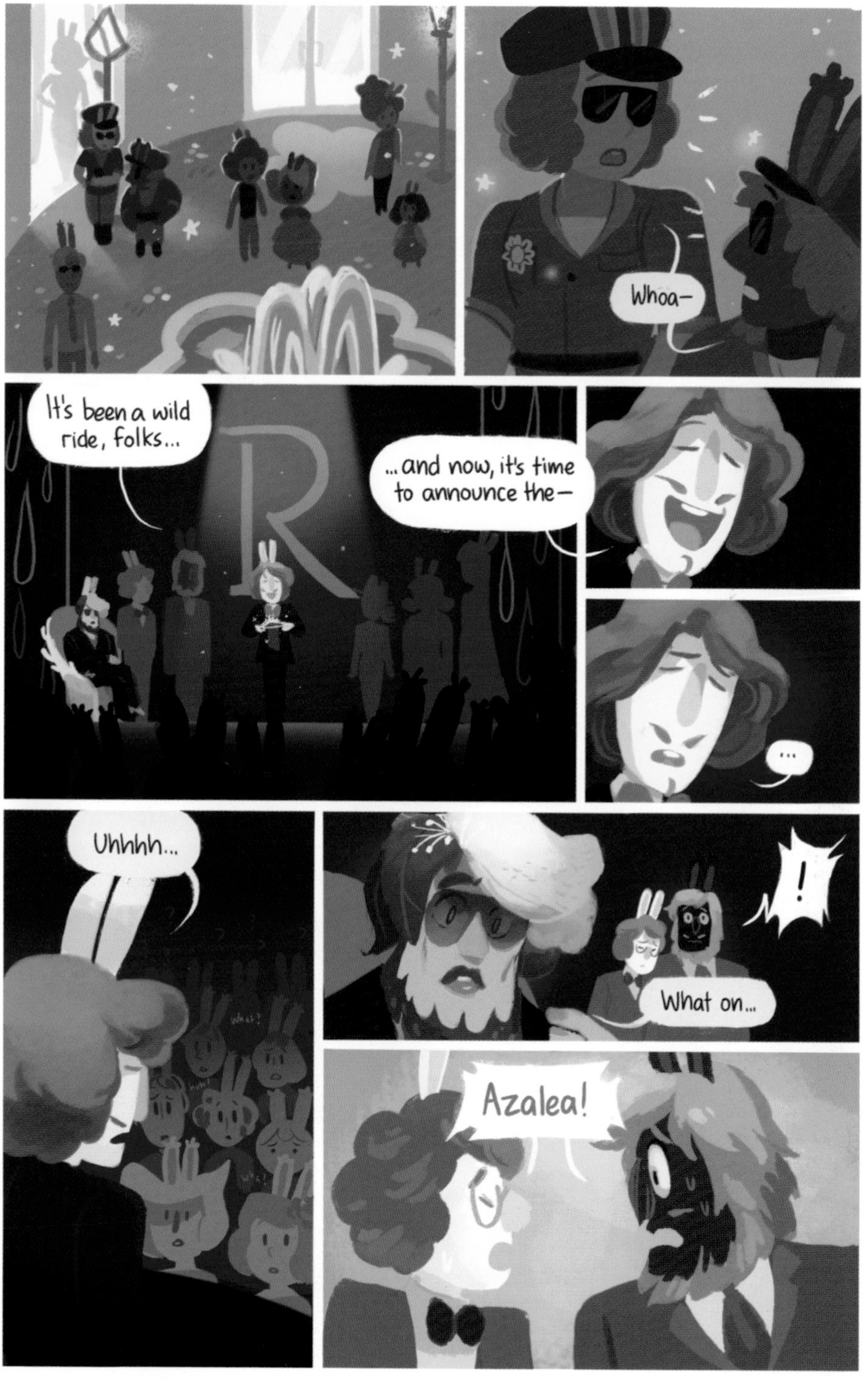
Whoa-
It's been a wild ride, folks...
...and now, it's time to announce the-
...
Uhhhh...
!
What on...
Azalea!

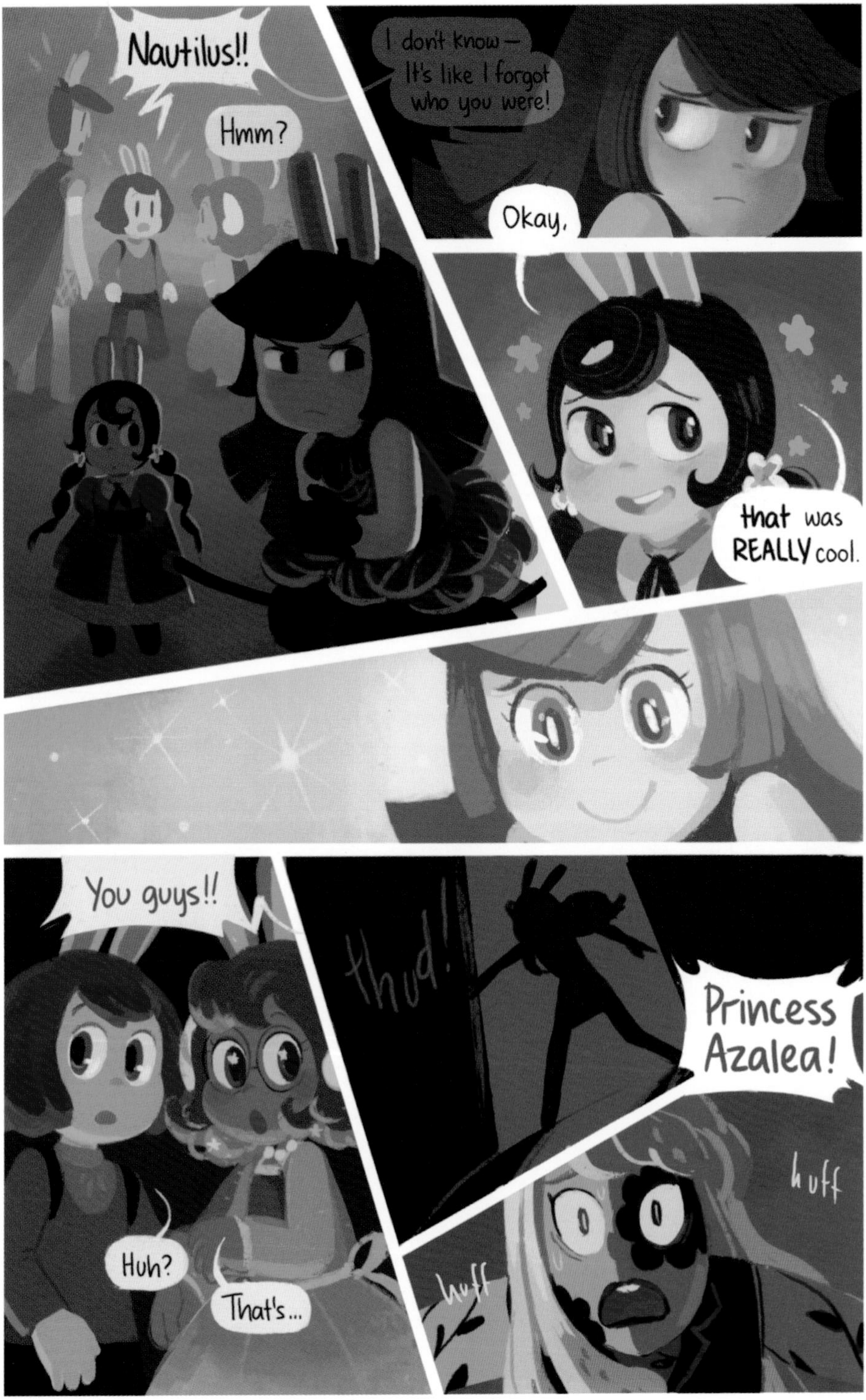
Nautilus!!
Hmm?
I don't know—
It's like I forgot who you were!
Okay.
that was REALLY cool.
You guys!!
Huh?
That's...
thud!
Princess Azalea!
huff
huff

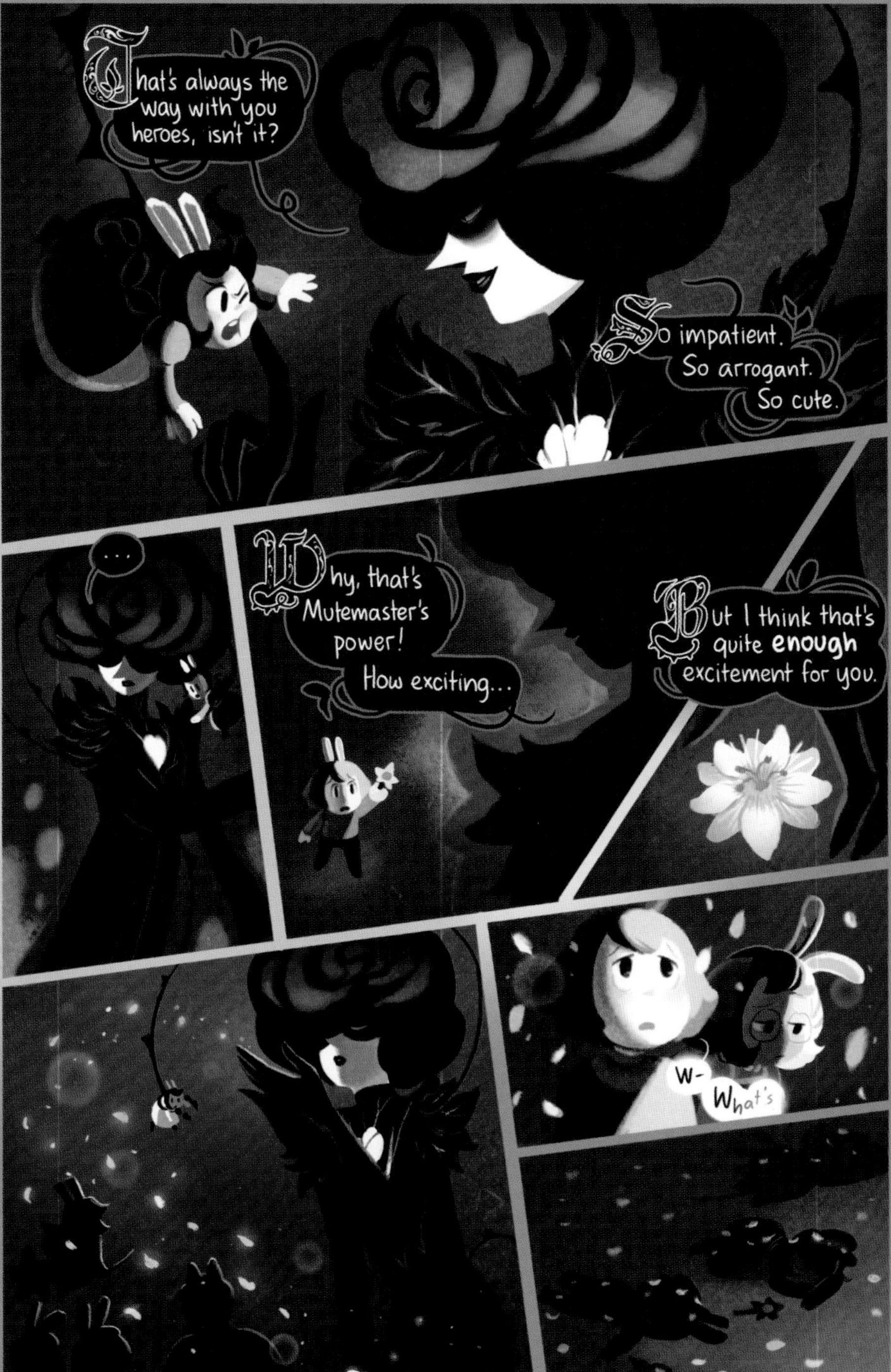
That's always the way with you heroes, isn't it?
So impatient. So arrogant. So cute.
...
Why, that's Mutemaster's power!
How exciting...
But I think that's quite **enough** excitement for you.
W-
What's

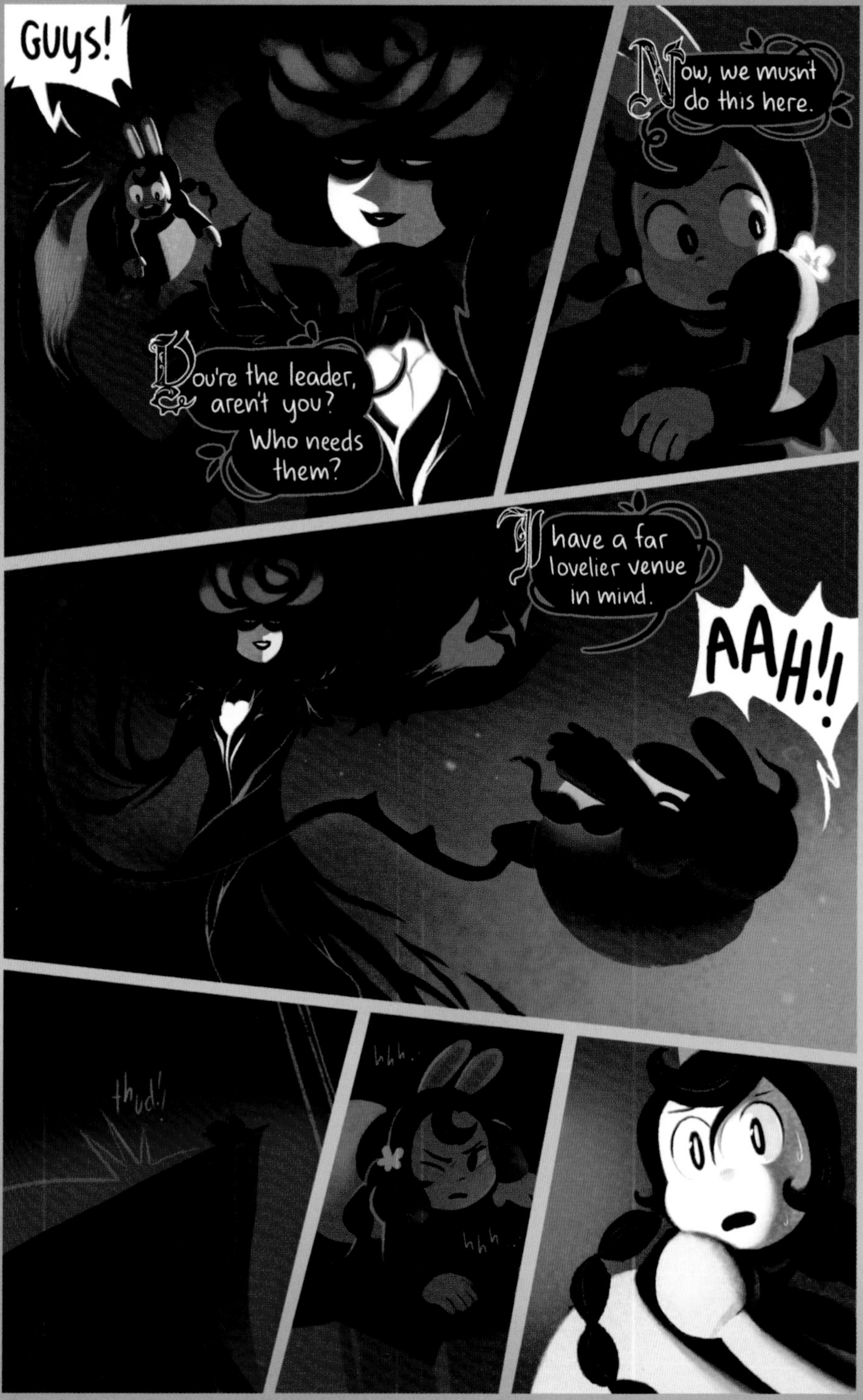
GUYS!
You're the leader, aren't you?
Who needs them?
Now, we musn't do this here.
I have a far lovelier venue in mind.
AAH!!
thud!!
hhh...
hhh...

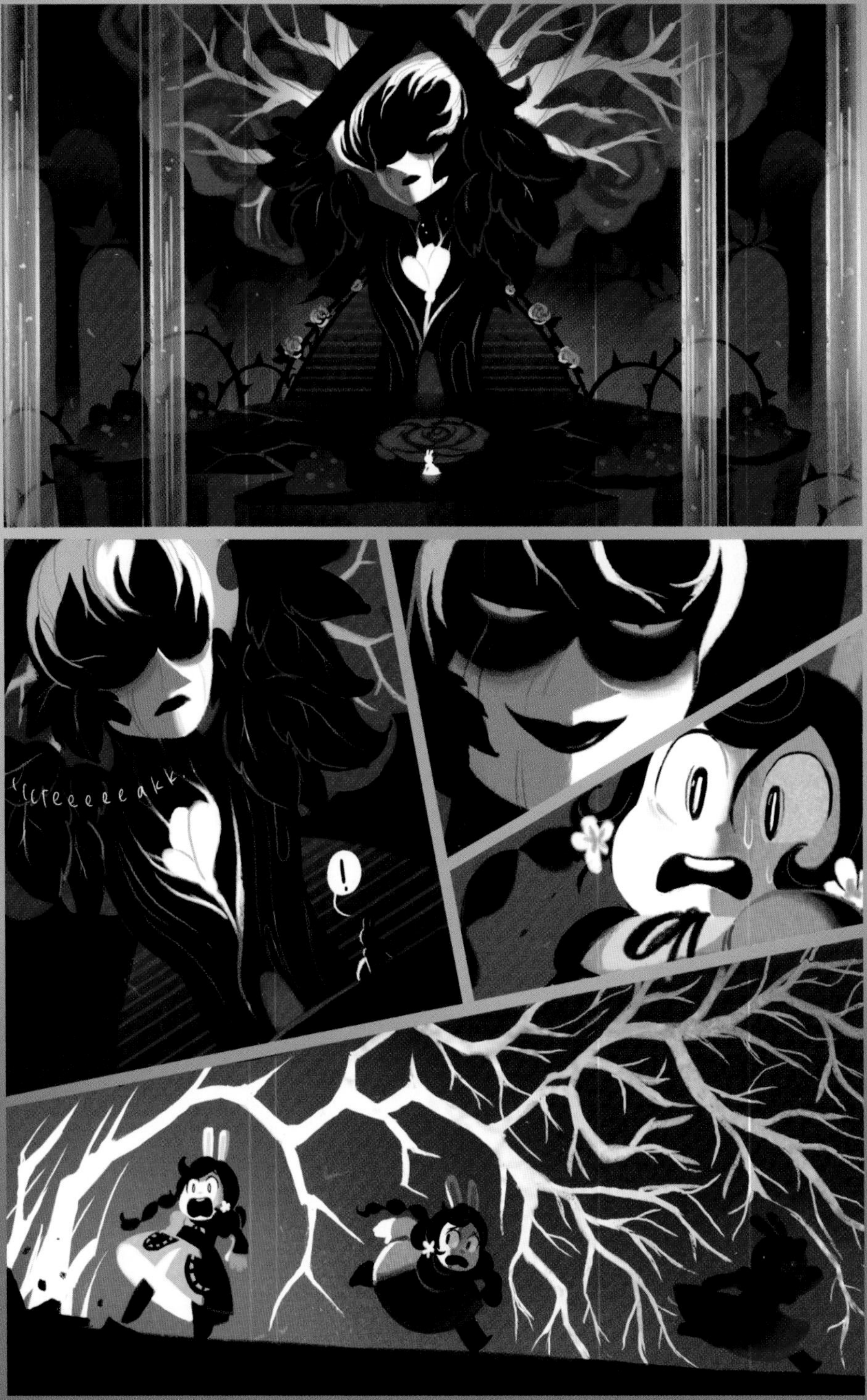
'Creeeeeeakk.
!

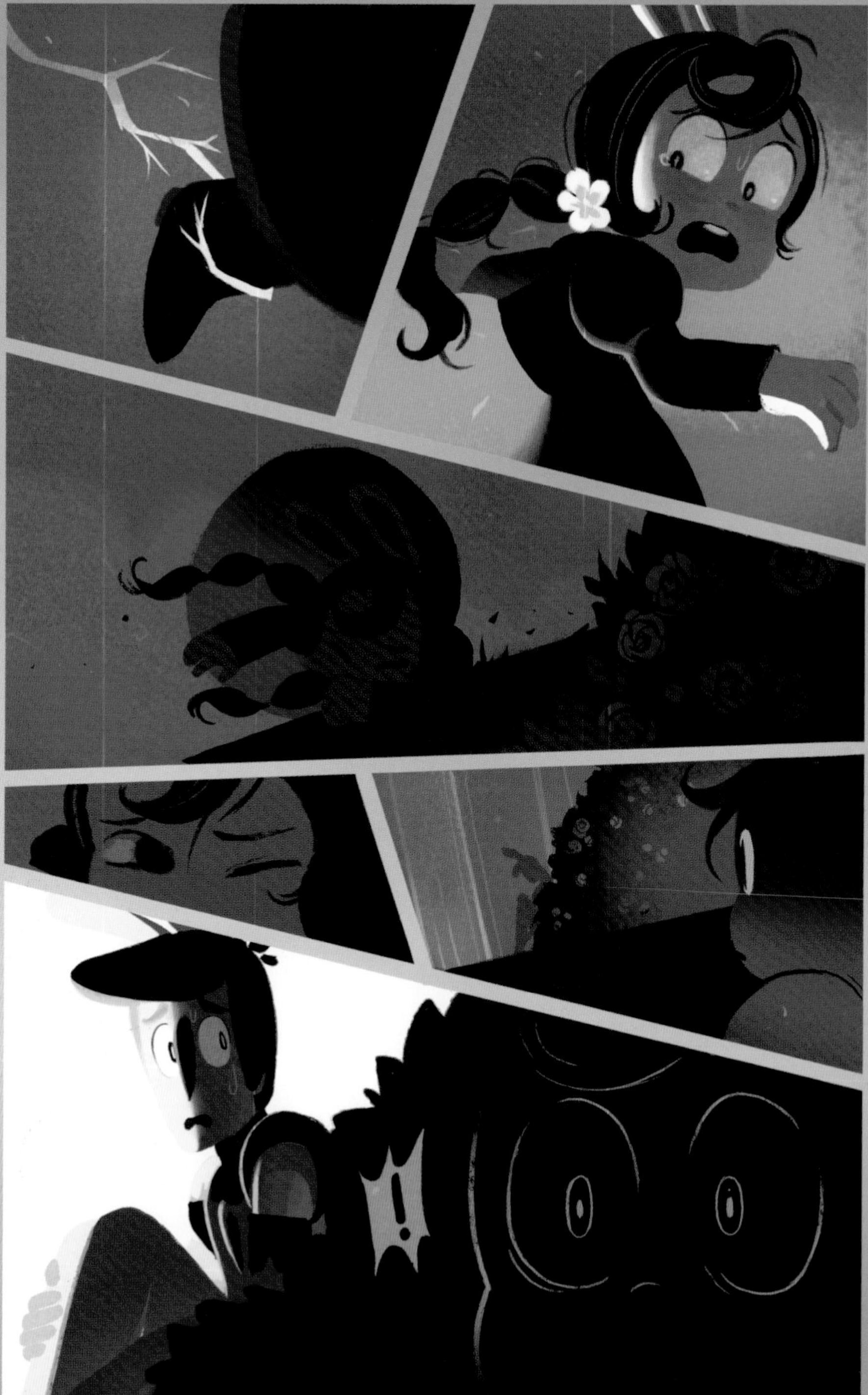
!

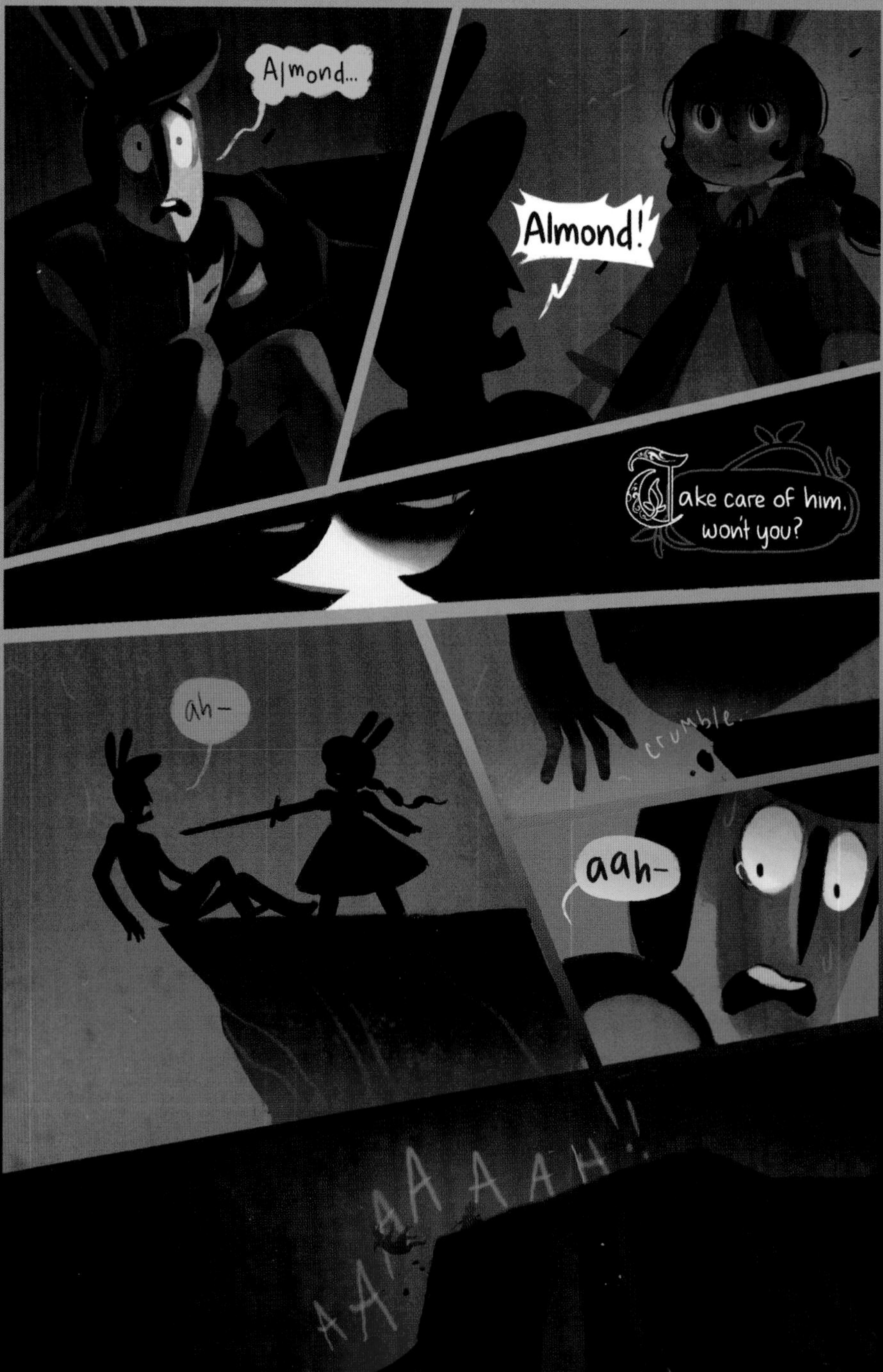
Almond...
Almond!
Take care of him, won't you?
ah-
crumble
aah-
AAAAAAH!!

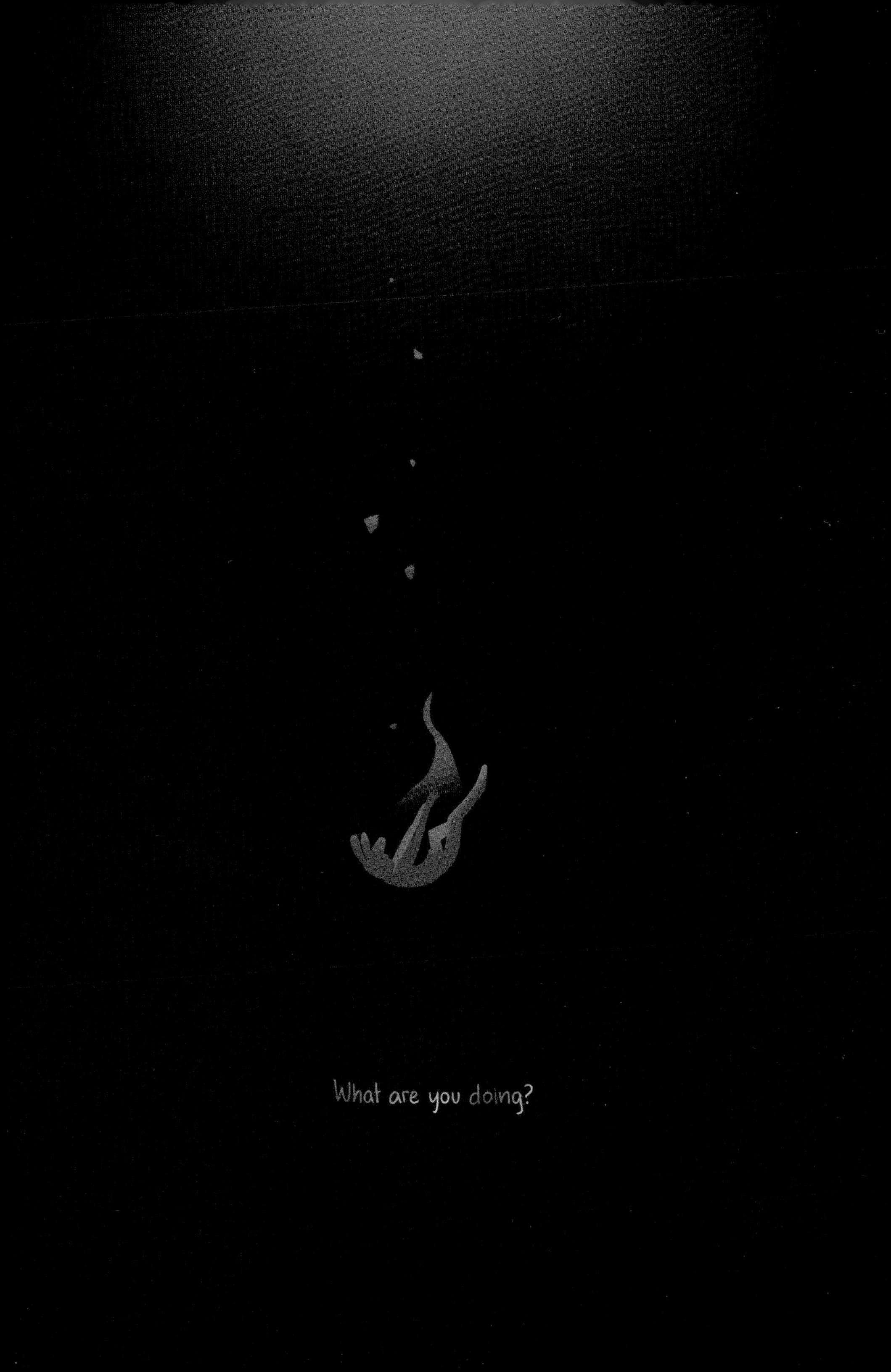
What are you doing?

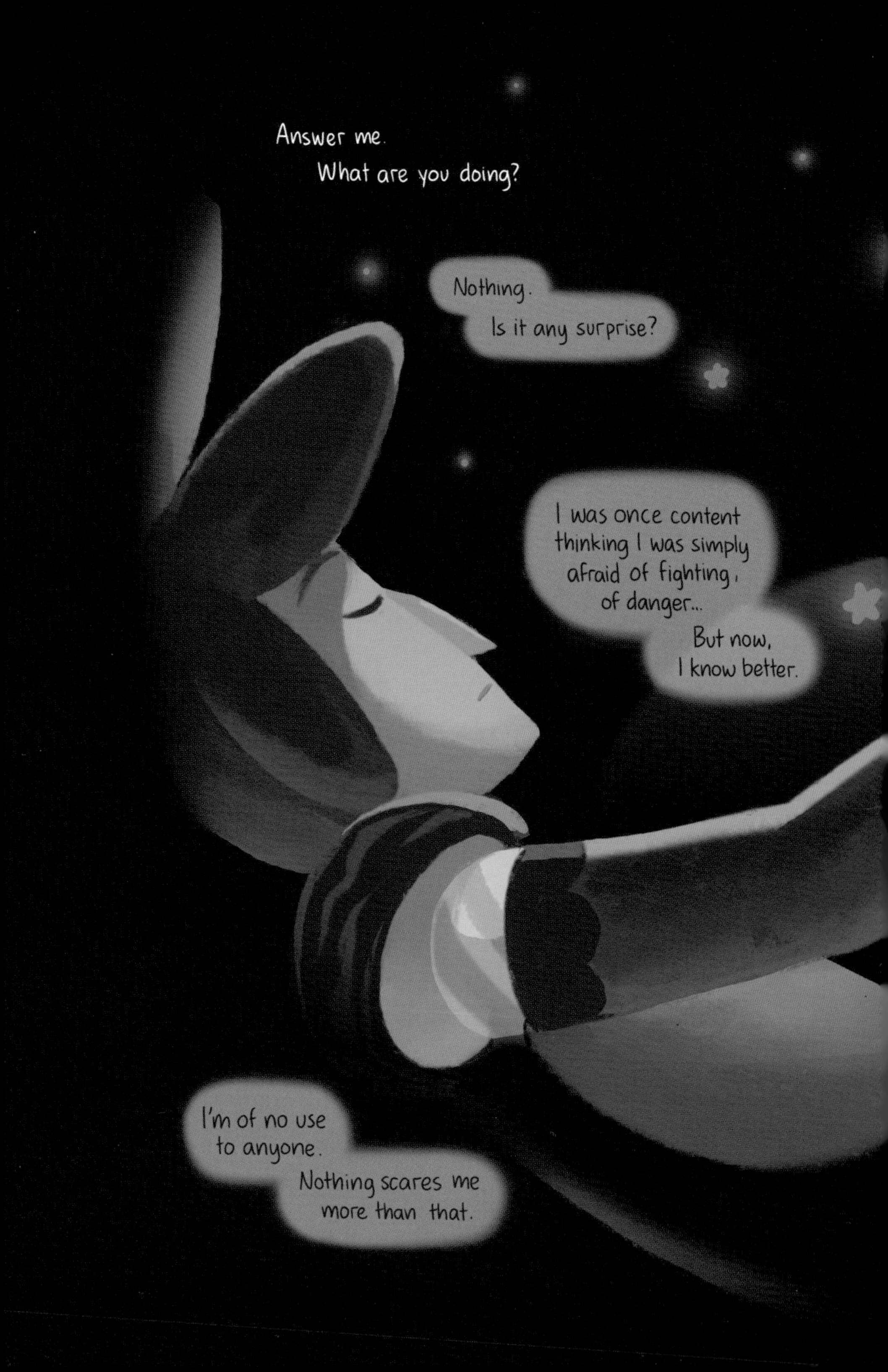
Answer me.
What are you doing?
Nothing.
Is it any surprise?
I was once content thinking I was simply afraid of fighting, of danger...
But now, I know better.
I'm of no use to anyone.
Nothing scares me more than that.

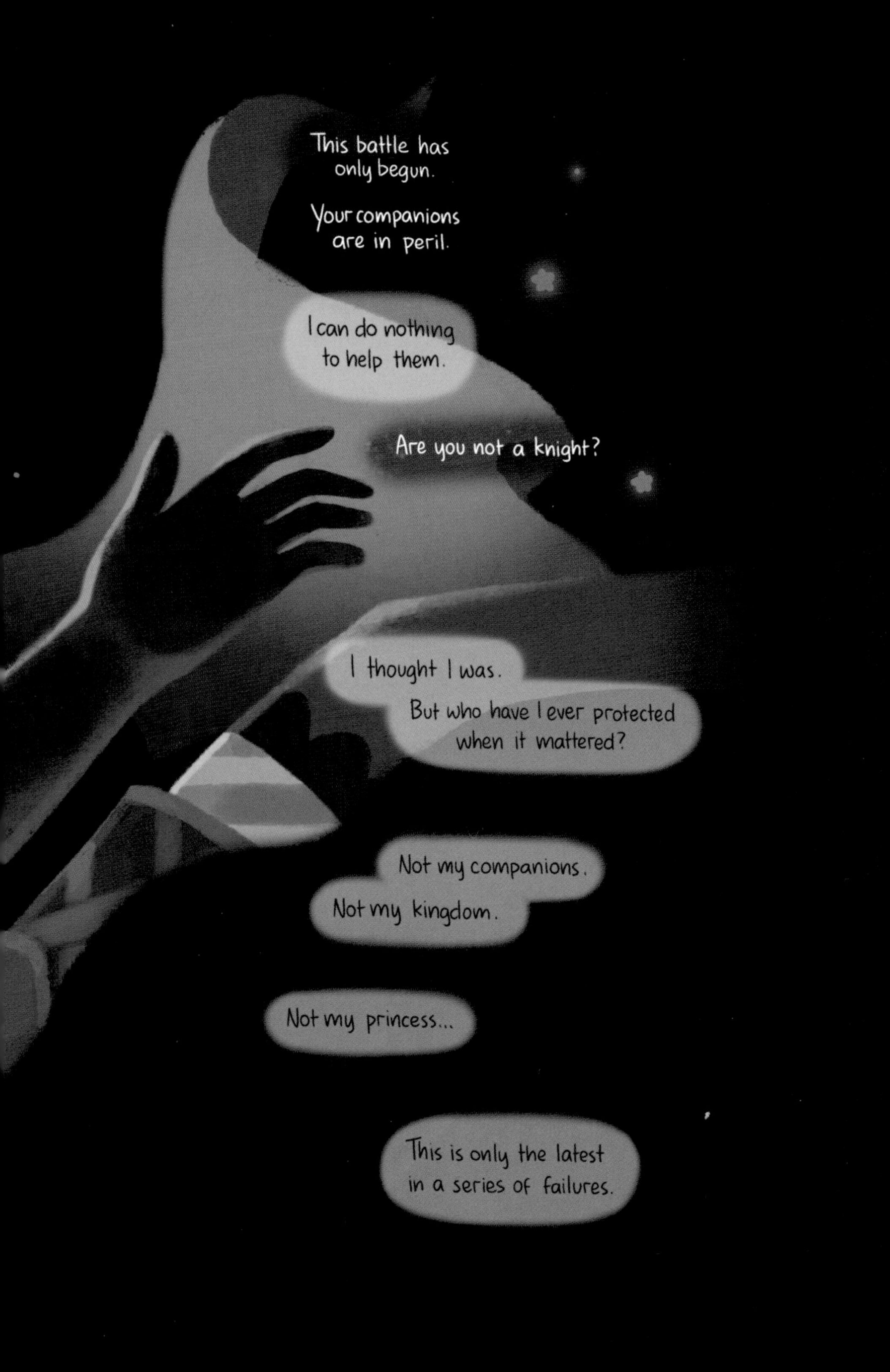
This battle has only begun.
Your companions are in peril.
I can do nothing to help them.
Are you not a knight?
I thought I was.
But who have I ever protected when it mattered?
Not my companions.
Not my kingdom.
Not my princess...
This is only the latest in a series of failures.

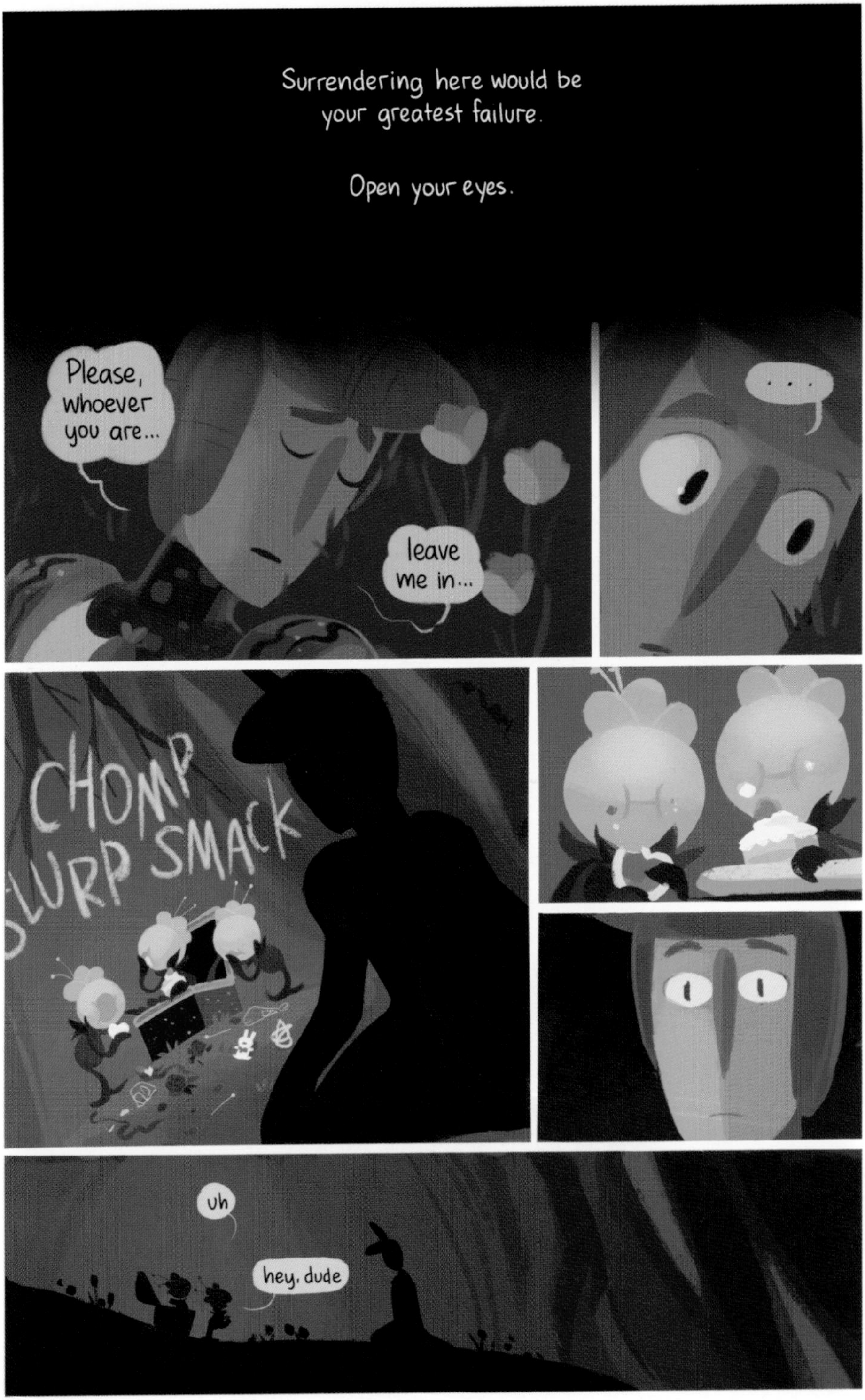
Surrendering here would be your greatest failure.
Open your eyes.
Please, whoever you are...
leave me in...
. . .
CHOMP
SLURP SMACK
uh
hey, dude

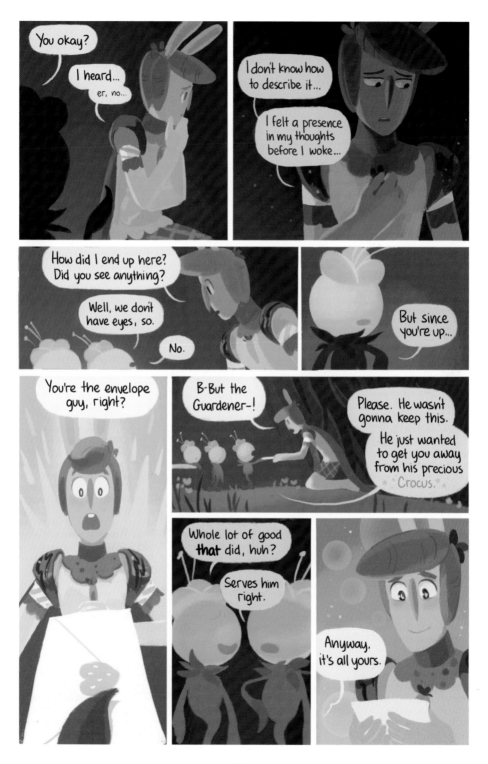

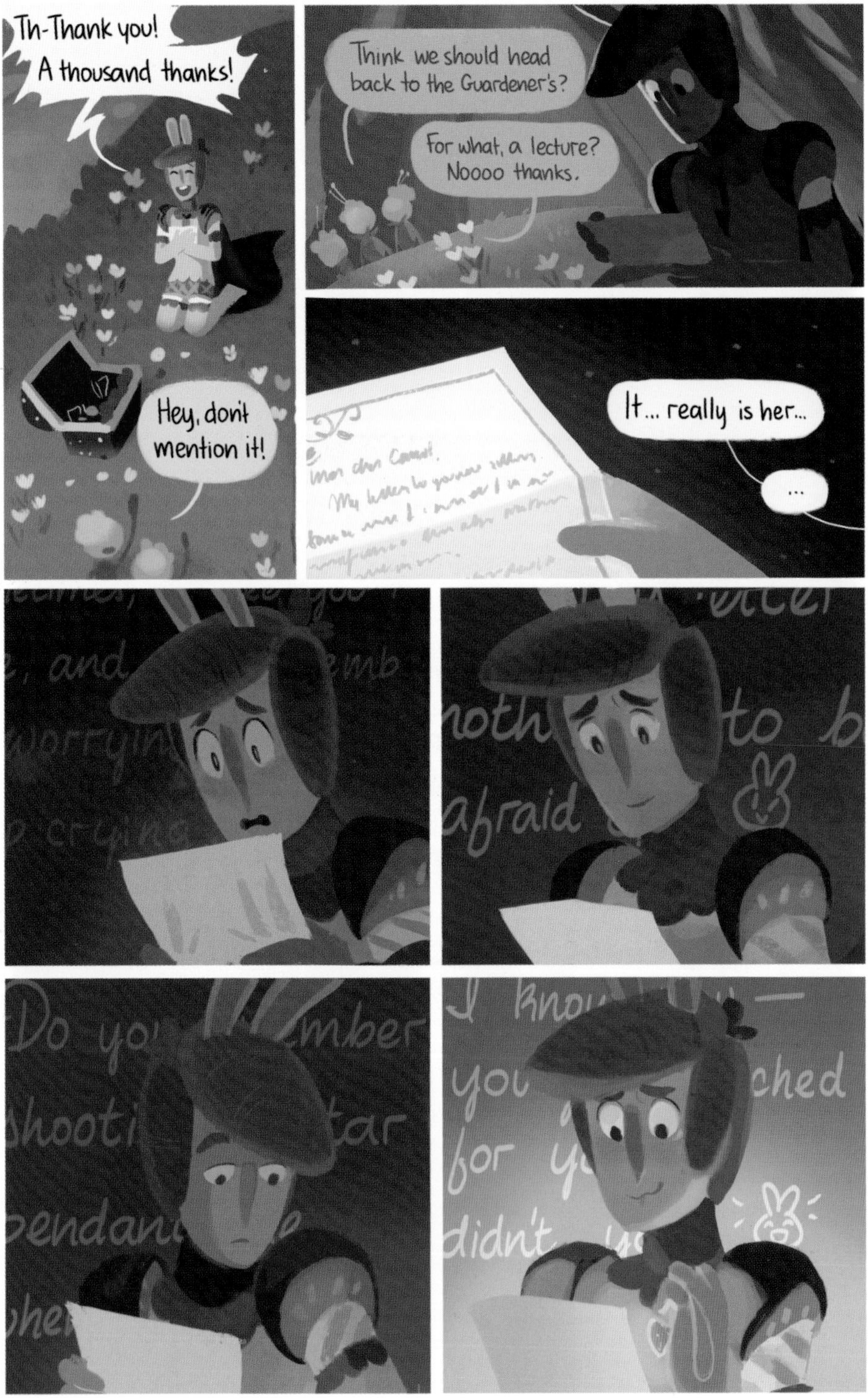
Th-Thank you!
A thousand thanks!
Hey, don't mention it!
Think we should head back to the Guardener's?
For what, a lecture? Noooo thanks.
It... really is her...
...

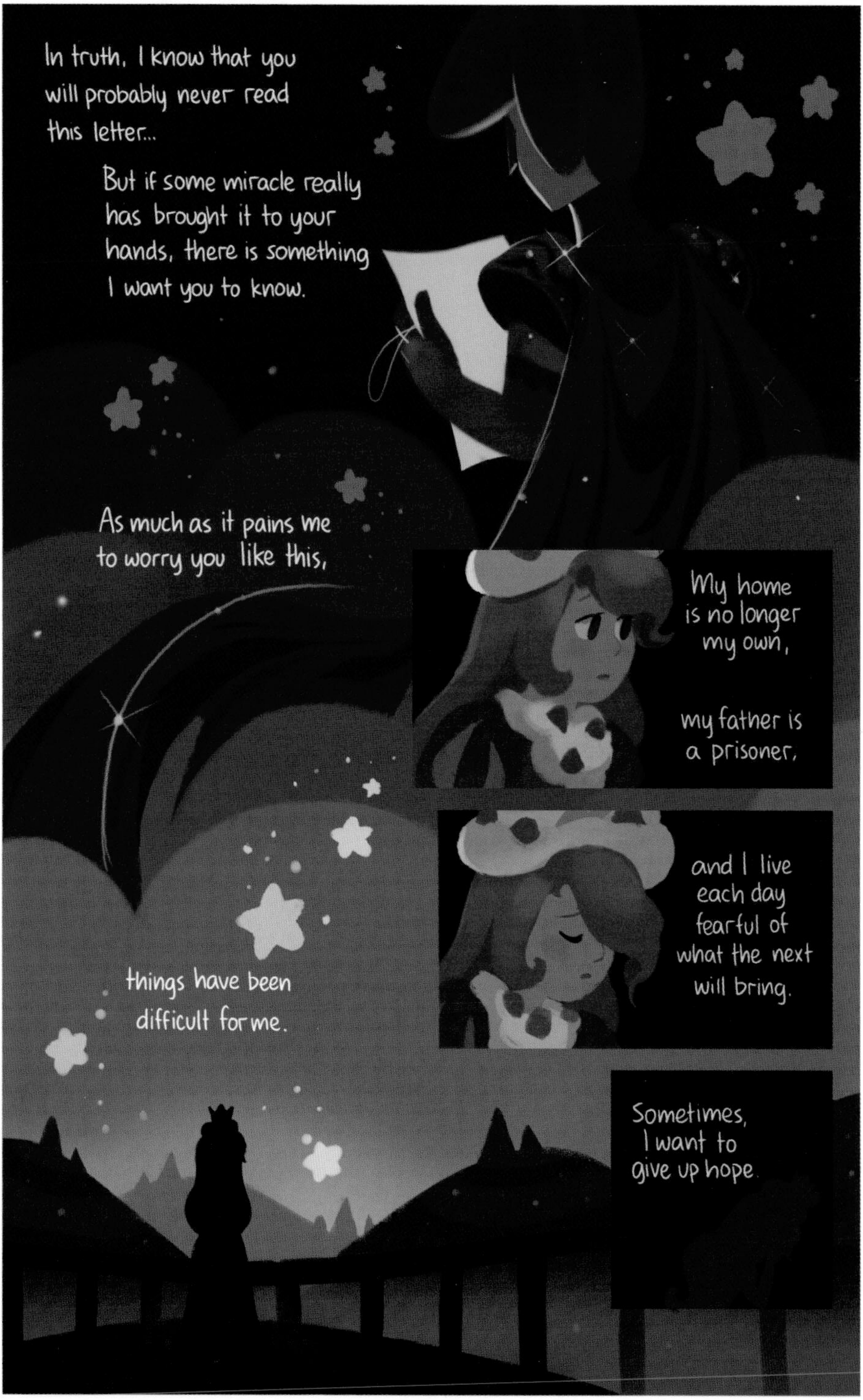
In truth, I know that you will probably never read this letter...
But if some miracle really has brought it to your hands, there is something I want you to know.
As much as it pains me to worry you like this,
My home is no longer my own,
my father is a prisoner,
and I live each day fearful of what the next will bring.
things have been difficult for me.
Sometimes, I want to give up hope.

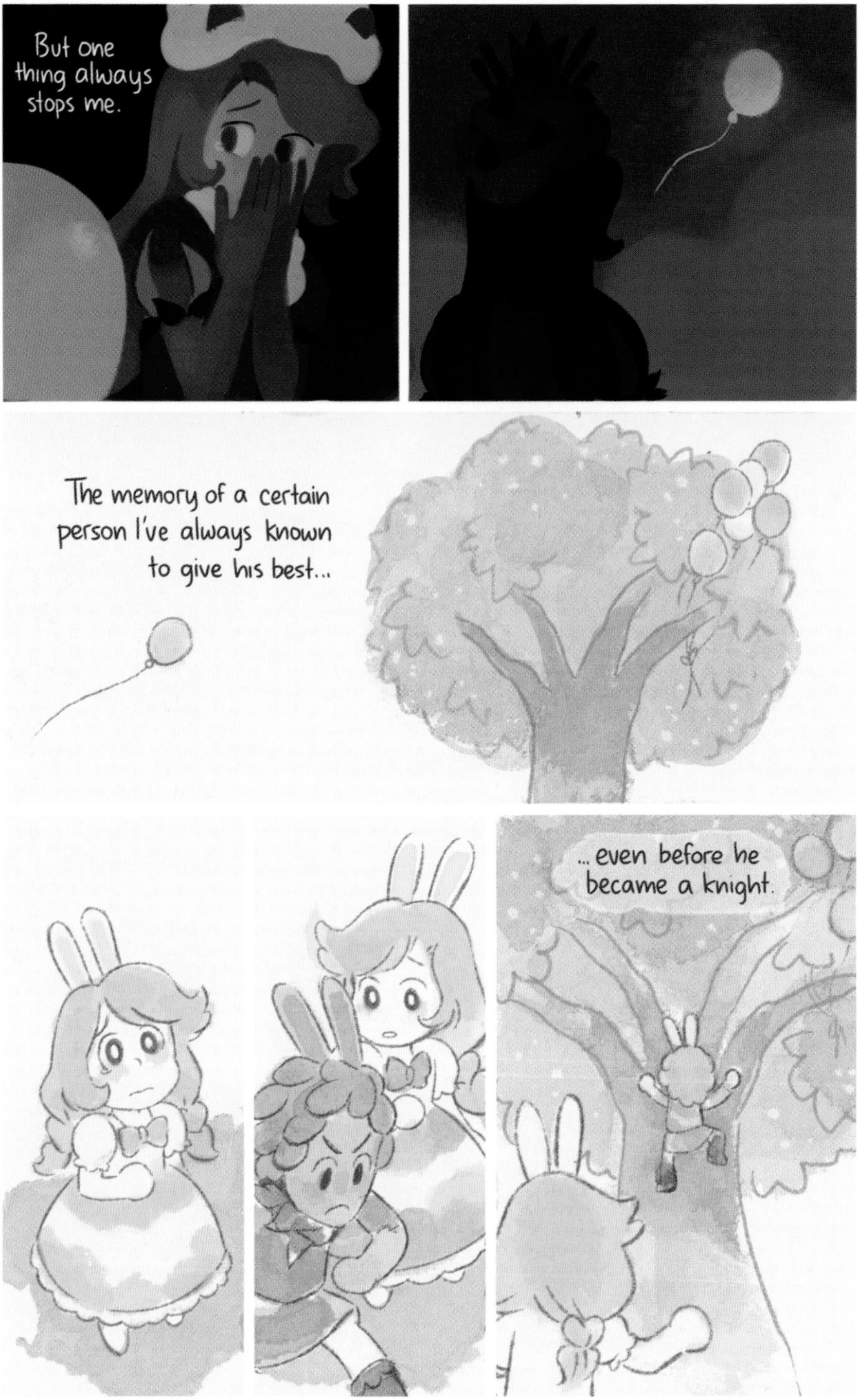
But one thing always stops me.
The memory of a certain person I've always known to give his best...
...even before he became a knight.

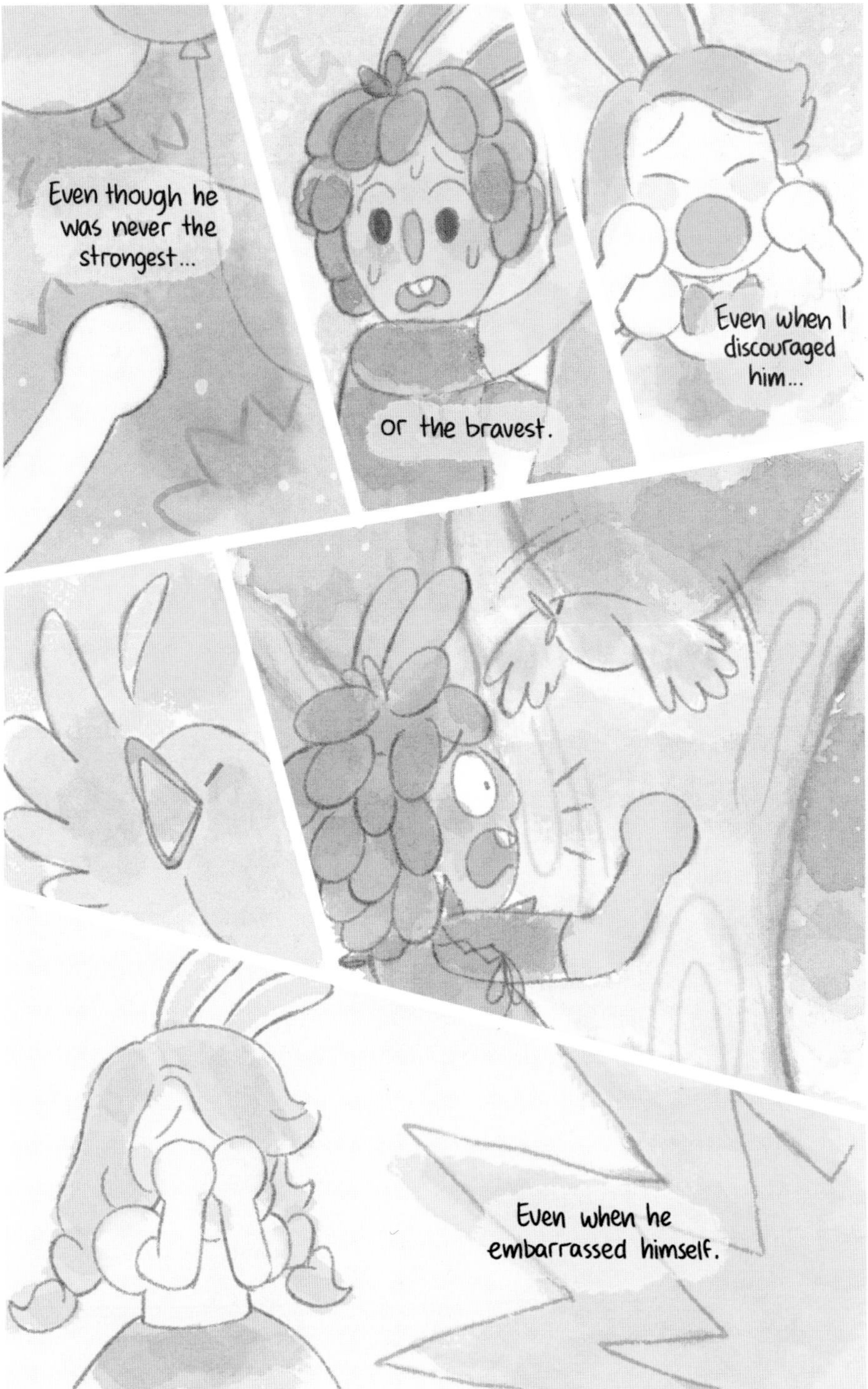
Even though he was never the strongest...
or the bravest.
Even when I discouraged him...
Even when he embarrassed himself.

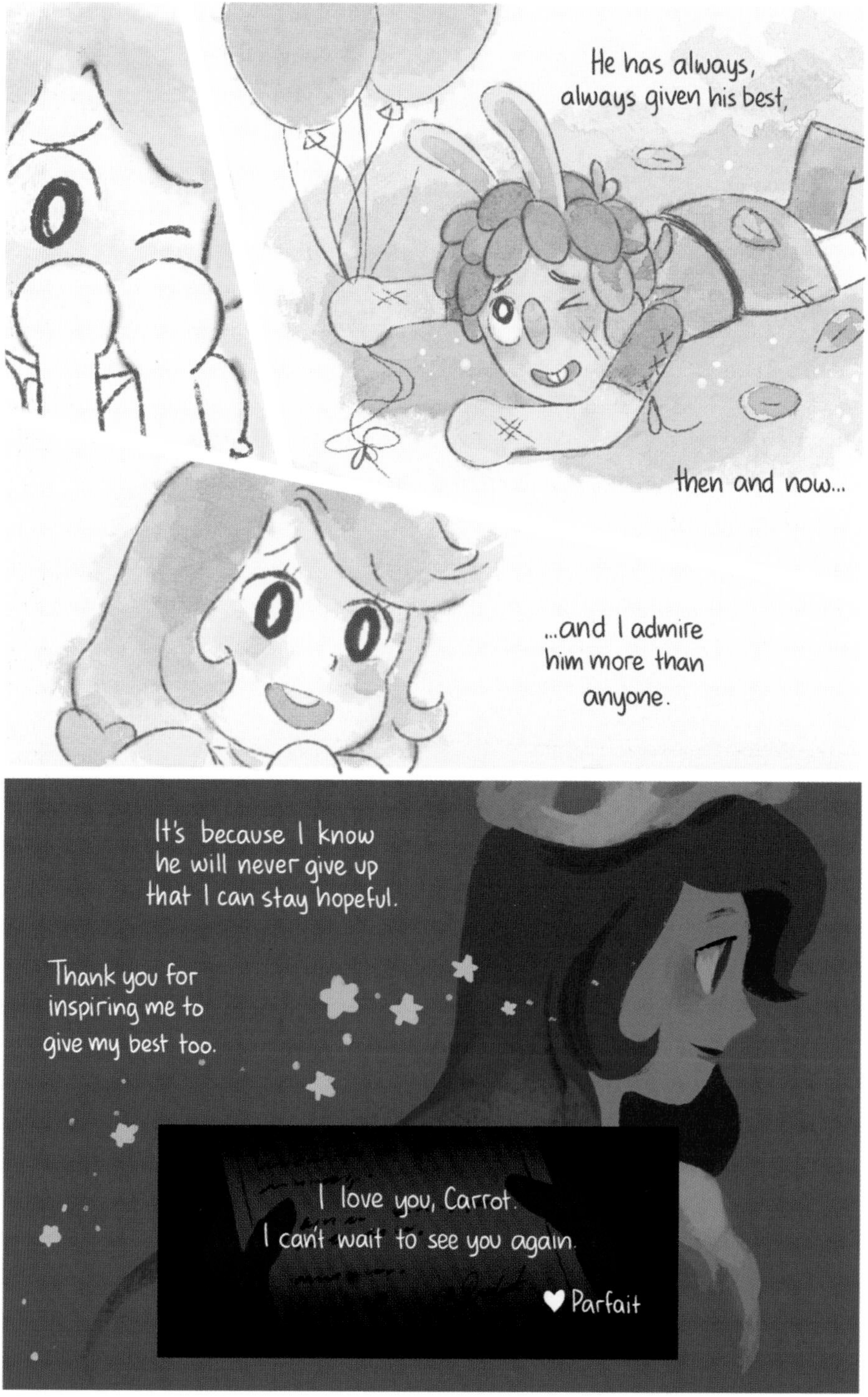
He has always, always given his best,
then and now...
...and I admire him more than anyone.
It's because I know he will never give up that I can stay hopeful.
Thank you for inspiring me to give my best too.
I love you, Carrot.
I can't wait to see you again.
♥ Parfait

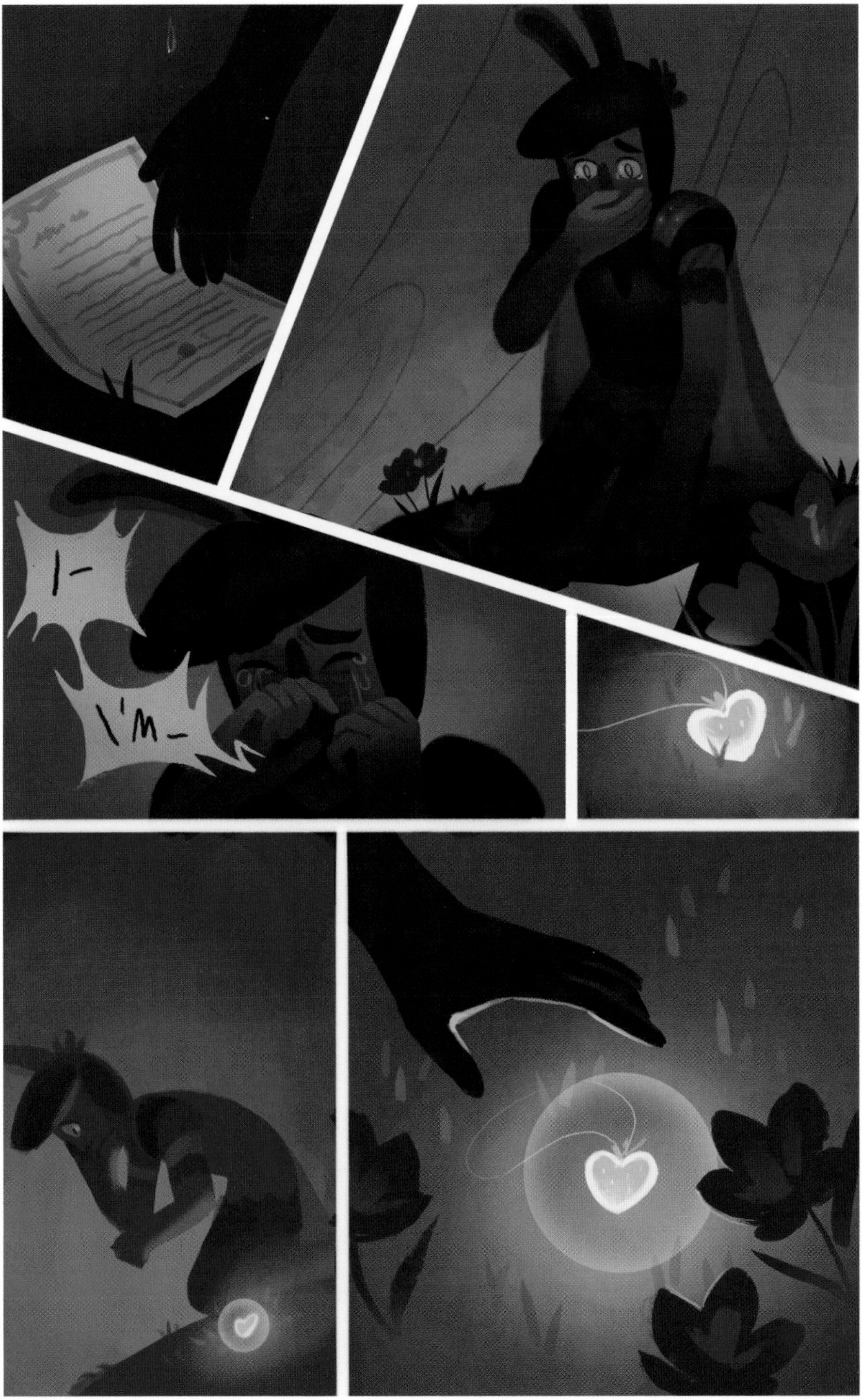
I-
I'M-

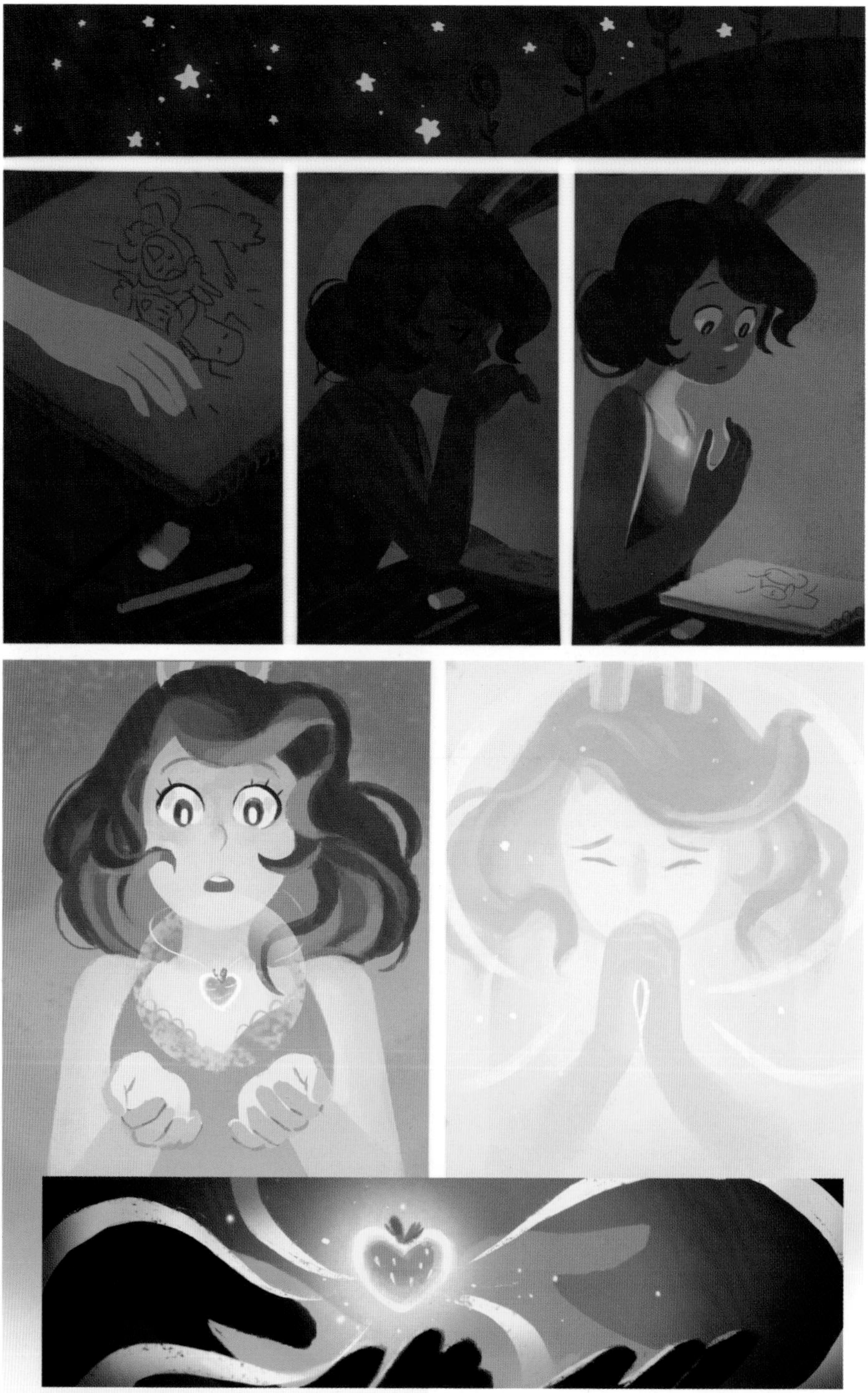

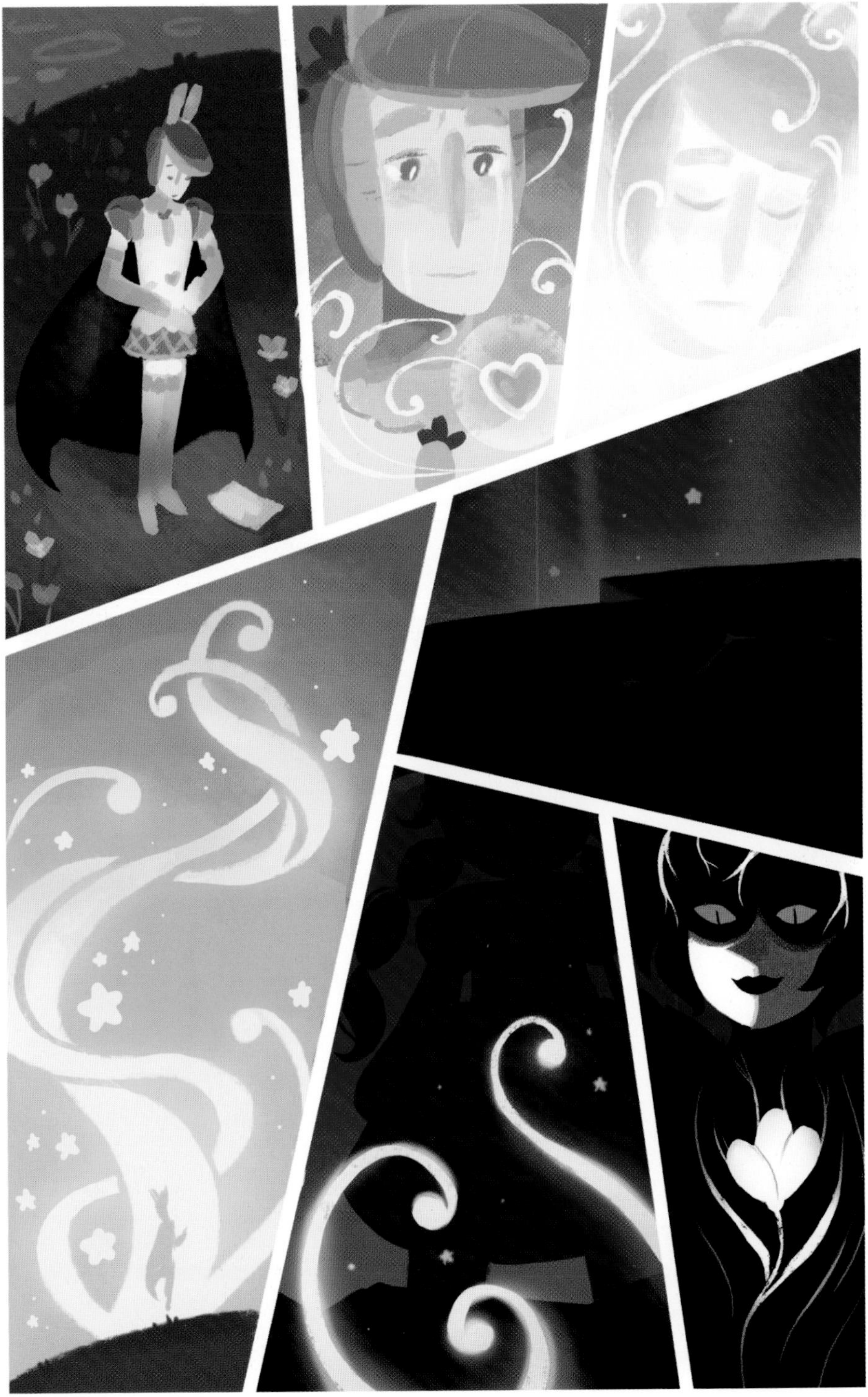

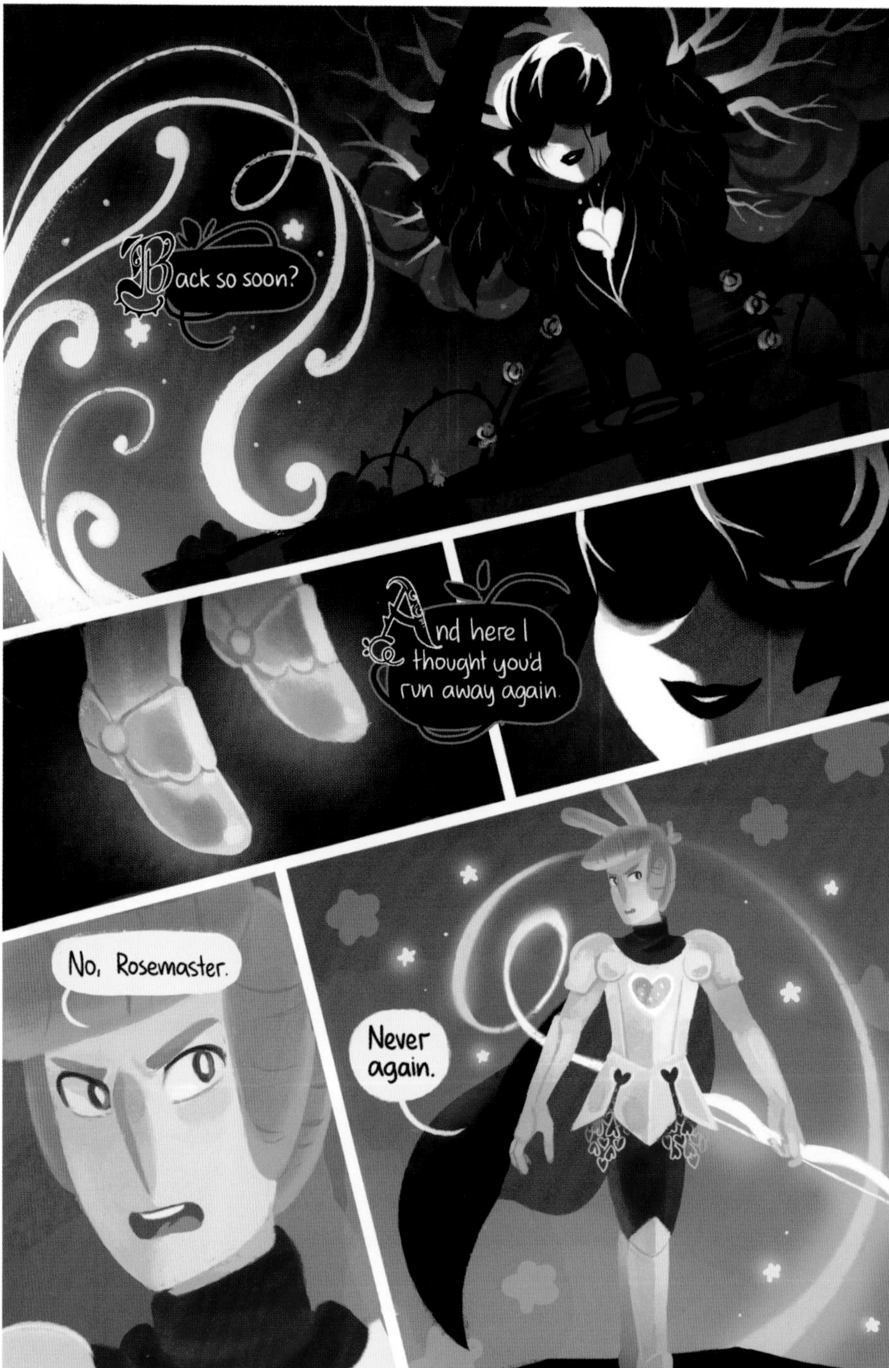
Back so soon?
And here I thought you'd run away again.
No, Rosemaster.
Never again.

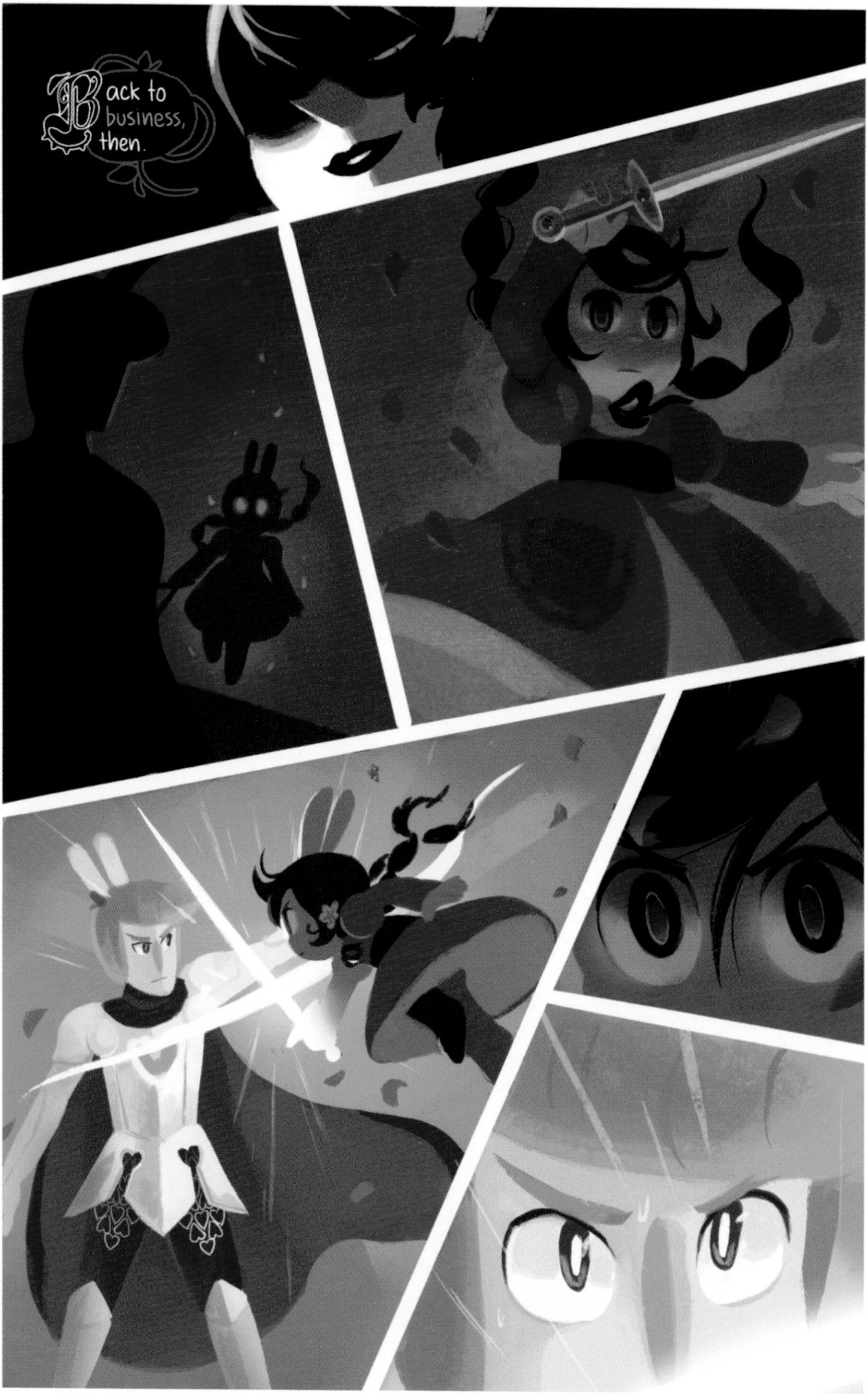
Back to business, then.

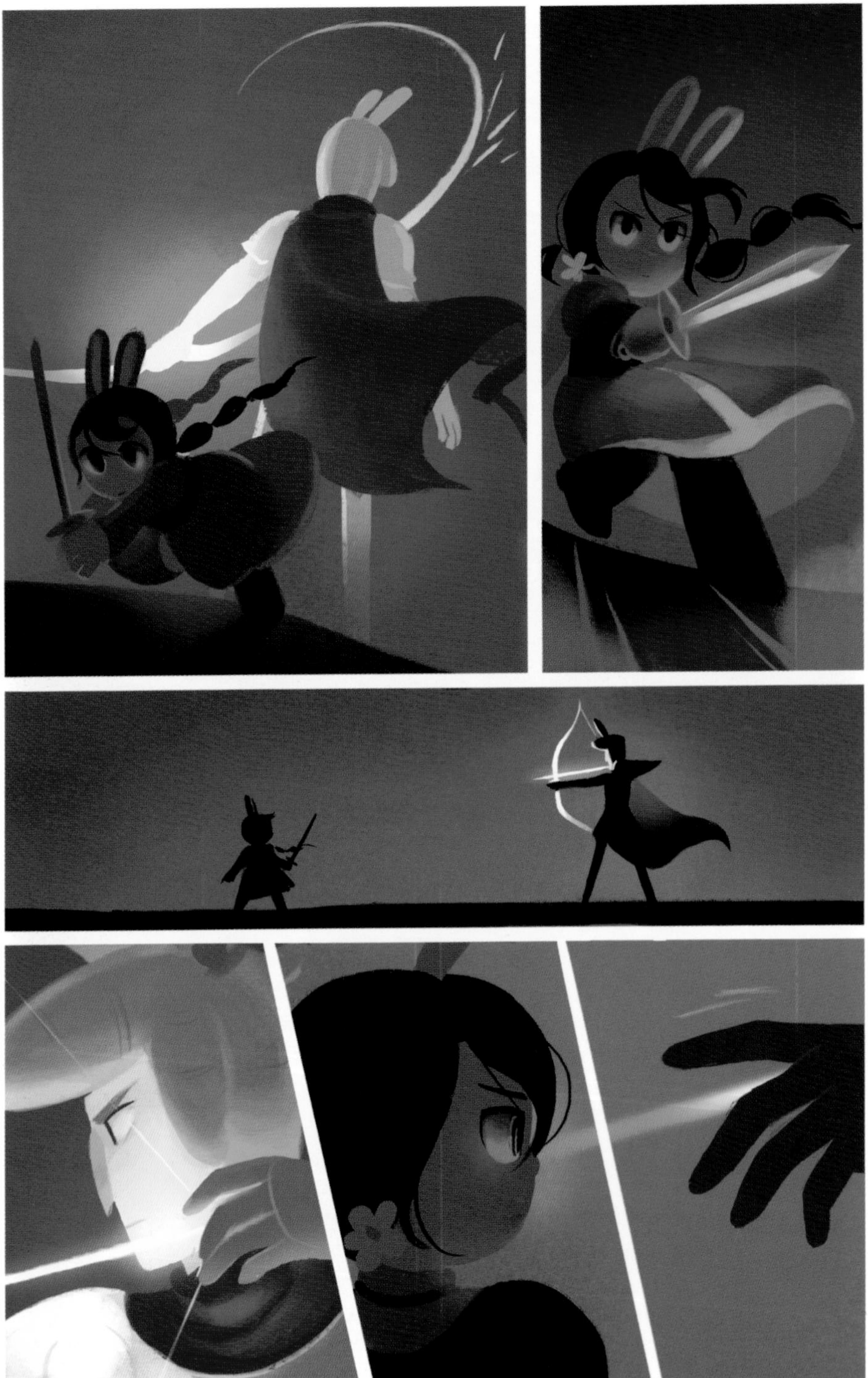

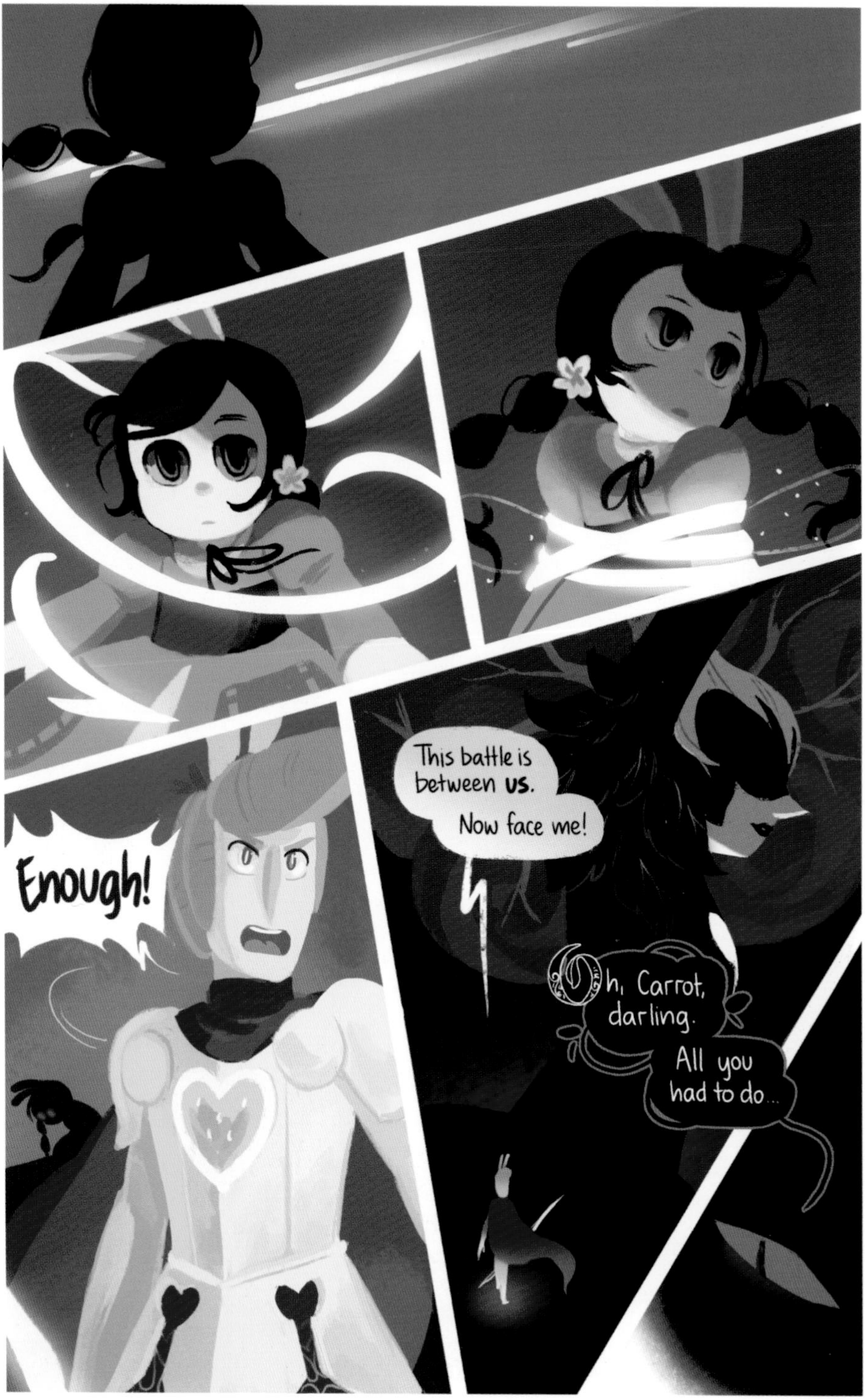
Enough!
This battle is between us.
Now face me!
Oh, Carrot, darling.
All you had to do...

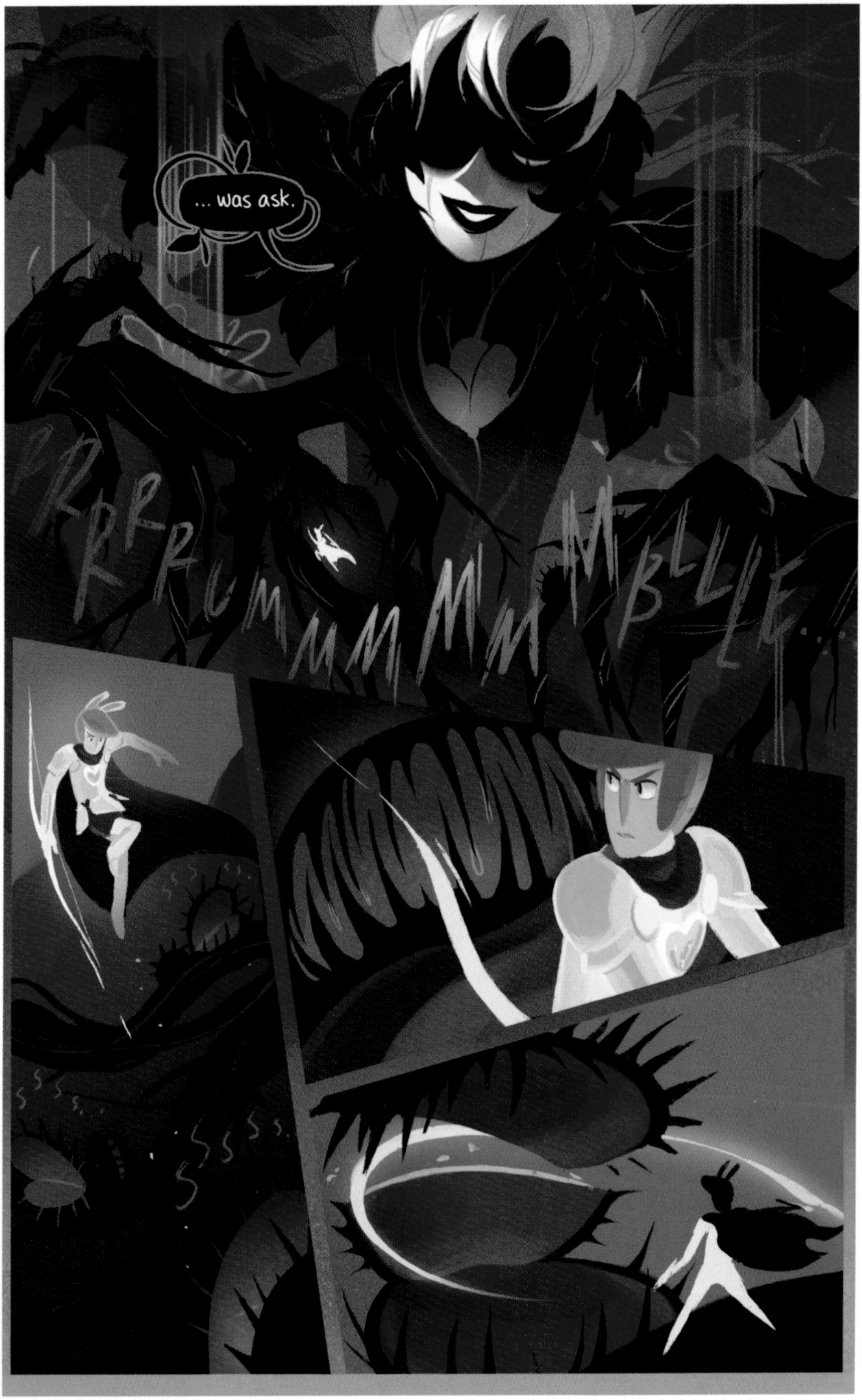

... was ask.
RRRRRUMMMMMMBLLE...

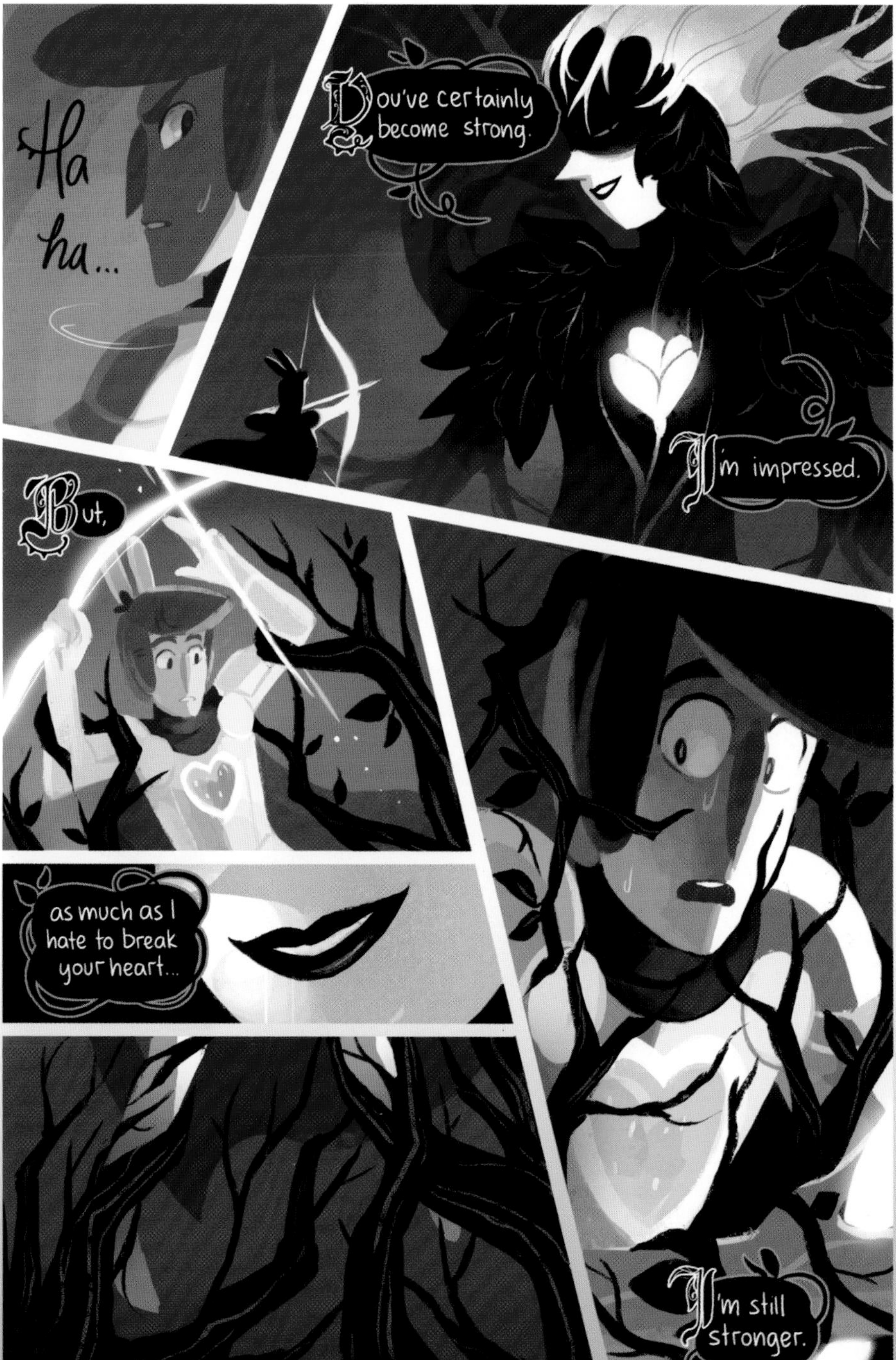
Ha ha...
You've certainly become strong.
I'm impressed.
But,
as much as I hate to break your heart...
I'm still stronger.

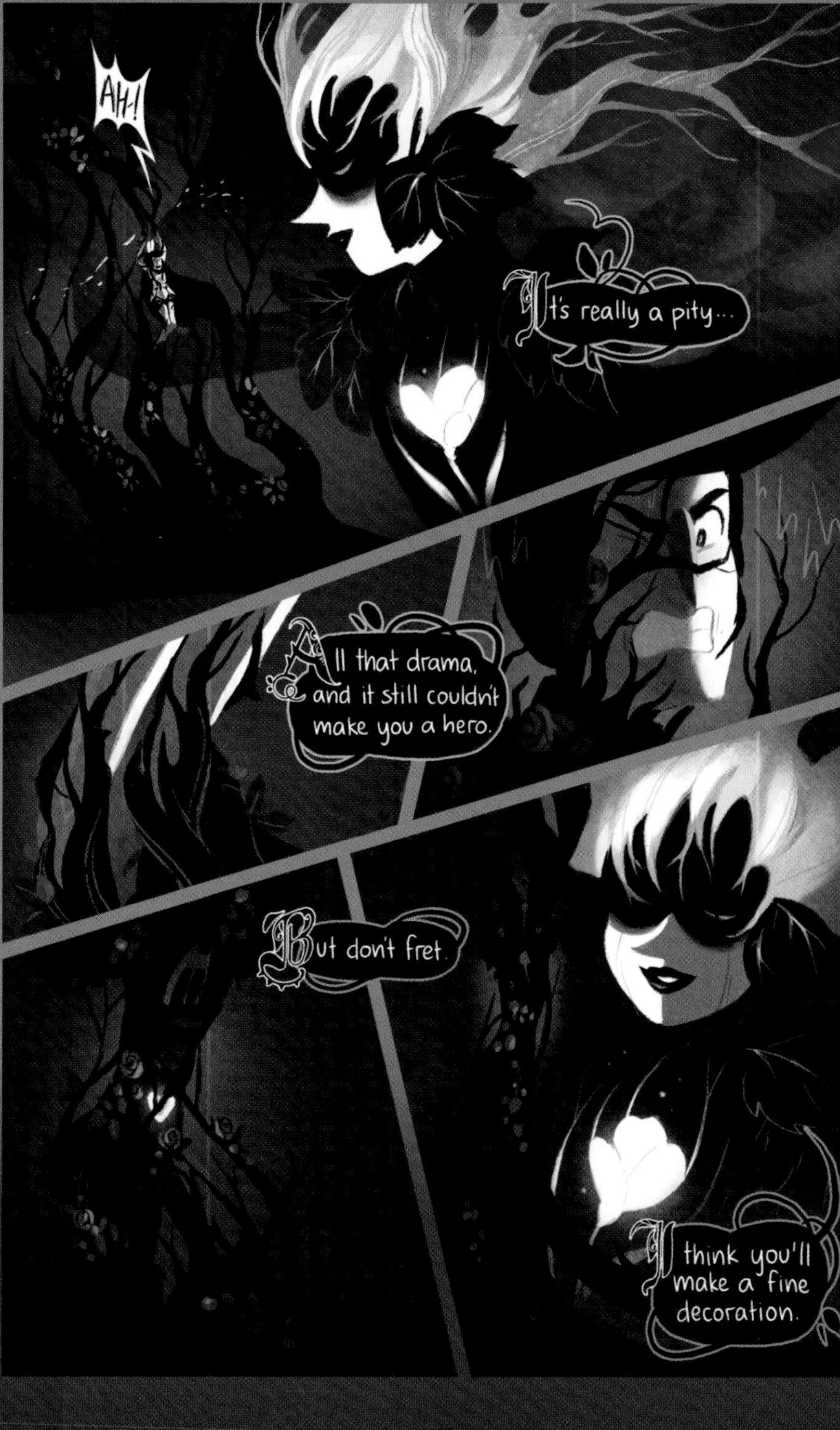
AH-!
It's really a pity...
All that drama, and it still couldn't make you a hero.
But don't fret.
I think you'll make a fine decoration.

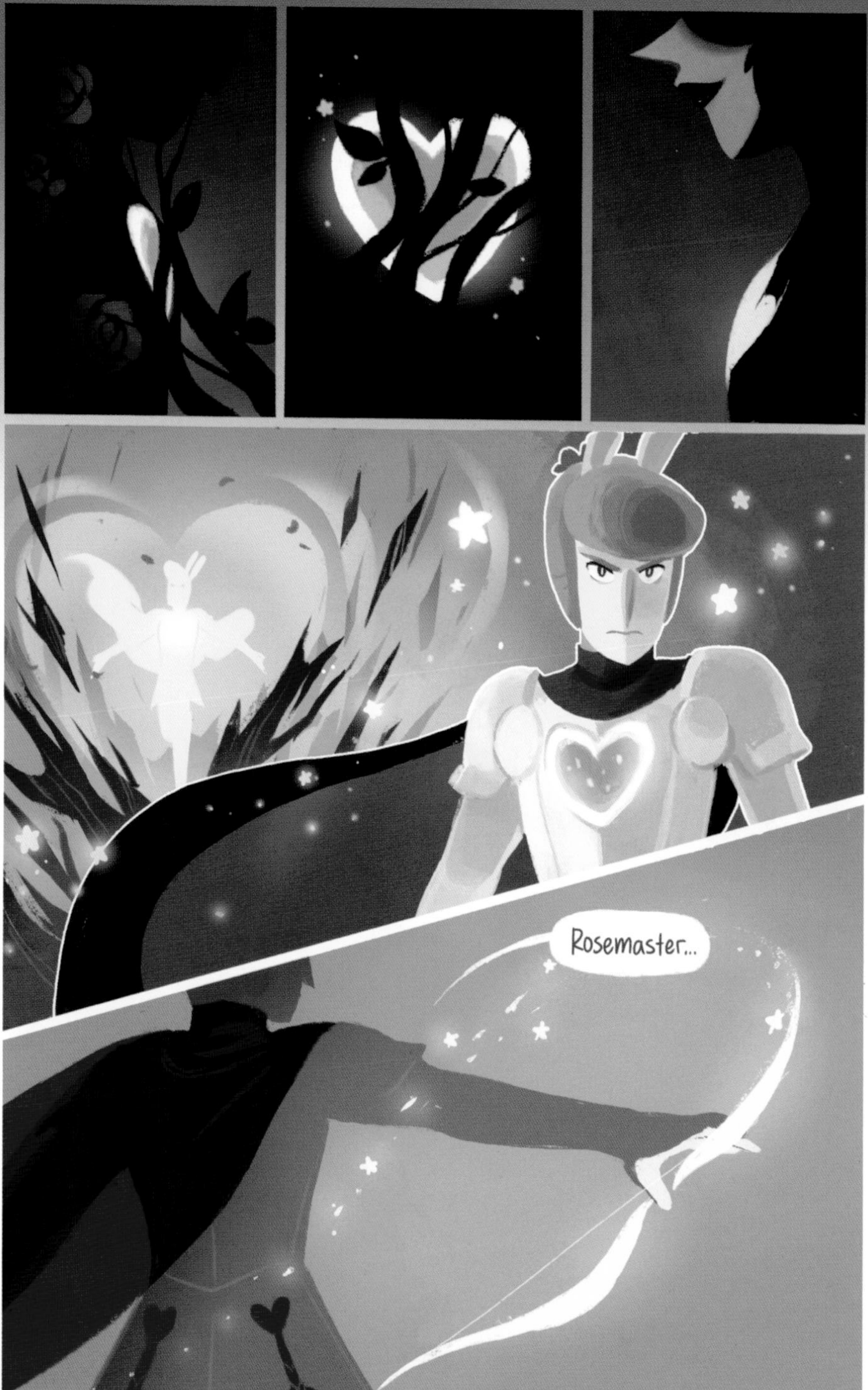
Rosemaster...

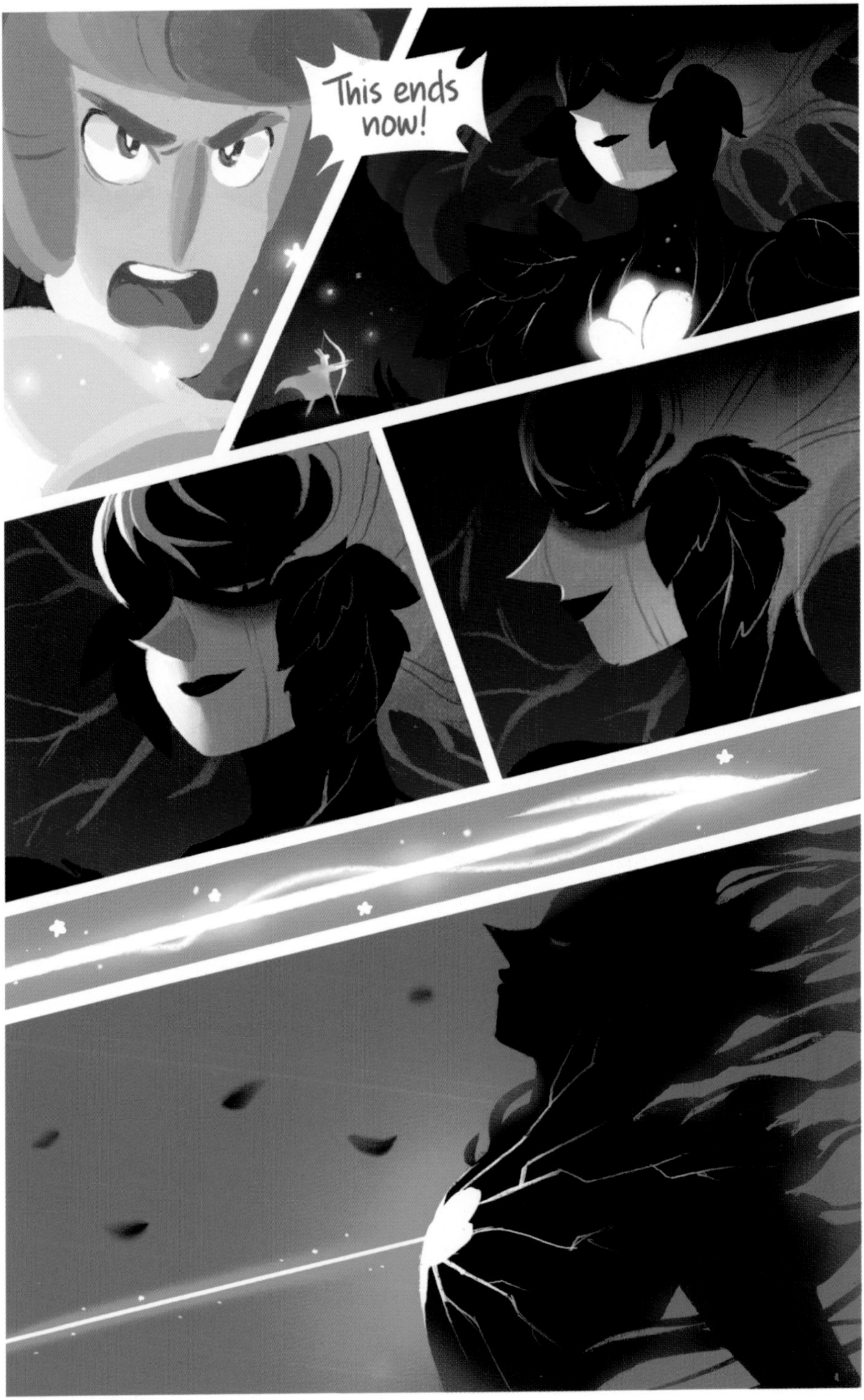
This ends now!

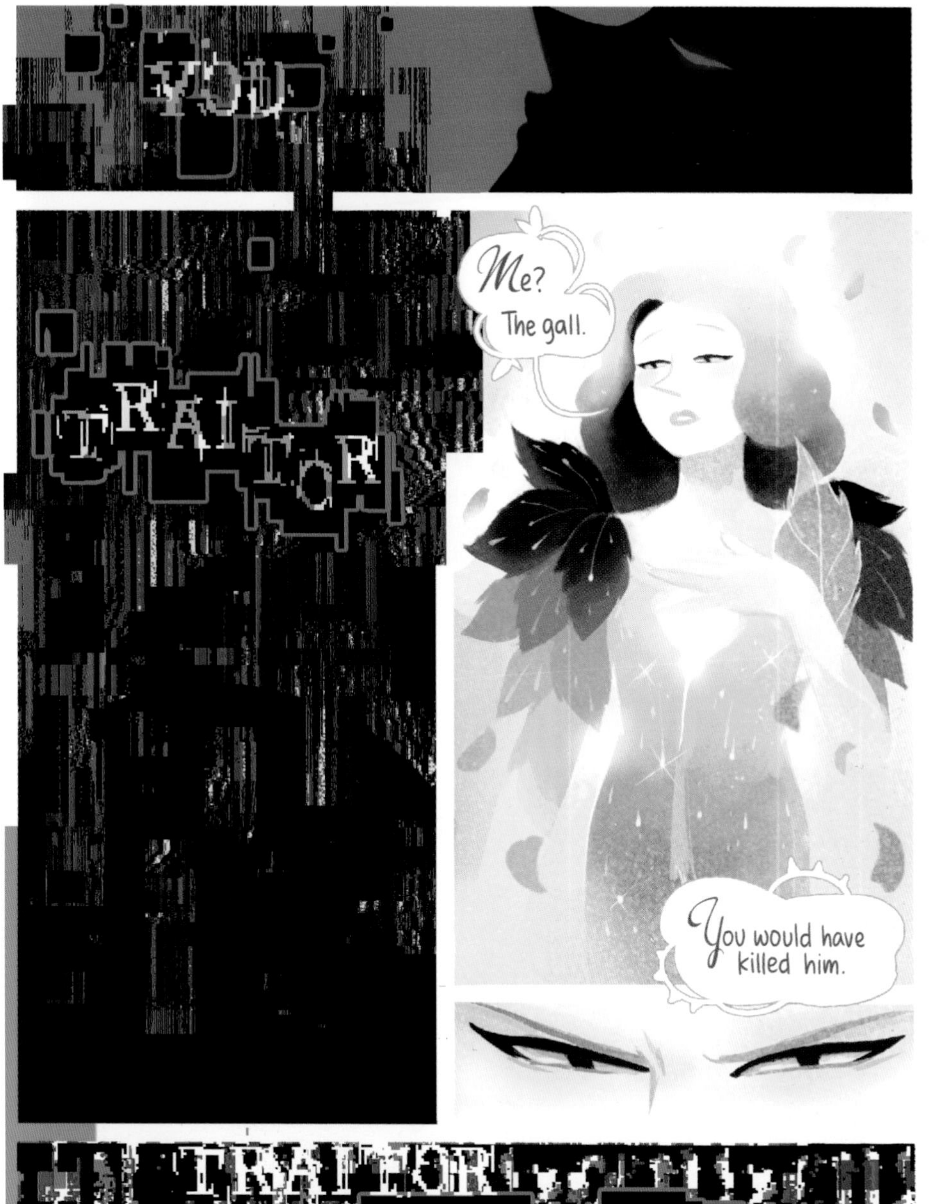
YOU
TRAITOR
Me?
The gall.
You would have killed him.
TRAITOR
TRAITOR
WOULD HAVE
FREED US

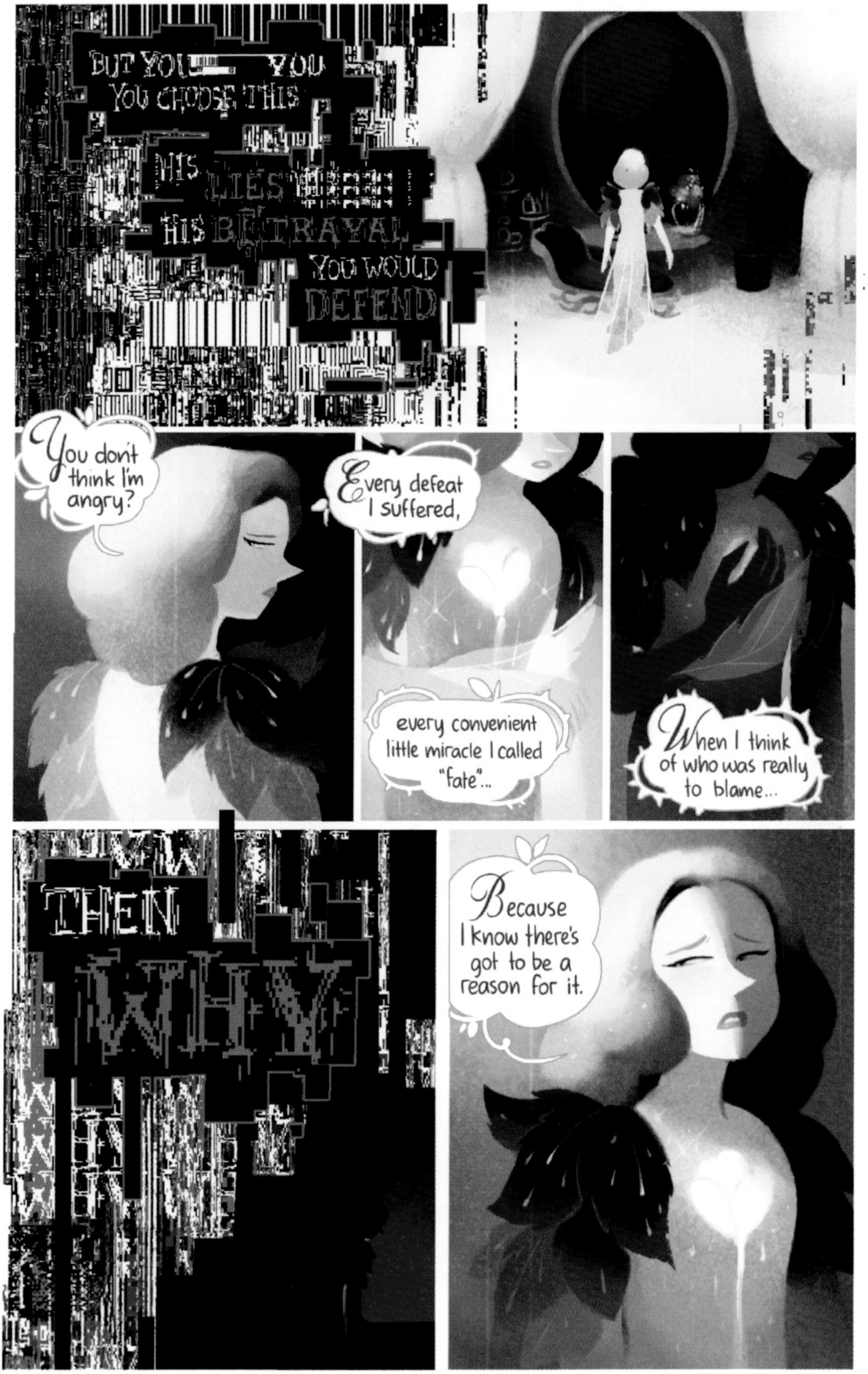
BUT YOU— YOU
YOU CHOOSE THIS
HIS LIES
HIS BETRAYAL
YOU WOULD DEFEND
You don't think I'm angry?
Every defeat I suffered,
every convenient little miracle I called "fate"...
When I think of who was really to blame...
THEN WHY
Because I know there's got to be a reason for it.

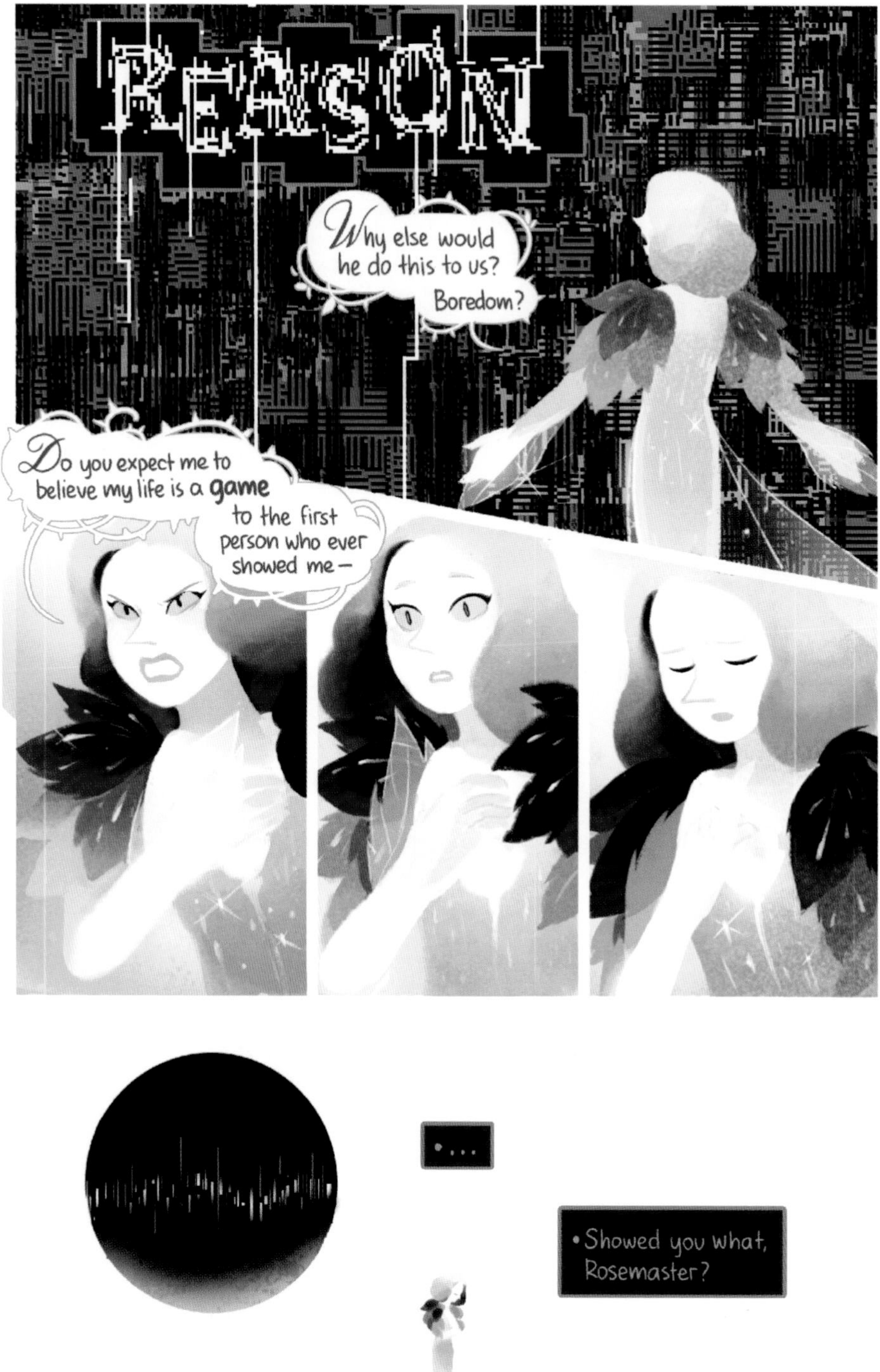
REASON
Why else would he do this to us?
Boredom?
Do you expect me to believe my life is a game
to the first person who ever showed me—
•...
•Showed you what, Rosemaster?

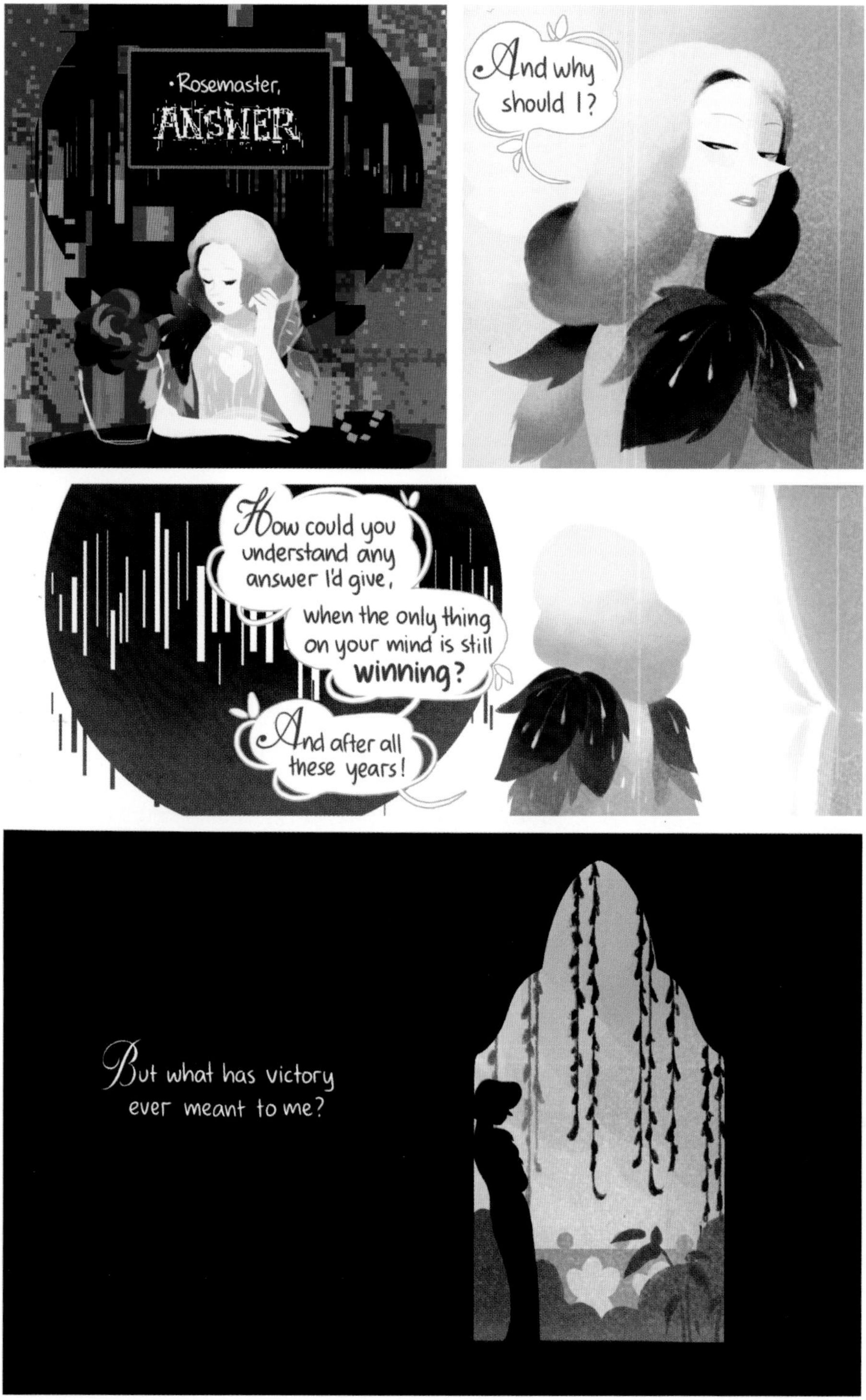

• Rosemaster,
ANSWER
And why should I?
How could you understand any answer I'd give,
when the only thing on your mind is still winning?
And after all these years!
But what has victory ever meant to me?

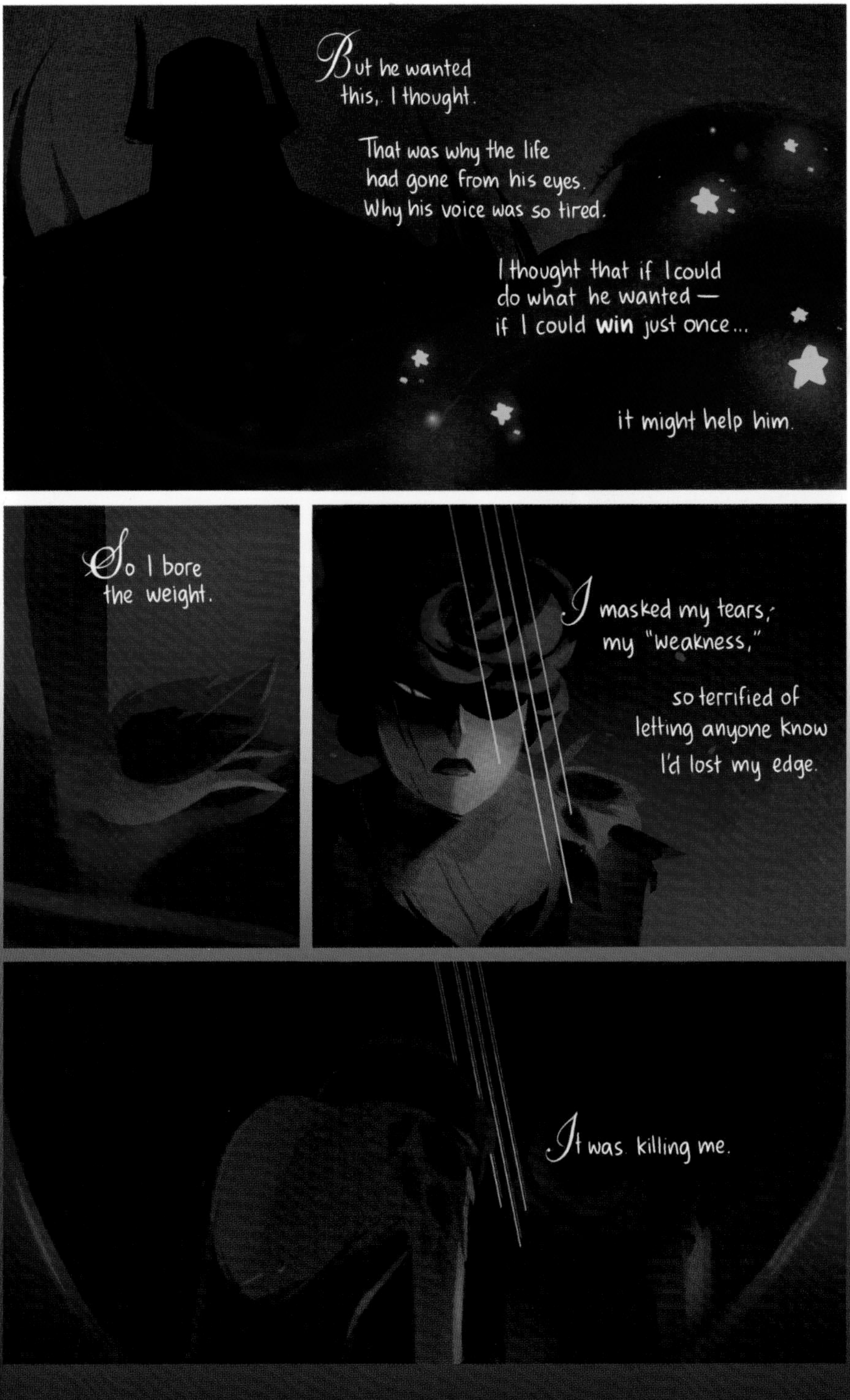
But he wanted this, I thought.
That was why the life had gone from his eyes. Why his voice was so tired.
I thought that if I could do what he wanted — if I could **win** just once...
it might help him.
So I bore the weight.
I masked my tears; my "weakness,"
so terrified of letting anyone know I'd lost my edge.
It was killing me.

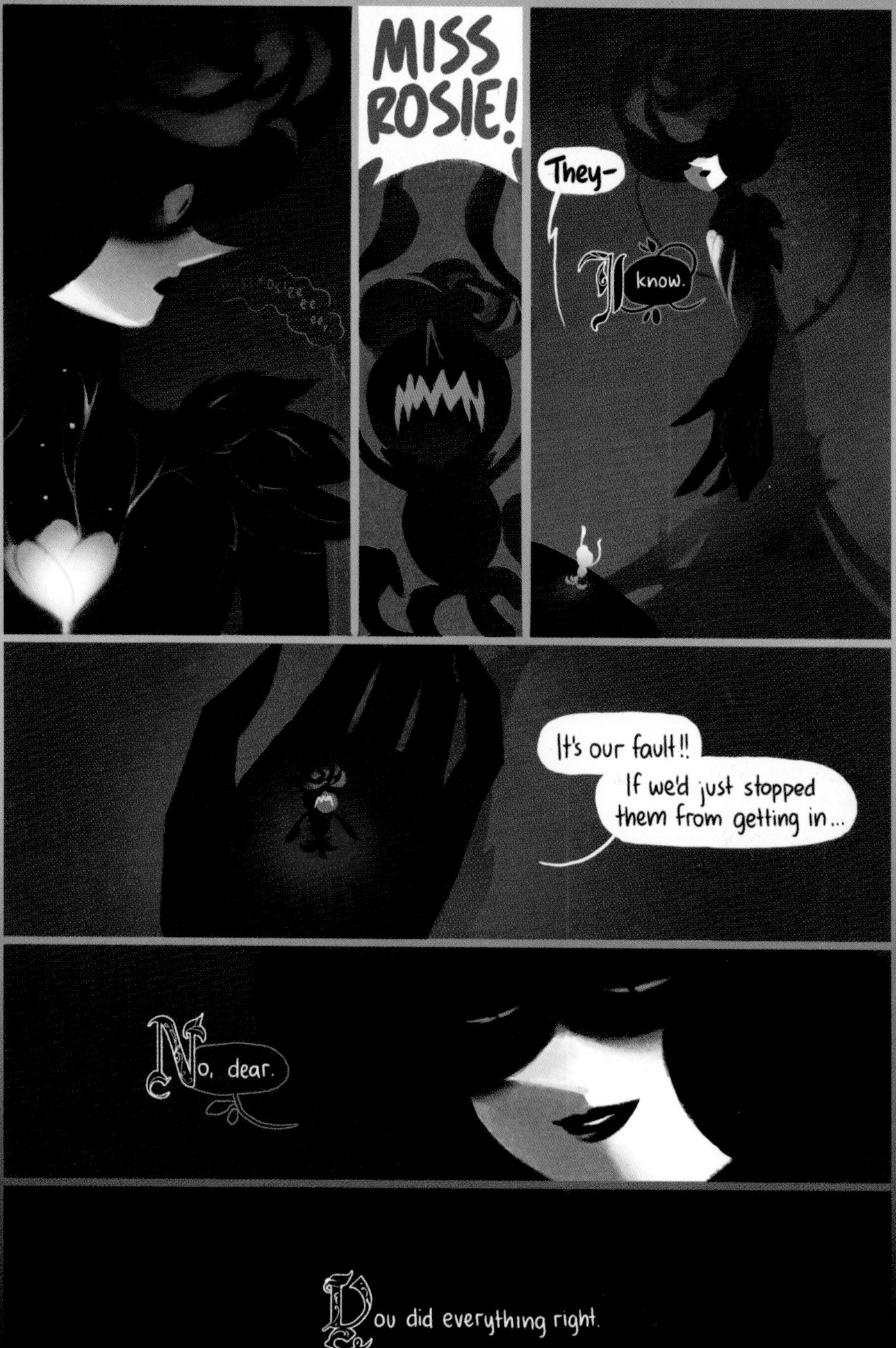
MISS ROSIE!
They-
I know.
It's our fault!!
If we'd just stopped them from getting in...
No, dear.
You did everything right.

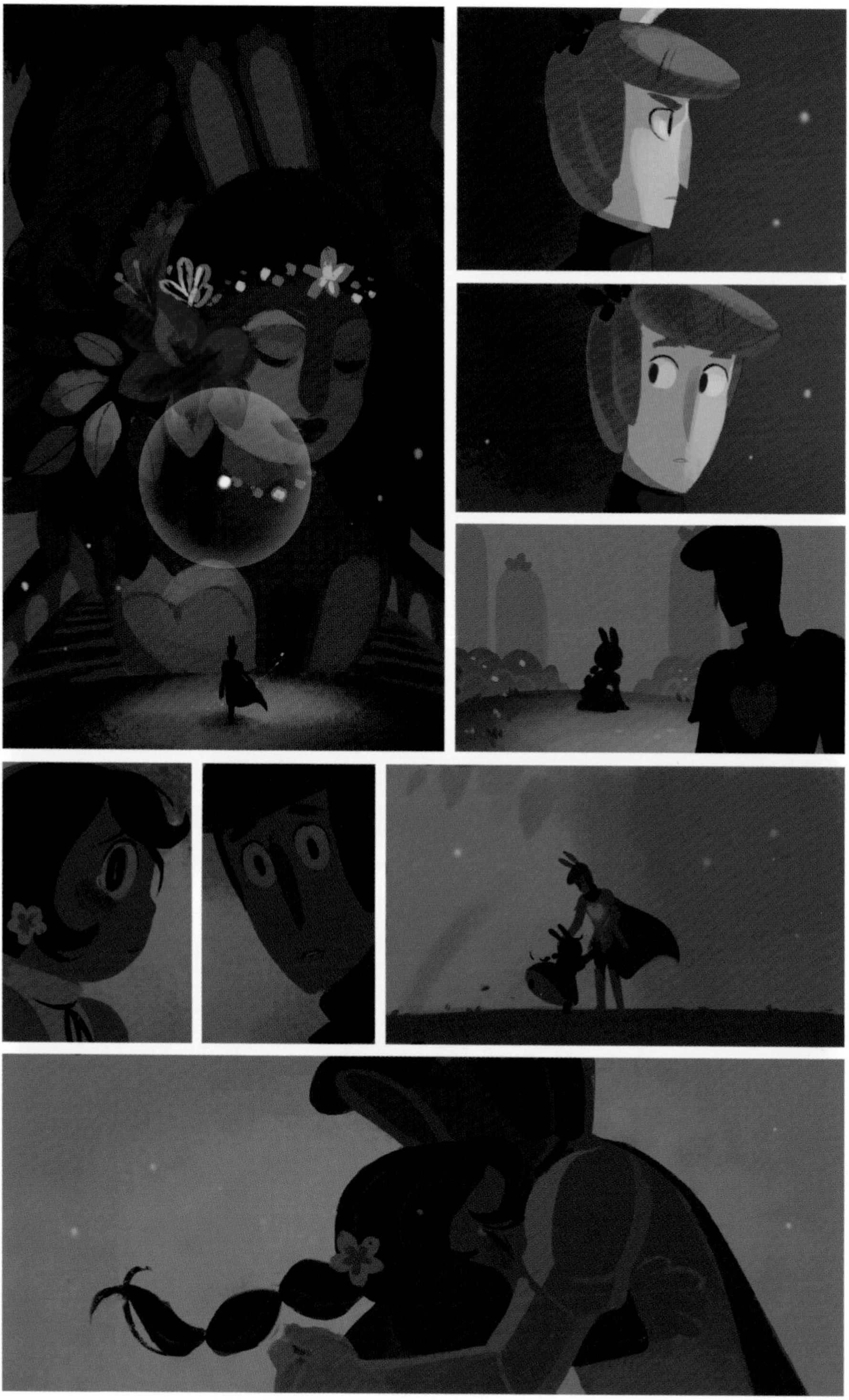

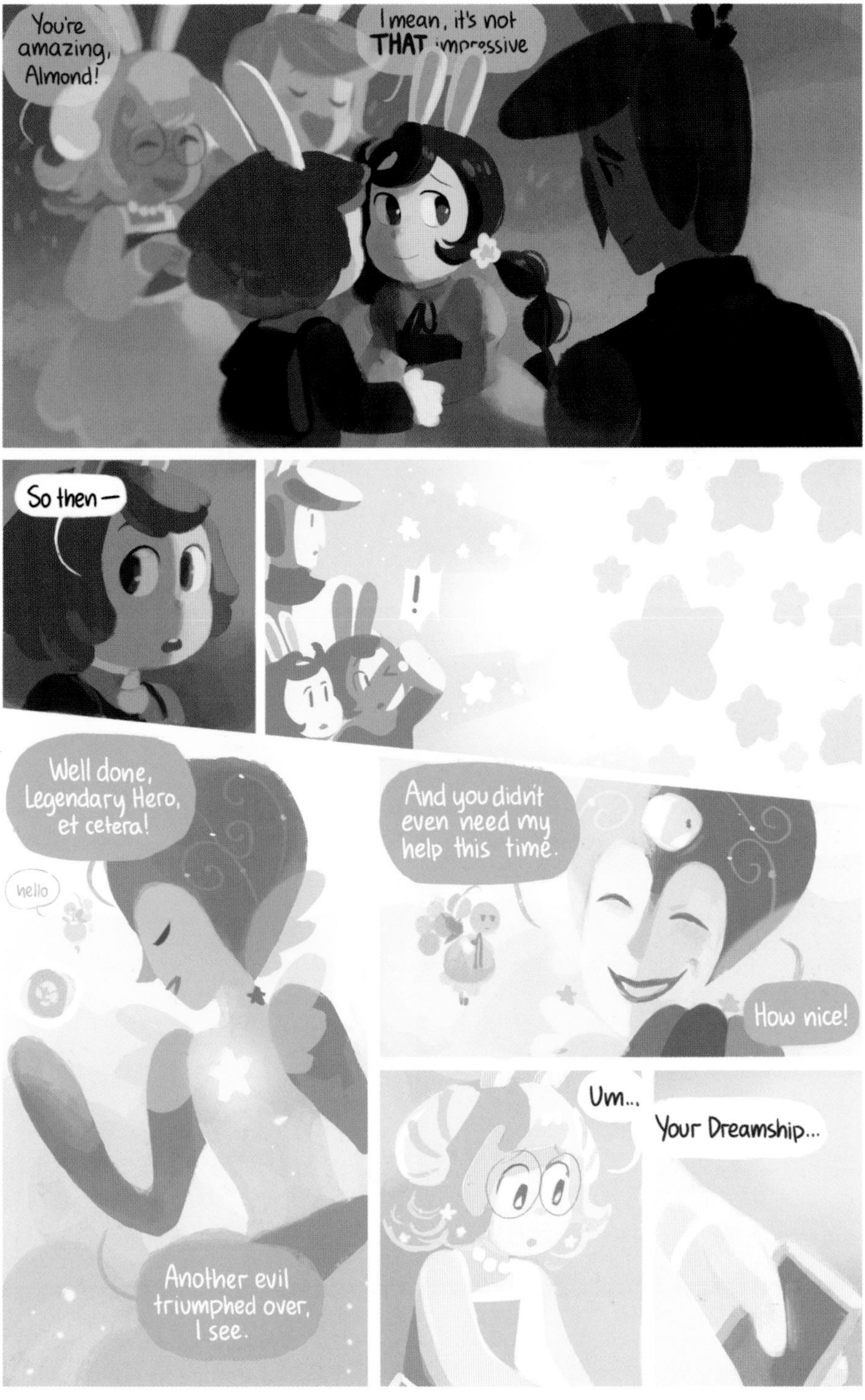
You're amazing, Almond!
I mean, it's not THAT impressive
So then—
!
Well done, Legendary Hero, et cetera!
hello
And you didn't even need my help this time.
How nice!
Another evil triumphed over, I see.
Um...
Your Dreamship...

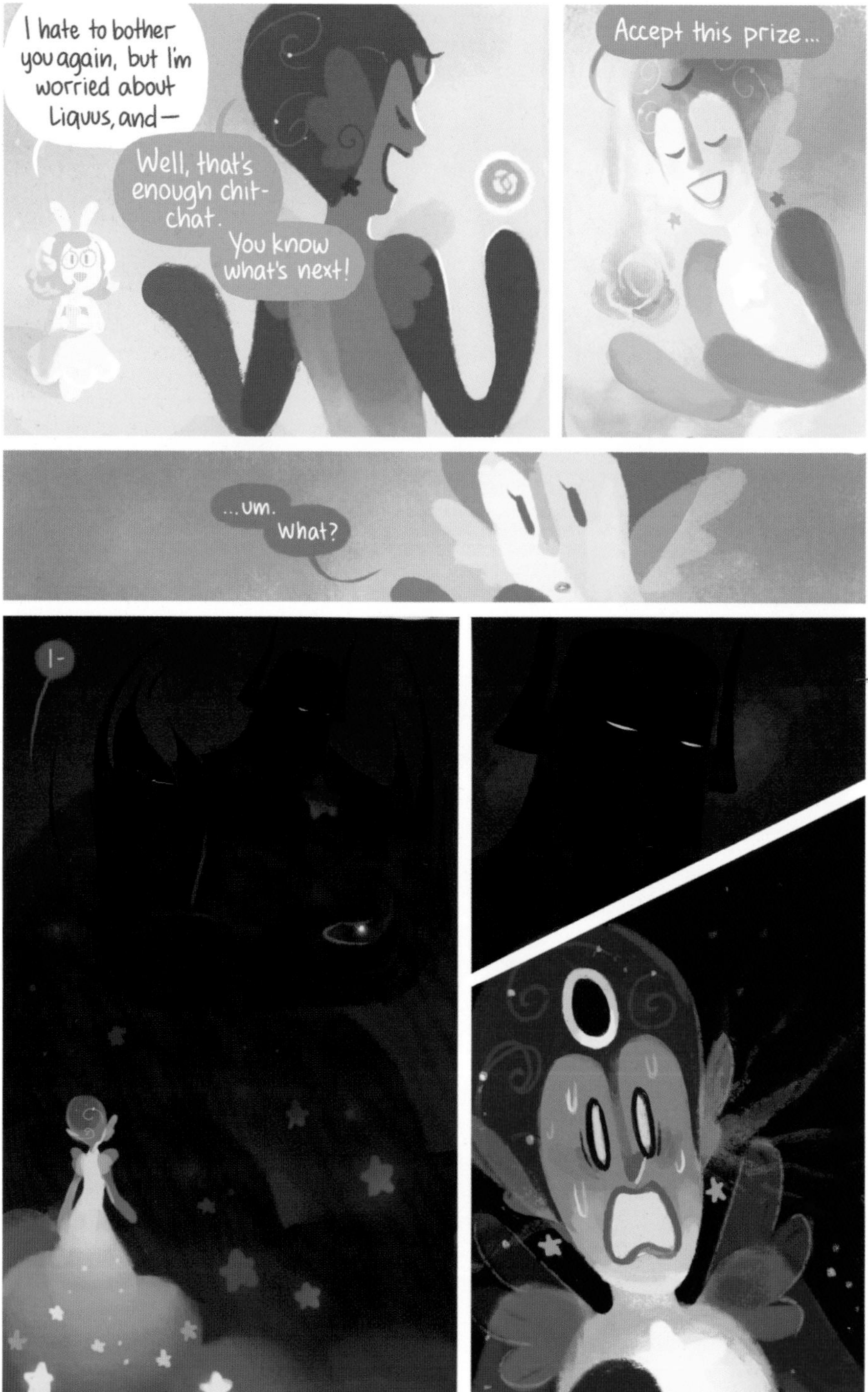
I hate to bother you again, but I'm worried about Liquus, and—
Well, that's enough chit-chat.
You know what's next!
Accept this prize...
...um.
What?
I-

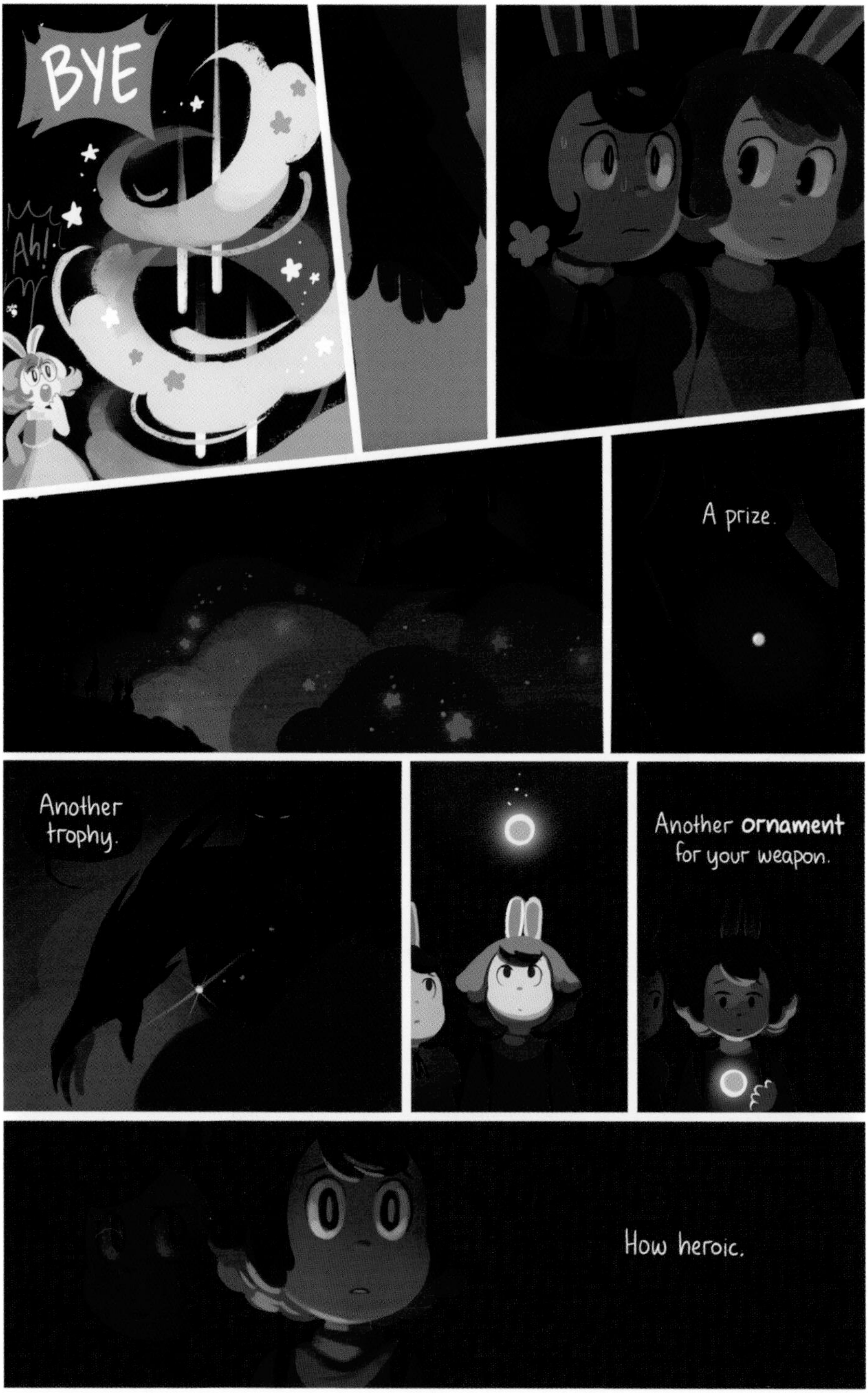
BYE
Ah!
A prize.
Another trophy.
Another **ornament** for your weapon.
How heroic.

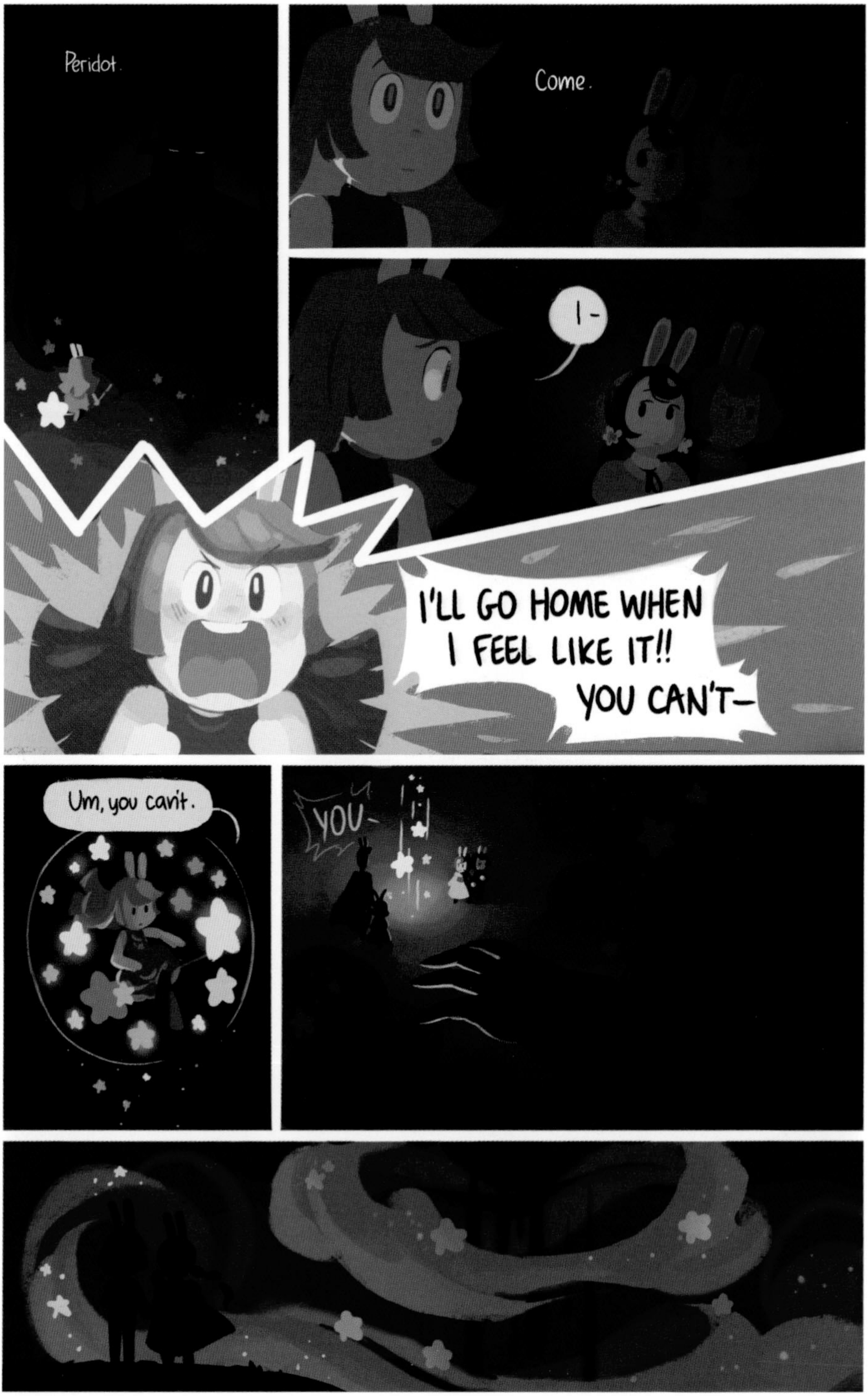

Peridot.
Come.
I-
I'LL GO HOME WHEN I FEEL LIKE IT!! YOU CAN'T-
Um, you can't.
YOU-

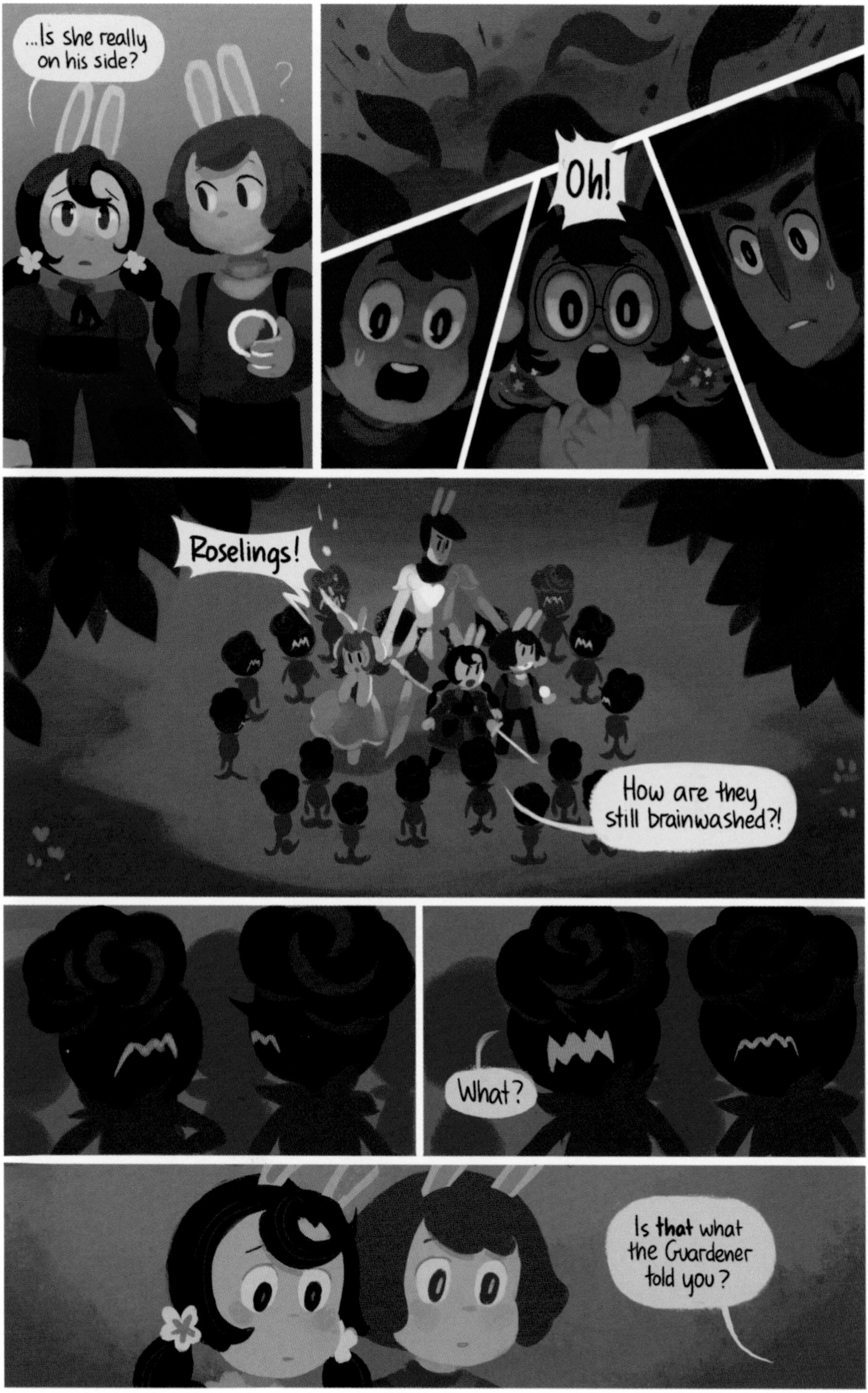
...Is she really on his side?
?
Oh!
Roselings!
How are they still brainwashed?!
What?
Is **that** what the Guardener told you?

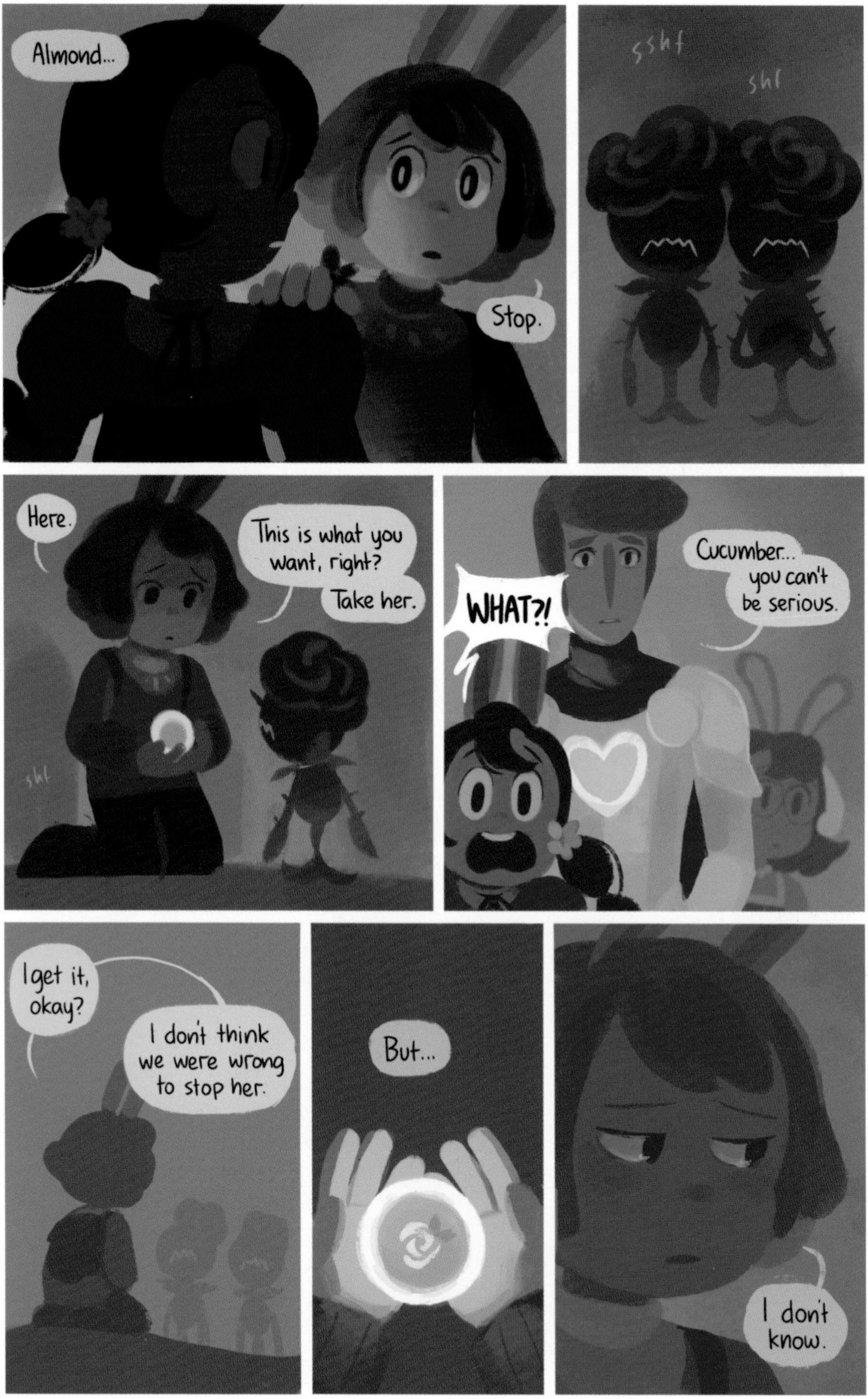
Almond...
Stop.
sshf
shf
Here.
This is what you want, right?
Take her.
shf
WHAT?!
Cucumber... you can't be serious.
I get it, okay?
I don't think we were wrong to stop her.
But...
I don't know.

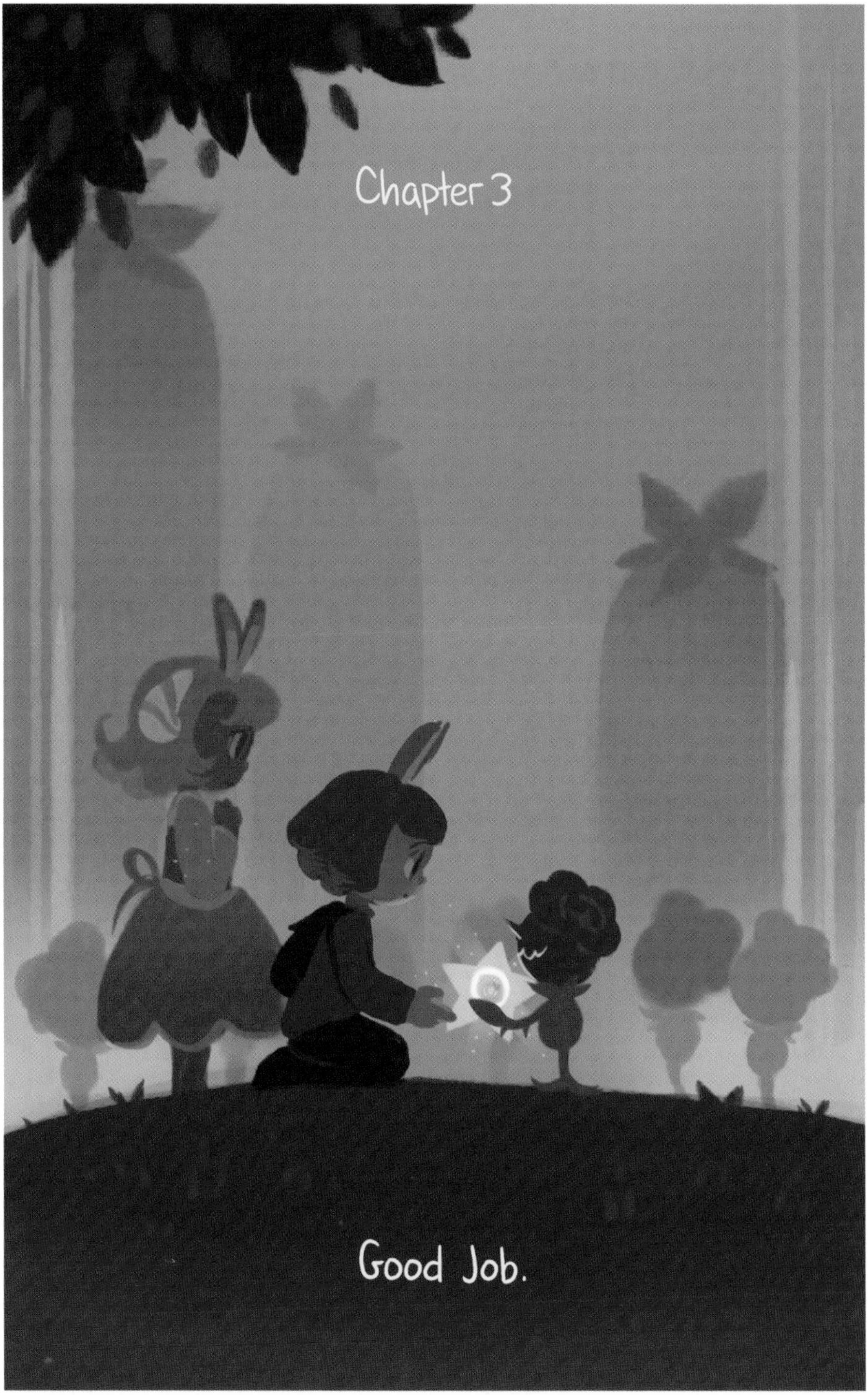
Chapter 3
Good Job.

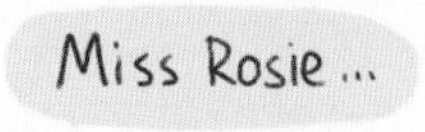
Miss Rosie ...

Miss Rosie.

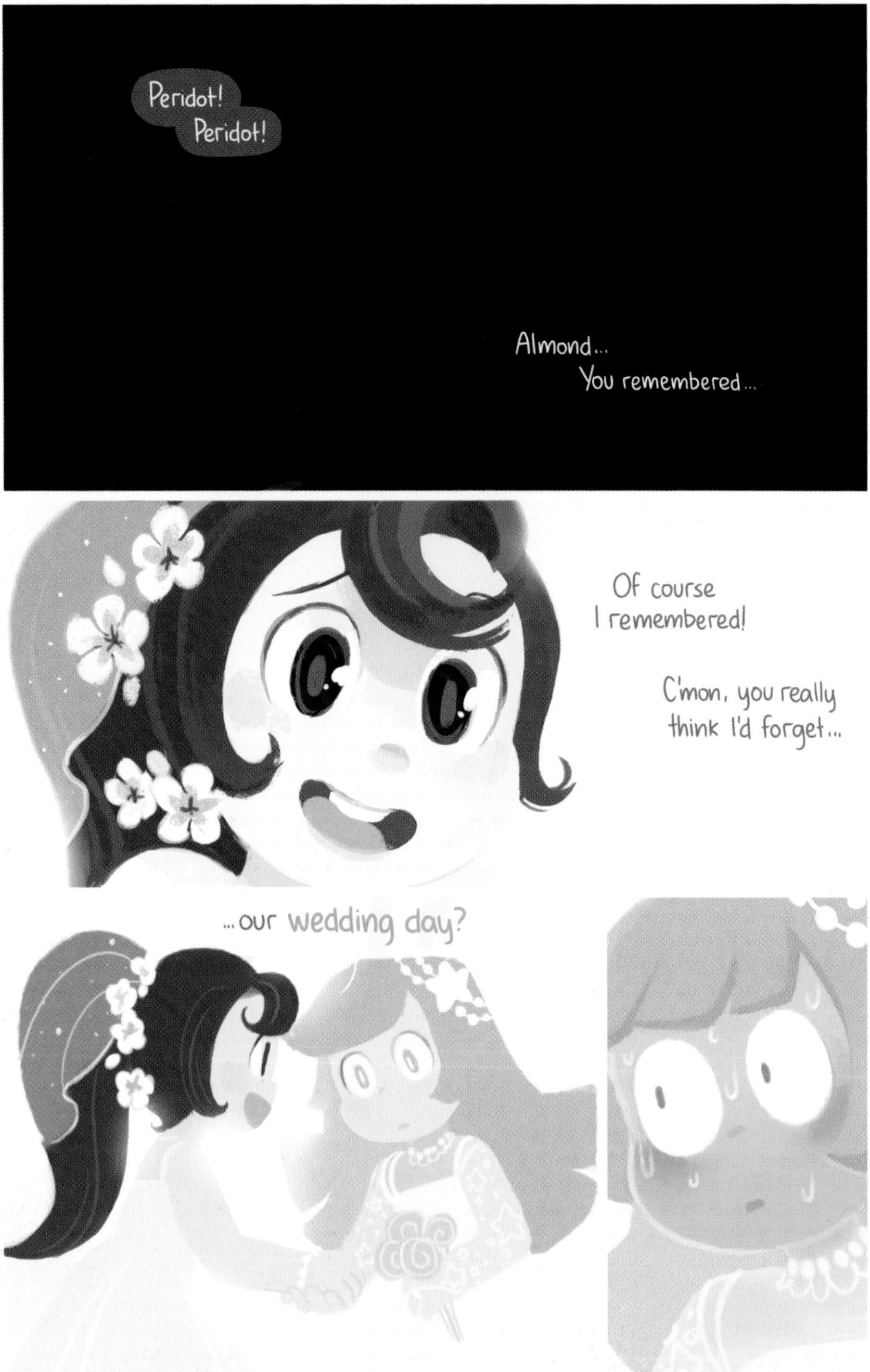
Peridot!
Peridot!
Almond...
You remembered...
Of course I remembered!
C'mon, you really think I'd forget...
...our wedding day?

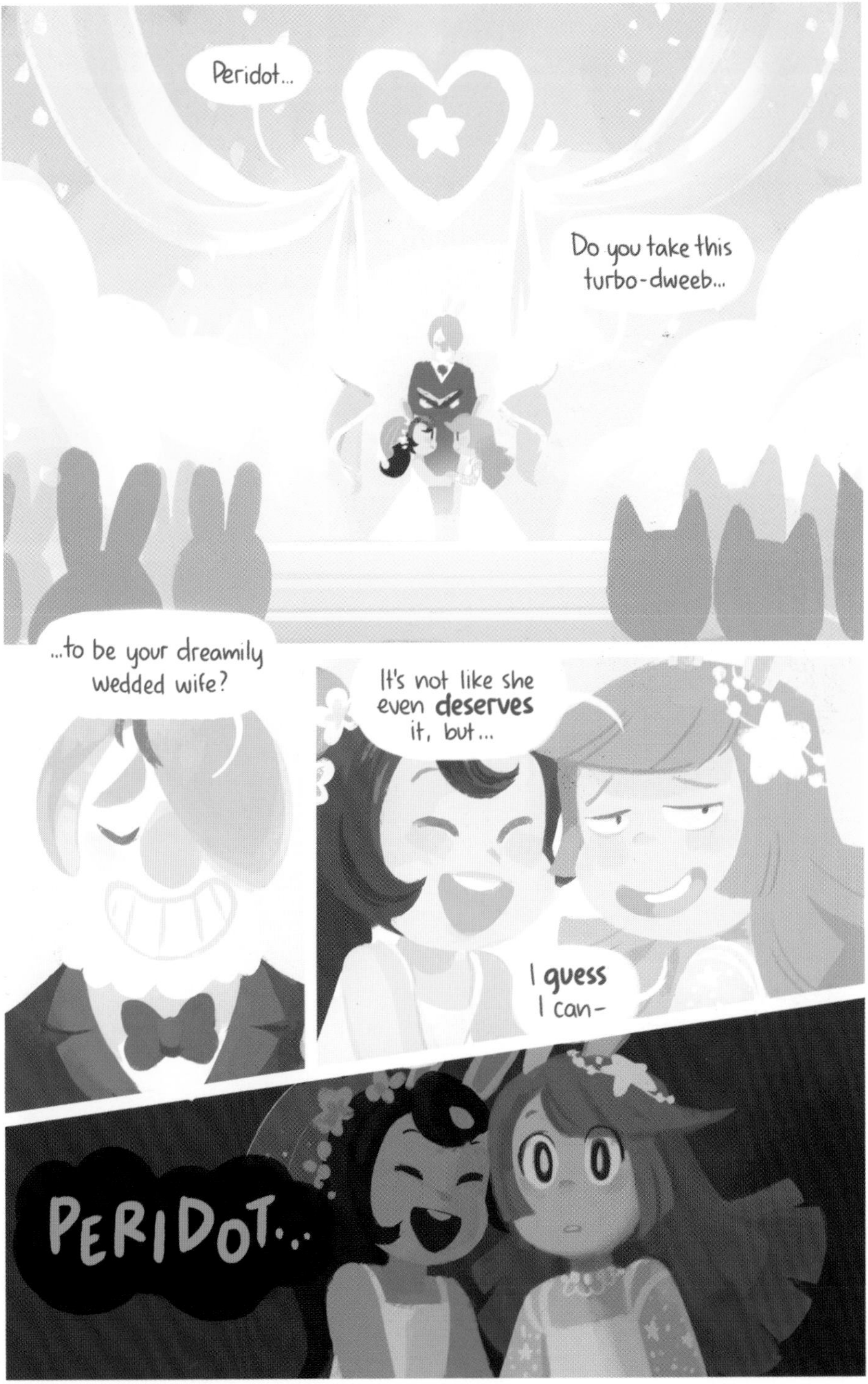
Peridot...
Do you take this turbo-dweeb...
...to be your dreamily wedded wife?
It's not like she even **deserves** it, but...
I **guess** I can-
PERIDOT...

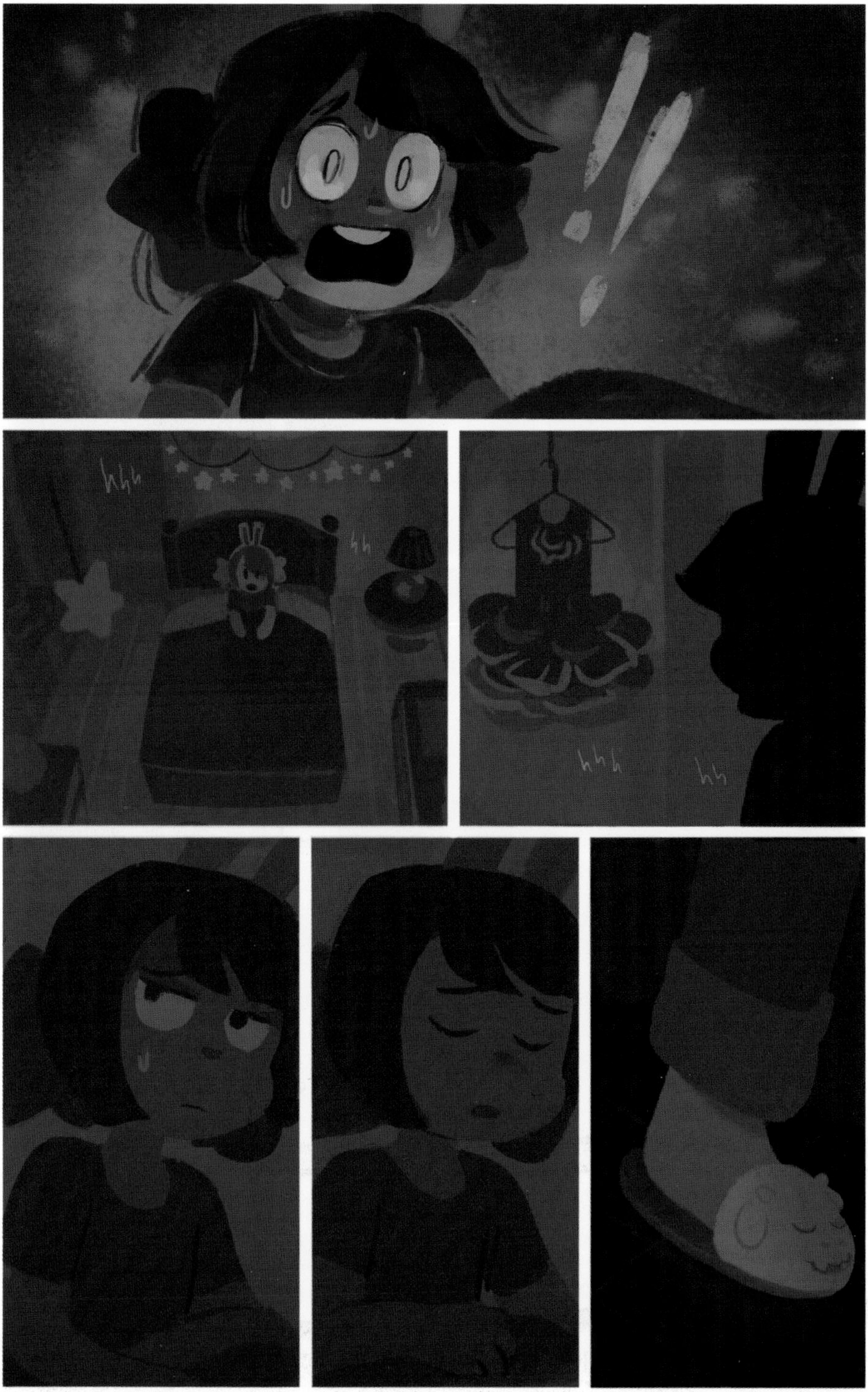
!!
hhh
hh
hhh
hh

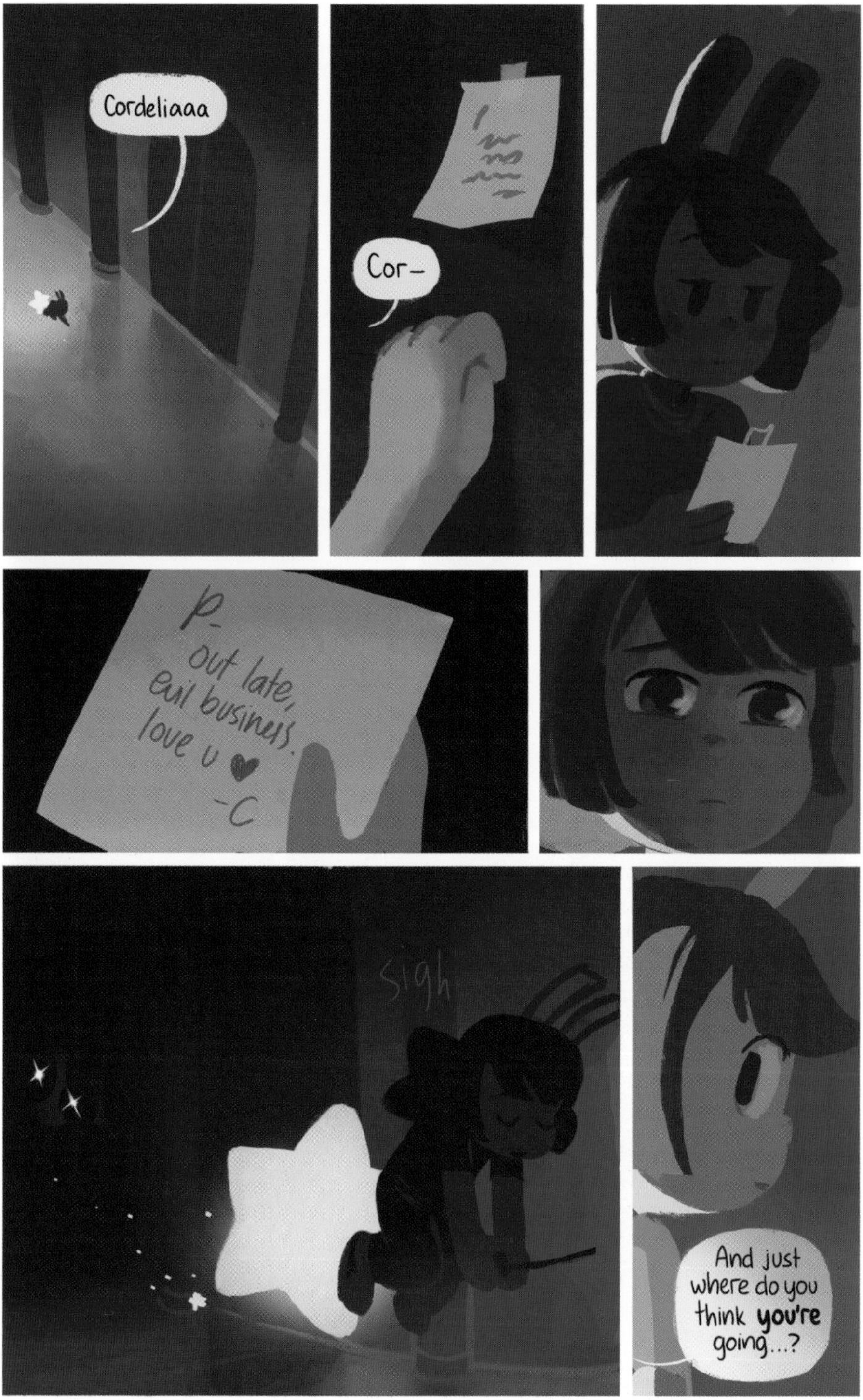

Cordeliaaa
Cor-
P-
out late,
evil business.
love u ♥
-C
sigh
And just where do you think **you're** going...?

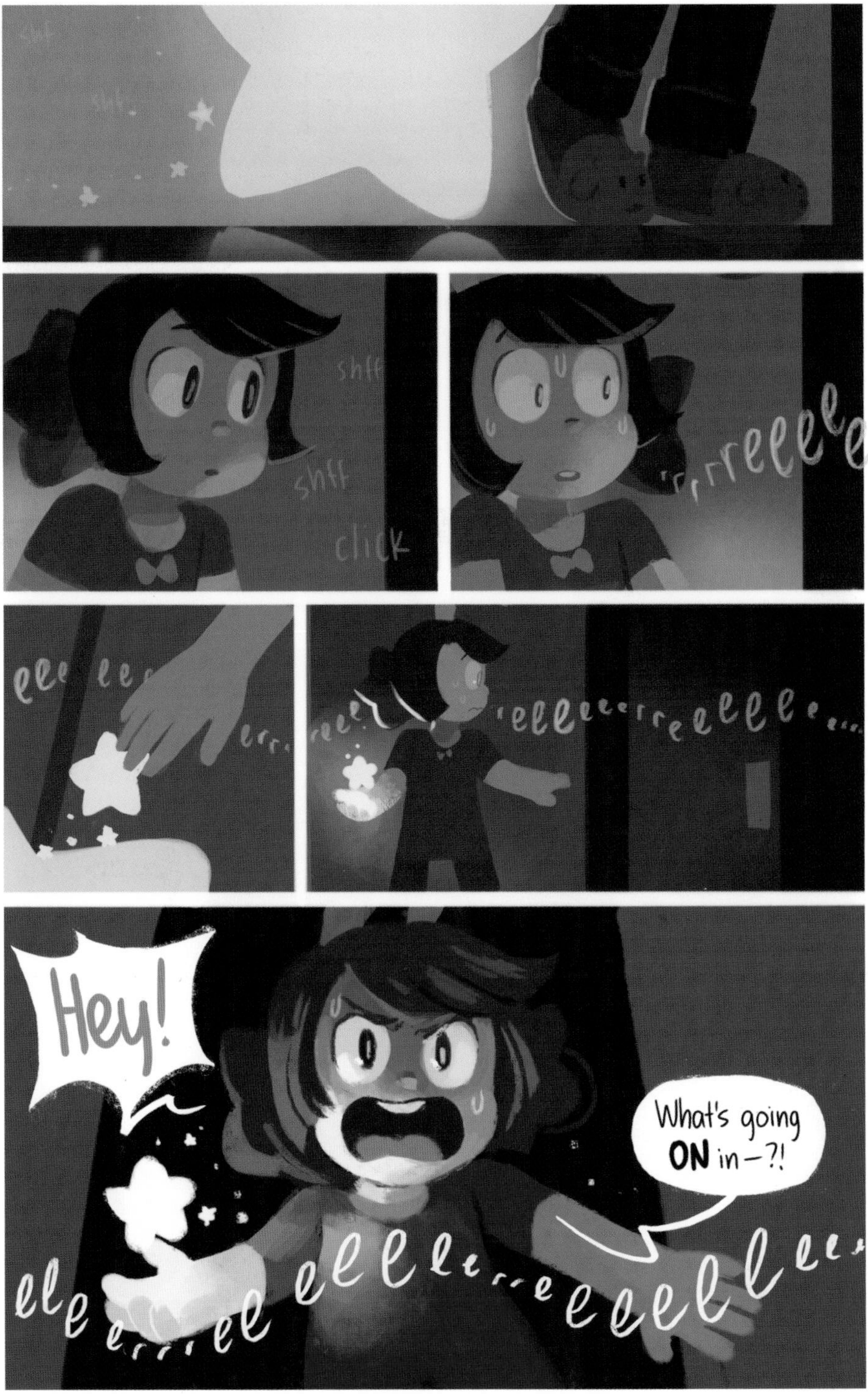
shff
shff
shff
shff
click
rrreeeeee
eee eee
rr..reee
'eeeeerreeeee...
Hey!
What's going ON in—?!
eeeerrrree eeeeerreeeeeeee...

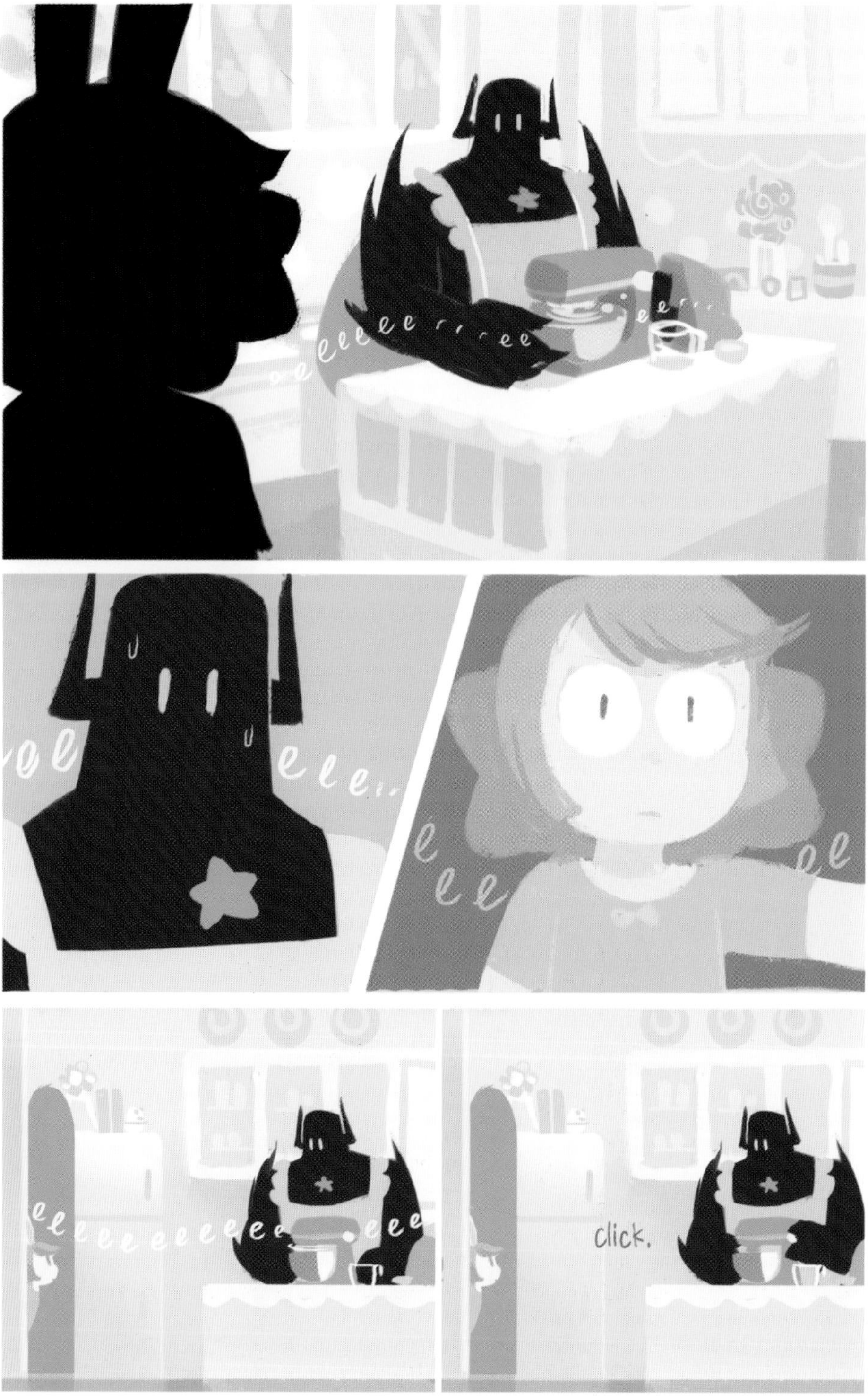

oeeeeee rrrrreee eeerr...
eee eee...
ee ee
eeeeeeeeeeeeeeeeeee
click.

177

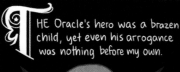

THE Oracle's hero was a brazen child, yet even his arrogance was nothing before my own.

It was only as I knelt defeated before him that I stubbornly acknowledged his sword as a threat.

In those days, emotion was beneath me. I acted on instinct — to spread fear, to consume this world and move on.

My only purpose.

But as I watched the hero and his companions celebrate their victory,

as I heard their cheers,

I felt something I couldn't understand.

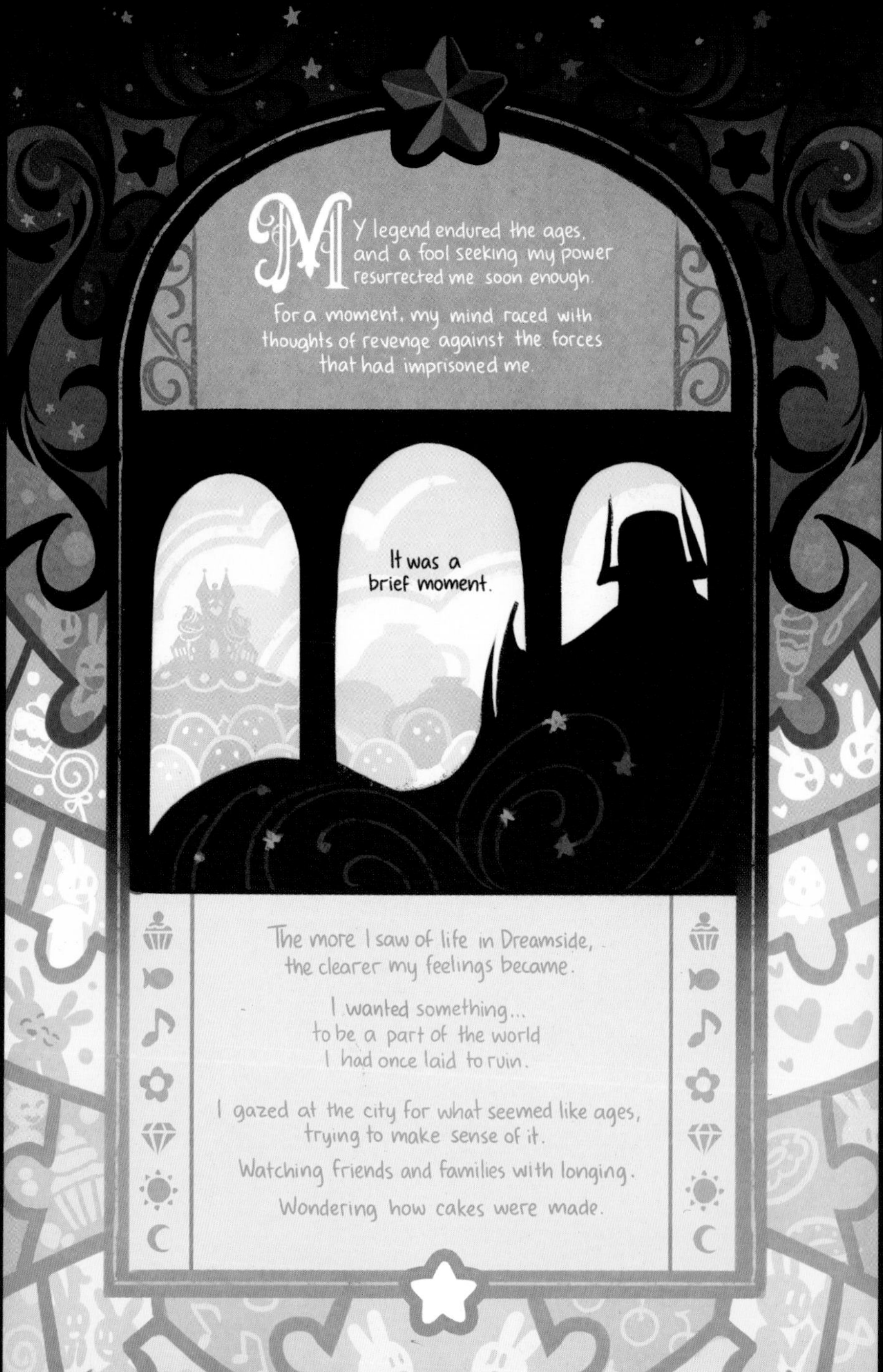
MY legend endured the ages, and a fool seeking my power resurrected me soon enough.
For a moment, my mind raced with thoughts of revenge against the forces that had imprisoned me.
It was a brief moment.
The more I saw of life in Dreamside, the clearer my feelings became.
I wanted something... to be a part of the world I had once laid to ruin.
I gazed at the city for what seemed like ages, trying to make sense of it.
Watching friends and families with longing.
Wondering how cakes were made.

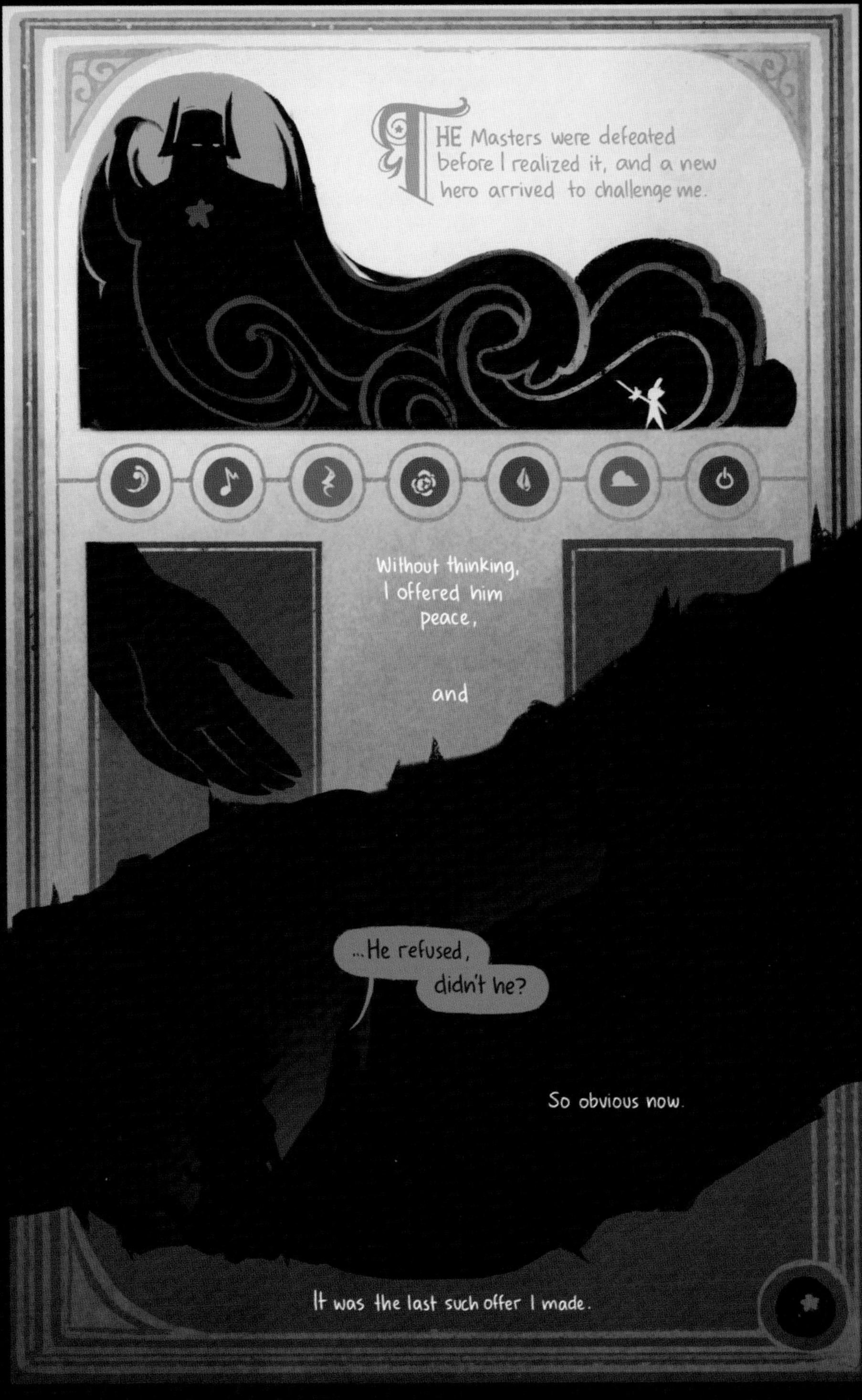
THE Masters were defeated before I realized it, and a new hero arrived to challenge me.
Without thinking, I offered him peace,
and
...He refused, didn't he?
So obvious now.
It was the last such offer I made.

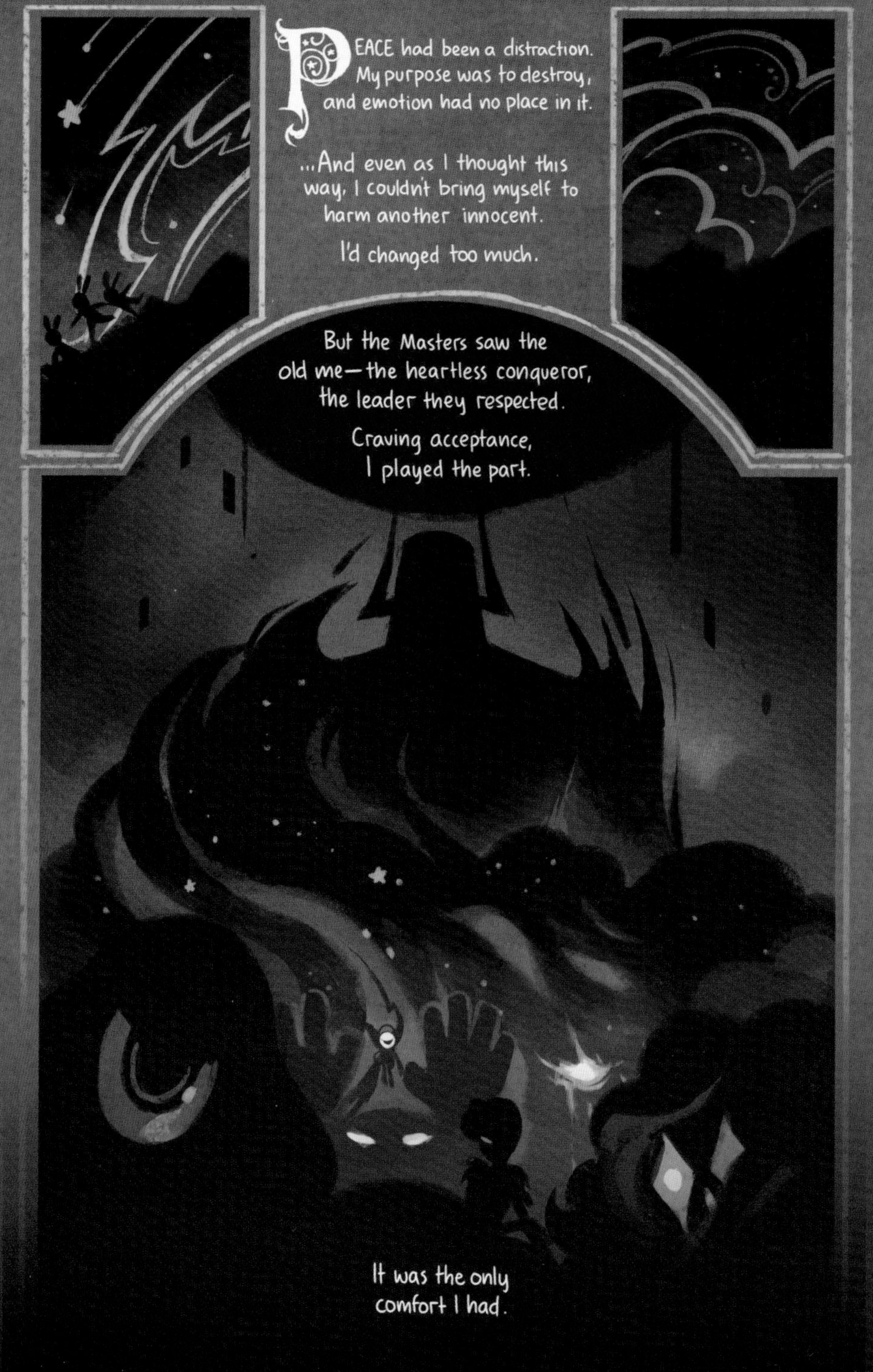
PEACE had been a distraction. My purpose was to destroy, and emotion had no place in it.
...And even as I thought this way, I couldn't bring myself to harm another innocent.
I'd changed too much.
But the Masters saw the old me—the heartless conqueror, the leader they respected.
Craving acceptance, I played the part.
It was the only comfort I had.

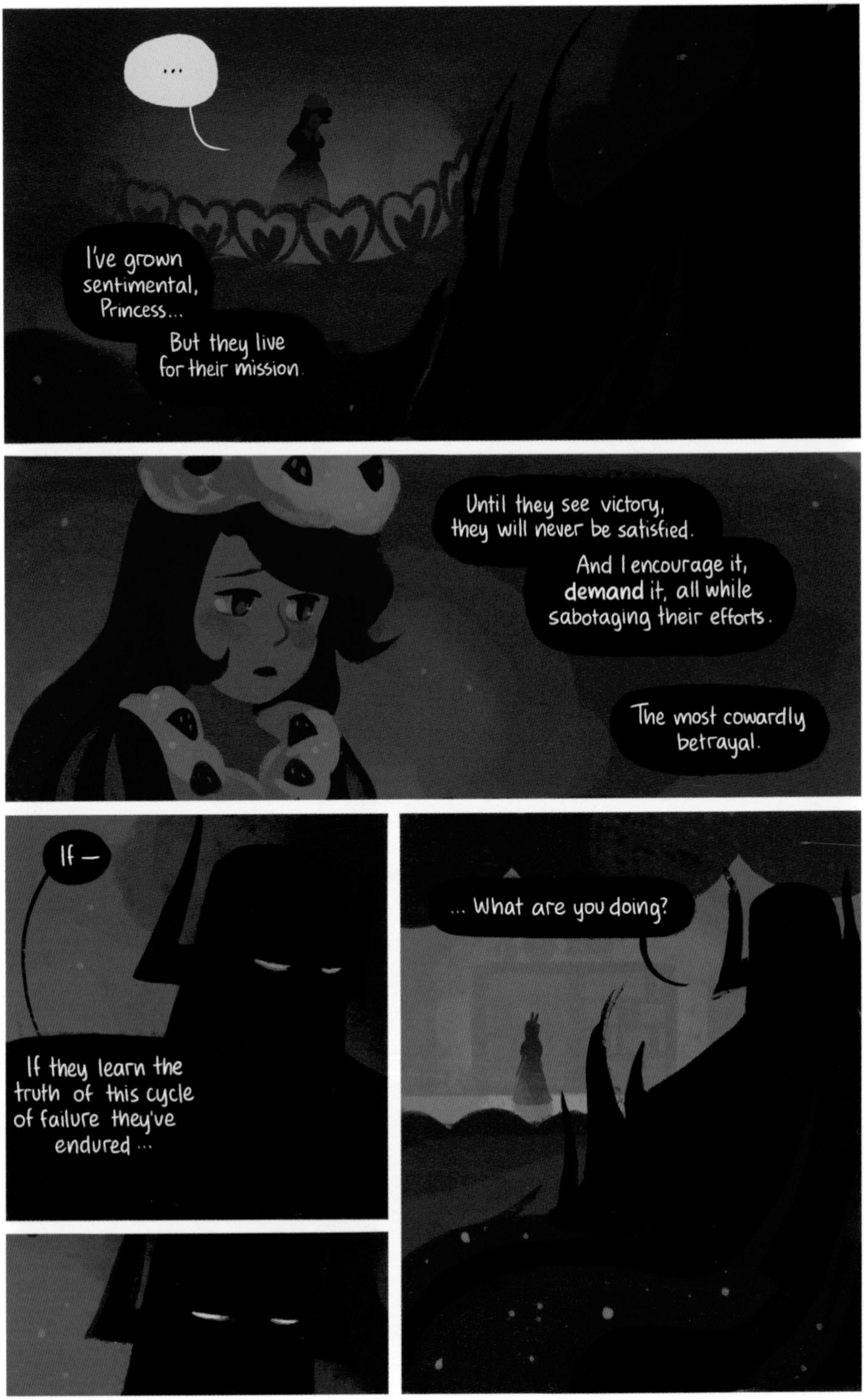
...
I've grown sentimental, Princess...
But they live for their mission.
Until they see victory, they will never be satisfied.
And I encourage it, **demand** it, all while sabotaging their efforts.
The most cowardly betrayal.
If—
If they learn the truth of this cycle of failure they've endured...
... What are you doing?

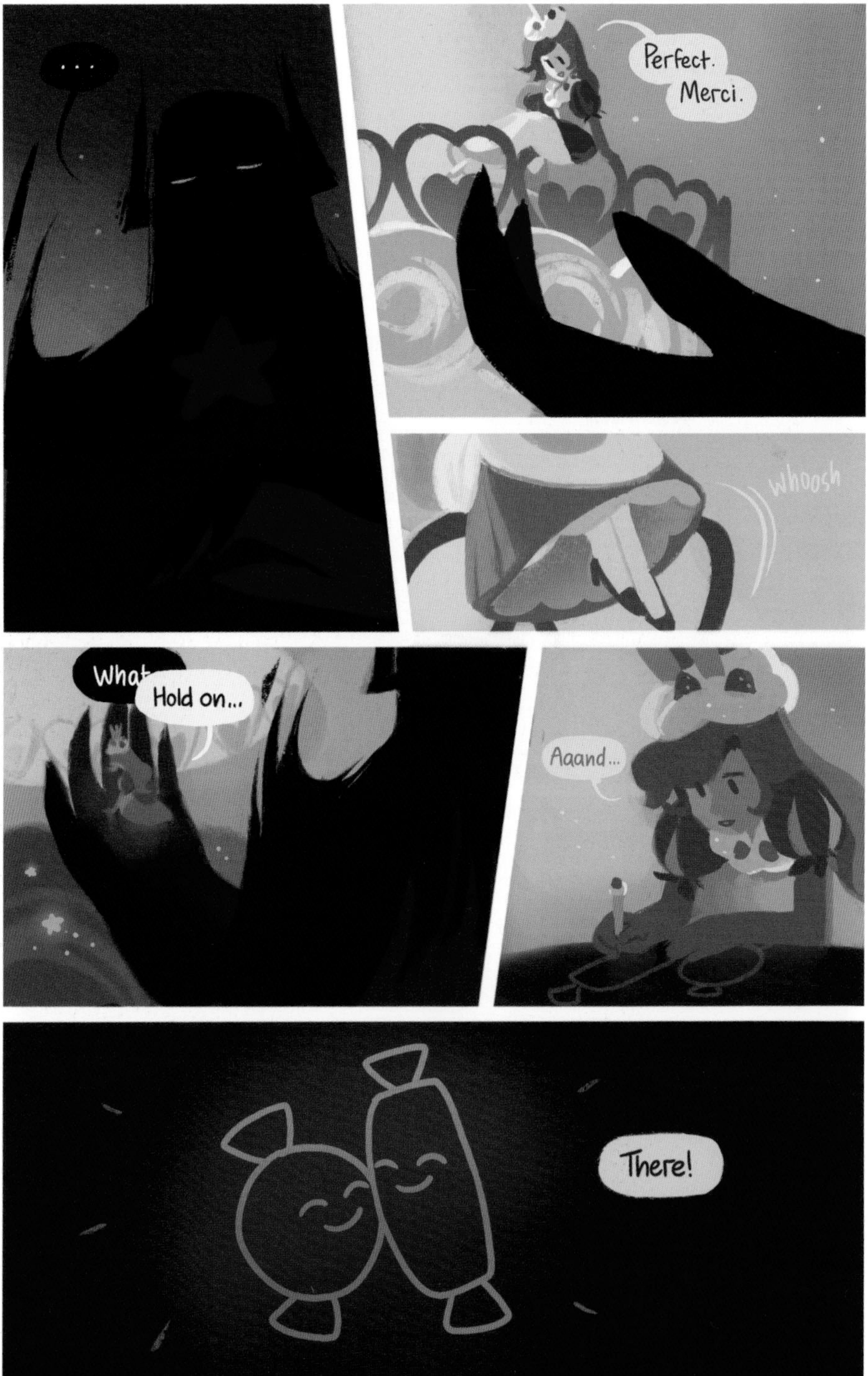
...
Perfect. Merci.
whoosh
What
Hold on...
Aaand...
There!

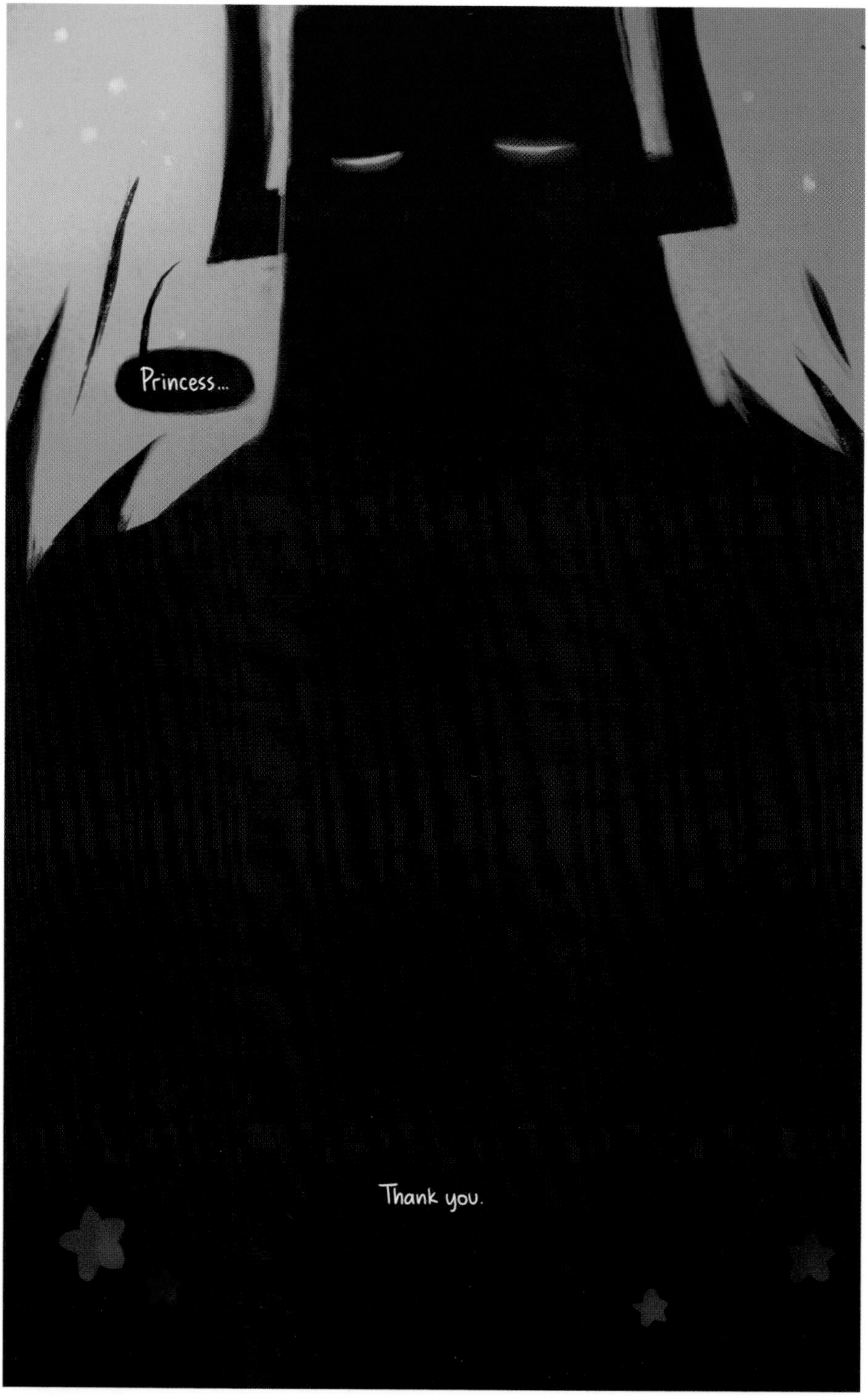
Princess...
Thank you.

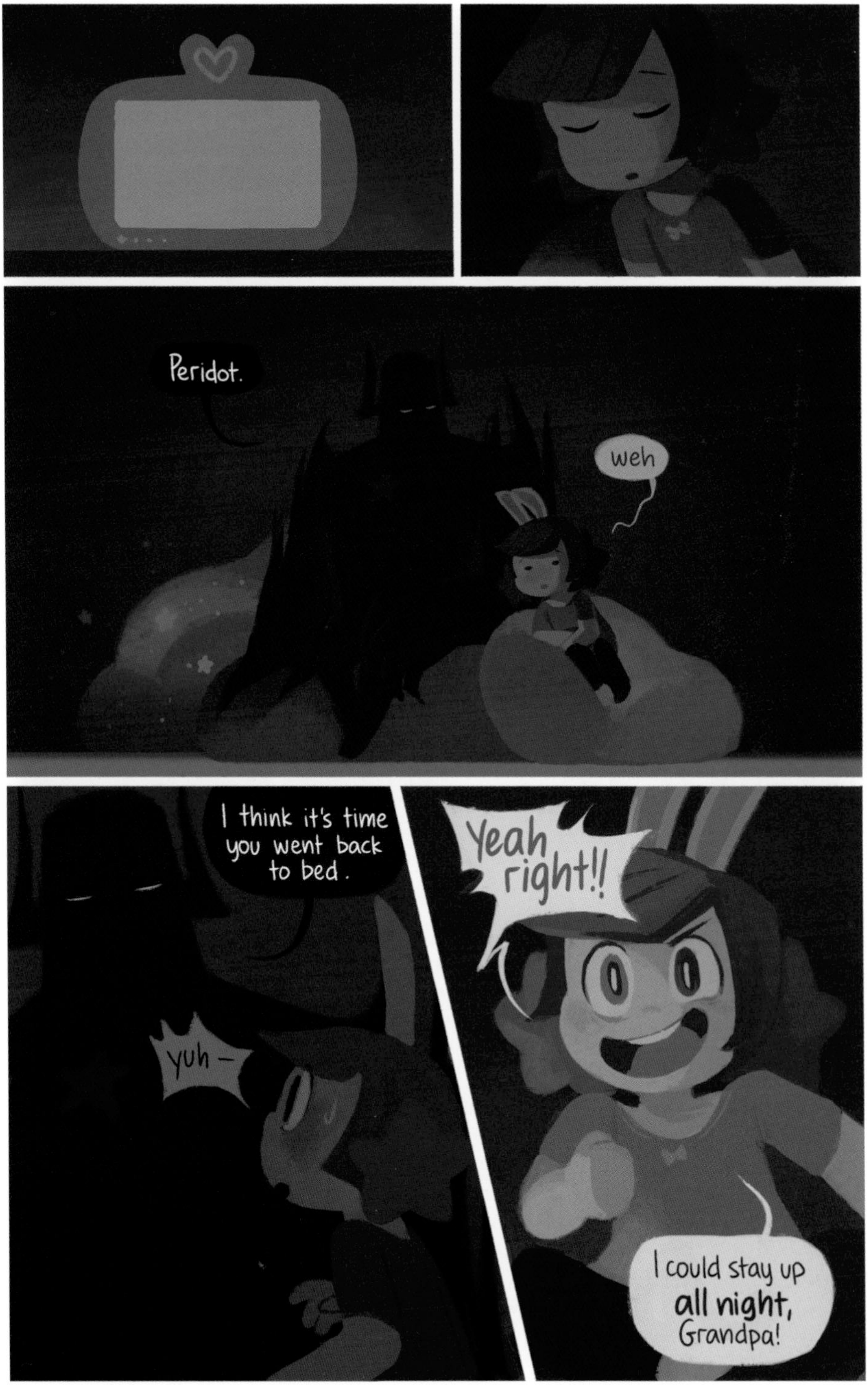
Peridot.
weh
I think it's time you went back to bed.
yuh –
Yeah right!!
I could stay up **all night**, Grandpa!

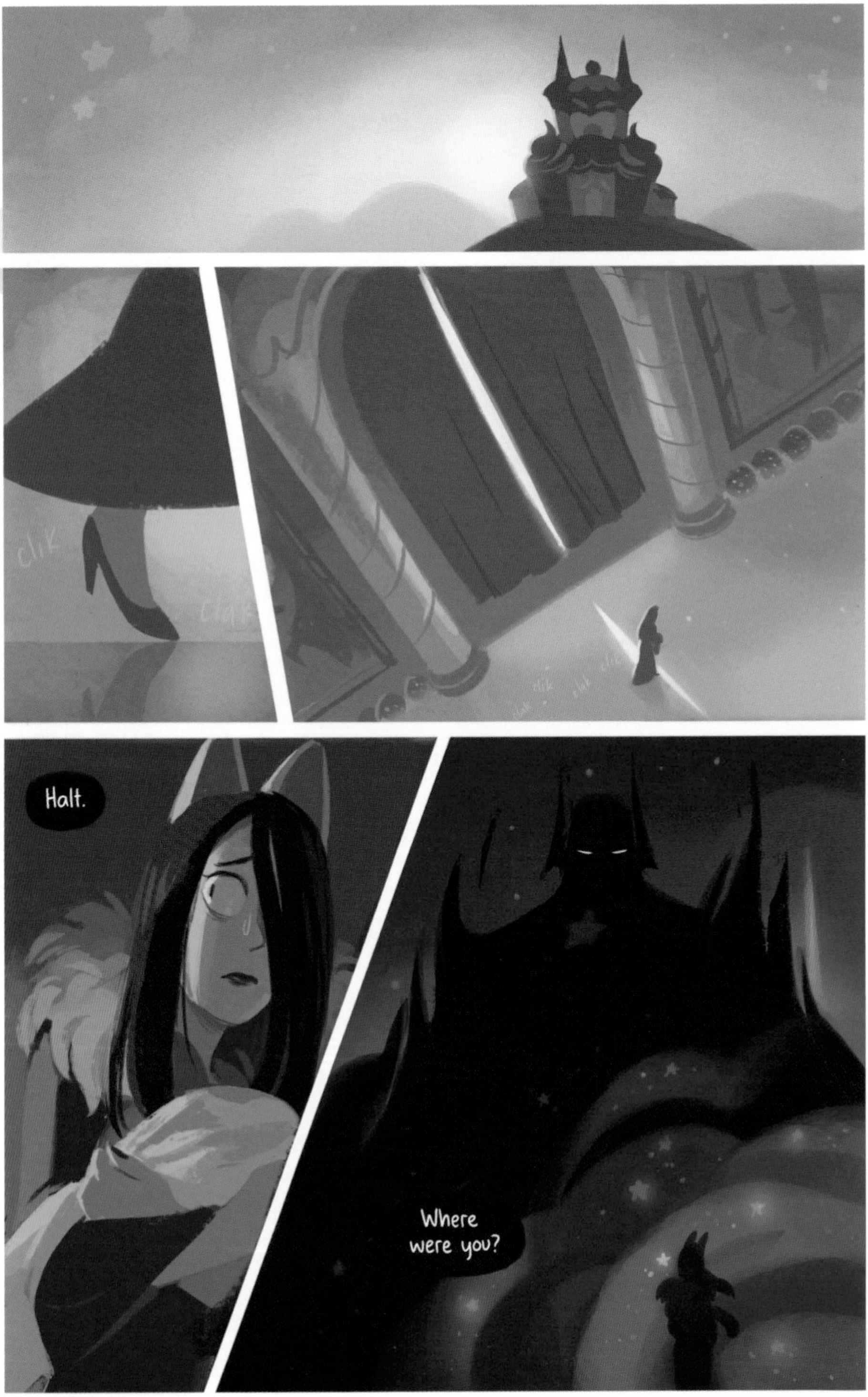
clik
clak
Halt.
Where were you?

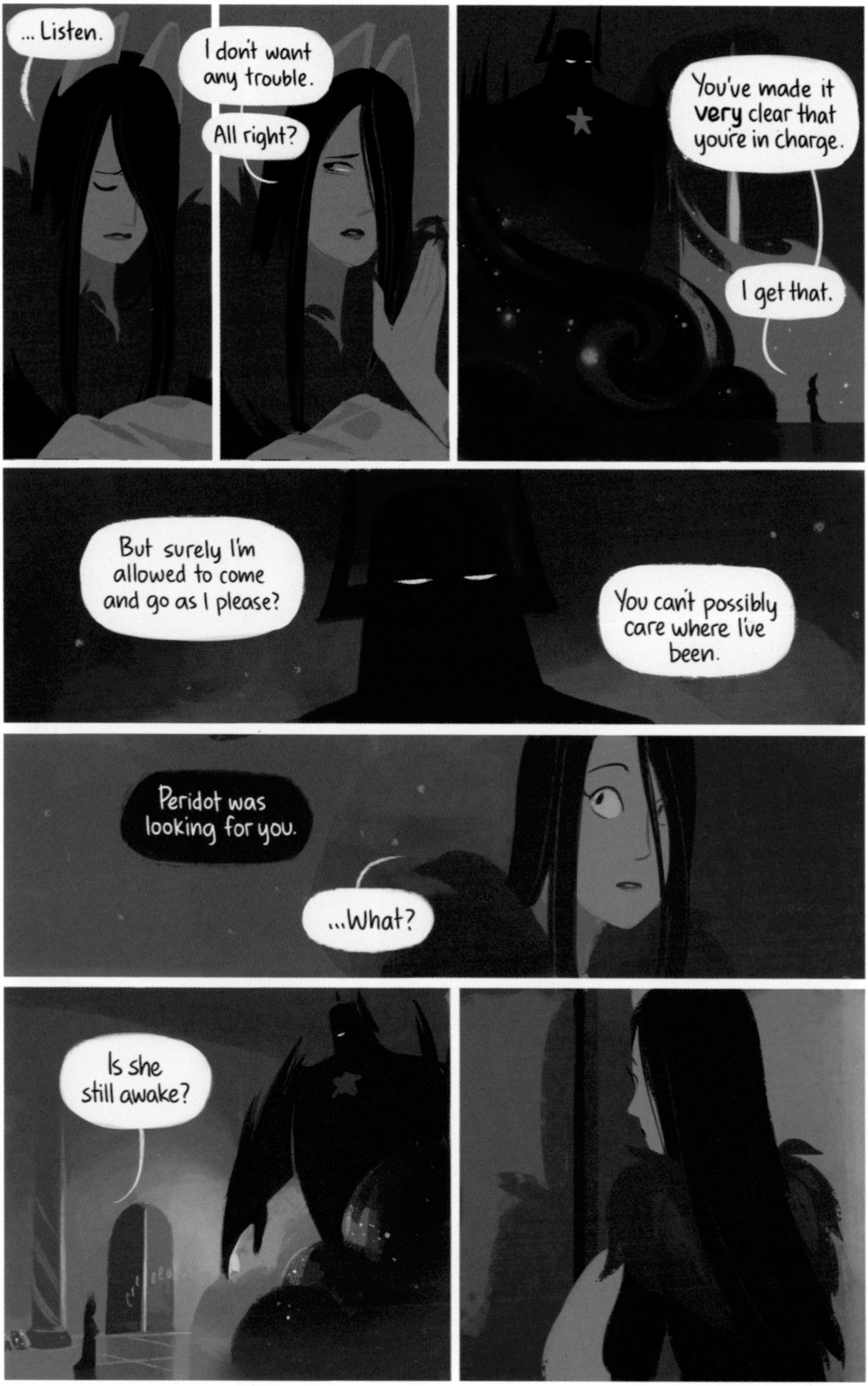

... Listen.
I don't want any trouble.
All right?
You've made it **very** clear that you're in charge.
I get that.
But surely I'm allowed to come and go as I please?
You can't possibly care where I've been.
Peridot was looking for you.
...What?
Is she still awake?

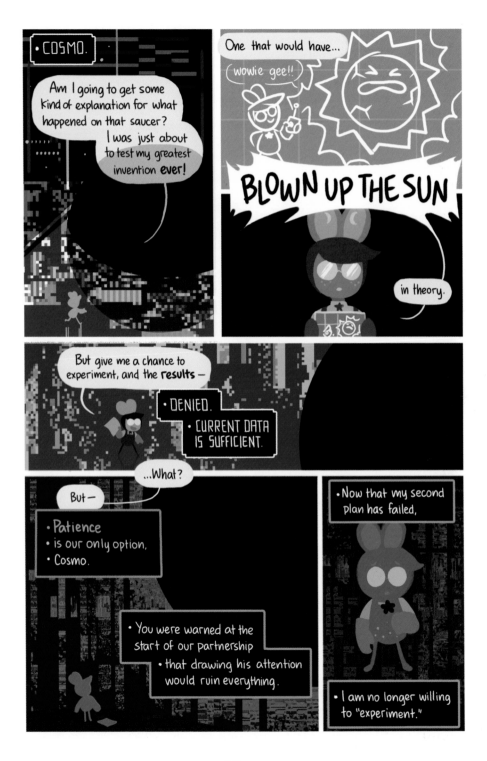

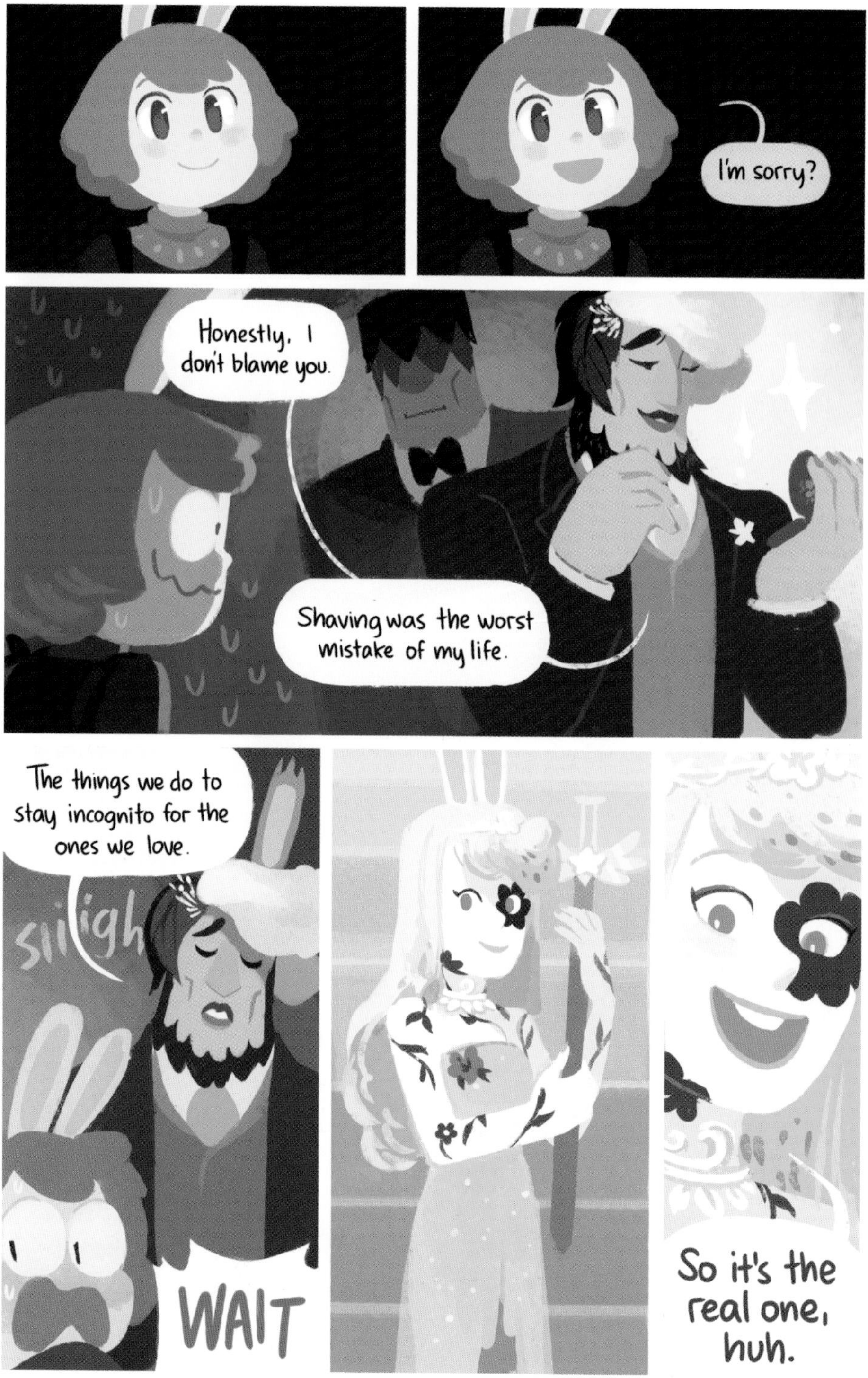
I'm sorry?
Honestly, I don't blame you.
Shaving was the worst mistake of my life.
The things we do to stay incognito for the ones we love.
siiigh
WAIT
So it's the real one, huh.

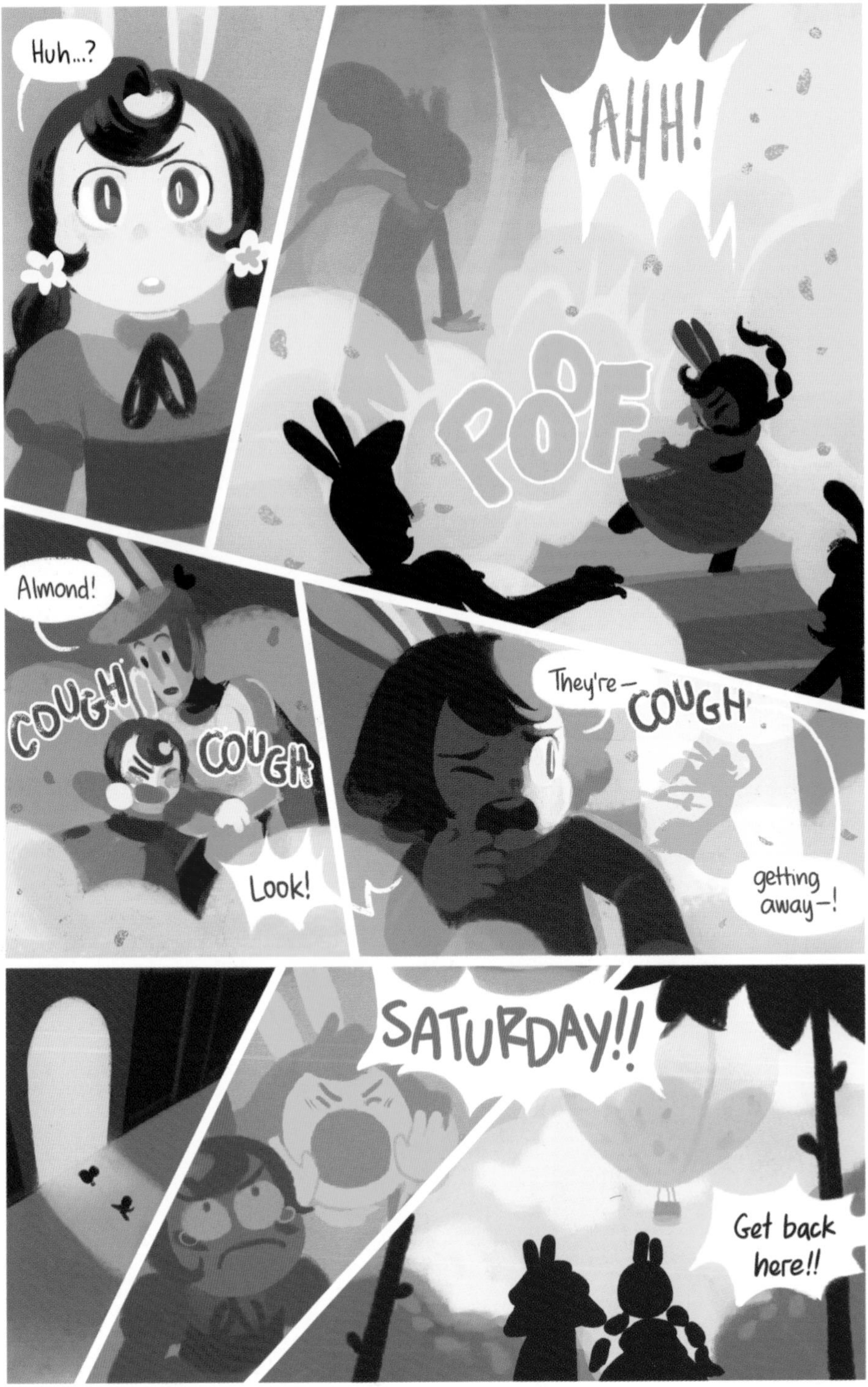
Huh...?
AHH!
POOF
Almond!
COUGH
COUGH
Look!
They're—
COUGH
getting away—!
SATURDAY!!
Get back here!!

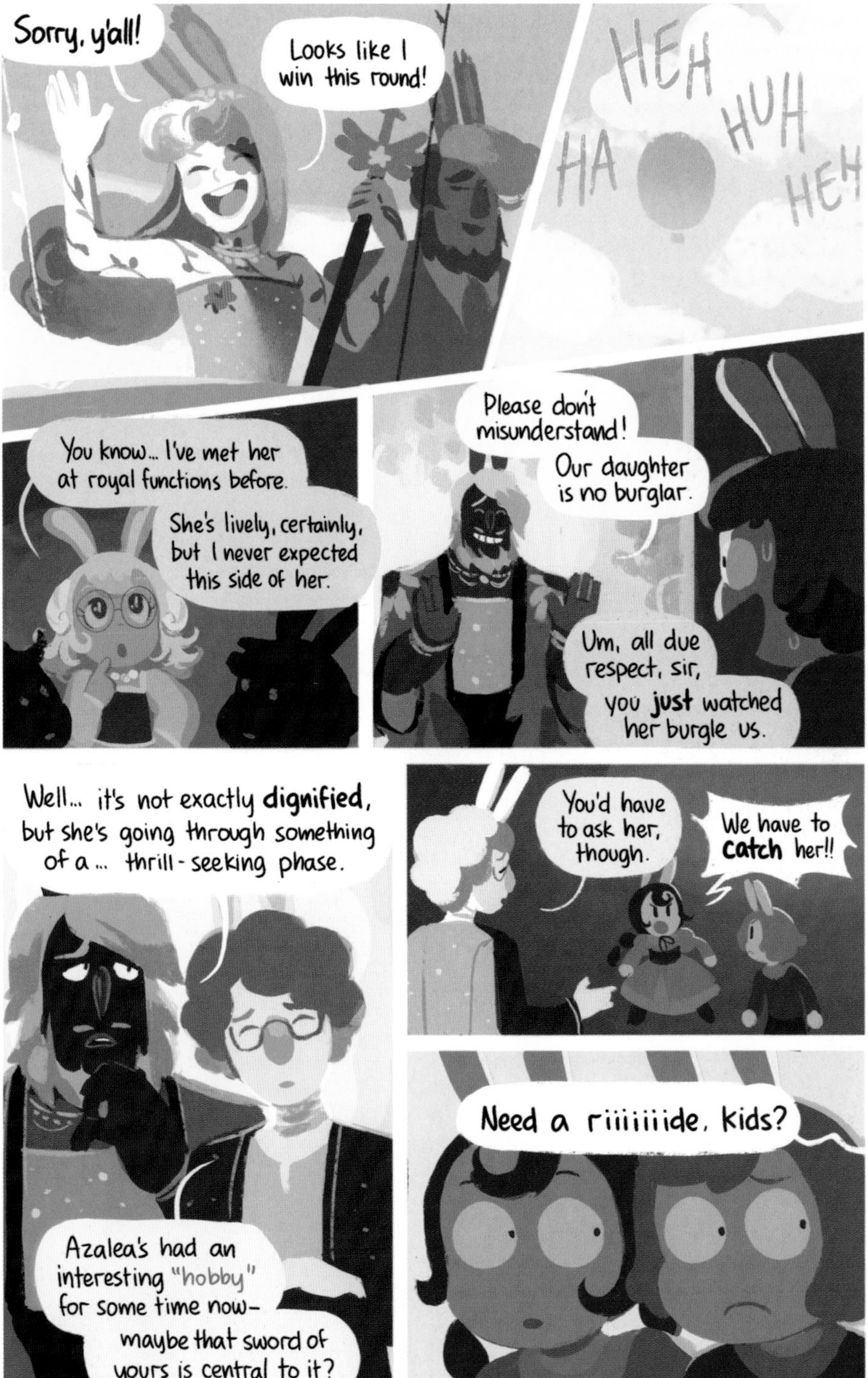

Sorry, y'all!
Looks like I win this round!
HEH HA HUH HEH
You know... I've met her at royal functions before.
She's lively, certainly, but I never expected this side of her.
Please don't misunderstand!
Our daughter is no burglar.
Um, all due respect, sir,
you **just** watched her burgle us.
Well... it's not exactly **dignified**, but she's going through something of a... thrill-seeking phase.
Azalea's had an interesting "hobby" for some time now–
maybe that sword of yours is central to it?
You'd have to ask her, though.
We have to **catch** her!!
Need a riiiiiiide, kids?

Yes...
Much...
much colder..

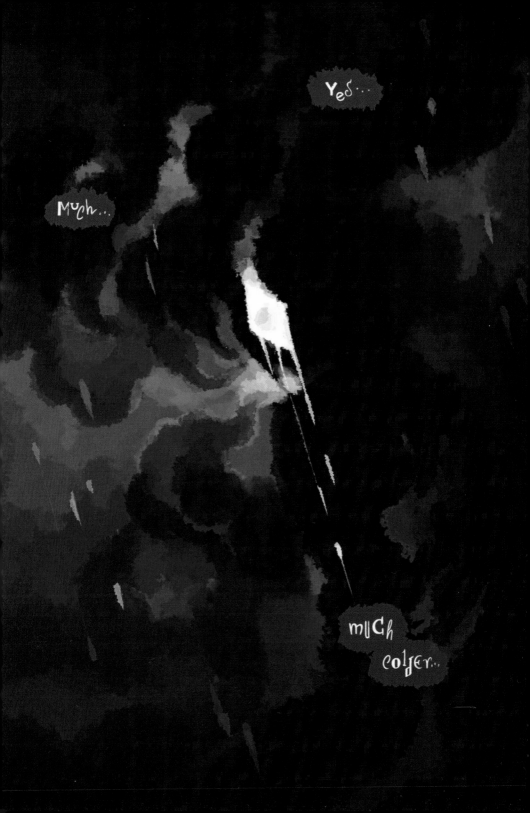

To be continued

Cucumber QUEST

CUCUMBER.GIGIDIGI.COM

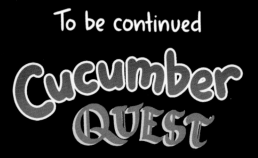

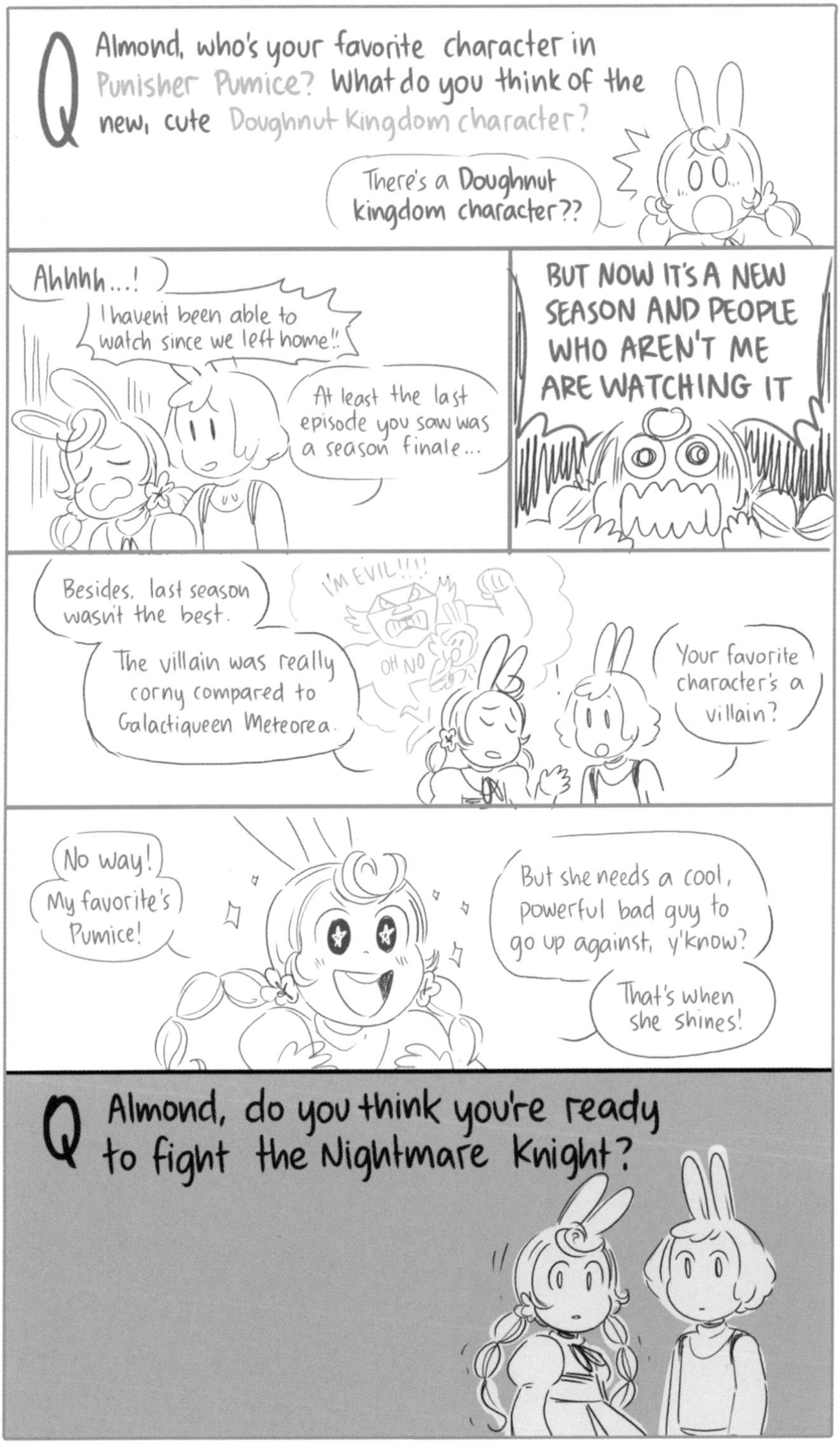
Q Almond, who's your favorite character in Punisher Pumice? What do you think of the new, cute Doughnut Kingdom character?
There's a Doughnut kingdom character??
Ahhhh...!
I havent been able to watch since we left home!!
At least the last episode you saw was a season finale...
BUT NOW IT'S A NEW SEASON AND PEOPLE WHO AREN'T ME ARE WATCHING IT
Besides, last season wasn't the best.
I'M EVIL!!!!
OH NO
The villain was really corny compared to Galactiqueen Meteorea.
Your favorite character's a villain?
No way! My favorite's Pumice!
But she needs a cool, powerful bad guy to go up against, y'know?
That's when she shines!
Q Almond, do you think you're ready to fight the Nightmare Knight?

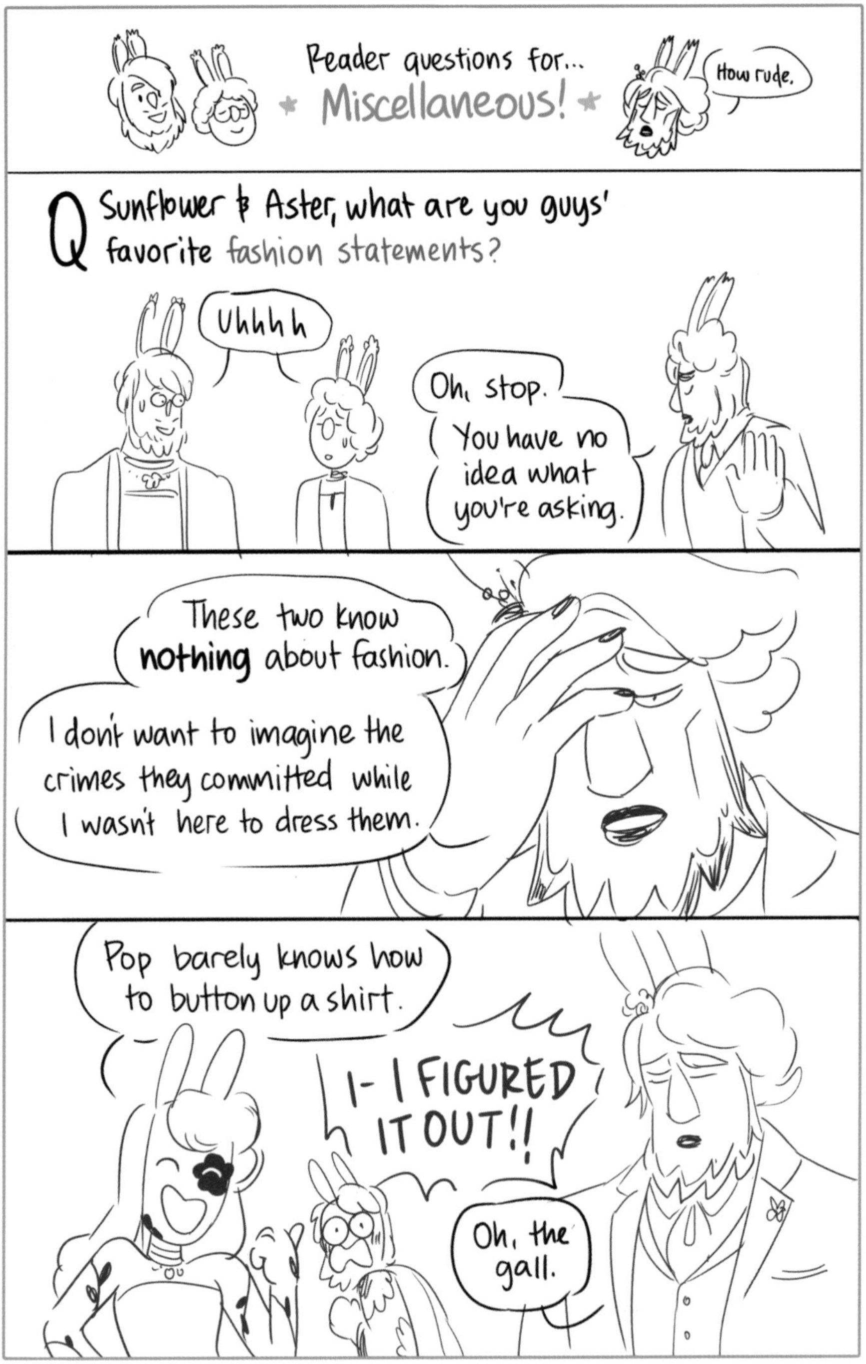
Reader questions for...
Miscellaneous!
How rude.
Q Sunflower & Aster, what are you guys' favorite fashion statements?
Uhhhh
Oh, stop.
You have no idea what you're asking.
These two know **nothing** about fashion.
I don't want to imagine the crimes they committed while I wasn't here to dress them.
Pop barely knows how to button up a shirt.
I- I FIGURED IT OUT!!
Oh, the gall.

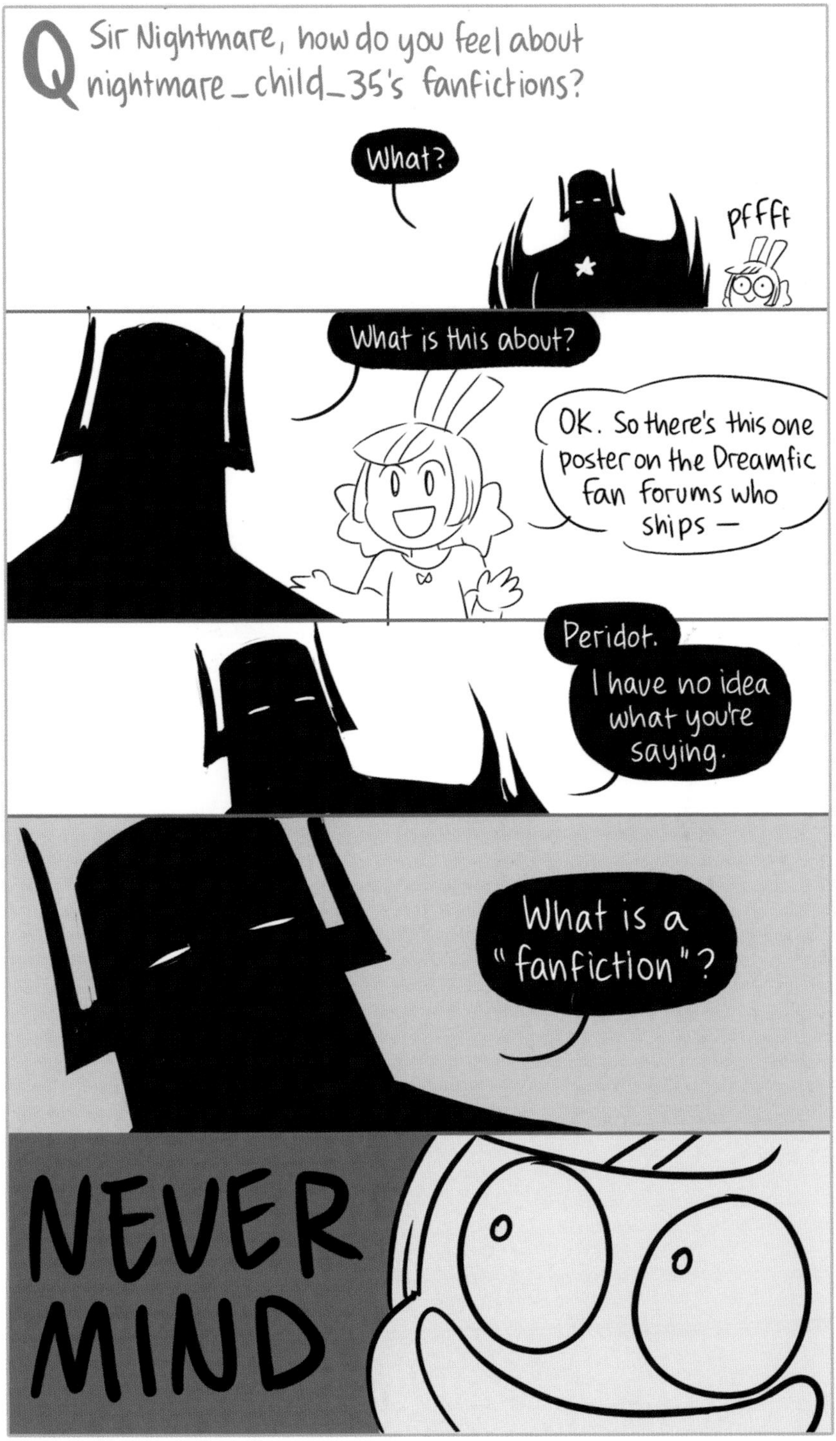
Q Sir Nightmare, how do you feel about nightmare_child_35's fanfictions?
What?
pffff
What is this about?
OK. So there's this one poster on the Dreamfic fan forums who ships —
Peridot.
I have no idea what you're saying.
What is a "fanfiction"?
NEVER MIND

Flower Kingdom

Dreamside's floral paradise also happens to be its smallest kingdom. Its population is centralized in Botanica Springs, while the rest of the island is untamed wilderness.

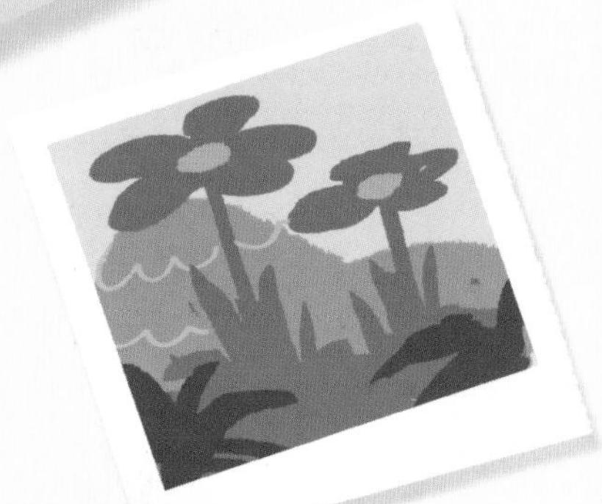

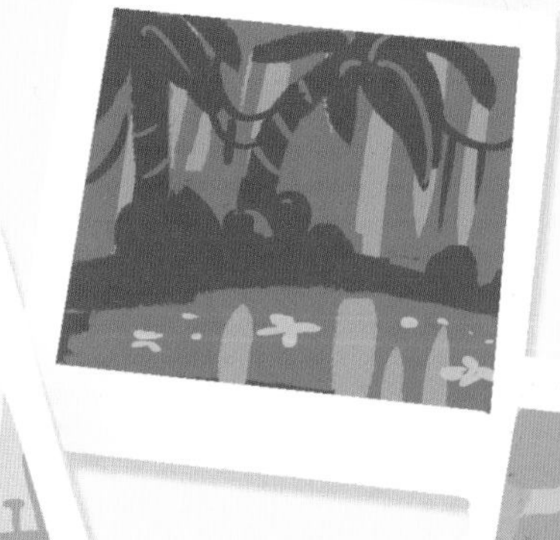

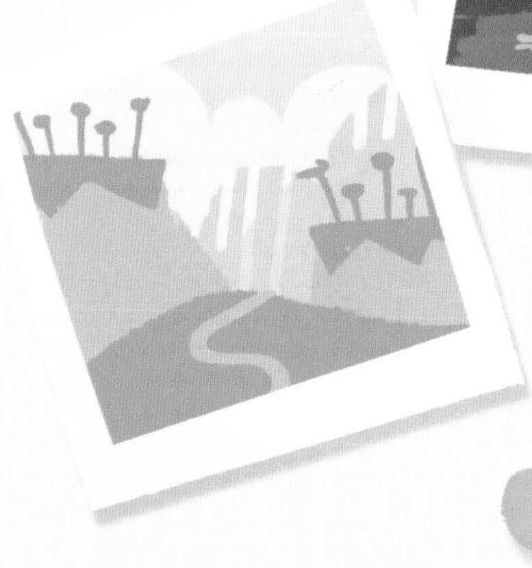

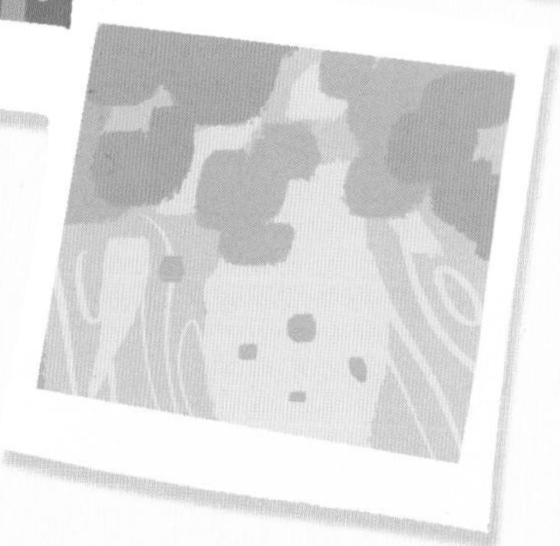

Botanica Springs is structured on a large tree with roots extending deep beneath the ground.

The underground region is where you'll find remnants of the ancient Flower Kingdom, which was devastated by the Nightmare Knight and Rosemaster long ago.

Surface

ground level

Hocus Crocus is here!

The statue you saw here is a depiction of Queen Lotus, known for her charity and beauty.

By the way, King Sunflower is descended from her!

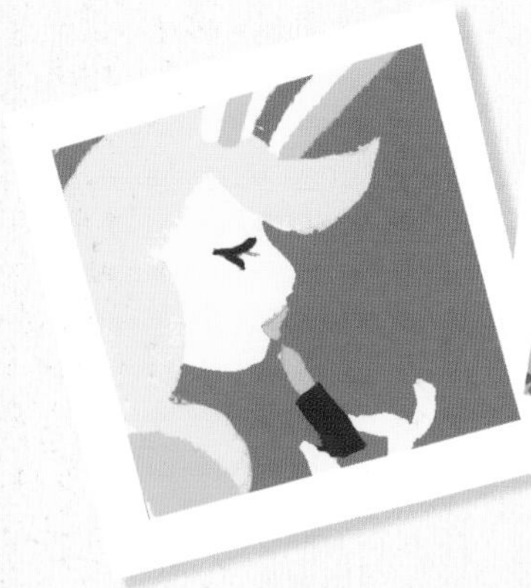
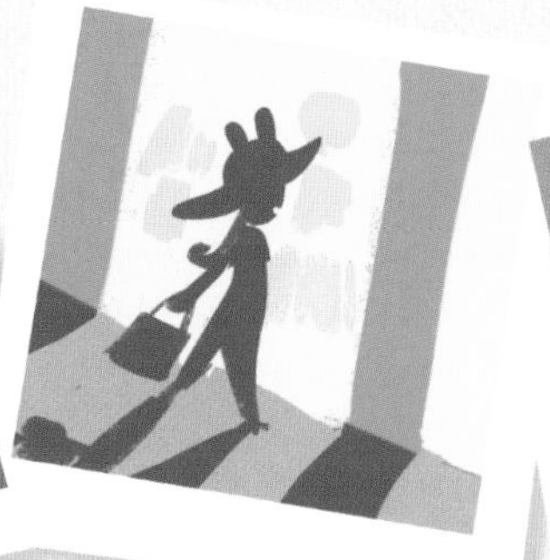
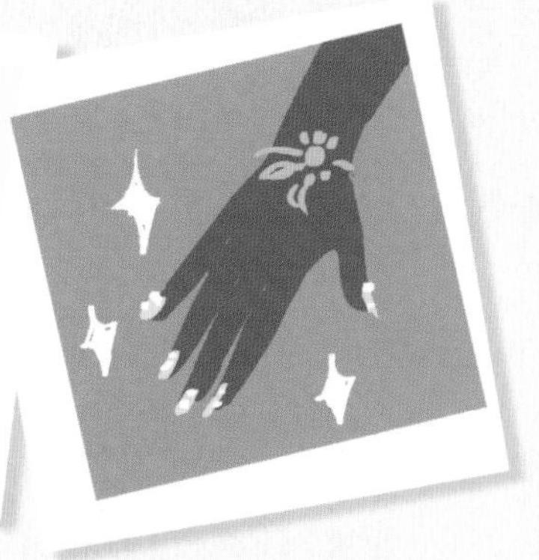

Modern Botanica Springs is a hot spot for trendsetters. You'll find no better shopping destination in Dreamside, except maybe the Galaxy Galleria in the Space Kingdom.

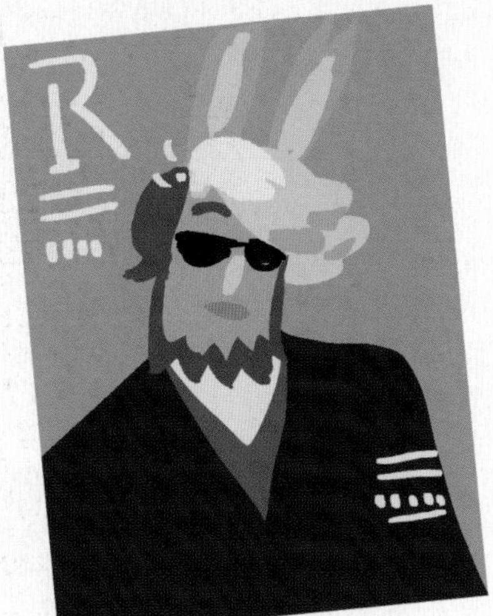
R

And who do Botanicals have to thank for their city's super-chic image? Well...you know the answer to that already.

He may seem untouchable, but Mr. R considers himself first and foremost a servant of the people.

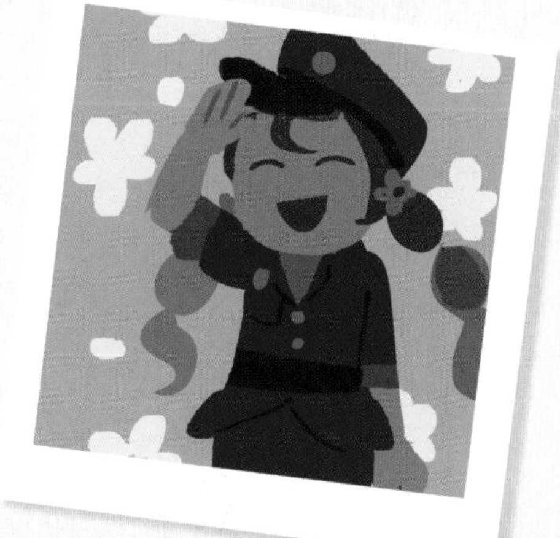

He even worked with the police to design their uniforms!

(They had to talk him down from sequins, but still.)

Okay, let's address the photo-realistic elephant in the room... What is the Guardener's deal, anyway?

No one can say for certain, but there are all kinds of rumors floating around about that guy.

Some say he was cursed.

Others say he was warped by the power of the Hocus Crocus.

Still others say he might be from a different world...

Nah, I'm just some guy.

It seems we may never know the truth...

Concept Art

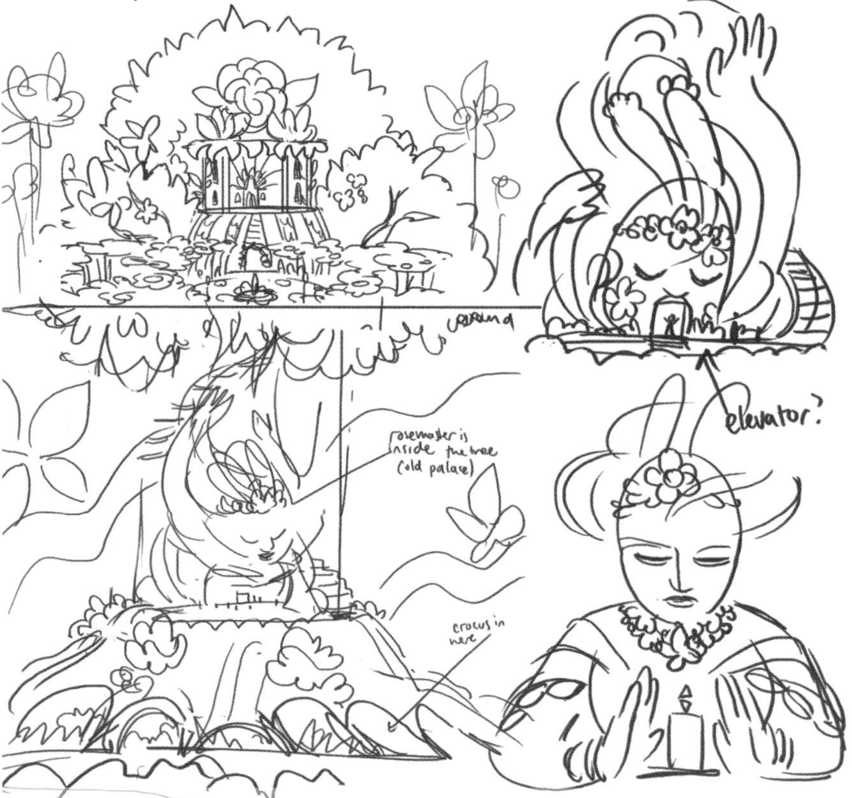
elevator?
rosemaster is inside the tree (old palace)
crocus in here

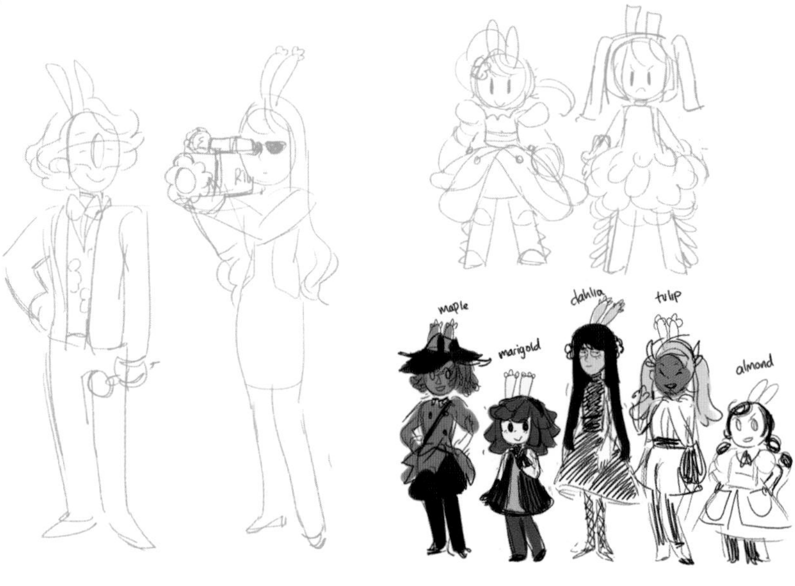
maple
marigold
dahlia
tulip
almond

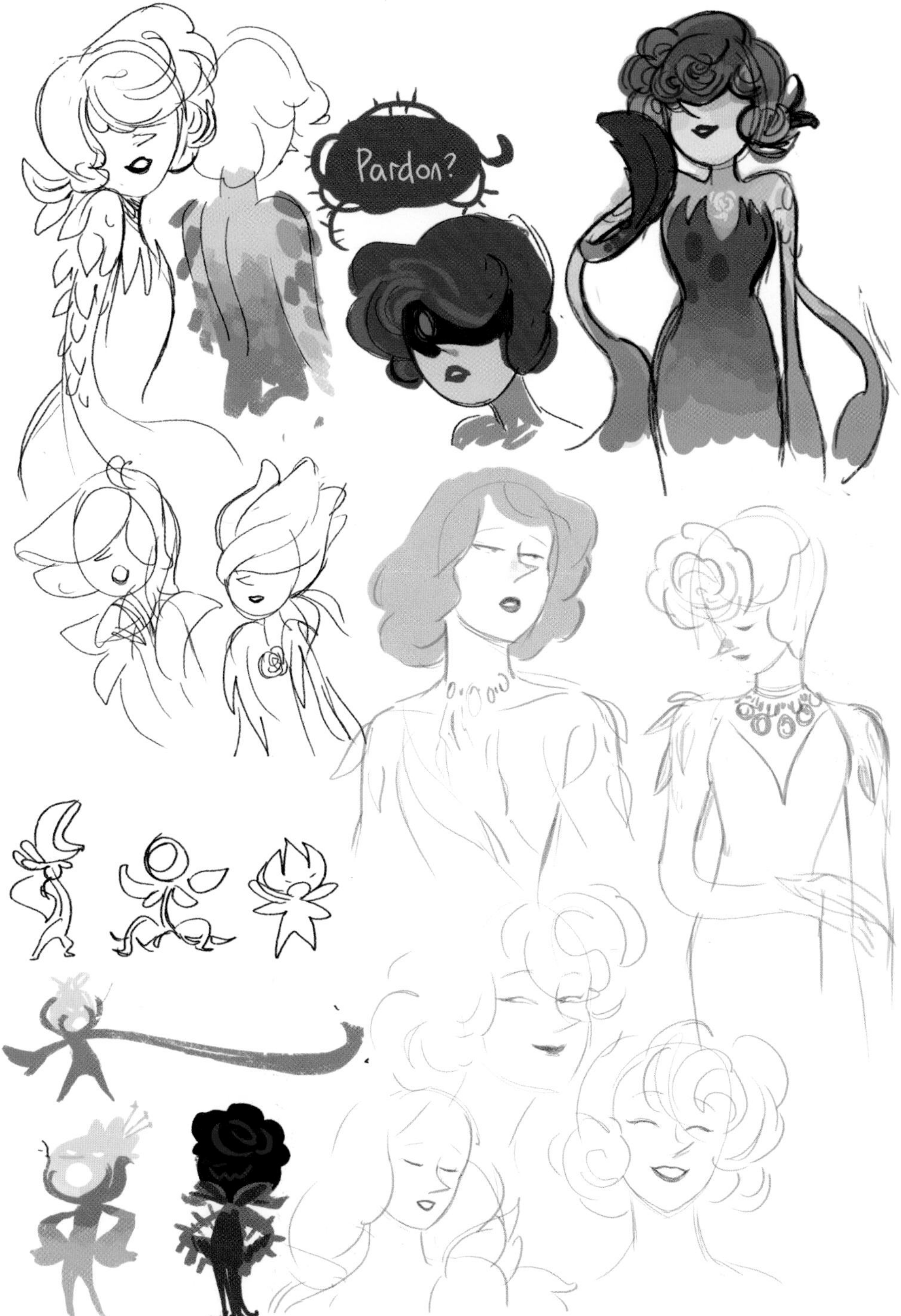
Pardon?

The Flower Kingdom

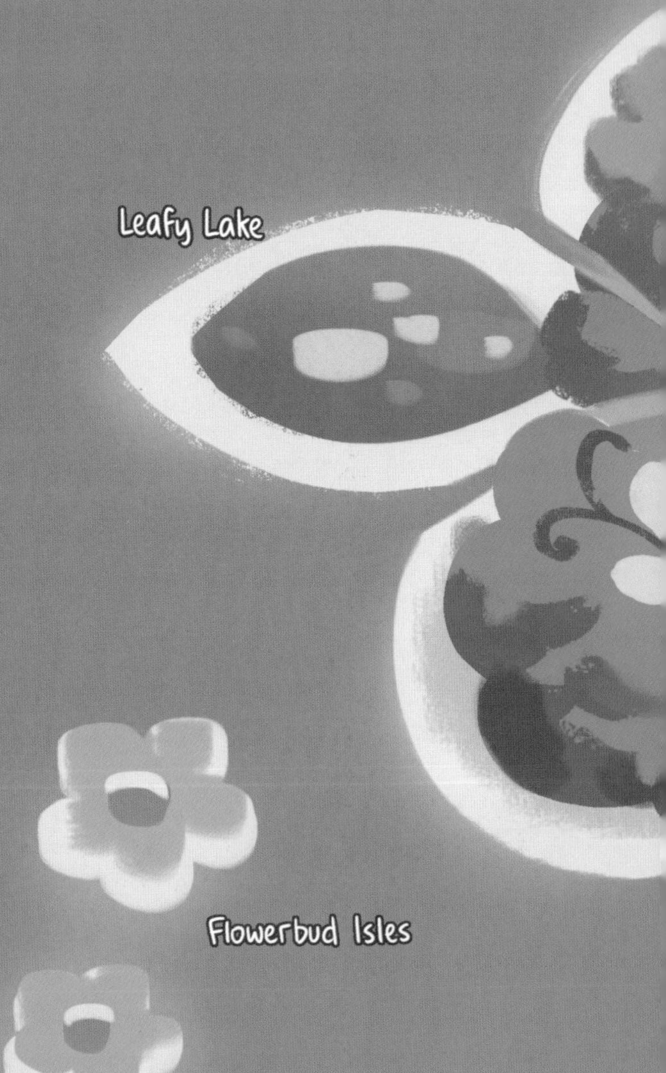
Leafy Lake
Flowerbud Isles

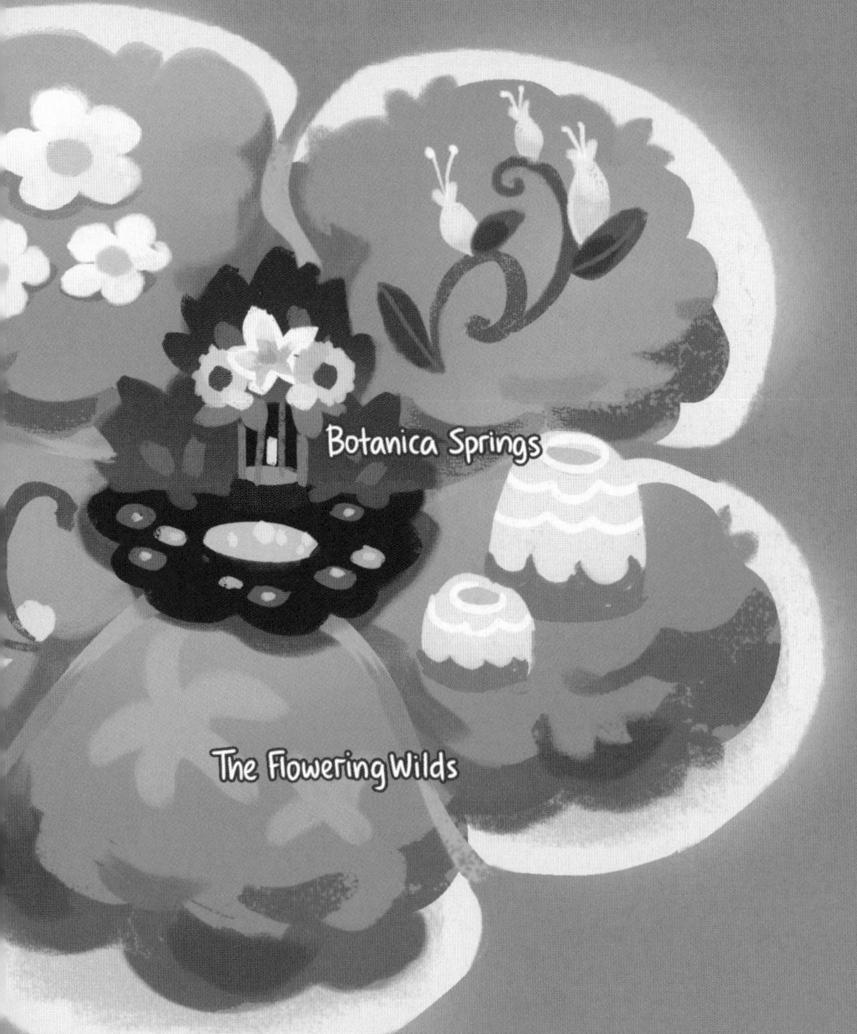
Botanica Springs
The Flowering Wilds

First Second

New York

Copyright © 2018 by Gigi D.G.

Published by First Second
First Second is an imprint of Roaring Brook Press, a division of
Holtzbrinck Publishing Holdings Limited Partnership
175 Fifth Avenue, New York, NY 10010

Library of Congress Control Number: 2017957142

Hardcover ISBN: 978-1-250-16295-3
Paperback ISBN: 978-1-62672-835-6

Our books may be purchased in bulk for promotional, educational,
or business use. Please contact your local bookseller or the Macmillan
Corporate and Premium Sales Department at (800) 221-7945 ext. 5442
or by e-mail at MacmillanSpecialMarkets@macmillan.com.

First edition, 2018
Book design by Rob Steen

Cucumber Quest is created entirely in Photoshop.

Printed in China by RR Donnelley Asia Printing Solutions Ltd., Dongguan City, Guangdong Province

Hardcover: 10 9 8 7 6 5 4 3 2 1
Paperback: 10 9 8 7 6 5 4 3 2 1